PRAISE FOR ETHAN BLACK AND

DEAD FOR LIFE

"Exceptionally engaging . . . readers of the previous [Voort] stories won't be surprised at the quality and depth of this one."

—Denver Rocky Mountain News

"An intense, intelligent thriller, *DEAD FOR LIFE* is well written, gripping. . . . And it moves. Don't pick it up if you have other things you should be doing."

—Detroit Free Press

"Black upends the standard conventions of good cop versus bad killer [and] paints a vivid picture of day-to-day life in New York. . . . Another strong performance by a crime writer who has created an unusual and realistically fallible police protagonist, one readers will follow for years to come."

—Publishers Weekly

"[The] suspense remains high."

—Kirkus Reviews

"Intriguing."

—The Oklahoman

ALL THE DEAD WERE STRANGERS
A Selection of The Literary Guild

"Dead on. . . . Black nails the cops' esprit de corps, but the baddies are even better, at once diabolic and heroic. . . . [He has a] flair for action."

—People

"Black writes nearly perfect thrillers."

—Library Journal

"Gripping . . . fast-paced . . . riveting. . . . Black's timely thriller addresses questions of terrorism and government corruption with intelligence and flair. The social underpinnings never get in the way of the supercharged suspense as the novel proceeds to a flawless, slam-bang conclusion."

—Publishers Weekly (starred review)

"A good mystery novel is more than a simple whodunit. At best it's a morality play that wrestles with the ambiguities of life and its various shades of gray. In that regard, Ethan Black's *All the Dead Were Strangers* is as good as it gets."

—Milwaukee Journal Sentinel

"The best entry yet in this excellent series. . . . One of the best page-turners of the year."

—Amazon.com (A Penzler Pick)

"The vulnerability of the U.S. to terrorist attacks—homegrown or imported—is the foundation for this book. . . . Intelligent and believable."

—American Way

"An exciting, carefully crafted novel."

—Booklist (starred review)

ALSO BY ETHAN BLACK

All the Dead Were Strangers
The Broken Hearts Club
Irresistible

ETHAN BLACK

DEAD FOR LIFE

POCKET STAR BOOKS

New York   London   Toronto   Sydney

This book is a work of fiction. Names, characters, places and incidents are products of the author's imagination or are used fictitiously. Any resemblance to actual events or locales or persons, living or dead, is entirely coincidental.

 A Pocket Star Book published by
POCKET BOOKS, a division of Simon & Schuster, Inc.
1230 Avenue of the Americas, New York, NY 10020

Copyright © 2003 by Ethan Black

Originally published in hardcover in 2003 by
Simon & Schuster, Inc.

ISBN: 0-7434-6420-6

First Pocket Books printing July 2004

10 9 8 7 6 5 4 3 2 1

POCKET STAR BOOKS and colophon are registered trademarks of Simon & Schuster, Inc.

Cover art by Christoph Wilhelm

Manufactured in the United States of America

For information regarding special discounts for bulk purchases, please contact Simon & Schuster Special Sales at 1-800-456-6798 or business@simonandschuster.com

For FDR, JFK, & LBJ, who understood that to privatize public good is to destroy it.

ACKNOWLEDGMENTS

A very special thanks to Chuck Adams, Patricia Burke, Ted Conover, James Grady, Bob Leuci, Bill Massey, Esther Newberg, Steve Rabinowitz, Jerome Reiss, Wendy Roth, and Eli Wallach.

ONE

"You'd think I'd get the shakes, considering what I'm planning today. But I'm okay. Last night I worried that I wouldn't be able to follow through on things, but now as the saying goes, so far so good."

At 6 A.M. on a bright, happy, blue-skied morning, Wendall Nye—failed father, failed husband, failed servant of the vast metropolis—steps briskly along the cobblestoned sidewalk bordering Brooklyn's Prospect Park, its jewel of public places, jauntily swinging a battered leather attaché case like any well-adjusted citizen and speaking softly into a neck mike suspended two inches from his mouth. From a distance he looks like one more preoccupied early morning commuter talking on a cellphone, reminding his wife to pick up his shirts at the laundry or giving orders to his secretary or to the harried broker who buys his stocks.

Wendall Nye, striding toward the subway, joining the trickle of type-A workaholics hurrying toward Manhattan well before rush hour begins, appears to be a man not wasting one second of time that can be spent on potentially profitable commerce, on moneymaking plans.

"The real commuters would throw a fit if they knew what I'm carrying in this attaché case. They'd run."

He speaks into a tape recorder hidden in his shirt pocket, addressing only himself and the man who will eventually hear his tapes. He says, "Laws distinguish between crimes of passion and premeditation. But what is premeditation but the coldest passion? That drums into you for months, that drives you to sleeplessness and turns your dreams red, that makes you follow strangers on the street, diagram exits of their houses, phone them and lie about your name?"

He falls silent as a real commuter passes from behind, talking loudly into a cellphone about the Hong Kong stock index, which seems to be diving. The man passes, recedes briskly, and then Wendall starts up again.

"*Passion's* the link, and when I am finished today and *you* hear my tapes, *you* who never had to deal with failure in your miserably privileged life, remember that. Last night I stood at my window looking toward Manhattan . . . at thousands of lights without warmth . . . and I was afraid I would chicken out this morning. I was filled with despair. But then, thanks to you, I felt passion surge inside me, as if I was sucking up all the intensity off the island . . . and I knew then that I would use every one of the items in my attaché case. I hope you remember that every day until you die."

Electronics are wonderful. One little invention changes the whole way that thousands of strangers perceive each other in the street. There was a time—not long ago—when the sight of a lone man talking and gesturing to himself caused passersby to stiffen or move away.

Now the few commuters paying Wendall any attention at all admire his foresight in wearing the neck mike so as to free a hand to carry his *New York Times* or bag of Krispy Kreme donuts or, once he enters the subway, for gripping a pole in the packed car so he can keep chatting stupidly to his kids, wife, mistress, plumber. Any one of the people who, in the modern city, careen down sidewalks as obliviously as carnival bumper cars, shouting inanities inside their cellphone cocoons.

"What are *you* doing at this moment, birthday boy? Having sex with your blonde girlfriend? Opening your expensive presents? Sleeping in that fucking grand old historical house of yours?"

He halts, pauses, breathes, calms. It will be counterproductive to release his monumental rage too soon.

Across from the park, in ones and twos, men and women who are not contemplating murder emerge from the fine, refinished brownstones and condos lining Prospect Park West. They are visions of success. They have reaped the rewards that the city offers: season tickets to the Knicks; country homes near Stockbridge, Massachusetts; four-wheel-drive Range Rovers, and access for their little Johnnies and Lolitas to the finest private schools.

Suits crisp, bodies smelling of expensive musk, they form a cocky parade of surgeons, lawyers, publishers, and more prominent journalists making the daily pilgrimage to whichever tower of commerce serves as the source of their worldly success.

"But you fear failure," Wendall whispers. "Your good looks don't fool me. Fear keeps the city going. You're afraid you'll lose your retirement savings because you bought IBM instead of Municipal Bonds. That your ten-year-old will hate you one day because you hit him with a belt, or because you never punished him sufficiently for him to understand the consequences of nasty acts. That your boss will downgrade you because you took a bad risk, or missed a good one, or because you hesitated when you should have done something aggressive, or failed to remove yourself from his line of vision on a day when he was in a surly mood.

"The city enhances failure. It is a magnifying glass for falling short. The city's invisible millions have always gone through life muttering, 'I should have been better. I could have been grander. I almost became famous. Why wasn't I something more?'

"But not *you*," he adds, picturing the blond man, the object of his hatred at the moment. "Asshole, bastard, ingrate. Everything came easy for you."

Blending in today, Wendall has dressed in a brand-new black-and-charcoal tweed jacket with leather elbow patches, a crisp button-down white shirt and World Wildlife Fund tie with a cute panda logo above the gold tiepin. The slacks are pleated and cuffed to brush tasseled loafers. The hair, thick brown with strands of premature white, is combed to the side and falls midlength beside large ears in a boy-scoutish style.

But the chest beneath the jacket seems to push dangerously against the fabric. The eyes—the pale green of buds forcing their way into life around the park's perimeter—reflect force metamorphosing into something that cannot be stopped. Faint thought lines meander across Wendall's blocky forehead to enhance a natural look of innocent befuddlement. Yet from close-up, if he turns to the right, the plaintive aspect is blunted by facial damage that has healed to leave small scars: a nailhead sized crater— in the cranial bones—beneath the skin. Literally a small hole in the head. A pinkish half-inch-long seam corresponding to stitches that once ran between the lower lip and thrust of roundish chin, reattaching skin that had been smashed, cut, ripped away.

"I've read a lot about serial murderers over the last few months. Seen the documentaries. Pored over the books. One thing is clear when it comes to these people. They got caught because they spread their work out over time. Hell, give even a dumb cop, a moron law enforcement agent, months to find you, *years* to track you, and he will do it eventually. It's only natural.

"I won't make that mistake."

Smiling faintly with resolve, Wendall shows a stretched, shiny quality in the skin of his cheeks, a paperish sheen that even the most skillful plastic surgeon leaves. Even with the damage, thanks to the surgery, he does not stand out.

He pauses at Grand Army Plaza, at the huge traffic circle and gigantic Civil War arch. The self-help books all stressed the importance of paying attention to everyday pleasures when planning a large project. *Small Acts Have Big Payoffs*, Simon & Schuster's current smash-hit seller, had read: "If you're designing a big job, don't get so caught up in logistics that you stop appreciating daily pleasures. Small pleasures calm you down. You'll be surprised how much they help you keep perspective."

So he wills himself to look around and take a last glimpse of this lovely plaza before he leaves it forever. If the plan works today he will not be back.

Which will avoid another mistake . . . leaving patterns.

The May air feels wonderful. The sky is so blue. He suspects that these simple pleasures will seem different within hours. He tells himself, *How fine and huge the great oaks look. How peaceful and lovely this neighborhood.*

It works! It's amazing how a disciplined change in perspective can cheer you up. The gleaming yellow cabs cruising Prospect Park West suddenly epitomize the best of a smoothly bustling city. There's the scrumptious aroma of a young woman's perfume as she passes him, heels clicking on cobblestone, ass shifting back and forth nicely, shoulder blades flicking with feminine perfection beneath the loose fabric of her lime-green silk dress.

"Gotta go now," he says loudly into the mike, as if telling a spouse good-bye, when in fact this message is for the blond man. "I'll be back later. I'll give you a full report. You'll get every detail. Bye."

Heartbeat picking up, he joins the crowd funneling across the black tar expanse of Grand Army Plaza and down the portals into the subway station, through the turnstile, to the packed platforms below. The entry to hell may be such a line.

He wonders with some tension, as the number 3 train barrels into the station, *Did I remember to put all the right things in the attaché case?*

But no way will he unsnap the case with people around.

He surges with the hungry crowd through the opening doors, reminding himself to tell the tape later, *If the cops ever checked out bags on subways the way they do at airports, they'd drag me out off to Riker's Island and I'd never get out.*

But police never check bags of commuters. The city could never function under such a level of scrutiny. The simplest trip would become a nightmare of security. The whole transportation system would be disrupted into collapse.

Now the automatic doors close and the train lurches forward, lights flickering, hurtling Wendall beneath Brooklyn toward the East River . . . the chance to back out diminishing with each minute . . . and the signs of the familiar stations rush by . . . Nevins Street . . . Hoyt Street . . . Borough Hall, and he is tunneling beneath the great, black East River, to

Chambers Street in Manhattan, where he switches to a local line, the number 9 train.

His resolve is rising with his heartbeat. The train drops him at Sheridan Square, and when he climbs up to Seventh Avenue, blinking in the intense urban sunlight—rays magnified on the street by a thousand windows, light fractured into shards by a thousand pointy roofs and cars and white concrete edifices—he's moving like a military scout in enemy territory, slipping through Greenwich Village. Wendall checking his watch, monitoring the crucial schedule. Wendall thinking, *Every person on the street is a potential witness. Change into the first costume, now.*

He does it in the bathroom of the Parthenon Diner, open twenty-four hours a day. As Muzak plays, and waiters wash their soiled hands, joking with each other in Greek, Wendall, in a locked stall, fits on the dark wig and the tortoiseshell glasses and makes sure that the nine-millimeter is on top inside the attaché case, safety off. He also removes from the case a small paper bag filled with bread crumbs and places it in his pocket. He limps when he emerges into the main room.

The place is packed with NYU students, neighborhood types, unemployed actors. Over the incessantly playing radio, people are talking about deals—New York's favorite subject—as they sit on stools, in vinyl booths, or wait on line for tables. They are telling each other: I wrote a new film script; I got a line on a new stock offering; I know of a two-bedroom apartment that will be available for rent soon, and in return for some key money, cash in my hand, I'll give you the phone number of the old lady vacating the place.

Nobody even glances at Wendall Nye as he walks among them, past them, back outside.

His heart is thundering louder even than the traffic on West Fourth Street. Three short blocks later he's on Sixth Avenue, Gabrielle Viera's street, where he slows as he reaches a small urban park—an asphalt basketball court inside a chain-link fence— between Bleecker and West Fourth.

Sit on the bench and wait for Gabrielle to arrive at work. Look busy.

7:10.

The basketball court's at his back. A row of businesses—drugstore, movie theater, pizza place, donut shop—is across the street. The paper bag filled with bread crumbs comes out of the pocket. Wendall Nye feeds pigeons, head down, face averted except for when he checks one second-floor window across the avenue. One thing that struck him about the serial-murderer books was that witnesses notice strangers on streets when the strangers are doing nothing. Maybe it's some instinct left from caveman days, a vestigial ability to sense predators. Wendall remembers the story of one Chicago murderer, Jerome Vincent Beck. Beck knifed six women in Windy City parking lots and was finally caught because of what he did before the crimes, not during them. *Before* the crimes, Beck lounged around the parking lots. It was the doing nothing, the obvious watching, that got him noticed, identified, and in the end, hanged.

So Wendall Nye spreads bread crumbs on the warming sidewalk. Pigeons gather at his feet, cooing and pecking and staring into his face with their pink little eyes, begging for more. Dumb as murder victims.

Wendall is growing nervous.

Gabrielle should be at work by now.

Five minutes pass. The schedule is getting tight. Has she gotten sick, he frets? Has she changed her routine? Has the subway broken down? He keeps glancing across the street, at a darkened second-floor window, at a banner reading, ASK ABOUT OUR PATAGONIAN ECO-TOURS!

Inside his head he screams, *Where is she?*

Wendall's starting to sweat.

What's *supposed* to happen, what he's planned for is, she's supposed to get to work early, like he made sure she would. She's supposed to click on her high heels into that doorway between the movie theater and the donut shop, and then, after three or four minutes, the lights upstairs are supposed to go on in the Viera Travel Agency. But the only light there now is the orangy polluted tinge from reflected sun.

Wendall uses up the last of the bread crumbs, and careful not to litter, places the crumpled bag back in his case. His nervousness is rising. His senses seem more acute. All around him, from conversations of passersby and from the headlines of the newspapers they carry, he gets snatches of today's version of the city's perpetual preoccupation with success. Which opening movie will succeed beyond box office expectations? Which Yankee second baseman will be traded to the Cleveland Indians in exchange for a more successful left-handed hitter? Which advertisement for a "successful" partner in the personals section of *New York* magazine will attract the wealthiest respondent?

She's not coming! Even after I phoned her yesterday and made an appointment!

But at that moment he sees a light go on inside the Viera Travel Agency, and then to his vast relief the window glides upward and he is looking, from his bench, at what appears to be a very attractive woman watering potted daisies, flashes of bright yellow that line wooden boxes on her fire escape.

The woman's long blue-black hair hides half her face. Her neck is white and slender. Her crimson sweater stands out in a very alluring way.

She must have walked in when I was looking in another direction.

Sweat pouring under his arms, Wendall rises and steps across Sixth Avenue, watching carefully so as to avoid the taxis and trucks zipping northward. He steps into the doorway of the travel agency.

Last chance to change his mind.

He presses his index finger to buzzer 2B.

"Viera Travel!"

"Hi, it's Robert Roth," he lies. "I phoned yesterday about your Argentina packages. You said to drop by early because I had to be at work."

"Come up!" responds the bright, sexy voice, thirty-ish and Latina. A buzzer sounds. Wendall pushes open the screened, locked door and mounts the steps to a second-floor landing, where Gabrielle Viera, even more lovely in person, has opened the door and stands beaming at him. Black eyes. Glossed lips. Dress long and tight. Her pumps are black Italian leather. Her bracelet, thin and gold, highlights the tan. The long hair tosses when she moves, and she moves quite nicely.

She closes the door behind him. She tells him that it was no problem for him to come early. In the travel agent business, which is very competitive, she says as if he gave a damn, every little bit of work gives an edge.

"If you want to be successful, you must get to work early and stay late," she says, shaking his hand, letting him feel the smoothness of her almond skin.

In fact, she tells him, not knowing that he has studied her every move for weeks, she often arrives at work hours before official opening time, to catch up on e-mails from other countries and to familiarize herself with dozens of airfare changes that may have been announced while the city slept.

"I'm interested in the ecotours," he says, scanning the bull-pen-style office, confirming that they are alone, but counting three desks in all, meaning that two other employees may arrive at any time. He also sees lots of potted plants, hanging ferns, a small alerce tree, and attractive outdoor posters of the Aegean, Costa Rica, Rio.

Do it now.

But he hesitates as she goes to her desk. He can't help it. He has never killed anyone before. His confidence—so high an hour ago—is fading now that he is here.

"You couldn't have picked a better time of year to travel to Patagonia," she says, holding out a glossy brochure. "Especially if you are," she adds, repeating the lies he told her over the phone yesterday, "a kayaker. Patagonia is an outdoor paradise. I myself just returned from there. May I ask what level of difficulty you prefer when paddling?"

"Average," he says, having never been in a kayak in his life, but having chosen this particular misrepresentation because the blond man, who Wendall hates, is an enthusiastic kayaker. The irony amused Wendall Nye.

Gabrielle's face glows with promise. "Then you will be happy with the many rivers to explore in the area around Bariloche."

Pick up the gun.

He is paralyzed, in agony. He just nods stupidly. It's different when a real person stands in front of you, not a picture you drew in a notebook. Her stupid voice drones on and on.

"The Argentinean economy is in trouble at the moment, so even the best accommodations and guides will cost you less. I used a terrific one. Diego Efron is his name."

"The pictures looked great," he manages to get out.

She winks, coming closer: "Normally travel photographs are better than the real place. But in Patagonia the opposite is true. See?" She shows a series of tantalizing shots of snowcapped mountains. It looks like Bavaria. No wonder the Nazis hid here after killing the Jews, he thinks. And here's a touristy shot of Gabrielle herself, wearing a yellow helmet and life vest, waving from an inflatable raft filled with shouting vacationers as it churns down Andes rapids.

"Should I turn on the AC? You're sweating a bit," she says. "It's hot for May."

He snaps open the attaché case while she fidgets with the thermostat. He raises the lid so she cannot see what is inside: the nine-millimeter and two silencers, ammo clips, and beside them an S & W S.W.A.T. knife, shiny sharp but not to be used at this address. There's a length of pipe stuffed with concrete and a blue velvet case that contains a pair of hypodermics filled with formalin. The small thermos carries Folgers coffee, and he's included a sandwich of Swiss cheese and Italian hard salami with deli mustard—on seven-grain bread.

"Good diet keeps your head clear," he'd been advised by the Ballantine paperback *Eating for Success.*

Stalling while he mentally screams at himself to move, he asks, "Is the water safe to drink in Patagonia? My wife's picky about what she eats."

"Absolutely safe! And the steaks! These are grass-fed Argentinean animals! The meat is so flavorful!

You will not have a better steak in the whole world."

"The airfare seemed high."

Suddenly he hears a door open out in the hallway. One of the other travel agents has arrived for work!

But then the door slams out there. Someone apparently arrived at one of the other offices on the floor.

What the hell is the matter with me? Coward! Stupid! Do it!

"Those prices *could* be reduced," she says, "if you can travel between Tuesdays and Thursdays."

His hand refuses to move. It is not attached to his brain, it seems. It hangs there like a dead animal.

"I sense some hesitation," Gabrielle remarks, stepping back, downshifting gears so that her voice becomes more modulated. Sitting, she crosses her legs. They are very nice legs, and he has a feeling that they have helped her make plenty of sales.

7:28.

"It's just that my family hasn't taken a vacation in years. I want it to be perfect," he says, thinking she'll never believe this pathetic, time-wasting lie.

She nods. "It is normal to reappraise a choice. But if you don't mind me saying so, especially after hearing the eagerness in your voice over the phone yesterday, I've found in life there comes a point which separates those who do things from those who merely consider them. You reach this border and to go any further must tell yourself, I will do this! That's how I bought this agency. I made a decision and it changed my whole life."

"Changing your whole life must have been difficult," Wendall remarks with some actual interest.

"Difficulty makes a decision more rewarding," Gabrielle says, laughs, and adds, "But this is just a vacation. You know, I grew up in Buenos Aires. My parents took us to Bariloche for vacations. Later I moved to New York and had many jobs before I bought the agency . . . and now I send people to the country where I lived. Life's funny."

"Filled with surprises, that's for sure."

"What else can I tell you? Ready for the trip of your life?"

Wendall Nye, big strong man, fists closed, grinding his muscles. Wendall thinking miserably, *I could never follow through on anything.*

He hears himself say, "I guess I . . . I suppose I'm just not ready yet for this."

Humiliated, he asks for her business card, puts it in his wallet. He reaches to snap closed the attaché case when he hears her say, still selling, "A wife and a son, isn't that what you said? I have a boy too."

He thinks, you have no children. You live alone.

"There is so much for a boy to do in Patagonia. Hiking. Mountain biking. When you return from this vacation, he will never forget it. The loving memory of a boy for his father is a precious thing," she says.

"I said I'll think about it," he says, wanting to hide his face, the burning shame traveling from his skull into his chest. She puts a light restraining hand to his wrist, a soothing touch. "Do you have a photo of them?"

"My family?"

"The people you wish to surprise. A picture of them. May I see it?"

"A picture," he repeats, slowly, and he envisions a picture, all right. It is a gray-and-brown-mottled cat running in a Brooklyn street. It is a cat scurrying under an old Ford Fairlane. He thinks of the cat and his rage returns full force.

She says, "Is something wrong? Don't you have a photo of your lovely wife and son?"

In one swift move his hand drops into the attaché case, grips the handle of the nine-millimeter, and lifts. Gabrielle must have thought he was going for a photograph. Her lovely face looks puzzled but not afraid. In her mind, she must be trying to understand what she is looking at, thinking, "But that is a gun. That is not a photograph."

The report sounds thunderous to him when he pulls the trigger, even with the silencer on. She never says anything more, just stares uncomprehendingly as the light goes out of her eyes. The blood spurting from her skull is darker than the red of her sweater. Wendall smells ammonia in the room. Woolite and urine. Sheep and vinegar. Something cared for mixed with something ruined.

I did it, he thinks in massive surprise, staring down at the gun.

He waits for remorse but it does not come. The room now seems smaller and yet appears to him as if from a great distance, as if it has become a still-life diorama in which he is the doll star, watching himself through the wrong end of a long telescope. Here is the woman slumping backward, in a swivel chair, arms thrown back at a rag-doll angle. Here is her carefully arranged furniture, in her stupid fucking travel agency, dotted in places by red spray. Bits of ruby color, shiny dots, soak into a desk blotter and trickle down the computer screen and have spread in an uneven arc to smear the glassed-in tour poster showing vacationers screaming with frightened pleasure as they navigate a turgid mountain river below the headline ARGENTINA! YOU MUST COME!

He feels, actually, a kind of triumph.

A phone is ringing somewhere. He realizes he must hurry, get out of here, and, returning the nine-millimeter to the case, sees that Gabrielle Viera, in the closing minute of her life, was right about moving on to new things. He has crossed a border. He has embraced the new world. From the attaché case he leaves, beside the body, the addressed envelope he prepared earlier, at his home.

Outside, at 8:01, commuters are pouring from the subway entrances in bigger streams now. They push and bump against each other, hurrying toward their offices. They are everywhere, like mice, eyes open but seeing nothing.

By the time he joins them he is calm and determined and fairly sure that no one saw him leave the building, and even if they had, within minutes, the wig is gone, dropped down a sewer near NYU. The glasses have been replaced by today's second pair, aviator wire rims that make his face seem narrower.

A clock has been set ticking. Hour by hour, thinks Wendall Nye, I will teach that bastard a thing or two. His hesitation is gone. In its place he experiences powerful certainty.

Next appointment: 12:20.

He envisions one of the other travel agents, maybe the short fat man who usually arrives at 8:15, strolling in, stopping in shock, groping for the telephone, screaming panicked words at the operator who answers the call to 911. He recalls the message he left for the blond man, which the police will see before he does, in minutes probably, and which they will undoubtedly pass on to him.

First the personal part, for Mister Voort.

Then the part that, within the hour, will put the city in thrall.

TWO

Voort feels a hand caress his shoulder and knows even before opening his eyes that the woman rousing him is not the one he slept with last night. The perfume is more subtle, the nails sharper. Brushing his shoulder tenderly, they set his nerve endings throbbing and fill his belly with unwanted warmth.

"Happy birthday, blond guy," his dead cousin's widow says.

What's the worst thing you've ever done to yourself? The worst choice you've ever made? Was it so big that you knew instantly that your life would never be the same afterward?

Or was it deceptive enough so you could convince yourself it was unimportant? A smile at the wrong person, perhaps. A few minutes' delay at a bar. A tiny wager. A hesitation in love that seemed so innocent, minor, and private that it was impossible to comprehend the enormity of the crossroads to which it brought you and the rolling years of unhappiness it would set in motion, stretching to your final hour.

Trouble now. But what is he supposed to do? Kick her out of the house? From the muted sound of running water, he knows that his girlfriend, Camilla, is only fifteen feet away, showering in the bathroom. The shower shuts off. He hears Camilla humming. She likes to hum rock tunes as she towels off.

"Wake up, sleepy," Julia persists.

Voort opens his eyes in his hundred-year-old four-poster bed. The widow—sitting beside him—is small and ash blonde, the hair pixie cut, the blue eyes light as the Caribbean sea, the skin Scandinavian white, and the shadow of legs and hips beneath her baby blue nightgown as slender, petite, and fetching as every mistake a man ever made.

She's a widow, for Christ's sake. And I'm hard as a rock. Maybe it's from being asleep.

Right.

Widows are supposed to be elderly, not twenty-seven, or at least that's what Voort used to think when he was a boy. Widows are supposed to be sad and used up. But Julia's lips are glossy and cupid-shaped, as Voort has heard more than once during the months she's been his houseguest, snatches of conversation in supermarkets, in restaurants, as men noticed Julia's lips.

"Seems there's a party starting downstairs, old guy," she smiles.

"I'm only thirty-three," he says.

"You look ancient," she says.

"What party?" he says, thinking, I'm flirting with her.

She flashes a killer smile. A smile that only eight years ago had high school boys fighting each other, racing each other in cars to impress her. A smile that had gotten cousin Don Voort to propose marriage. And now he hears a slamming door downstairs. A stereo playing something classical. Handel. He smells bacon. He hears children laughing down there.

"Camilla said you didn't have any particular plans this morning so I made some calls. I hope that's all right."

Actually, Camilla was going to take me out to break-fast, and then we were going to the boathouse to build kayaks. This is my first day off after two weeks straight of working overtime, filling in for cops arrested up in the Bronx. Camilla and I were going to have a quiet day. We were going to eat and make love and take in the traditional birthday Mets game tonight.

Despite Julia's presence, the thought of Camilla fills Voort with a different kind of warmth, a solid happiness that has marked his life since they got back together six months ago, reuniting after spending over a year apart. First they'd become friends again. Then more than friends again. The rocky history between them has settled into a loving consistency that gives Voort contentment. Into the kind of excitement that comes from knowing a woman well, as opposed to the dangerous, spicy kind that comes from not knowing one well enough.

"I was thinking," Julia says, little hips on his bed, fingers lingering on his shoulder, robe open enough so that he can see the rounded tops of those apple-sized breasts, "Why do birthday parties always start at night? Why not make the whole day special? We all wanted to celebrate," she says, and by "we" he knows she means the whole extended family. The Queens Voorts. The Tugboat Voorts.

"That was thoughtful," he says, sliding back enough on the bed so her hand drops to her side.

"You've been a lifesaver to let Donnie Jr. and me stay here. I'll find an apartment soon. I promise. I've been looking hard."

Voort the detective in his two-hundred-year-old house. That's how long the building has served as a haven for family members who lost their farms, or were out of work, or needed to get back on their feet again after fighting the nation's wars overseas, or who simply needed a sick bed because they feared the dirty New York hospitals of the past.

These days, Voort cops who find themselves, at 2 A.M., exhausted after working overtime, use the spare key and crash in one of the second-floor bedrooms. It's easier than making the long commute to Nassau or Suffolk counties, when they have to be back at work in a few short hours.

"What's the point of having three floors of space if I don't use it," he tells Julia. "It's more important that you love where you end up."

The townhouse and the land it was built on was bequeathed by the Continental Congress to his ancestor, Admiral Conrad Voort, as reward for blocking a British landing in New Jersey during the

American Revolution. The original grant, framed on the brick wall of the living room, says, "For actions beyond the call of duty, and in lieu of payment, Admiral Voort and his descendants are hereby awarded, in perpetuity, lot 28 on the island of Manhattan, in the City of New York. The land or structure will never be taxed, by federal, state or city authorities. Home and land may be handed from generation to generation. This edict will remain in effect until the last Voort dies or sells the property, at which time all monies from the transaction will remain in family hands, not to be subject to any tax levied by any government authority, federal, state or local. Thank you, Admiral Voort. Signed and witnessed."

Voort, at the moment, is easily the richest cop in New York, thanks to two centuries of smart investments, including his own.

And now, behind Julia, the bathroom door opens and Camilla steps out amid billowing steam onto the polished plank floor, as she vigorously towels herself. She's taller than Julia, hair longer than Julia's, down to her very fine ass, belly flat from running and kayaking, eyes flashing northern Irish pissed-off blue when she sees the woman sitting on Voort's bed.

Julia says brightly. "I was saying hi to the birthday guy."

"He's so cute." Camilla doesn't look as if she is thinking about how cute he is.

The window is open and a May breeze wafts past three-hundred-year-old oil paintings and the antique

night table, marble cherub, and porcelain basin that
Admiral Voort plundered from British frigates as he
raged up and down the coast. But Voort's eyes linger
on the far wall. His problem at this moment is better
represented by the newer painting hanging there,
which he commissioned. It shows modern New York
cops and firepersons digging in the wreckage of the
World Trade Center, after terrorists destroyed the
towers.

In the painting, men and women silhouetted in
smoke and dust bend and sift beneath the last half-
standing section of superstructure, a fan-shaped
skeleton of melted steel rising like a pipe organ
behind the crews. Rescue workers, the newspapers
had called them. But there had been almost nobody
to rescue. Nobody to send to hospitals in hundreds
of ambulances standing by.

Voort and his partner, Mickie, had been among
them, looking with agonized urgency for survivors
among the three thousand vanished people—residents and visitors who had been innocently at work
in the offices one moment. And who had watched
ceilings crashing down on them the next.

Voort flashes to himself, working beside his uncles
and cousins and hundreds of fellow officers and
detectives. Buried below had been, among the dead,
three Voort cops, including Julia's young husband, a
foot patrolman who had been running into the tower
to help evacuate it when the building collapsed.

"Oh, Donnie," Julia murmurs, following Voort's
gaze and twisting her wedding band unconsciously.

Voort's eyes meet Camilla's. He asks her with the look: *What am I supposed to do?*

Out loud he tells Julia, "I love that you made me a party. Camilla and I will be right down."

He supposes that he could have put the painting downstairs, because why place such a terrible vision where you wake up? But for the present at least he has decided he wants it there to remember, each morning before going to work, the consequences of lack of imagination and preparation. Wants to remind himself and, later, any children who will inherit the house, why you must always ask the extra question, make the extra phone call, fill out the extra report, even if you are exhausted, and whether or not you think it will do any good.

Julia pulls his attention back, as she holds out a small package wrapped in shiny blue paper.

"Happy birthday. I wanted to give this to you in private. Not in front of the rest."

"Oh, open it, honey," Camilla urges, taking Julia's exact place beside him on the bed.

"It's his badge," Voort breathes, picturing his cousin, who in truth he barely knew: an awkward, gangly, smart cadet in the academy. A respected patrolman who'd racked up a decent record on arrests.

Donald Voort's badge, or the remnant of it, rests on purple velvet, which enhances the shiny part and makes the tarnished one more dull. Voort runs his thumb over gouged, half-melted metal. It reminds him of the tie rods and melted girders he sifted past.

It produces a sick feeling in his stomach and strengthens his resolve to help Julia and her five-year-old son, Donnie, Jr., any way he can.

"I can't keep this."

"It should go with the family artifacts. Put it downstairs with the old revolvers and nightsticks and awards." She wraps his hand around the charred metal, "You don't need other presents. You have your house. You have a terrific lady. You have all the physical things you need."

Her flesh is as warm as the badge is cool. She says, stepping back but leaving the sensation of her skin on his knuckles, "Sorry to interrupt, but I figured you'd want to know there were people downstairs."

"No problem," Voort says.

"We'll be down in a jiff," Camilla says.

"By the way," Julia says, turning that pixie smile on the taller woman except, woman to woman, it seems to convey a different meaning than when flashed at him. "Do you know, Cam," Julia says, using the hated nickname, "what the other Voorts are starting to call us?" Julia giggles. "The sisters. Isn't that funny? I guess, because of the blonde hair. I guess they think we look alike."

"What do you know." Camilla remarks.

"Like you're the older sister and I'm the younger."

"How about that? The older sister," Camilla repeats.

"Bye," Julia sings. "Happy birthday to youuu."

By now, if Julia hadn't shown up, Voort and Camilla would have made love. They might *still* be making love. They'd be lying in bed one way or another, that much is for sure, instead of regarding each other flatly over the quilt as traffic sounds drift up from Thirteenth Street, cabs honking, kids laughing, a dog barking . . . noise to fill the awkwardness in the room.

"I can't just ask her to leave."

"Of course not. You couldn't even ask her to take two steps back."

They've been living together for the last two months—not as long as Julia has been bunking with her five-year-old on the second floor—but enough time for him to have started relishing Camilla's little rhythms. Like, when they're not squabbling, the way she plays imaginary guitar when she thinks he isn't looking. The way she sets up a pot of decaf coffee before she goes to bed with him each night.

The way, now that she's lost her investigative TV producer job in the recession—contract nonrenewal, they call it at NBC—she likes to make love each morning and laze around reading the *Times* before slipping into denim coveralls and heading down to the boathouse where she's building a kayak.

Tough TV producer Camilla turned into a boatbuilder. Working with resin and wood each day instead of cameras. She's always loved kayaks, paddling them, racing them, winning awards in them, and he finds he likes the new Camilla even more than the old. She's softer.

"Her robe was open. She knows what she's doing," Camilla says.

Doggedly, he says, "There are always going to be family staying here."

They are both getting dressed instead of making love. Covering themselves instead of touching each other. Happy birthday, pal.

She says, "Don't pretend this is about family."

Happy birthday to youuuu.

She says, as she bends at her dresser, takes out folded blue jeans, slips them onto her long, beautiful legs, "They were going to be divorced before the towers went down."

"That's rumor, Camilla. And even if it's true they could have gotten back together. *We* did. Not to mention, what about Donnie Jr.? Not to mention, she's practically broke."

"I always hated that expression. First someone says *not* to mention it. Then they mention it."

Camilla's holding a baby blue cotton spring-weight turtleneck. She's still nude on top. Half-dressed women look fetchingly naked, Voort thinks, amazed by his permanent chemical connection to Camilla, even when they are fighting.

Half-dressed men look like clowns, shirts flapping, socks clinging.

More softly, she says, "I'm turning into the heavy here. What can I say without looking like I don't have sympathy? A terrible thing happened. I covered the story. I *saw* what was left of those bodies. My upstairs neighbor was never even found. And I know the role you have in this family, but," she says firmly, "Julia got over a million dollars, *minimum*, between the Red Cross Fund, the city, and the federal reward system. A million three probably, tax free, and I'm not saying that's even the beginning of compensation but . . ."

"She lost it in the stock market. She got bad advice."

"She made bad choices, which you can't be responsible for. And she's making another mistake now, coming after you. What am I supposed to do? Pretend it isn't happening?"

"Isn't it possible you're imagining it?"

"As possible as you imagining it's not."

"The point isn't what she wants. It's what I do and . . ."

"No," she interrupts. "I'm not going to let her screw up your birthday. But we have a history now, you and me. I made a mistake that I regret and we both punished ourselves over it. That we're back together means we have something strong and powerful between us, but *listen to me*.

"Before I was married, my ex-husband courted me like crazy. He was nuts over me. He called me, wrote notes, brought flowers. He was there all the time for me, and the second I fell for him it started to change. Maybe that's what all guys do," she says with some bitterness. "Maybe you all get bored. But if that's the case, no one is ever going to be bored with me again. Even you. I'm not going to live like that. Once was too much."

"Camilla?"

"What?"

"I love you."

"Right."

"Camilla."

"What?"

"The party can wait."

She says nothing for a moment, which is her way, he knows, of telling him that she meant every word of what she just said. Then a slow smile spreads over her face.

"It certainly better wait," she says.

From downstairs come the smells of coffee, of cinnamon. Voorts will be setting up long tables in the dining room. The Hudson Valley crew will have driven down with salted hams and fruit pies and homemade hard and soft ciders. The Tugboat Voorts will have chugged over from Staten Island with cartons of liquor from one of Cousin Marla's discount stores. The party, Voort knows from happy experience, will go on all day. Voorts will take over the house, whether or not he is here. Cops on duty now will drop by when their shifts end. The kids will play foozball and knock hockey in the basement. The retired cops will bring their whiskeys out to the greenhouse, or up to the roof, and they'll look out over the skyline and tell stories until midnight. The women will turn the Dutch kitchen into a lush-smelling proving ground for recipes that have been in the family since George Washington sat listening in his tent to advice from Voort scouts in buckskin, since the first Voorts to land in the New World worked as night watchmen in New Amsterdam.

By tonight, there will be over two hundred people here. Voorts stopping in will bring foods from all over the city: hummus from Brooklyn, cannoli from little Italy, sweet and sour pork and moussaka and pad thai, paella, fried okra, and twenty kinds of sugary pies.

His eyes flicker again to the World Trade Center painting, and he feels by the way that his chest constricts with emotion how for all of them the house has somehow become even more important since the World Trade Center was destroyed. He supposes each generation has coped with its own terrible disaster, and that for past cop generations this house was a gathering place after John Kennedy was assassinated or Pearl Harbor was attacked or while the country was swept by flu epidemics. The house is the family touchstone. And Voort, its keeper, is the involuntary family prince.

Now Voort the cop prince is having a birthday, and the prince's birthday is always a patriotic occasion. On the prince's birthday, citizens celebrate all kinds of things. During hard times, the prince's birthday enables his subjects to celebrate the best of themselves.

"You're so beautiful," he tells Camilla as the phone starts ringing. He ignores it.

And now their clothes are coming off, which is much, much better than the other way around. The baby blue turtleneck is gliding back over her head. He pulls in his breath at the way her breasts perk away from her lovely rib cage, and the way her slim arms come down as she unbuttons her jeans. All her angles seem to heighten his lust. The arc of her neck. The delicate bone line beneath her lightly freckled shoulders. The tapering legs. The round curve of hips.

The phone stops ringing. Either someone downstairs is answering or the machine is picking up.

Camilla crawls toward him over the quilt on all fours, like an animal. He pulls her close and her tongue slips into his mouth, rimming his teeth. Her long fingers caress his neck, chest, thighs, balls. Belly to belly, he relishes the hardness of her abs, the jut of her hips.

"Oh Voort," she says as he fingers her wetness, kisses her, licks her, moves to enter her. "Voort," she whispers over a knocking on the door.

"Julia'll go away," he says, but instead it's another voice out there, his partner Mickie's voice calling, "Yo! Long John! Make the porn movies later. We gotta go!"

Voort rolls away from Camilla, and she sticks her tongue out at him like a nine-year-old girl. They're both panting and sweating. His dick seems as hard as the cherub statue's, and his balls are already starting to throb with pain from lack of release.

"Julia called you too?" Voort gets out.

"What's a birthday bash without the best buddy present, Con Man. But I'm not interrupting for personal reasons. I want to live."

"Go away."

"Get your pants on. There's a squad car downstairs for us, sent by Generallismo Eva," Mickie says, naming the city's new chief of detectives. "She wants us, forthwith."

"It's been two weeks. We *can't* be working again."

"Maybe we're filling in for more scumbags arrested by the mayor's avenger, Tommy D."

A feeling of dread begins in Voort's belly and rises sourly up to his throat. "If we were filling in, Mick, the call wouldn't come from Eva."

"Then maybe she wants to give you a birthday present. Maybe she bought old Con Man a tie."

THREE

Nine minutes later Voort is bouncing around the back of a squad car as it shoots west down Thirteenth Street, siren blaring, running traffic lights so fast that the pedestrians staring out at them blur. Speeding to work is not an unfamiliar situation, at least on the surface. Cops live with trouble so much that its rhythms seem normal. Phones ring at 3 A.M. Murders interrupt dates. Robberies break up pizza parties, Monday night football games, French movies, weddings.

But something about this particular summons seems wrong, Voort thinks as they run another red light.

"You gonna tell us what this is about?" Mickie practically shouts at the driver. His ringed fingers poke through the wire-mesh seat divider. The blue and white smells of ArmorGuard, curry, wet dog hair, peach air freshener, and a wedge of carrot cake that the driver's half wrapped in tinfoil on the front seat.

"They said get you. They said fast," the Blue Guy says, keeping his eyes on the road.

It's the way he's acting that's bothering me.

Mickie leans back, his ease at odds with the frantic speed with which the car careens through Manhattan. He's a powerfully built ex-marine who picks his clothes out of *GQ* magazine. As the steppes look is in this spring, he's wearing a soft, expensive Cossack-style fawn-colored cotton shirt beneath his Calvin Klein suede jacket. Sharply pleated chinos end at shiny Bass loafers. But the soft look doesn't go with the black eyes, thick black hair, and Mickie's black Irish temper, which he rarely loses, always to the detriment of anyone on the receiving end.

Voort's in soft blue jeans, a white button-down shirt, and a black Calvin Klein two-button jacket. The two richest cops in the city don't usually ride in the back of squad cars. Called in on cases, they transport themselves. And normally on a day off Mickie would be out in Roslyn at his waterfront home, playing the market on his guest cottage computer or fishing for sea bass or sharks in his new Grady twenty-five footer.

"Hey driver, who'd you have back here last? It stinks."

No answer.

"My advice, Con Man, is move Julia out of your house," Mickie says as the car hits a pothole, misses sideswiping a trash truck, and leaves behind three fist-waving garbagemen screaming at them. If the Blue Guy's going to keep quiet, Mickie figures he might as well turn his attention to other things. Why worry before it's necessary?

"Since when are you a fan of Camilla's?" Voort says.

"The Valkyrie grew on me when she committed herself to you. But the point is, both ladies are not going to stick around much longer, old buddy. You wanna make the choice who stays? Or should they make it for you?"

"I've never turned away a Voort."

Mickie issues a deep mocking sound from the back of his fullback-sized throat. "What is this, goddamn *Gone With the Wind?* There'll always be Tara? Look, I've been married so long I don't even remember being single any more. But if you want to sleep with our little Britney Spears, that's your business, but do it with your eyes open. If you don't, admit you can't fix her life and send her on her way."

"Watch out for the van," Voort tells the driver.

Mickie says, "Con Man, I'd love to have five minutes with the fuckers who did the World Trade Center. I'd gladly spend a century in hell for five minutes alone with them. But victims are not saints just because they're victims."

"Maybe we should give personality tests before helping out."

They shoot past discount stores, hot dog stands, bars. They screech sideways onto Seventh Avenue, providing a moment's entertainment for the stationary cyclists pedaling up in the second floor window of the Village Health Club, the newsstand owner on Twelfth Street unwrapping a stack of *Posts*, a restaurateur hosing down the sidewalk in front of The Blue Ostrich Café. Cabbies pull over to let them pass, glad that whatever tragedy has summoned the police, whatever murder, subway fire, car crash, gas leak, they themselves escaped it.

Voort catches the driver's glance in the rearview mirror and frowns, and Mickie nods at him, meaning, *I saw it too.* Blue Guys, they know, are exquisitely sensitive to the mood of their commanders, and any uniformed cop who's been ordered to fetch two detectives, forthwith, *detectives who have their own car and didn't need to be driven,* knows that his passengers are probably either about to be decorated, handed a crucial assignment, or that some big-time shit has hit the fan.

Accordingly, Blue Guys escorting winners tend to radiate the respect that was conveyed when they got the order. They do their job with quiet attentiveness or buddy up to the passenger, asking questions, telling stories, basking in the glory radiating off the adjacent seat.

Blue Guys baby-sitting a screwup, on the other hand, project suspicion or amusement, depending on their level of knowledge. If they're friendly at all, it comes across as relief that the department's wrath is about to fall on someone else.

What Voort just saw in the rearview mirror was a kind of appraisal that cops rarely give other cops. What he saw, for a fraction of a second, was the stare you see in an interrogation room, cop to suspect, not cop to cop.

Mickie adds to the alarm by observing, as they career off Bleecker back onto Sixth Avenue, "That's the commissioner's car."

They pull over between Bleecker and West Fourth, joining the collection of squad cars, Crown Vics, and TV vans that marks a major crime scene. Vehicles are parked in a fan shape, like animals at a feeding trough, in front of a donut shop and closed pizza parlor.

Voort says, "Captain's car. Inspector's car. Mayor's office. What the hell happened?"

A crowd of bystanders clusters outside a taped-off door between shops that clearly leads to the upper two floors of the building. Blue Guys guard the entrance. Traffic on Sixth has backed up because only two lanes are moving, and both are clogged with gaping drivers. That's why Voort's Blue Guy took the long way around.

Reporters run toward him when he gets out of the car.

"Hey Voort! It's Ritchie Awls from New York One!"

"One question!"

"How'd they get here so fast?" growls Mickie, who hates journalists. "Air drop?"

The Blue Guy escorts them under the yellow crime scene tape, and, ignoring the newsmen, they head up a narrow flight of linoleum stairs.

And now they are passing through the open door of the Viera Travel Agency, as the plaque reads, and the unbelievably foul smell hits them. And now, in the bright sunny room, Voort takes in the familiar view of white-coated technicians, fingerprinting detectives, a photo guy moving around the bull-pen-style office.

Men and women open drawers, examine papers with tweezers, dust glass cases containing travel posters, peer behind desks, beneath wastebaskets, or onto computer screens that have been switched on.

An inspector converses with the captain of the Sixth Precinct, who Voort knows, in a corner.

His eyes go to the desk closest to the window, where an ME leans over a victim slumped back on a chair, and whose bare foot protrudes from the edge of the lab coat. Voort sees the hem of a red dress. A painted toenail. He sees a spray of red dots on the window behind the woman, as if a housepainter shook a wet brush nearby, splattering the double-strength pane.

Despite his disquiet, he notes, *No sign of break-in. Electronics still here and drawers tidy, so it probably wasn't a burglary. Pocketbook open and I see a wallet, so forget robbery. Rape? She's dressed. And from the smell, this just happened.*

The sun, pouring through the big windows, heats up the room and glows across the bent shoulders of the ME's lab coat. It reflects off framed posters to shimmy in tiny tricolored rainbows on walls and potted plants.

Mickie starts to hum softly, but not a tune. A warning. A low three-note warble like an alarm going off.

Voort picks up on it, notices the speculative glances coming their way from the crime crew. The ticking in his chest accelerates. Normally crime scene staffers concentrate on their jobs, not on visitors.

"The chief said Detective Voort only," grunts the Blue Guy escort. "Not Detective Connor." He points to a small glassed-in conference room, where the new police commissioner, new chief of detectives, and a young deputy mayor named Tommy Lamond Deans are clustered around a table, focusing on something on top while the commissioner talks. The chief nods agreeably, liking whatever the commissioner is saying. Tommy Deans emphatically shakes his large head no.

They stop conversing when Voort walks in, and Voort notes the way the chief slides her arm over a sheet of paper on the table. Three expressionless faces look back at him. *If it was a job*, Voort thinks, *they'd be explaining logistics. It feels like I'm in trouble. But why?*

He takes in the faces. Eva Ramirez, New York's first female chief of detectives, is a slim, hard-faced woman of forty, who came up through the department by compiling an award-winning record stretching back seventeen years. Her petite body is encased in a conservatively cut gray business suit, and her normally jawlength copper-colored hair is fixed back by a large tortoiseshell pin. Her green eyes are bright with directness. She neither wears nor needs any appreciable degree of makeup. She's widely admired for fighting recent staff cuts, and has a reputation going back years for backing up subordinates who got caught in a jam.

Even Mickie—who respects very few brass—likes her.

Commissioner Warren Aziz, next closest to Voort

and a former DA, is an unmarried workaholic with ambitions to run for mayor, senator, or governor, whichever position opens first, whichever race gets the blessing of Democratic party leaders, according to a recent *Times* editorial. The paper approved of Aziz's balance of a concern for civil liberties with a record of prosecuting crime. Son of Iranian refugees, the new commissioner lives in a four-story walk-up on the Upper East Side. He wears off-the-rack suits that he buys on sale. He has no car, and during off-hours takes public transportation, where he is said to be accessible to anyone who wants to talk to him. Aziz is the only one here that Voort has worked closely with, and Voort considers him shrewd, fair, and farseeing, but hesitant if potential encroachment on civil liberties is involved.

Deputy Mayor Thomas Lamond Deans is the least familiar to Voort of the three, but possibly the one with the most power. A lawyer, and the son of a Harlem couple—tobacco store owners murdered by an off-duty cop in a stickup, Deans is a former federal prosecutor said to dine regularly with the mayor. A hard-liner on crime, he heads city hall's anti–police-corruption task force, which has been responsible for a wave of firings in the South Bronx. The city is in the midst of one of its periodic department scandals and unforgiving moods. Over a dozen officers have been indicted in the last month for taking bribes, and the mayor has promised to "root out any bad apples left."

"You look like your picture in *New York* maga-zine," Deans remarks, referring to a widely read profile that ran after Voort's arrest of the killer John Szeska last year. "Big Apple's Hero," the magazine called him then. Deans doesn't seem to regard him as a hero now.

Eva waves him into a seat as Aziz nods noncommittally and Deans crosses his powerful arms.

"We have a problem," she says.

"Maybe I can help," Voort says.

"Gabrielle Viera," Eva says, and the scrutiny of Voort in the room seems to ratchet up a notch. He searches his memory.

"Who's that?" he says, liking the looks from Deans and Eva less with each second that goes by.

"You never heard the name?" Like he's lying.

"Viera was the name on the plaque on the door. She's the owner, I take it."

"Think," Aziz says more calmly. "Viera."

Deans spells, "V-I-E-R-A," as if that might change his mind.

Voort shrugs. "I said no."

"Ever do any business with this agency?" Eva asks.

"I use my own agent."

"But you do travel a lot, huh?" Deans says, as if that's supposed to mean something.

"So what?"

Eva lays a framed photo of a sexy-looking Latina woman on the conference desk. She's sitting in the back of a powerboat, in a string bikini, smiling. She's got a frosted drink in her hand, with a straw and a paper umbrella in it. She's probably the woman in the chair outside.

"Maybe you know her by sight, not by name," Aziz suggests.

"If I ever met her, I don't remember."

Deans tells the others, "Let's move this along. We don't have time."

Eva nods without breaking eye contact with Voort, and tells him, "I want to ask you something and I want a straight answer." She holds up a hand to stop any protest he might make, any claim that he'd never lie. "Tell the truth now, even if it involves a lapse on your part, I'll do right by you. The commissioner too. Right, Warren?"

"I always liked you," agrees Aziz, who radiates sympathy if not warmth at the moment, and who last year worked on the famed Szeska case with Voort. "People make mistakes. Everyone does. The point is, do you have some involvement in this thing?"

"Mistakes?" Voort says, as the throbbing in his throat picks up and small pinprick pains erupt along the tips of his fingers. "Involvement?"

"Now's the time to tell us. If it comes from you, things will go better," Eva says, as if he is some kind of suspect, which, he realizes with shock, he is.

Throw out an open question. Let the target squirm, lie, protest, bluster.

Deans says, "I think you know what we want."

"You can't think I did this," Voort says.

Deans's chair scrapes as he pulls it out. The deputy mayor stands, a big man whose energy will not let him stay in one spot for long.

He tells Eva, "Show him," and glances at the

paper that is mostly hidden beneath her arm. Voort understands that whatever is on that sheet is the reason he's here.

The room is hot, and he's started sweating, but thankfully the wetness seems confined to his back. How many times has he looked in on an interrogation, watched a first bead of moisture form on a suspect's forehead, turned to Mickie and whispered, smiling, "Guy looks hot."

"Take a look," says Eva, and pushes the paper across the walnut table so words in black magic marker jump out at Voort. The writing is jagged and childlike, which might mean a socially retarded person wrote it. It might also mean that a sophisticated author is trying to mislead police. Both scenarios have happened before.

Voort feels more perspiration erupt beneath his underarms as he reads. The first part of the note says:

WHAT WILL YOUR SUPERIORS DO WHEN
THEY LEARN HOW YOU SCREWED UP, VOORT?

And the second:

YOUR FAULT CONRAD. HAPPY ANNIVERSARY.
BIRTHDAY BOY. THREE MORE BY MIDNIGHT.

"Today your birthday?" Deans asks, as if that fact would confirm the truth of the rest of the note.

"Yes."

"What mistake does the note refer to?" Eva asks in a low, extremely interested voice. This case will be the most public one of her new job, and whether she believes Voort or not she doesn't want to mess up.

"I have no idea."

"Not even a guess?" Aziz says. "Anniversary points to some shared experience. Anniversary of what?"

"The writing's crude, but the word 'superiors' tells me the author might be military," Voort says, knowing that's not what Aziz meant.

In the pause they all stare at the note as if their collective will might force some revelation from it. Voort's unsure which part is the most horrifying. The threat? Or the claim that he's responsible.

Don't even consider it.

He repeats, in a whisper, "Three more by midnight."

9:21, reads the digital clock on the windowsill, buzzing softly and giving rhythm to the passage of suddenly crucial time.

"Clearly," Eva starts out again, "the writer believes that when we learn about something you did, it will explain what has happened here. Start making sense, Voort. Why is this addressed to you?"

"How do I know? He's a nut, whoever wrote it."

"We never said it's a he," Deans says.

"He, she, whatever," Voort snaps, even though he knows that, were he the deputy mayor he might be acting the same way. All Deans has been doing for the last month is listening to crooked cops lie.

The letters seem to get bigger and blacker and

float off the page to hover before his eyes. The paper is a plain sheet, as white as he has probably turned. That it is not inside an evidence bag tells him there are no prints on it.

Deans, the mayor's friend, adviser, back-watcher, fix-it guy, says, "Well, the starting point for this threat, on the face of it, seems to be you."

"Some con's getting back at me for an arrest."

"Why Gabrielle Viera? Why today?" Deans says.

"Come on, Voort," Aziz says, "You're a hero. Everyone likes you. Your family's been cops before there even *was* a department. Maybe whatever you did wasn't even wrong. Maybe it's perfectly explainable. The shooter thinks it's a screwup but it's not. Give it to us now. Don't make us find out later."

"We find out later," Deans says. "We'll crucify you."

"I think I get the point."

"Anyone threaten you recently? Phone calls? Letters?"

"No."

"Any cases coming up in court, as in, someone wants you discredited," Eva suggests.

Voort thinks. "No."

"Maybe it's Mickie who made the mistake. Your partner. *You* didn't do anything but you're helping him out."

Aziz tells Eva and Deans, "I believe him."

"Give me a polygraph test," Voort says.

Both Aziz and Eva look startled. Police unions have fought hard to guarantee that cops never have to take lie-detector tests. In fact, unions forbid their members to take the tests. Civilians? Hook them up to the machine as fast as possible. Cops? Forget it. Not us. Never.

"You're sure," Aziz says, liking it. "You'll sign something that it was your idea?"

"I'll waive the lawyer. You're wasting time on me."

"We'll decide what's wasting time," Deans says. "And lie detectors aren't always right. You practice, control the heart. How do you feel about we send some people to your house, to check around a bit?"

Voort envisions detectives arriving at his birthday party. Opening closets. Questioning Camilla and Julia. Emptying boxes. Peering into drawers.

His sick feeling begins to turn to anger.

"If you haven't done it already, I'd say that's a screwup on your part," Voort replies.

"You want to be a hard-ass? Good. I love dealing with hard-asses."

"Don't take your frustration out on me."

He sees that Mickie is no longer visible in the bull pen outside, which means detectives have taken him elsewhere to grill him. If you and Voort took money, they're telling him . . . if there's a gambling, drug, or woman problem . . . if Voort slept with Gabrielle Viera, if you're both involved, give him to us. Coaxing him, bullying, offering deals. Making the same promises that Voort and Mickie offer suspects all the time.

"Tommy, go easy," soothes Aziz, holding up his hands like a referee at a fight, shrugging to Voort apologetically while Voort suddenly wonders if they're doing a high-level good cop/bad cop. Wonders if Aziz doesn't believe him at all.

"You have to understand," Aziz continues, "we're under pressure. We have to ask these questions."

Voort calms a little, and knowing Aziz, sees what else the new commissioner is going to do. "You giving a press conference?"

"We can't keep this secret, can't have people later saying we sat on it, we had information and didn't release it. *Maybe somebody can help before this thing gets worse.* We need to give them the opportunity."

"Let me make the announcement," Voort says.

A pause, then Eva sees it, nods. "You go on. You look sorry. You say, 'I don't know what I've done but clearly I've done something that was a terrible mistake.'"

"I ask the shooter to get in touch with me. I guarantee a secure phone."

"I'll start it. You take over after that," Aziz says. "After about ten minutes."

Voort feels nauseous.

"If it turns out to be nothing, everyone will know," Eva says. "You won't be left hanging."

"This whole thing could be a bluff," Voort says, hoping more than believing it. "Hell, that magazine piece mentioned the date of my birthday."

"Is that house of yours really worth four million bucks?" Deans says in a way that tells him the deputy mayor is suspicious of any cop who has that much money, whether the article explained about his terrific investments or not.

Voort is thinking, *Is it possible that I caused all this somehow? That I did make a mistake?*

"We have a polygraph expert standing by," Eva says with a first sign of softness. "He's very good. He used to be at the Defense Department. He debriefed Soviet defectors."

"I'll be in good company then."

"We won't say you actually did anything. We say it's a possibility. We mention your splendid record. We say it's possible the note is a false clue, that the writer simply has a grudge." `

We, he thinks. She sounds like a cancer doctor telling a sick man, *we* need an operation.

And never mind what they *say*. The fact is, he's going on TV to tell a city that's angry at its police department to start with that somehow he may have caused a murder. He knows that the city, within the hour, will be in a panic, especially since no one knows whether the killings are planned or random. Newscasters will break in on regularly scheduled broadcasts. Drinkers in bars, shoppers in markets, construction crews on break will be poking their fingers at headlines or TV sets, staring at Voort's photo, asking each other, "What did that stupid fucker *do?*"

Voort tells Eva, "I want to work on this case."

"You are," she says, but they all know the policy. When a cop is under an investigation, he doesn't conduct it. Eva says, "The press conference will be a big help. You can help with your records too, you know, go through them. Maybe you'll find something. Trigger a memory."

"That's not what I meant," Voort insists, and Deans shakes his head firmly as if to say, no way will this man be permitted latitude here.

Voort's heart is pounding. His legs feel weak. He has never until this instant felt suspicion coming at him from inside the department. Hell, as a schoolboy he spent afternoons at One Police Plaza, wandering halls, playing with the commissioner's dog, learning how to fill out reports from detectives, even going out on cases with his dad. He spent weekends listening to his uncles tell stories about the way Voort cops broke up Civil War draft riots and arrested prohibition-era gangsters. He went to his first union meeting when he was seven.

"What if the writer of that note *wants* me off duty?" he says.

"Oh, he wants it. The question is, Why?" says Deans. "You go home. Sit it out. I want you where we can see you, where we can get to you when the thing breaks. No way later will people be able to say we covered up for you."

Voort lurches to his feet and goes to the window. At least it's closer to the action than the table is, and further from Deputy Mayor Thomas Lamond Deans. Out there, beyond the growing crowd, whomever left the note may be getting into place, Voort fears, for a second killing. Moving around the city while on Sixth Avenue a police van pulls up and a couple of Blue Guys haul out a portable podium. It looks better on TV to hold a press conference from behind a podium. That stiff block of wood gives speakers a protective shield. It makes confusion look official. It gives assurance to lies.

"Here's what'll happen if you keep me out of it," he tells the deputy mayor, moving back toward the guy. "Some detective'll dig up something good but it'll seem like nothing to him because only I'd recognize the connection, and I won't learn about it until too late. An important address. A bar I visited. What'll you tell *them,*" Voort says, jerking his thumb at the window, "when that happens?"

"I said no."

Voort observes the crime crew working in the big room outside. Their faces, hard with frustration, give him another idea.

"You're not finding much, are you? Prints, hairs, nothing."

Deans unfolds his arms.

"No break-in," Voort says. "No struggle. Looks like he was standing right next to her. File cabinets closed, so our shooter wasn't looking for something. Pocketbook on the table, neat and closed. No witness, right? Just whomever, a coworker maybe, found the body."

"What's your point?"

"That I'm your best connection," Voort says. "Three more by tonight? That's one every couple of hours, unless he or *she,*" he says, smiling at Deans, "does them all together. Starts a fire in a house, maybe. Blows up a car. He didn't say he'd do the other three separately. How you going to explain it if the screwup is yours, not mine?"

At a new sound in the room, a buzzing cellphone, Eva reaches into her bag, pulls out the Nokia and flips it open. "Yes?"

She listens. She says, "Thanks, Hazel." Hanging up, she tells the others, "That was the computer people. Gabrielle Viera had a record. One arrest. Seven years ago. Soliciting at the Plaza Hotel. She changed her name but kept her social security number."

She's eyeing Voort like this is supposed to mean something to him. "The charges were dropped. Gabrielle Ramos. You recognize *that* name, Voort? You ever work vice?"

"No. But what's the first thing you did when you found it out? *You ran it by me.* You need me. You can't selectively tell me things."

"Let him work on it," says Aziz.

"Or maybe I could tell the reporters that the new policy is to yank anyone off the job if they're accused of something. Never mind who does the accusing. Never mind if they don't even mention what you did. Want to screw a cop? Write an anonymous letter."

Deans shakes his head, but wearily, blunting the extent of his opposition. Aziz shrugs at Eva, needing her backing to overcome Deans. Eva reconsiders the note.

"Okay, *if* you pass the polygraph. *If*," she tells Voort. "Parallel investigations. You report directly to me."

"Thank you."

"You'll wear a bracelet," Deans says. "That's the only way I'll go along with this. If you leave the city, if you do anything screwy, if you disappear for even ten minutes I'll come after you with everything I have."

"I'll pass the test." Voort's thinking, "I'll pass because even if I did screw up I don't understand how. There's nothing to lie about."

Eva sighs and says, "I'm sticking my neck out for you," which she is, whether she believes him or not, and Voort can see, outside the window, more spires of TV broadcast antennas pushing their way upward into view as more vans pull up.

"He wants us to catch him," Aziz announces as Voort reaches the doorway. "Otherwise why leave a note? Why not finish the murders *before* he contacts us? Why make things tougher on himself?"

"Because the asshole wants attention," says Deans.

"He wants to outsmart us," says Eva. "He wants to get Voort."

Voort feels the presence of the invisible opponent. He feels pure hatred coming off the note on the table. Does he even know the author?

Three more by midnight.

He tells the others, "I wish to God I knew what he wants."

FOUR

"When on a key project," Crown Publishers' *The One-Day Business Trip Manager* advises, "don't underestimate the importance of renting a hotel room. Although you will not spend the night, you need a place to unwind and review strategy as a day progresses. The difference between feeling harried and rested—taxed or alert—will reflect itself in your performance. Guaranteed."

Now Wendall Nye sees that the Montenegro Hotel is small and dark but blessedly quiet, the perfect sanctuary for resting between tasks. The clerk had taken cash without demanding to see a credit card. He'd told Wendall while examining the hundred-dollar bill offered, "You better be out by noon like you promised. And without a MasterCard imprint from you, I can't turn your phone on or unlock your minibar."

"I have a snack right here," Wendall had replied, holding up the brown paper bag.

"I spotted this place when I was on one of my late-night scouting trips," he tells the recorder. "I watched where the prostitutes working streets near the Hilton take their johns. Those hotels always accept cash."

The window faces a brick wall four feet across an airshaft. The bed is single but the mattress quite firm. The wool carpet, spotted with cigarette burns, is the same olive hue as the surprisingly new paint job. There's a framed oil painting of two fishermen in a rowboat. One has hooked a leaping bass. The other reaches for it with a net.

"I can't stop eating. I . . . I feel like I haven't eaten for years."

With time counting down to his departure, he sits in front of the TV, in his boxer underwear, showered, shaved, gorging himself on junk food from a deli down on Fifty-eighth Street. Entenmann's chocolate donuts. A KitKat bar. A cherry danish with vanilla frosting. The crazy hunger is a surprise to him, and the food seems to make no impact on his digestive system. It doesn't even feel like it's going into his stomach at all. It seems to evaporate as soon as he swallows each bite.

"Where's the egg sandwich?"

Then his heart begins to race because on NY1, the all-news Manhattan cable TV station, Conrad Voort is stepping up beside the chief of detectives outside the Viera Travel Agency. Just the sight of the man's face sets Wendall's blood rushing, and the number of journalists present—more than he can count—raises Wendall's level of excitement even more.

Chief Ramirez tells the scribbling journalists, "The detective to whom the note was addressed has an announcement to make."

I bet you're going to ask me to call a special private phone line, shithead. And beg me to stop, Wendall thinks.

Voort sends his plea out over the airwaves. "Please talk your grievance out with me instead of taking it out on innocent people . . ."

You'll get answers my way, not yours.

Voort's trying to sound caring, professional, on top of things, but the strain in his voice is a joy to hear. "I'll get your call wherever I am."

Just wait till my tapes reach the papers. They'll publish every word. The whole city will read about what you did, you miserable sack of shit.

Wendall uses the automatic channel clicker to check NBC, ABC, FOX. Voort fills the screen continuously, the camera angle a little different on each network, but the unrelenting scrutiny the same. Wendall grins. This is the best possible result he could have hoped for.

Voort pleads with his invisible opponent. "If I've hurt you in some way, done something to drive you to this, let's work it out . . ."

Wendall turns the sound down, finding it pleasing to watch the blond man's mouth moving uselessly. Voort looks like a puppet, head jerking, mouth flopping, as Wendall unwraps a cellophane-wrapped egg 'n' cheese sandwich and bites into the warm, buttery mix. His body's been going crazy since he left the travel agency. First he'd grown cold—so much that he'd actually started shivering in the subway. To a woman who'd noticed it, a commuter, he'd said, "It's a spring cold. The air-conditioning gets me every year."

The woman had nodded. "The AC is always too high or too low," she'd said.

Then the cold had gone away, but he'd been seized with dizziness when he climbed out of the station at Columbus Circle. He'd just frozen in place at the top of the stairs, gaping at the city as if he were some aborigine materialized here from New Guinea. The noise had been earsplitting. The skyscrapers had seemed to waver, the air to squeeze from his esophagus. Taxi horns had sounded like jackhammers, jackhammers like missiles going off.

But again he'd gotten himself under control, willed the horrible sound, after a few terrifying moments, down to an acceptable decibel level. The truth was, he'd been expecting *some* kind of physical reaction so he'd not been that surprised.

As the *Closing the Deal Primer* had predicted:

"You may find on the big day that your body will act in funny ways. Nervousness can show up as exhaustion, forgetfulness, or a tendency to lose your temper at little things. Keep your eye on the prize! Take a deep breath, a quiet walk, or listen to soothing music for five minutes. After the deal is closed all those silly symptoms will disappear as if they never existed!"

True.

And now he sees that the reporters' question-and-answer session with police is starting, so he turns the sound back on as the cute blonde from Channel Five asks Chief Ramirez, "Is Detective Voort under investigation?"

Great!

"When will he be taking the polygraph test?"

Blah, blah, blah.

Wendall shuts off the set because it is almost time to go. On goes the tape recorder. It's time to continue the official record—to tell the real story—so that later the reporters can pore over every detail, publish little maps, photograph this very room perhaps, in the aftermath of what will happen to Mr. Phillip Hull in . . . why, *time is flying* . . . in a very short while.

"I will leave the hotel to make the second change," Wendall says, neatly cleaning up the room to spare the maid work, disposing of the wrappings and napkins and used coffee cup in the wastebasket. "I've given myself extra time to get ready in case there's a d . . . d . . . delay. Ohhhh, shit."

He feels his stomach rising.

He makes it to the bathroom as the nausea slams into him full force. His head burns. His vision blurs. He throws up every bit of food he has just eaten, and when he finally stands, dizzy, thinking, *I'm wasting time,* his bowels cramp and his intestines clench and he sees that his body is betraying him again.

Damn.

There's nothing he can do about it. Cursing, he

sits on the toilet and spends even more precious minutes voiding himself, sweat pouring from his face and neck and finally, almost a third of an hour later, he's in control again.

I better watch what I eat for the rest of the day.

He showers the sweat off. He dries himself and chews an Altoid to rid himself of the foul taste.

Comb your wig. Don't leave the room until you look completely at ease. Put the TV back on for a few minutes while you catch your breath, in case there's been some new development while you were sick.

By now Voort is off the screen, probably rushed off to his lie-detector test, and the cute blonde from Channel Five is saying, "This will be one of the biggest manhunts in the city's history. So far police have no answers. But what they *do* know is that somewhere in New York, by midnight, the 'Voort grudge killer' may strike three more times."

Voort grudge killer!

He tells the tape recorder, as he gathers up the attaché case, "The poet Keats said 'There is not a fiercer hell than failure in a great object.' I'll be interested in Voort's thoughts on this later, but right now it is time for metamorphosis number two."

The maid doesn't see him leave and the clerk's back is turned when Wendall slips across the lobby. The Montenegro Hotel was so dark that when he reaches Fifty-sixth Street the day is so dazzling he has to shield his eyes, a lucky development because now lots of people will be wearing sunglasses. The sky is a rich, dark blue. Turning west, toward the slightly seedier area off midtown, he goes into the phony "cellphone" routine again, making sure to keep his voice low.

"I considered buying all my props in Brooklyn but didn't want to lug around shopping bags. They're noticeable."

He feels safe, actually. As invisible as one more innocent pedestrian. If on TV, Gabrielle's murder had seemed to be panicking the city, on the street the sense is that it never even occurred. The metropolis has absorbed one more tragedy. The city entertains itself regularly with odd or tragic tales, and passersby here have more personal things on their minds, or probably never heard of Gabrielle Viera at all.

At length he reaches Eighth Avenue and the Hide 'n' Seek theatrical prop store where he purchases a curly black wig and matching beard and mustache, a glue-on mole for his face, and wire-rimmed sunglasses that look like something John Lennon wore.

Then he heads east again, to the new Salvation Army store on Fifty-fifth Street, where he buys secondhand jeans, running shoes, a knapsack with a "Geraldine Ferraro for Vice President" sticker on it, a chocolate brown lightweight turtleneck, and a Crew brand button-up denim jacket, frayed at the hem. It's unlikely that the old woman at the cash register will remember the items as he clumps them together on the counter. She runs the electronic scanner over the price tags, barely looking up at him. She's more interested in getting back to her paperback, *A Brief History of Time*.

Even if she remembers me later she'll describe the disguise.

At the Fifty-seventh Street McDonald's, Wendall uses the bathroom to change, taking his time in the stall until the two men who were at urinals when he entered have left the room. He switches his paraphernalia from the attaché case to the knapsack.

Emerging, he's stuffed his old disguise in the Salvation Army bag, which he gives to a homeless man wheeling a shopping cart down Sixth Avenue.

"Thanks, man! You're even my size!"

The attaché case—prints wiped off—goes into a trash Dumpster fronting a construction site a block from Central Park.

"Hey you! You can't throw that in there!"

Wendall jerks up to see a foreman type in a yellow hard hat gesturing at him angrily from three stories up. In New York, even trash Dumpster space is valuable. But the man is too far away to do anything to stop Wendall Nye.

"Now I really have to concentrate because Phil Hull poses special problems, because keeping quiet will be extra crucial in the park. I guess if there are people around I'll try again when he gets off work at five. But now would be better. I don't want to pack the afternoon with too many things to do."

Excitement rising, he strolls into Central Park from Fifty-ninth Street, half an hour before Phillip Hull's usual lunch hour begins.

The morning is getting lovelier. Small puffy clouds drift in the sky. The trees are blooming and he inhales a sweet, mulchy odor of fertilizer, budding trees, and spring flowers tinged with a whiff of animal dung wafting west from the Central Park Zoo.

Unhurriedly, Wendall takes the meandering paths, past the softball fields and the merry-go-round. In his neat beard and denims he could be taken for a tourist or artistic type, an actor maybe, off work today. Or maybe a painter or writer taking a pleasant walk.

Again, there is no evidence of any "panic gripping the city." On the contrary, the playground is filled with toddlers. Park benches are spotted with tourists, lovers, and retirees reading the *Times* or *Post*.

Phillip, keep your usual schedule today. Please.

From a boom box tuned to all-news radio he catches a few words about a "huge police mobilization," but it all seems far away.

He strolls past joggers, sunbathers, a three-card-monty artist. A trio of roller skaters weaves along the park drive, bending and straightening as they set down pink plastic cones along the side of the road so they can race each other slalom-style before a gathering crowd.

Closing on the target site, Wendall experiences a stab of tension. He leaves the main path, climbs a small grass and boulder hill, pushes through a clump of bushes to find that luckily the little knoll is empty. He's in a squarish plot surrounded by oaks, with a fine, unobstructed view of the sky.

The ground is warm against his haunches. He settles back against an oak. Unbuckling the knapsack, he pulls out the binoculars and bird book, and he watches the sky as if he could care less what he will see there. Wendall waits.

Right on schedule he hears a slight shaking sound in the bushes. Someone is coming.

Phillip?

Someone coming into view now. Ahhh.

Then, *Who the hell are you?*, Wendall thinks, enraged.

"Have you ever committed a crime of any kind?"

"I told you. No."

"Ever drive faster than the speed limit?"

"Everybody does that once in a while."

"Ever cheat on your income tax?"

Voort sighs at the technician. "I said I'd give you latitude on questions, but what are you saying, the IRS offed her?"

"I'm testing your responses, detective."

"For half an *hour?* Look, we're wasting time, and why did we have to go back to headquarters for this anyway?"

The technician turns and looks at the mirror, as if to complain to whoever is watching from behind. The top polygraph expert from John Jay college—as Eva described this guy—is a small, lithe man with a deep smoker's voice, military bearing, a handsome cleft chin, and an accent that makes Voort think Boston or Rhode Island.

"Have you ever taken a bribe, detective?"

"I told you three times! And I have no knowledge of other detectives taking them either."

The technician's voice remains as impersonal as the black needle that he always monitors but which Voort cannot see. Voort wants to scream.

"Are you gay?"

"No."

"Ever sleep with another man's wife?"

"Christ!" But it's a legitimate question, considering that a jealous husband would certainly carry a grudge. In fact, it's exactly the kind of question he and Mickie would ask, Voort admits to himself, gritting his teeth, feeling stripped, naked, enraged.

"Yes."

He gets a mental picture of Dr. Jill Towne, with whom he'd had a brief fling during the Szeska case. The gorgeous doctor—an expert on tropical diseases—had been under police protection when they started sleeping together. Voort reminds himself that he hadn't known at first that she was married.

But he hadn't broken it off when he found out she was.

Jill's supposed to be in Africa with her husband. Or have they come back? I never even met the guy. I took her word that their relationship was open. What a dope I was.

The technician clears his throat, "I said, please relate the circumstances of the affair."

When Voort hesitates the door opens and Eva strides into the ninth-floor interrogation room, looking annoyed. "You can stop this at any time," she snaps, "and go home and wait. You can call a lawyer. But decide now. I don't have time for your crap. You asked to take this test. You knew we'd be going over everything."

"Sorry." Within half an hour, he knows, other detectives will be making sure Jill and her husband are really out of town.

Or how about Kenny the dancer, who I took Camilla away from? Or the families of anybody I put in prison? What if I sent an innocent person away?

You could go crazy thinking like this.

Voort tells the story of how he broke regulations and slept with a suspect. It will do wonders for his career.

"A little louder, please," the technician says.

Voort speaks louder.

"Have you ever had business dealings of any nature with members of organized crime? Or taken gifts from anyone you knew to be in organized crime?"

"No."

You have to keep calm for a polygraph. But innocent people's heartbeats speed up too, he thinks, understanding now why the union prohibits cops from taking these tests. He flashes to the ABC quiz show *Hot Seat*, where contestants are cuffed into a swivel chair as flames roar around them, and an emcee shouts "Answer now!" and, if the contestant's heartbeat goes up, they lose the opportunity to win money by answering questions that are far less threatening than the ones Voort faces now.

"Have you ever planted evidence on a suspect?"

"I never planted evidence. I never struck a suspect without reporting it. I never conspired in any way to deceive the department. You want me to say it a few more times?"

The technician leans back, runs both hands through his longish hair, and begins unsnapping Voort's leather forearm strap. "You aced it, Voort. I knew your father, and I hated doing that to you. Congratulations."

He flashes a thumbs-up to the mirror. "If everyone who slept with a married person was in prison, there'd be no one to serve the damn meals, ha ha!"

In the hallway outside, Voort receives a cool congratulations from Eva, although she doesn't look convinced yet of his innocence, or maybe she's just preoccupied or pissed off about Jill Towne.

"We haven't learned anything new while you were in there," she says. "Mickie's in your office. Remember, report in regularly." She taps his brand-new electronic wristband. "And remember, this will tell us where you are."

You think I could forget?

He takes the elevator up to the sex crimes unit and the private office—a perk particular to their division—which he shares with Mickie. His partner barely looks up from two stacks of paper on his desk: one a computer printout, Voort sees, and the other a pile of photocopied forms.

"They had you in there long enough," Mickie says. "Grilling you about the Twinkies you stole when you were six?"

"They were more interested in the four million you got from the Mendoza brothers. But I explained that was for yard work."

"Arrest records," Mickie says, nodding at the computer printout. "Your own old logs, ten years' worth, from your birthday." Mickie taps the second pile. "We've got priority with the computer girls. It's amazing how fast you can get things when there aren't two thousand requests logged in front of you. I had these thirty minutes after you left."

Voort nods appreciatively at Mickie's thinking. "The other guys are concentrating on Gabrielle Viera, so you figured we'd do me, huh?"

"You ought to be a cop," Mickie says. "We need a one-day strategy, right? So I'm thinking 'anniversary,' right? The asshole wrote, 'anniversary' *and* 'birthday,' so maybe to him they're two separate things. I'm thinking today could be the anniversary of whatever pissed him off."

"So we check the old logs and see what I remember."

Mickie taps the copied pile. "Maybe he's been in prison."

"And just got out."

"Or he's been out and now something set him off. Hey Voort, remember ninety-nine, when we beat Midtown South in softball? That third baseman was pissed off when you snagged his ninth-inning line drive."

"Sergeant Lieberman. Put out an APB."

But the banter is more automatic than jocular.

Voort falls into a sitting chair and glumly reaches for his logs.

10:38.

Outside and below their office, tourist boats and tugs cruise the East River. Cars move swiftly on the ramps of the Brooklyn Bridge. The office is expensive, laid out by Mickie's interior decorator. The sitting chairs are rich Italian leather. The foldout couch shows a geometric southwestern motif. The walls are done in soothing terra cotta. The carpeting is so thick that the taupe-colored fiber holds impressions of their shoes.

"Just because we work in shit doesn't mean we have to live in it," Mickie, who loves luxury, likes to say.

There's also a silver coffee urn by the minifridge, which is stocked with juices, cheeses, and Heinekens. The room smells of fresh-brewed Blue Mountain coffee. The TV on the wall unit is tuned to NY1, which is showing a Murray Hill apartment building above the caption POLICE SEARCH GABRIELLE VIERA'S HOME.

"By the way, both your girlfriends left messages," Mickie says. "The widow says if you need anything, sweetie pie, just ask."

"I need for you to shut up."

"But the Valkyrie's swung into action," Mickie says with admiration. "Those producers love to produce! She's got about every off-duty Voort in the city standing by, got them organized by shifts if you need it. Call the house any time you want the army to head out. It's not a party anymore. It's a war room."

Feeling a flush of warmth, Voort says, "This is going to keep getting worse, isn't it?"

"Maybe not. Remember what Napoleon said. Sure the field marshal's talented, but is he lucky? I'll do the arrest reports. Hell, for the last few years we wrote 'em together. Maybe I'll remember something myself. You check the logs. It's only ten day's worth. If something big happened, it should be there. But my opinion is, this whole thing's gonna be bullshit."

Voort opens the minifridge, takes out a cold apple cider from the Hudson Valley Voort farm, and pours a glass.

Slumped in the sitting chair he tries to concentrate on the logs, but the odds against finding anything quickly seem so vast that he has to will himself to pay rigid attention. He's sat in this office with Mickie hundreds of times, looking over printouts, diagrams of crime scenes, chalkboards, schedules, transcripts, videotapes. But he's never been examining himself.

"Are the computer girls running CARS?" Voort asks as he works.

"CARS, CRIMS, NITRO, WOLF, BADS," Mickie says, referring to local and federal data systems available at One Police Plaza. The computer-assisted robbery system, CARS, is probably the best, since it holds information on every murder, robbery, and sex crime in the city over the last twenty years. With the touch of a button it can cross-reference even small bits of information and match up crimes and criminals. Punch in a nickname, weapon type, time of day, even partial description and CARS sifts through hundreds of thousands of solved and unsolved crimes.

"They lifted a lot of prints at the travel agency. Maybe El Grudgo left a few," Mickie says, working.

"It's not just a grudge. It's that he also seems so sure that whatever I did will piss off the department."

"What you *did*, Con Man?" Mickie snaps. "You didn't do shit. Don't you think if you did something you'd remember it? Or I would?"

"Yeah."

"He's fucking with you."

To change the subject Voort says, "I guess we'll miss the Mets tonight." The family has a field-level box at Shea Stadium. Traditionally, on Voort's birthday, if there's a game, he goes. Mickie and his wife had been invited to go with Voort and Camilla tonight.

Mickie slams the desk with his palm. *"He's doing a head trip on you.* Come on, Con Man! Gabrielle was arrested for vice, dammit, and vice means she hired out to nuts. You were a public figure even before that magazine piece came out, and public figures *attract* nuts. An imaginary relationship. That's what this grudge is going to be. Voort sends me radio signals in my tooth fillings. Voort used black magic to make my dick shrivel. Voort came from Mars to torture me. Voort's Satan disguised as a cop."

"I never thought anyone would find out."

Voort goes back to his old logs, written in his own

hand. The writing casts him back to when he was a Blue Guy, ten years ago. He has no memory of the day he's reading about, but the notations bring back a setting, a period, and he sees, doodled on the edge of the page, *raining*. So he imagines a hard May rainfall. He smells the odors of Brooklyn's Flatbush Avenue: mixed-up hummus, Chinese food, car exhaust, street tar, all tinged by the underground smell of diesel and dirt coming up from the subway.

In his mind, the rain batters a windshield as Voort rides a squad car with an older partner named Jay Attanasio, his first partner, dead from cancer four years ago. Voort sees himself and pudgy Attanasio taking turns driving the wealthier part of the precinct, Park Slope, with its brownstones and well-kept apartment buildings. Then rolling into the higher crime areas abutting the north side of Prospect Park near Grand Army Plaza.

"Domestic disturbance," he reads in his own hand. Apparently no arrest was made, and he has no recollection of the incident. He remembers the street, since he regularly patrolled it. Garfield Street, two blocks from the park.

Nice street.

But as for the people, or argument, all he sees is a collage of angry faces from those years. Black, white, Chinese, Lebanese. Men and women screaming at each other over paychecks, sex, jealousy, illness— ranting at 2 A.M. while their neighbors groaned and fumbled for phones.

He flips a page. "Purse snatching on Montgomery Place."

He remembers the exceptionally lovely tree-lined street, where an exgirlfriend, Shari, lives, but again he has no recollection of the particular purse snatching. By the time his squad car would arrive at the site, the perp would usually have long ago fled back across Prospect Park West into the park.

"Loud party at Sixth Avenue near Eighth Street."

"Vandalism at Synagogue Beth Israel." He finally remembers something here, black swastikas, dried, dripped paint on yellow brick. A broken window. A bent lock where the vandals had tried and failed to break in before the alarm scared them away. He remembers a thin, stooped rabbi wearing a white yarmulke telling him something about Germany. Or was it a different rabbi at a different time who had told him something about Germany? Had the rabbi been born in Germany? Or had the desecration reminded him of Hitler's Germany?

Such a long time ago.

"Burglary at Harvey's Shoe Store. Three boxes of Reeboks taken—men's, white, size nine."

No arrests.

Voort finishes the first three pages of the report written on his birthday ten years ago. He'd finished up at the Seventy-eighth Precinct house at 6 P.M. that night and probably driven off to Shea Stadium. Met the cousins outside gate B, under the loudspeakers. Drank cups of Bud and screamed at the pitchers from box F123J. Maybe brought a date, although back then birthdays usually meant a guys' night out.

He can't remember. It's no use.

He turns to the log for nine years ago. Ten minutes later he tries eight.

"Whoa!" Mickie says, looking up, flushed. "How's this name for memory lane? William Neems."

Voort sits up, feeling a slight ticking start up in the back of his neck. "The water inspector."

"Right. The city water inspector. Big, powerful guy. We beat the shit out of him when he resisted. We broke his jaw. He was still screaming at us when they carried him off, remember?"

"Yeah. He assaulted prostitutes in areas where he was inspecting pipes."

Mickie sits up, more excited. "He said he never did it. Said someone who *looked* like him did it."

"He said I came on to his wife," Voort says, "and wrecked their marriage."

They freeze at an interruption—Voort's special-line cellphone ringing. Heart hammering, he flips open the phone.

"Detective Voort," he says, keeping his voice calm, wondering what sort of voice he will hear next.

"Oh, hi. It's Louis in communications. We're testing the line."

"It works." He hangs up, dry-mouthed, and tells Mickie, while he punches in the computer room number, "Neems said I ruined his life."

"I'd say that's a grudge."

Ten minutes later Hazel calls back from computer-ops to tell them in her German accent: "Willie

Neems was released on parole six months ago. MINX parole system has him back in Brooklyn, working in an asbestos-removal company named Clean Living." She gives the address of the office. "And Voort?"

"What?"

"I know you didn't do anything wrong. I don't need them to check it. I know it."

"You'll say anything to get refrigerator privileges, Hazel."

"Got any more of that Louisiana Voodoo Beer up there?"

Hanging up, Voort frowns. "But we didn't arrest him on my birthday, so what anniversary could he be talking about?"

"Hell, a day you testified. The day he was convicted. The day he got raped in the shower in Sing Sing. Who knows what happened to him in jail. And then he reads about you in a magazine, right? He's in prison, rotting and steaming and you're grinning away like a cover boy. I like this, Voort."

"And Gabrielle Viera? Why her?"

"He used prostitutes. Maybe he had a grudge against her. The point is, do you have a better idea?"

"Me? I don't have any idea."

Mickie screws up his face so that Voort knows he's about to do an imitation. Mickie cries in Neems's distinctive, hoarse voice, "I'll get you, Voort!"

"His lawyer said he really didn't remember anything," Voort recalls. "In the courtroom hallway, after the trial, when it didn't make a difference and we were alone. He said Neems really didn't do it."

"The jury took twenty minutes to decide otherwise. So do we keep reading or visit Slick Willie?"

Normally Voort makes decisions easily, but now he hesitates. With so little time, the importance of every decision seems magnified.

"We could phone," he starts to say, but then shakes his head. If it *is* Neems, you don't phone. You show up. You watch his face when you talk to him.

But driving to Brooklyn and back could take over an hour.

"We keep reading," Voort says. "And list the best possibilities. Then we follow up on them after we check the whole thing."

"You da boss." Mickie looks disappointed.

Voort stands up. "No, let's go. I'll make the list on the way out."

"Good. If we wrap this up, we can make the Mets/Reds tonight, except, hmmm, I bring Syl, but are you sure you want to bring Camilla, buddy? The widow's all alone. She's frail. She's lonely. She likes the Mets."

Voort thinking, *Nothing will come of this. It would be too lucky.*

The clock by the minifridge says 11:10.

FIVE

Pedestrians walking across the bridge move faster than the autos. "For chrissakes, where'd all this traffic come from?" Mickie says, staring out at what appears to be a solid mass of exhaust belching, idling steel. "We look out the office window, the bridge is clear! We get in the car and suddenly half the city's here!"

"It looks like more than half," Voort says glumly, trying to concentrate on his old logs.

Mickie's running the siren even though cars ahead have no space to pull over. Make enough commotion and maybe reality will change. But all he accomplishes is the forcing of the people in nearby cars to press their hands over their ears. Voort imagines other drivers turning up their radios, trying to drown out one sound with another, transforming each vehicle into a cocoon of noise.

"How's this for an investment," Mickie says. "A chain of fast-food restaurants right here in New York. We build 'em alongside the Long Island

Expressway, the Belt Parkway. As cars crawl by people rush in and order. We call it Burgers on the Run.

"Beats the tech fund you pushed last week."

Voort goes back to his log, but so far at least it's remarkable how little of note had occurred on his birthdays. He had responded to lots of domestic disturbances, he reads, but made no arrests. Lots of burglary and robbery calls—after the crimes were over. Voort the Blue Guy took down information from victims, then handed the interviews to detectives for whatever follow-through occurred.

He reads, "Stolen dog reported."

The Caprice jerks forward and stops, gains six inches and halts. The bridge casts Voort back to age five. He remembers sitting in his parents' LeSabre, possibly in exactly this spot, staring fearfully up at the latticed array of turn-of-the-twentieth-century cables that rise on both sides of the road and seem to fill the sky. Voort the kid, fearing monsters, feeling as if the Buick was traversing an enormous science-fiction spiderweb, like one he'd seen in a comic book. Feeling like the spider waited for him on the other end, maw dripping, glittery eyes watching the tiny humans in cars passing below.

Mickie—shouting into his cellphone—brings Voort back to the present. "You found out what? Good girl!" And, to Voort, "Con Man, it's amazing how efficient the system is when thirty thousand people are looking for the same perp. Neems is working a job on Eastern Parkway. Hazel got the address so we'll skip the office, go right there."

Experiencing a sensation of being watched, Voort looks left and realizes that two couples in the Nissan four-door beside them are staring at him excitedly, jabbering, pointing.

All four people glance away when he looks back.

"Go ahead, give 'em your autograph," Mickie says, grinning. "Know what I hate? It's when a guy gets famous and right away he forgets regular people."

"I see what my mistake was, Mickie. It's right here!"

"What?"

"Teaming up with you."

And now traffic begins to flow with no hint, as usual, as to why it ever slowed in the first place. They crawl off the span onto the wide, busy avenues around Brooklyn Borough Hall, turn left on Atlantic, right on Flatbush, and head toward Grand Army Plaza, zipping past streets that Voort used to patrol.

But the traffic slowdown has dampened any earlier optimism. *It would be too lucky to hit it on the first try.*

They pass the clock tower of the Williamsburg Savings Bank building and shoppers headed for the Fulton Mall. The view provides a montage of memories. Here's Dominico Grocery, where he once answered a burglary call, but not on a birthday. Here's the Knossos Diner, where his partner used to gorge himself at 3 A.M. on cherry pie. Here's Conover's Mobil, where they pulled in one night for gas and broke up a robbery. Again, not on his birthday. Here's the apartment building where he used to ring buzzer

7F after work and wait with a hard-on for his Korean girlfriend—an opera singer—to buzz him up.

Now Voort's special phone line rings, but it turns out to be a detective named Santini working the main investigation, asking if he's ever heard of someone named Bea Zemen.

"Who?"

"Gabrielle's neighbor. She works the newsstand at the Delta Terminal at LaGuardia."

"No. Why?"

"Just checking. By the way, Chief Ramirez wants to know how things are going in Brooklyn?"

Voort realizes that one reason for the call is to remind him that he is on a leash—as if he could forget it. He regards the bracelet on his wrist, with its tungsten lock and pinprick light on top. It's impossible to mistake it for an innocent adornment.

"Brooklyn," Voort says, "is the birthplace of one out of ten people in the U.S." He hits END.

"Give those assholes back what they give you," Mickie says as they pass the tree-lined border of the Brooklyn Botanic Garden. They have reached Eastern Parkway.

"There's the building." Mickie kills the dome light and they pull into a miraculously open parking space. Voort remembers working the Caribbean Day parade here each year, remembers the steel bands moving down the wide road, the dancers in feathered costumes, the stands selling jerk chicken and Jamaican beer and spicy tuna and coconut-flavored ice.

A squad car passes, its uniformed occupants nodding hello. Fellow cops, except he has the feeling that they've been dispatched to observe him. He shakes off the paranoia as the car drives away.

Concentrate on the scene. Botanic garden on one side. Apartment buildings across the street. A hulking string of midsized, boring-looking, faded-brick buildings, as unique and individualistic as a Stalinist housing project.

Voort actually had been on this block when he was a kid, during one of the Sunday drives to see neighborhoods of historical interest to the family. A Queens beach where Voort smugglers had landed muskets for the Continental Army. A church in Tribeca where a Voort had slipped silver coins into a British sergeant's pocket in exchange for information on enemy troop movements in the Bronx.

Voort sees himself on a crisp fall Sunday on this block, holding Dad's hand, imagining the story as Bill Voort tells him, "The revolution started on Eastern Parkway and almost ended here. This is the highest ground in the city. Washington assembled his army in Brooklyn and the British marched through forest to attack. The colonists ran."

"Did Voorts run too?"

"As scouts we were out front, ha ha. But under orders."

We, Voorts always said when discussing history. *We* beat the Spanish in 1898. *We* helped break Tammany Hall.

"The Brits were professionals and we were new at war. They drove us down to the harbor but then they became too confident. When the sun went down they decided to wait 'til morning to finish the Americans off. But that night Washington's army escaped by rowing over to Manhattan. Guess who found the boats?"

"Voorts," he'd said, feeling the ever-present pride in the ancestors.

"So what's the lesson?"

"Never give up, even if you're losing?"

"There'll be plenty of times like that when you grow up. But feeling like you're losing and actually doing it are separate things."

"Then how do you know if you lost?"

Voort's dad had smiled. "Maybe you never do."

Now the forest is gone and no marker commemorates George Washington's passage here. Voort and Mickie cross an urban landscape filled with belching oil trucks and rattling cars and late-morning pedestrian traffic of predominantly elderly women pushing handcarts to or from shops.

A young, Hispanic doorman in the lobby—Mauricio, his name-tag says—eyes their badges and says, "The asbestos team's in the basement. But dust is everywhere. You oughtta wear a mask."

"Got any extras?"

"You wouldn't catch me dead down there. Maybe you can buy some at the hardware store a couple blocks away."

No time, Voort thinks, and tells Mauricio not to alert the work crew that police are here. The stairwell to the basement echoes with the grinding of mechanical saws and the calls of men shouting orders at each other. When Voort pushes open the swinging door the decibel level shoots up and the dust is so thick he and Mickie have to put handkerchiefs over their mouths.

It would be great if we broke this right now.

"I hope these guys have good health insurance," Mickie says. "Not some shitty HMO."

They find the work crew removing pipe insulation in the boiler room: a half-dozen men and women on ladders, hard hats on, eye guards on, tie-on masks over their mouths and noses. People who do this kind of work are new immigrants, probably. High school dropouts. Guys with no education and new babies. Add an ex-con or two.

"We're looking for William Neems," Voort shouts over the noise at the foreman, a small, tough-looking Asian of indeterminable age who squints at Voort's badge with flat eyes beneath his plastic eye guard.

The man turns the badge upside down as if checking for forgery. Cops, Voort understands, are not popular in this room.

"*Who* you want?" the foreman asks, but Voort is sure he heard it right the first time.

"Neems!"

The foreman yells to a white guy stacking cut-up sheets of insulation in a corner, "Is Billy?"

"Is Billy *what?* Speak English, you gook." It's like some invisible signal has passed through the room. Let's screw around with the cops.

"Policeman want Billy!"

The noise is tremendous. The walls seem to be shaking and dust is everywhere and someone turns up a radio. Eminem music blasts off the concrete walls.

"Ohhhh, Billy! I saw him."

"Where?"

"You ought to get a mask on," the white guy says in an Eastern European accent but indifferent tone that tells Voort he couldn't care less if Voort caught lung cancer or not. Neems is apparently not working in this particular room.

"Where is he?" Voort watches to make sure no one picks up a cellphone or slips down the hall to alert William Neems.

"This dust," the man says, delaying, sliding a rubber-gloved finger across his throat, and Voort has a feeling the man is smiling beneath his mask. "It gets in your lungs but you can't get it out. Can't even see it with a microscope. Later you get sick, guy. Like the coal mines in Romania!"

"If you want to go back to Romania," Mickie says. "I can arrange it with the INS."

"What kind of attitude is that? I'm a citizen! I try to do you a favor and you give me shit."

The guy's brows are chalky above his plastic face shield and below his hard hat. But his pale blue eyes have registered the threat.

"You're about as much a citizen as the president of France," Mickie says.

"I saw him last Friday. Or was it Monday? Hey Marcella! Did Billy work here last on Monday or Friday?"

"You mean he's not even *here* today?" Voort says.

The foreman chuckles as if Voort is a fool for not knowing it. "Why he work if home with Shanghai flu all week?"

Mickie turns the boom box off. The grinding noises stop, one by one. Dust drifts over strips of cut-up asbestos lying in piles around the stepladders.

Voort tells them, "If we check Billy's phone records and find that you called him after we left, we'll be back. So will the INS."

"You are worse than Ceauşescu," the Romanian says.

Six minutes later, in the car, Mickie says, "Neems has the flu, my ass."

"Go faster."

They're shooting south down Seventh, the siren clearing traffic from the intersections with Union Street, President Street, Fifth Street, while both men hack up flem on their way to Neems's home address.

Voort remembering the ex–water inspector clearly now. Seeing him at the coffee machine at the water department, where they'd arrested him. A heavy man, but fit. An ex–high school halfback with coarse, ruddy features, an auburn crew cut and thick lips sucking coffee from a Styrofoam cup he flung at them as he ran with surprising nimbleness for the stairs.

He sees Neems in the interrogation room with his lawyer, slumped but glaring at Voort and whispering through teeth Voort had broken when he resisted. "You like my wife?"

"We asked her questions."

"How often we have sex? What kind of question is that?"

"Billy," Mickie had said gently. "You're a sex offender. You're a pervert. We want to know exactly how perverted you are."

The lawyer snapping, "I'm stopping this now."

Neems at the trial had told the disbelieving jury, "That detective came on to my wife!"

By the time they reach Sunset Park—Neems's neighborhood—and pull over halfway down September Eleventh Place from his address, the cellphone's rung twice more, both times with detective Santini asking if Voort remembers people he cannot recall.

The area is populated by cops and firemen, an odd location for a sex offender to take up postprison life. The block consists of small clapboard homes fronted by small, well-kept lawns behind chain-link fences. The rule is, walk toward the suspect's home casually in case he's watching. Nod hello to the moms on stoops and ignore the kids riding razor scooters on the sidewalk.

Voort tells Mickie, "Take the back."

Mickie hurries down a narrow alley separating Neems's green clapboard house from an aluminum-sided one next door, as Voort ignores the again-buzzing cellphone and opens the chain-link gate. The sun feels hot on the back of his neck. He makes sure the safety is off on his new Sig Sauer.

NEEMS, 2B, says a sticker on the mailbox, and a

little arrow beside it points at stairs going up the side of the house.

This is it.

He hates outside stairways. They're visible from above. His cousin, Officer Steve Voort, was shot in the leg while walking up an outdoor stairway in Little Neck a year back.

At least in 2B, Voort sees, slipping up the railed stairs, the shades are drawn. He hears no sound from above, just the cheeping of small birds behind a rain gutter and the squawk of the angry mother wheeling in the sky.

Voort knocks and gets no answer.

Heart beating faster, he raps on the window. The shades prevent him from seeing inside.

But then a lock clicks and the door is swinging open and it's Neems, all right, a little older, a little grayer, a lot fatter, standing in the doorway wearing a faded plaid bathrobe and cotton pajamas, blowing his nose in a paper towel. The bloodshot eyes widen when he realizes the identity of his visitor.

"You."

Behind the man, in the dark living room, Voort sees a hissing vaporizer, a TV tuned to NY1, crumpled blankets on a couch that seems too short for the man. A rancid odor wafts from the room—part sweat, part steam, part fever.

Neems rasps. "I shoulda made *you* take a lie-detector test."

He tries to say more but breaks out hacking, as Voort's hope dies. Neems doubles over. His nose is dripping. He wipes his palm on the hem of his robe.

"Seven-thirty. You want to tell me where you were at seven-thirty this morning," Voort says, knowing that preliminaries are useless with this man. *But you follow through just in case.*

Neems laughs silently. His belly shakes beneath the robe. "This is rich," he gets out, voice raw and painful-sounding. "You think I killed her."

The laughter degenerates into more coughing. He manages to get out, "Nice bracelet. My cellmate had to wear one of those after he got out."

The damn cellphone keeps buzzing but Voort ignores it, and the sun seems hotter on his neck.

Neems says. "I was eating soup, that's what I was doing. The landlady was with me. She brought me split-pea soup. Little onions. Little potato. Lotta peas. You like split-pea soup?"

Voort will check out the story, of course, but has a feeling it will be true.

"Got a warrant? Otherwise, I'll see you on TV," the sick man says, and slams his door. Voort hears coughing on the other side.

Reaching for the phone, he has a bad feeling that this time the call is not going to be a mere inquiry; this time, now that Neems looks innocent, things are going to get worse. And an instant later the premonition is confirmed when Eva tells him, "We found another note for you."

"Does that mean there's another body?"

"Get to Central Park, the entrance on Fifth and Sixty-sixth. You'll see the squad cars. I'll be there."

I can't be responsible for this. I can't have screwed up that badly.

Two dead now, probably.

12:46.

Forty minutes earlier, on the top floor of Manhattan's prestigious Forty West Fifty-seventh Street, Phillip Hull, Ph.D., sits gazing out his window at the rooftops below. His excitement is rising because in minutes his favorite part of the day will begin.

I can't wait to see her, he thinks as his phone rings.

"Senator's on line two," his new secretary says.

"Which one?"

"Gravitz, from Massachusetts."

"I'm in a meeting. I'll call her this afternoon, any time she wants after three."

As he hangs up the phone rings again. It's been that kind of nonstop morning. Like every morning.

The secretary says, "Tim Ott on line one." Ott, new, young CEO of Disney, looks out at Hull shrewdly from the cover of the *Forbes* magazine on his desk. The secretary says, "He wants to know if you're free for lunch any day next week."

"What was the first thing I told you when I hired you, Brenda?"

"Excuse me?"

"The very first thing."

"That you never make lunch dates."

"How excellent of you to remember."

"That you always have a standing lunch date and

I should never even try to get you to change it."

"Then why *did* you just try to get me to change it?"

"I thought, you know . . . Disney . . ."

Phillip Hull tells her that he'd love to have a breakfast with Ott, or a dinner, but not lunch.

Ott's a pompous asshole and I hate my life.

But before he can leave the phone screams. His wife, Patricia, is on line six, raving about some furniture maker she met in the Berkshires. She's on a Smithsonian Artists-of-New-England tour, with other big donors, driving around in a luxury bus and stopping to inspect "American crafts" and order custom-made cabinets, paintings, quilts, bed frames, clocks.

"We really ought to buy one of Ken Smith's tables, Puppy," Patricia tells him. "He's got the cutest shop in Becket. His work is handsome, and a great investment," she adds, as if "investment" has anything to do with it. She would never part with anything once she got it into their apartment. Her goal in life is to acquire more things.

Ringgggggg.

In the last eight minutes before lunch he fields calls from the archdiocese, asking if he's finished his report on the demographics of Staten Island churchgoers. ("We're particularly interested in the racial breakdown.") From the senior partner of Cobb & Bowes Advertising, asking if the report is finished on lemonade drinkers in the United States ("Men or women, Phil? Who likes lemonade better? The hard sex or the fair one?"). And from the chief aide to New York's state senate majority leader, asking about Hull's report on voter makeup in Schenectady, an area due to be redistricted under court order ("Between you and me, we Democrats have to know where to draw the lines, capish?").

I need to see her, now.

Phillip Hull, demographics consultant to *Fortune* 500 companies, coal company lobbyists, and even Hollywood film corporations takes from the tiny top drawer of his thirty-six-thousand-dollar French antique desk ("Napoleon once used it, Puppy, so I bought it for you at Sotheby's!") a plain brown paper bag in which, this morning, he packed his usual noon repast of an avocado and mushroom sandwich, a sliced kiwi fruit, a bottle of Nantucket cranberry juice, and two Gas-X pills.

He thinks, making sure to slip binoculars into his pocket, *I need to see her.*

He thinks, *Numbers never lie. They trick. They confuse. They deceive. But they need help to lie.*

He's been growing sick of numbers for the past few years and now, riding down in the elevator, watching the doors slide open and reveal, floor by floor, dioramas of waiting rooms of companies that occupy this prestigious address . . . law firms . . . literary agency . . . modeling agency, he thinks, *I should have been a park ranger but my parents said no. The truth was, I was poor and I wanted money.*

Hull smiles, squeezed in the elevator. A ranger! A lowly paid ranger who couldn't care less about

Napoleon's fucking desk, driving a pickup in Yellowstone and seeing real animals instead of the Yalies he dispatches regularly to all areas of the country to ask residents questions like "Would you be willing to pay ten cents a gallon more for gasoline if that cut global warming? Twenty cents?"

Out on the street, at the corner of Fifty-ninth and Central Park South, stopped for a light, Hull imagines himself as part of a special Ranger team, rereleasing a captured Canadian wolf into Yellowstone. In the vision he is tan, not pale, and fit, so that he does not need blood pressure pills, which make his balls numb, sinus medication, which makes him drowsy each night, back pills, tendonitis pills. He doesn't even *have* a wife and daughter in the vision.

Beside him, as he waits for the light to change, he hears one woman tell another, "*Anyone* could be the next victim! *We* could be victims if we don't watch out."

In Hull's mind the wolf bounds off toward snow-capped mountains but turns and regards him with gratefulness—in a real bond between man and beast. Then the light changes and ahead, beckoning like a green oasis, is the quiet expanse of Central Park. Entering it he feels the pressure in his head ease and space open up. Sometimes Phillip thinks he'd go crazy if he didn't have his private daily hour in the park.

Strolling east, he reaches the brushy area where he likes to have lunch—and sometimes gets a nice view of *her.* As he pushes into the bushes an old woman is coming out . . . bent . . . white-haired . . . a homeless person whose unwashed odor hits him from six feet away. He prays inwardly that she hasn't decided to make the clearing her bedroom . . . that when he pushes the rest of the way through he won't see a soiled bedroll or cardboard box where she plans to sleep tonight . . . a pile of ashes where she made a fire last night . . . a discarded tin of Dinty Moore . . .

Fortunately there's none of it. But a man is sitting in the clearing instead.

Can't I even have privacy here?

A stranger is sitting, back against a tree, knapsack open beside him as he looks down at a book. A shaggy-haired man in denim and sunglasses. Disappointed, Phillip turns to leave.

But the man says, from behind, "My God! Is that a peregrine falcon up there?"

Hull turns and the man's got binoculars to his face, and, following the line of sight, Hull thinks, heart leaping, *I see her!*

She is small and slate gray and climbing the thermals with strong, deep wing beats. In his own binocs he makes out her long wings and the midnight slash of blue on her crest. Her whole aspect, everything about the muscle and aerodynamics, screams of sleekness, freedom, wildness.

"She's beautiful," he says as the man holds out the bird bible, the waterproof, plastic-covered Audubon guide.

"I understand several pairs nest in the city," the man says. "We don't have them in Iowa. It's too flat."

Moving closer, Phil nods, eager to talk about *this* subject. "One pair nests on the Brooklyn Bridge. One on the MetLife building. Mind if I sit here? I actually eat lunch here most days."

The man says, "Join me, please," and looks up, following the magnificent flight of the falcon. It eats up the air in great arcs.

"Peregrines in the wild nest on cliffs. New York's filled with man-made ones," Hull says.

The man asks, "Do they really eat pigeons?"

"You'd be surprised, because pigeons are actually faster in straight flight. So the falcon," he says, sitting a few feet from the man, opening his bag, pulling out his sandwich, "uses strategy."

"Flies above it, hey?"

"Folds its wings and drops at speeds up to two hundred miles an hour."

"Punches right into the pigeon with those claws," the man says, and whistles admiringly as Phillip notes the man's free hand going into his knapsack, maybe reaching for a sandwich too, a snack, a Coke, or bottled water.

"Drags its prey onto a rooftop," Phil tells his new friend. "Sometimes I watch them from my office, hunting over Times Square. They bring the pigeons they catch onto rooftops."

"It's amazing that predators can live in the city. Hey, isn't that another one?"

"Where?"

"Right there," the man says eagerly, pointing.

Phillip Hull raises his binoculars, craning. His

heart is beating fast. He can't see the other bird yet but he yearns for release. He feels his neck elongating, stretching.

He is only vaguely aware of a shadow on the ground, sweeping toward him, before the awful pain explodes in his throat.

SIX

The afternoon is starting to get muggy now, the heat to rise to uncomfortable levels with a moist, sticky haze that thickens and pollutes the city's air. A gray pall hovers over the skyscrapers. Joggers move slowly around the park's periphery. Voort sees a runner bent over at the curbside, throwing up.

"There are no clear choices today," Eva tells him when he climbs into the department's mobile command center, as if she is wrestling with some personal decision herself. "Just instinct, and half my best people are second-guessing themselves with the clock running down. So tell me," she asks. "You a Mets fan?"

It's a bad question because of the odd intensity with which she asks it. Because she's ordered him here before letting him see the body. Because why is she talking about baseball now?

Eva's so tiny she can stand in the van packed with

communications and surveillance equipment, but rather than looking vulnerable as another person might, she appears filled with energy. The air-conditioning is on blast to protect the equipment. The van is freezing, Voort thinks, as sweat dries on his neck.

"I go from time to time."

"Follow pitching changes?"

"Who was killed?"

Her look says, I'll tell you when I'm ready. "Manheim for Aguilar. Stuff like that?"

"That's a minor league trade the Mets considered making a few years ago, and didn't. Neither outfielder turned out to be good. Neither ever reached the majors."

She grunts and turns to face the bank of TV screens showing the park outside and squad and detective cars, medical examiner cars, and TV vans, the electronic vultures of crime. The park drive has been closed to normal traffic. Crowds of gapers are growing by the minute. Blue Guys block off a hedgerow halfway up a grassy rise.

"Show me the note, Chief."

She looks angry now, and alone, battling her own departmental demons. She's risked herself to back him on her first major case, and he feels a wave of gratefulness for her loyalty, or at least enough of it so he's stayed on. Finally, she's holding out a copy of the note.

"You tell *me* what it means, Voort."

Stomach churning, he reads:

MANHEIM FOR AGUILAR? DOESN'T SEEM SO IMPORTANT NOW. BIRTHDAY BOY. DOES IT? SCORE SO FAR: VISITORS TWO. VOORT. ZIP. HAVE A BUD AND A COUPLE OF DOGS WITH KETCHUP AND PEPPER. ON ME.

Voort realizes his hands are shaking.

"Zip," she says softly.

"Pepper," he says. "I always put pepper on hot dogs. It's a joke in my family."

"That's what we gathered from your cousins. So tell me, since you're the only man I've ever met with this particular diet. Tell me how the person who wrote this note knows what you eat?"

"Want me to take another lie detector test?"

"What I want is for you to remember something, because our writer is looking more like someone you know. A fight at Shea? A bet on a game? What I *want* is for you to walk through those bushes and recognize the way the body lies, an angle of attack, anything that links our dead man to your life. And do it before more people lose theirs."

"It would help if you told me who got killed."

Or are you watching me to see if I already know?

"Phillip Hull," she says.

Voort sucks in his breath. Even without the death of Gabrielle Viera, Hull would rate the news vans. "He works for half the major politicians in the state."

Eva shivers against the AC. "He was discovered by a dog walker. Her borzoi gets off the leash and disappears through the bushes. Starts howling like crazy, then goes nuts. By the time the hound of Baskerville's under control we got teeth marks on the body, ripped clothing . . ."

"Fingerprints?"

"The dog owner's."

"Footprints?"

"Just impressions on the grass from about thirty pedestrians who came running when she screamed. But we have a witness. Detective Paul Santini dug her up."

Voort brightens until Eva shakes her head. "It's a bag lady who's drunk as my uncle Jaime, but at least she's sure she saw a man. The sketch guys are coming up with something. Any information is an improvement, I guess."

"I was at a fundraiser with him once at the Met," Voort says, and Eva brightens.

"But I never talked to him." Eva slumps.

In his memory, "In the Mood" reverberates through the lobby of the museum. A live jazz band plays up on the balcony, near the new Greek vase display. Voort and Camilla eat smoked oysters on water crackers as he spots the tall pollster in the crowd, while a speaker from Save the Hudson lambastes Corriston International's chemical-dumping policy over the past ten toxic years.

Voort says, "Add politics now. Add sports. This is getting wider."

"Go check the body and surprise me with facts I don't know, not problems I do."

1:28.

The second he climbs from the van, reporters start shouting questions from behind the police line, and the crowd quiets so they can hear juicy accusations and denials. Voort's become entertainment, a good story to tell at home tonight.

"Hey Voort, is it true you're involved in insider trading?"

"They're saying you planted evidence on the Lopez case!"

He heads up the knoll, sweating lightly from heat and from Eva's revelations. Breaking through the bushes, he sees detectives, medical examiners, photographers.

Paul Santini—who has been put in charge of the main part of the investigation—is on the far side of the clearing, talking with other detectives. Voort's only met the man once, but he's reputed to be a smart investigator, a bird dog. Certainly Eva must trust him if she gave him this case.

TV helicopters hovering now, overhead.

Work slows as Voort passes, headed toward the man-sized lump beneath the plastic tarp at the foot of an oak. He's aware of cops eyeing him, muttering to each other. He knows the tone. He's used it on screwups who've embarrassed the department. He knows the look. He's given it to detectives who got fired, arrested, demoted, or transferred to places where you never heard from them again.

It never occurred to me that I'd ever be the target of those kinds of looks.

A young medical examiner with whom he's played

poker flashes him a thumbs-up, and Voort finds himself absurdly grateful.

An older detective from the sex crimes unit glares and turns away. Voort wants to shake the guy, explain things, but what the hell can he explain?

"Hey Con Man, good news!"

Mickie, coming toward him like a guided missile of support, stops at the foot of the tarp at the same time.

"Little moneymaking opportunity here, Con Man. Lieutenant Saito's giving three-to-one odds you screwed up. Two-to-one you took graft. I put down a hundred."

"You *bet* on me?"

"After the way my tech fund plunged again last week I'd rather invest in you. Voort, meet Phil Hull. Phil, meet Voort."

Mickie slips the tarp back and Voort gags at the damage. He's seen lots of bad beatings, but this was one of the worst. Whoever killed Hull did so in a gigantic rage, didn't stop hitting even after the numbers expert was dead. Flies dot the smashed skull and protruding bone shards. The left ear is only partially attached. The right eye socket is oozing. The legs look broken in at least three places. The torso's caved where ribs were smashed. The neck seems oddly deflated, as if the cartilage was bashed in and collapsed.

Voort forces himself to probe, to examine wounds and fingertips and feel for loss of body temperature, but other detectives have already done this and in the end he finds nothing that reminds him of any previous case.

"They found a pipe stuffed with concrete, Con Man."

"He's getting rougher," Voort says. "Or is it even the same guy?"

Voort tells Mickie about the note then. "Two franks with ketchup and pepper. That's what I always have. Two Kahn franks. Two Buds."

"What's the last game you went to, Voort?"

"A couple weeks ago." Two copters are thwacking overhead.

"You think he's watching now?"

Voort imagines a con out of prison, tracking him at the ball game and bars and restaurants and the supermarket.

Voort tells Mickie, "Let's hit the crowd."

Bursting through the hedges, they head for the police line, trying to see the faces behind it. But the reporters surge forward to meet them, shouting questions and blocking their view of anyone else.

"Voort, is it true the murders today are tied in to the bribery scandal in the Bronx precincts?"

Both men pushing back. "Get out of the *way!*"

It's no use. Someone grabs him. It's like he's a rock star mobbed by paparazzi. He sees more Nikons than faces, and with each turn into the crowd the reporters flow around him, re-form like some new collective life form, the hundred-footed journalism amoeba. Voort glimpses strangers' faces over shoulders, past microphones.

Staring, fascinated people, none familiar, look back.

Voort says, as they fight to return, "Mickie, if he goes to my house, Camilla's there."

"Don't worry. I called the cousins. They won't leave her alone."

They break from the crowd, cross the police line, and head for the van to make their disappointing report. Voort straightens his clothes as Mickie tells him, "I hate to say this, but what if *you're* one of the two targets he still wants to hit? Ever think of that?"

"What does he think I did to him?"

"Con Man, the guy who shot John Lennon never even met him. The guy who shot Allard Lowenstein thought he was sending messages through fillings in his teeth. Nuts fix on people. He's fixed on you. You didn't do a goddamn thing."

"What'll he use next time, a flamethrower?"

Mickie says, "An asbestos suit'll go great with your birthday tie."

Deli bags lay beneath the mobile switchboard. Cellophane-wrapped pickles lay beside the banked TV screens. Cans of iced Lipton sweat beside the police sketch artist's rendition of the killer, which is going out over the airwaves, and maybe, considering the latest victim's identity, reaching the whole northeast United States.

"Eating helps you think," Eva says. "If you don't want the food now, take it with you."

But the notion of eating seems repulsive to Voort.

Mickie grunts at the sketch. "Big glasses. Shaggy hair. I bet it's a wig. You think it's a wig, Con Man?"

"I have no idea."

"Try the turkey," Eva says. "At least I'll feel I'm accomplishing something that way."

But in his mind's eye Voort's going over the baseball angle: he's at Big Shea seeing the hordes pushing through the turnstiles on a fine May night, the neon sculpture of a pitcher rising up the outer wall in yellow and green. Neon knee raised wa-ay up, arm held high for a neon fastball. Voort seeing the beer man popping open an ice-cold Bud and tilting a paper cup so the suds don't run over. Box F123J is so close to the field he can hear fastballs hit the catcher's mitt.

Eva saying, "Senator Ryker's brought up the possibility of terrorism. Interference in elections."

"By killing a pollster?" Mickie says. "Give me a break. And if it's terrorism, how does Viera fit in?"

"Hull was working on a contract for the White House," Eva says with a sigh. "The FBI wants to come in."

Don't think about the political stuff yet, Voort tells himself. *Not until you finish with Shea.* But all that comes to him is a memory of "Mister Met"—the mascot with the gigantic baseball head—running out on the field during the seventh-inning stretch with an air bazooka, shooting folded-up souvenir T-shirts into the mezzanine while "Lazy Mary" blasts through the stadium.

Did he ever have a run-in with people in a nearby

box? An argument with someone who might have noticed how he put pepper on hot dogs or heard the cousins teasing him about it?

"What was Hull doing for the White House?" he hears Mickie ask as he conjures up name plaques on the seats running down his aisle. Shaw Lyman, *Esquire*. Gennaro Brothers bakery. Tokyo Bank Trust. Easy to remember, since he's been seeing the same plaques since he was fourteen.

Eva saying, "He was working with census numbers to calculate federal aid to states. Like ninety million goes to Texas because they have a higher birthrate. Sixty million to Connecticut. People there have fewer kids. The formula is important because federal aid is drying up."

Mickie whistles. "Where there's meat, there's flies."

But Voort's doing it right, concentrating on one line of thought at a time, like Dad taught him. Bringing up the faces in nearby boxes now, which is easy because giving up a box at Shea is like surrendering a rent-controlled apartment. You don't do it. Owners die, but their friends, kids, and business partners tell the Mets they're still alive. Each December, all over New York, bills from the Mets' organization, addressed to dead men, arrive at their "new addresses" so the boxes stay in the family, so the faces stay the same.

Hell, Voort thinks, *Shaw Lyman was over ninety years old when I first saw him twenty-five years ago, a half-blind divorce lawyer groping down the aisle. Yet his name's still up.*

Is it really possible this relates to baseball?

Why not? More trivial complaints have driven people to murder. You put mustard on my sandwich instead of onions. You called my son a jerk at the hockey game.

"Ever bust a bookie?" Eva asks suddenly. "Betting and sports?"

"No."

Mickie eyes the TVs, which give the van crowd-surveillance capability. The new cameras up top are on because perps tend to stroll away if they see cops coming. But they hang around a crime scene sometimes if they think nobody is looking back.

"A former prostitute and a pollster. You can connect a former prostitute and anyone," Mickie says. "Anyone could have dipped into that well and probably did."

"We're not sure she was a prostitute," Voort says. "The charges were dropped."

"Since when did you join the ACLU?"

"We're checking connections," Eva says, but what she really means is "hoping for," and, wracking his brain about the pepper, Voort glances at the screens too and is surprised to see Julia Voort out there in the front row of gawkers.

She's all I need right now.

The widow dressed in a conservatively cut gray calf-length spring dress/jacket combo that frames her cute little body nicely, enhances the sexy aspect as she chats up one of the Blue Guys at the line. Either he's trying to pick her up or she's identified herself as a cop widow, because Blue Guys at crime scenes don't make eye contact with prying strangers. No way. Leave me alone, is the message they radiate.

A slight ticking feeling starts up in his back. *What the hell is she doing here? How did she even find me?*

Voort asks Eva, "What exact year did the Mets consider those trades? You checked already, didn't you?"

Six years ago.

"So the idea," he says, crazy with frustration, "is, Mickie and I go back to Brooklyn, where I worked then."

"Retrace what you did on your birthday. Re-create the day. Hit the same addresses and try to remember things. You'll do it for all the years in the logs, but start with the one in the note. Meanwhile, Paul's people will be looking at other angles. And if you can't reach me, report to him."

"I'll need to know what Hull was up to six years ago, in case it dovetails with something I find."

"You'll get it when we do," she says. "But we may not reach those questions immediately." She holds up a hand to stop Voort's protest. "Paul doesn't interpret the note like you do. He'd also like to talk to you before you go."

"What *other* way is there to interpret it?"

"It could be a trick. Or you might have argued with someone but not during that same year. Paul's concentrating on more recent angles."

"I especially like the terrorist angle," Mickie says. "Maybe al-Qaida wanted travel discounts but

Gabrielle sent them regular fare on the planes they blew up."

Voort says stubbornly, "Let us visit Hull's office before we go back to Brooklyn."

"Remember that business with the mosques last year?"

Voort says nothing and Eva nods. "You remember. Two weeks of bomb threats so Manhattan North quadruples security at mosques. Half the force is watching mosques when a bullion shipment gets hit a mile away. A baseball trade, Voort, is what you have. The second you tell me how baseball ties into this, I'll give you what you want."

"What about the pepper?"

"An interesting guess is still a guess."

Mickie tears his attention away from the TV screens to argue. "Our boy gets off on danger. He figures he's smarter than us. *We* could never beat *him*, so he sweetens the odds. He gives us a real year to make it interesting. He spikes the dumb team points."

Chief Ramirez nods as if to say it's possible, but that doesn't make it true. "Before you take off for Brooklyn, Paul wants to check your log page from six years ago and see if your stuff ties into what *he's* doing."

"I'm still a suspect."

"Of course." Eva is frowning now, staring at the screens herself.

"I recognize that woman," she says, "from the funerals. She's one of our widows from the World

Trade Center. You lost family, Voort. Is she with you?"

Julia has managed to get through the police line somehow and is being escorted toward the van by a respectful Blue Guy.

Voort's unsure who or what he's more furious at: Eva, Paul, Julia, complexity.

"Yes, she's with me. I'll be right back."

"I had to come," she says. "I couldn't stand hearing what they're saying about you on television. I called your office and they said you were here."

Meaning you told them you were a police widow. That's the only way they'd tell you anything, and the only way the guys here would let you through the line.

She says, her big eyes on his, "I know you didn't do anything wrong. Whatever you need, I'm there."

"Thanks, but this isn't the time."

"That's what they said when the plane hit the trade center and I tried to call Donnie to tell him to be careful. His lieutenant said it wasn't the time. There'd be time later. Be patient, he said. Be a good wife. Wait."

Tears glistening in the corners of her eyes.

Asshole, he tells himself. Of course she'd show up. Of course she couldn't just sit at home again. And you tell her off.

Julia standing on tiptoe now, pressing cool lips to his cheek within view of the TV cameras, then the lips shift to *his* for an instant. Light, a touch. Julia's perfume wafts into his nostrils. Julia's cinnamon taste is on his mouth. He could close his eyes and still feel the lithe body a foot away.

"Donnie always looked up to you," she says.

"That means a lot to me. Give Camilla a message," he says, knowing she'll learn Julia was here anyway. Hell, if the TV's live, she could know already. Either way some kind of destructive female telepathic signal has surely gone out.

"Anything," she says. The cop Scarlett O'Hara.

"Tell her I miss her." Like the words are a drug to create amnesia. Utter the five-syllable incantation and loved ones forget wounds, hurts, grudges. He wonders if the message will sound as pathetic to Camilla as it does at this moment to him.

Julia's lips glistening. Julia nodding eagerly, like the kiss never happened. Like it was in his imagination or it had been a handshake and his words are the rightest thing in the world.

But you've given me an idea.

He steps off a bit, hunches to block out directional microphones, unsnaps his Nokia, and shifts stance because he doesn't want Julia to hear what he's going to say. Of course they're all watching but they can't hear the phone ring on Thirteenth Street, can't hear Camilla on the other end saying how glad she is to hear him, how she's wanted to call but knew he needed to concentrate.

They especially can't hear the detailed instructions he gives Camilla now.

"I can do that," she says when he's through. "And

when you catch this guy I have an idea for a birthday celebration. You. Me. Kayaks. The Adirondacks."

"Bed and breakfast on a lake. And Camilla, if you get an answer, and you can't reach me, *don't tell Mickie*. That way if things backfire I'll be in trouble, not him."

But Camilla's no Julia. "Lover, Mickie would kill you if you kept him out of it and so would I. Don't tell me how to report."

"Once a producer . . ." But Voort is smiling.

"By the way, Julia's disappeared; she left her guests here. I think she's going to try to see you."

"Actually, she's here."

A pause. Then Camilla says lightly, "Well, this is just like being on the job again." He's unsure which part of the job she's referring to, since she just got fired from it, just got screwed.

A click on the line.

Julia tells him, when he gets back, "I know you have to work now. Take care of yourself."

His face still burns where her lips had touched his skin.

The four of them sit in the mobile command center, staring down at Voort's log pages of six years ago. Paul Santini has finished the big grill job on Voort and learned nothing useful. Voort is to give full cooperation to Santini in his "parallel investigation."

Santini doesn't have to do shit for Voort.

If Santini is right and the baseball clue is screwy,

or I interpreted it wrong, I'm ending my chance to stop two more murders.

"Read the schedule out loud," says Santini, a dapper, dark, intelligent man; an athletic, slightly bow-legged ex–college wrestler who favors boxy Hugo Boss suits. "Maybe we'll get lucky and something will ring a bell."

Reading, Voort translates his official notations into plain English in his head.

From 8:15 to 8:35 that day, six years ago, he'd answered a false alarm—a phony phone call—about a woman screaming at 895 Swidler Street.

"We used to get half a dozen of those a week," Voort says. "They drove everyone crazy. Then they stopped."

From 8:50 to 9:35, he'd worked a traffic accident in Grand Army Plaza and ticketed Mr. Ralph M. Lieb of Great Neck for sideswiping a blue Dodge van. Nolita Massey of Third Street, the van's driver, had required hospitalization for a broken left leg. Voort had charged Lieb with reckless endangerment and running a light.

He asks Santini, "Can you send a detective to check out Lieb?" Meaning, it makes no sense for Mickie and I to eat up two precious hours driving back and forth to Long Island.

"My guys are pretty busy, actually," Santini says.

"Paul would be happy to do it," says Chief Ramirez. "Right, Paul?"

From 9:35 to 10:14, the notation "patrolling" tells Voort that he and Attanasio had been driving the precinct, making their presence known and discouraging crime. At least that was the hope. In fact, the city had commissioned a demographic study that year comparing robbery rates in neighborhoods patrolled by car versus on foot.

"Wait a minute. Did Hull's company do that study?" Voort says.

"I'll be happy to check," says Santini, who clearly learns fast.

At 10:25 Voort had responded to a robbery call at Paolo's Wine Shoppe on Brooklyn's Fifth Avenue, near Flatbush.

"I took the statement," Voort says, remembering the cheery Brazilian merchant from whom he used to buy cases of Oregon Pinot Noir, the pudgy Rio-born immigrant who for years had tried to set Voort up on dates with his sister Rose.

"She's sexy but she has a temper," Paolo used to say.

Voort had no idea if the robber was ever caught. He can only hope that somewhere in this parade of details will lurk a hidden link.

Dad used to say, "Always look at the back story. A murder is the end of things, not the start."

"Twelve o'clock to twelve-oh-nine," Mickie reads. "Ten whole minutes for lunch, huh? If you guys didn't spend your life goofing off, maybe you could cut down on crime."

"Keep going."

From 12:19 to 2:10, responding to an anonymous complaint, Voort and Attanasio had arrested Kimmy

White, eighteen, and Patricia White, sixteen, for prostitution on Fourth Avenue near Bergen, then spent an hour-and-a-half filling out arrest reports. Voort does not recall the arrests but envisions the strung-out, crack-addicted girls who work the corner. Two months on Bergen can turn a healthy teenager into an HIV-infected germ bag who gives blow jobs for eight bucks, minimum price of a doctored vial or shot.

"Are the sisters inside or out?" he wonders aloud.

"We'll check," says Santini, a regular brother now.

"Two-eighteen to two-fifty-seven. Kidnapping," Voort reads, but his pulse remains steady because, having studied this report earlier, he knows its happy outcome. He had reached 405 Harris Street to simply run into the missing five-year-old girl in the lobby. Victoria Washington had wandered off to the playground and, tiring eventually, had wandered back.

"Almost quitting time that day," Mickie says. "Time for Voort to hurry off to Shea for some delicious pepper."

"Two-fifty-eight to three-eighteen. Patrolling," Voort reads, and then, "Last call. Another phony emergency. This time a guy was supposed to be screaming in a brownstone. The old lady there had no idea why we came."

For a glum moment no one says anything. Then Santini says, "Maybe something happened that's not in the log."

"Maybe we *were* wrong about the year," says Mickie.

"No. We hit these addresses. We see if anyone remembers something I forgot. We don't have time to try much else, anyway."

"Since when do you forget anything?" Mickie says, and tells Santini, "Send someone good to check Lieb in Great Neck."

"Everyone working with me is good."

"Everyone with me too," Mickie replies, meeting Santini's gaze solidly as Voort hates that they're fighting about him, hates how the day is passing so quickly.

"Con Man, take a sandwich with you," Mickie says. "The chief's right. I'll drive. You eat."

"At least someone around here listens," says Eva.

Voort's stomach does flip-flops. The cellophane-wrapped pickles look to him like mold bars.

Voort checks his watch. It's 2:45.

SEVEN

The city paves over history, memory, continuity. A prison becomes a private school, a slave market a hospital. Dutch skeletons crumble beneath high-rise condos. Atoms rearrange themselves to suit the appetites of time.

The whole block looks different, Voort thinks in despair, parking in front of the apartment building where he'd responded to a phony emergency call six years ago. A co-op apartment building has replaced a tenement, a health food store the old tire shop. The packed playground across the street is as new as the saplings lining the curbside, the paint jobs on apartment buildings, the whole sheen of revival signaling good news for city planners. Bad news for a cop trying to make his memory work.

"Nobody home," Mickie says, finger pressed to 9A.

"Maybe they're not even living here any more."

At least whoever occupies 9L is secure or stupid enough to buzz them in without asking for identification. Riding up in the new elevator, smelling polish,

Voort thinks, *Who's even going to remember a call we made here for no reason. A woman screaming who wasn't there.*

As the elevator door opens, though, piercing screams erupt down the ninth-floor hall.

"Well, what do you know," Mickie grins. "It's coming from 9A. Again."

Voort hears a woman shouting, "Is there any nurse at that hospital you haven't screwed yet?"

The woman hollers, "She left an earring in our bed!"

The voice cuts off abruptly when Mickie knocks. Padded footsteps approach the door. It never ceases to amaze Voort how people who live in apartments believe their private affairs remain truly private, and when the voice comes again, this time from directly behind the door, it is soft with embarrassment, "Mrs. Feinstein? Is that you?"

"Police."

"Oh God." There's the scrape of a lock opening at eye level, the snap of a latch below that. The door opens but whomever the girl was screaming at must have retreated to the back of the apartment, leaving her to handle the police alone. Voort looks into the mortified face of a young woman—pretty in a flushed, freckled, Irish way. Voort cataloging: twenty-six maybe. Lean in jeans and a pink button-up shirt with the tails hanging out.

Then he realizes she's holding up a film or TV script.

"I'm auditioning for Cora in *Medical Practice*."

Another time it might be funny. Now Voort merely feels mocked, as if whoever killed Phillip Hull has gained control of even small circumstances and is twisting them for private amusement.

But he smiles, needing this girl's memory. "You fooled us. You're a good actress," he says.

"I was making too much noise, wasn't I? I told Mrs. Feinstein I get carried away. I said, Knock if I bother you. I'm *so* embarrassed."

"Don't worry. No one complained."

Anne Boyle, as she introduces herself, has only lived in this apartment for three years, she says. "The couple before me said they needed to move away from New York, fast."

"Why fast?" Voort asks. He takes in the small, cheery apartment. Low-cost Scandinavian furniture. Bright lemon-colored walls. Potted ferns and a summer stock theater poster from Provincetown, Massachusetts.

"She wanted kids. He wanted space."

"Where did they go for children and space?"

"Mrs. Feinstein gets postcards from Mountaintop, Colorado. Why? Did they do something wrong?"

"Everyone wants to live in the goddamn mountains," growls Mickie, who regards traveling anywhere outside the metropolitan area as a form of deprivation. "What do they do in the goddamned mountains after they've finished staring at the goddamned trees?"

"Check with Mrs. Feinstein, in 9G. But I never heard anything about police coming here six years ago."

"Good luck with your audition," Voort says. He and Mickie will check Anne's story, but just like six years ago, it seems there was no purpose in coming here.

At least Anne seems happy that nobody complained about her. "I really sounded mad, huh?"

"Furious enough to kill the guy."

She giggles. "That's funny. In real life I can't get angry with anyone. I'm a hopeless wimp."

The wineshop is unchanged, Paolo still stuffed into his purple, sleeveless Hofstra University sweatshirt, a pudgy fixture behind the cash register, grinning with recognition when his old customer Voort walks in.

"I am mad at you. You never come here anymore and you never called my sister for a date."

"I got transferred. I came to ask about the robbery."

"Which one?"

Mickie snorts as Voort says, "Six years ago."

"Ah, the *second* one," Paolo says, happy to have the matter clarified, clearly not a grudge-holding type. Voort wonders how many times he's been robbed? Eight? Twenty?

"Paolo, did they catch the guy who did it?"

"Yes! Three years later a detective phoned and I identified the man."

"Three years is a long time," Mickie says, more question than compliment. "That's some memory you have."

Paolo's smile fades a little. "I don't want to get anyone in trouble . . ."

"Meaning what?"

"This is important to you, Voort? Okay. The detective who called said he'd arrested someone for a different robbery, but he thought it was the same man who robbed me. He wasn't supposed to tell me but . . ."

Mickie breaks in. "He asked you to come to the precinct."

"As if you wandered in by yourself," Voort says.

"You wouldn't be there to eyeball the perp," Mickie says, "since nobody called you, right? You'd come in for another reason, like maybe you forgot the number of your old complaint report for insurance purposes."

"Yes! He said he wasn't supposed to suggest before I saw a suspect that he was guilty, but if I hurried I would be in the waiting room when he brought the man in. He said if I happened to be there by coincidence and identified him . . ."

"Paolo, *was* it the guy?"

"I'm almost positive!"

"Almost? What's 'almost'?"

"He looked scary," Paolo nods. "Besides, two other people identified him from a robbery at a different store."

Voort blows out air. "And were they *also* in the waiting room by coincidence when the suspect was brought in?"

But Mickie stops Voort by holding up his watch. "No time, Con Man. It didn't involve you."

Paolo beams, now that the unpleasant part is over. "My sister is married with a little boy now. Voort, do you have a special woman in your life yet or are you still alone?"

"Oh, one's not enough for Voort," Mickie says. "Voort's the Rudolph Valentino of Thirteenth Street."

Paolo laughs. "As long as you are here, Voort, I have some wonderful pinot noir in back."

The three prostitutes start running when they see the Caprice coming. "This car's as unmarked as a zebra," Mickie says, watching the girls totter into an abandoned building on six-inch-high heels.

If Anne Boyle's block has changed, Fourth near Bergen hasn't, Voort thinks. The day is going maddeningly nowhere. Pockets of New York hover in time. Residents move but the feel never alters. Cars get bigger, haircuts shorter. Losers stay losers whether their surroundings change or not.

Standing outside the abandoned building, Voort cups his hands. "We just want to talk, girls."

3:48.

The block is hot and silent and flies swarm from piles of trash. Passing drivers, all single males, speed up when they spot the "unmarked" Chevy's five-foot antennae and cop spotlight.

"It's amazing how the instant a hooker appears on a corner, horny guys materialize and start circling like fish," Mickie says.

Voort calls out a white lie. "We're investigating a murder! The victims are girls like you!"

Could Gabrielle Viera have worked here? But this

is the last stop for girls and Gabrielle was high-end, if she worked as a hooker at all.

They're hiding in that building, he knows, just like girls used to do when he patrolled here. The whole block is enemy territory. Pirated electrical lines disappear into top-floor windows. Pigeons line rooftops and cock their dumb heads. Somewhere on this block—probably in a basement—will be a steel door behind which boys sell powders and needles so the girls can smoke up earnings as fast as they come in.

Voort shouts. "Come out and we talk for five minutes. Don't and we call in the vans!"

"No money! No dope! No customers!" Mickie adds.

"Four . . . three . . . two . . ."

A high, thin female voice floats out of the building. "You promise just to talk?"

And here they come, like soldiers filing from a captured pillbox. Four girls—Voort must have missed one going in—pick their way up to the detectives, smiling like they'd planned to chat all along.

Will they remember something? Were they even *here* six years ago? He looks over two white girls, both older, in short skirts and tube tops, and both smoking filter tips. The black girl's in a lavender dress, eating a Twinkie, and licking cream off her fingers. The youngest and most attractive is Asian and so high on drugs she's barely able to walk. Evidently the corner's run by an equal opportunity pimp.

Do they even remember what happened six hours ago?

Out come the photos of Gabrielle and Phillip. No,

the girls say. Neither looks familiar. The man was never a customer. The girls you're asking about, Kimmy and Patricia White, never worked this corner while we were here. The old pimp's in jail. The old gang is gone. The old girls have scattered.

"Nobody stays in the same place anymore," the black girl complains.

Perhaps if a man were drunk these girls could seem sexy, but in the bright daylight the glitter of sequins is as cheap as the lashes, the leather skirts bunch because the girls are losing weight. Thin arms show needle marks. The hand that takes Voort's card shakes.

Five minutes after we leave it will be in the street.

But suddenly the taller white girl is frowning, trying to remember something.

"Did you say Kimmy *Knight* or Kimmy *White*?"

When he says "White," her red mouth opens wide and her laughter explodes out. *Ah-Ah-Ah.*

"*I'm* Kimmy. At least I used to say I was."

"Where's your sister?"

"We just told guys she was my sister. Some of 'em wanted sisters. Like Mister Pills. We called him that 'cause he got so excited when we were wit' him he ate pills for his heart."

"Do you remember me?" Voort says, hopefully.

She peers at him. She's getting restless, twitchy. She needs to work, or needs a fix.

"I don't remember faces."

The Asian girl giggles.

"That's not the part we look at," she tells Voort.

❊   ❊   ❊

The Caprice stalls at lights, grinding and moaning as if sharing human frustration. On all-news radio Commissioner Warren Aziz is announcing that police have received lots of calls from people claiming to be the killer, but none has known information held back by police.

A reporter asks, "Commissioner, with the Voort family so influential inside the police department, what kind of pressure are you under to keep him on the job?"

"Where do they get this shit?" Mickie says. "Or do they make it up to piss him off so he talks too much?"

"That's what we do in interrogations," Voort says.

"That's different. That's us," Mickie says, pulling over as Voort's cellphone buzzes and his mouth goes dry. Mickie says, "I'm going to check the goddamned engine."

4:09.

Camilla's voice says, "Are you listening to this press conference? It's unbelievable."

"What did you find out?"

"My pals at NBC came up with a partial list of Hull's clients six years ago. But he did pro bono work too, so we only know clients who paid, and not all of them."

"Go."

"Senators Axinn and Lehmann used him, on campaigns. Ford Motor Company on consumer demographics. No one in the world made a move unless this guy checked out numbers first. Health Department. Board of Ed. My favorite's the Yankees. How will you check all of them out in one day?"

"Why the Yankees?" Voort thinking hopefully, *baseball was in the note.*

"Projections for the future. Percentage of older fans, cable watchers. Fans turned off by baseball strikes."

Where do I even start looking for a mistake?

"Three more. Manhattan borough president's office. Wright & Nutter law firm and the sanitation union. In one afternoon, how do you figure which one to pick?"

"Can you find out what Wright & Nutter were working on six years ago?"

"I can try, but getting a straight answer from a lawyer—even on what she just ate—is tougher than getting the Pentagon to admit they sent troops to Peru."

"Which detectives are at the house?" he says as a radio reporter asks Aziz, "Is there any truth to the rumor that Venezuelan drug gangs may be linked to the killings?"

Camilla says, "Cousins Jack and Vann. Uncle Jeffrey."

"Absolutely no truth at all," Aziz's voice says, maybe lying, maybe not. No one's been telling Voort what the police are learning across the river.

Mickie gets back into the car and gives a thumbs-up. Voort tells Camilla, "Ask Vann and Jeffrey to visit the law firm. Maybe they'll get lucky."

Then off they go again, toward the scene of the

reported kidnapping six years ago. Voort goes over his notes as if looking long enough might reveal an answer.

"Manheim for Aguilar. Doesn't seem so important now," he repeats to Mickie. "Like I argued about it with someone. Like he heard me say it. Like he was there."

"Like he's a nut in dreamland," Mickie says.

"Then we might as well forget everything," Voort snaps. "If it's not a clue then let's go home."

"Sorry. You're right."

They're in Boerum Hill now, a less affluent part of the precinct, a mix of low-income public housing and urban settlers gambling their life savings on fix-'em-up homes. The neighborhood varies block by block, even building by building. A rebuilt townhouse sits beside a boarded-up health hazard. A renovated condo gleams next door to a burned-out shell. The battle between deterioration and progress reflects itself in the gap between bureaucratized poverty and urban pioneer hope.

"Why would someone be angry because I considered a baseball trade important? A logical reason for a change, Mick."

"Because it's not important."

"Something *else* was important."

"That you didn't see, or ignored."

Voort says, "A baseball trade that was never even made. How could that be connected to me screwing up in somebody's mind, even if they *are* imagining it?"

Mickie pulls the car over in front of a half dozen identical faded brick apartment towers. "Here we are. The scene of no damn crime at all."

The block is wide and busy, and at 4:19, with school out, the sidewalks fronting the renamed Clarence Thomas housing project are packed with kids, hundreds of them, in groups, pairs, singles. Voort wonders if one is the girl he found six years ago. She'd be in elementary school now.

"Conrad, you know what an investigation is?" his dad used to say. *"Nothing and nothing. And just when you're ready to give up, nothing again."*

Mickie puts the police visor sign down, not that anyone needs it to identify them as cops. Walking toward the gigantic project, they pass a Mister Softee truck dispensing ice cream, a basketball court where a game is in progress, benches filled with old people, and knots of teenage boys wearing oversized jeans and baseball caps. A few glance sullenly at Voort.

Foyers of public housing projects never contain any furniture to be vandalized. Only one of four elevators is working, but at least Mrs. Charlene Washington turns out to be home. Mother and daughter wait at the open door to 11A, Mrs. Washington slim-looking in a pressed floral-print-blouse-and-pleated-skirt combo, home from—according to the old report—work as a limousine service secretary. The girl in pigtails and a cobalt-blue dress, holding a math textbook. From her wide-eyed expression, Voort has a feeling she's been watching him on TV.

"I remember you," Charlene Washington says. "Some days just turn your life upside down."

That's for sure, Voort thinks, realizing that even the nature of hope seems reversed today. He'd rather sense anger here than gratitude. Fury, not welcome. Resentment. Accusation. Emotions that cause a grudge.

Mrs. Washington invites them into the quiet, neat apartment decorated with Senegalese pottery, Angolan weaving, banks of potted ferns. "When I saw you on TV this morning I thought, it's an anniversary for me too. Of when Victoria was gone and you brought her back."

"I ran into her in the lobby that day. She came back herself."

Victoria says shyly, "You looked pink."

Mrs. Washington offers tomato juice but seems unsurprised at their rushed need to ask questions, and sorry she can't help. "Every day is the anniversary of a thousand things," she says. "Since my husband died I have anniversaries three hundred sixty-five days a year."

"Nothing else stands out that you remember?"

"Victoria left. Victoria came home."

One more address on the log, and then we'll go to a baseball game because that's what I did six years ago. But what'll I do there—question everyone in other seats?

Victoria goes into the kitchen and comes back offering him a Milky Way bar tied with a blue ribbon.

"Happy birthday," says Victoria Washington.

Voort tells her he loves Milky Ways. He has no appetite. Eva's sandwiches are still in the car.

4:46.

Voort prays in church normally, but there's no time today. Shadows lengthen. The afternoon unwinds. He closes his eyes over the wailing siren as they head for the last address in his log.

God, help me see clearly, and remember what I need to know. Make it so I didn't cause what's happened. Keep Mickie out of it. Give Julia a new life. Dad? Are you there?

I am.

Voort imagines Big Bill, who died when he was nine, up on their roof on a hot July evening. Dad in his grill-master outfit of cutoff shorts and DBA T-shirt, spatula in hand as he tends a smoking Weber. Mom's downstairs, bringing up whichever Voorts have arrived to cool off. Iced Pabsts in a cooler for Bill. Mountain Dews for Voort and his cousins. Sizzling franks and burgers scent the evening.

On a boom box, Mets announcer Bob Murphy is shouting, "Mookie rounds third, trying for home!"

But in the memory, Big Bill isn't interested in baseball. He's peering over the rooftop, frowning.

"Feel like a lesson, Conrad? Or are you having too much fun?"

"A lesson *is* fun," the boy says, loving any story, rumor, wisdom about police.

"Then tell me what's wrong down there?"

Alerted, Voort stares down at Thirteenth Street,

sees cabs gliding past, shoppers coming back from the Food Emporium, tourists—they always walk slow—strolling and pointing out historical homes, like theirs. Voort feels tension rising.

"Hurry," Bill says, "or he'll get away."

Voort checks the loungers, the bus stop, and shadow areas where stairwells lead to basement apartments.

"Maybe I made a mistake depending on you, son."

For the boy the night gets hotter. Every fiber of concentration goes into gridding the street as he's been taught. He must not fail. He goes over each square, but observation is hard when you're rushing. He considers the whole picture instead of little things, searching for a pattern, a break.

"I better call in and report it," Bill says, disappointed.

"Wait! It's the tall guy on the corner!"

Dad rubs his head lovingly. "The correct answer was nothing, son. You saw nothing because there *was* nothing. So what's the lesson?"

"Don't believe what I don't see for myself," says a humiliated Voort.

Now Voort snaps out of it and looks up at the deteriorated brownstone across from where Mickie's parked. The old log says, "Caller hears shouts and noises from 811 Bryce Street, apartment 3E."

He faintly remembers the building, or is it another one in his mind? The blue paint has peeled so much that the number is barely readable. The broken front lock's enabled thieves to smash mailboxes and probably steal checks. In a way, he thinks, today matches his day of six years ago in its round of required snap judgments. This time an old lady's voice comes over the intercom. "Speak up, please."

When he's finished, she says, "Please speak up."

Mickie groans. "Why do I have a feeling people are shouting in 3E all the time?"

Voort hates whenever he comes across old people stuck in crappy apartment buildings. They haven't even the illusion that life might improve any more. Buzzed in by Estelle Moore, his anger worsens as he navigates her daily obstacle course, two flights of dark, creaky stairs.

Something is bothering me besides the building. But what?

His senses are ratcheting up, but all that comes so far is an acute awareness of the mildew that would be hell on an old person's lungs, the carpet so frayed it could trip Estelle Moore, the busted light at the top of the stairway that might cause an old woman to lose her balance, the incredible vulnerable-looking tininess of the white-haired woman leaning on a metal cane as she waits for him.

"My mother used to say, 'Estelle, you'll know you're getting old when policemen look younger than you.' Come in."

Blue, alert eyes. Hearing aids in both ears. What bends the spines of old people so badly? But the smile is amused.

Inside her apartment, knit comforters drape the Haitian cotton sofa. Bookshelves are filled with photos—of ballerinas mostly—along a far wall. A vaporizer spews steam by the hassock, even though the temperature in here has to be seventy. Headphones lying on the couch trail wire to a big screen TV, meaning that she watches with the sound turned up. Maybe a neighbor called 911 six years ago when the TV sounded like a fight.

"I see you looking at my ballerinas. You won't believe it, but I used to dance."

"I believe it, ma'am." 4:59.

"Then you must be a good detective, because you could never tell from looking at me now."

She has no recollection of Voort specifically, but recalls police visiting the apartment years ago. "That was you? You look like you were in high school then."

"Do you mind telling us what you remember?"

"I was at the window, watering plants. I saw the squad car park and two policemen—you, I guess—come in. The downstairs lock was broken so you didn't have to buzz up. I was surprised when you banged on my door."

"Was your TV on?"

"If it was, I rarely play it without the headphones. I remember that the officer I talked to said there'd been a lot of phony calls to the police that month."

"Nothing else stands out?"

"I can check my diary if you want."

"Diary?" Mickie says, sitting straighter, pleased. *What the hell is bothering me about this place?*

"Give me my cane. I fill one book a year with things that would be of no interest to anyone else. Recipes. Notions. Any odd happening would be there."

At 5:04 Voort and Mickie sit quietly in a small sewing room watching Estelle Moore searching through an overstuffed closet. A radio plays in the next apartment. Footsteps sound overhead. Voort thinks partial deafness is a blessing in this place.

Estelle mumbling, "Let's see, two years ago. Four . . ."

Hurry.

She straightens, holding a red leather book. "*You* read it. It's been years since I wrote anything embarrassing. Maybe something here will help you out."

He finds the proper date and reads, "Dalia Stein called from Israel. She and Mort are having a terrific time but Mort has indigestion."

Damn.

He reads, "TV special on Jacob's Pillow Dance Festival on Channel Thirteen tonight. Can't wait! ! ! ! !"

Voort says, closing the volume, "Nothing."

"Sorry."

Mickie's swinging an imaginary baseball bat, meaning, we'll find an answer, maybe at the ball-park. But when they say good-bye and return to the dark hallway Voort feels the ticking in the back of his neck worsen, feels a different sort of frustration, a straining and coalescing of infuriated energy toward some rational, possibly hopeful idea. *Don't leave yet.*

"What is it?" Mickie asks as they reach the street.

He doesn't answer, afraid speech will distract him. He crosses the street, plunks down on the curb and stares back at the house. Mickie comes back from the Caprice with a towel, spreads it on the curb to keep stains off his pants.

"Okay, take it minute by minute," Mickie says softly. "We reach the block . . ."

"We park. We're walking up the . . . shit!"

Voort seeing it now, not an answer but a bad possibility. Voort's heart pounding as he grabs the cellphone. *Hazel better answer this time.*

"Computer room! Oh, Voort. I'm sorry I haven't been here. Other detectives keep giving me things to do."

He tells her not to worry, but the job now is crucial. Tells her, "I need you to access 911 records. Copies of every Seventy-eighth Precinct emergency call on this date six years ago."

"*All* of them?"

"Schnell!"

While they wait, fretting, Santini calls to say that Ralph Lieb of Great Neck is in Ecuador on vacation. He also passes along the same information about Hull that Camilla did. But now Voort knows Santini's reliable, doing his job.

Voort paces the street. Three minutes. Five . . .

He tells Mickie, hoping he's wrong, "It was the number on the stoop. I could hardly read it."

The phone buzzes at ten minutes and Hazel says triumphantly, "They computerized 911 logs after the Zorovich case. It's on my screen."

Voort holds up his own copy and reads Hazel the address of the first apartment he visited this afternoon, and six years ago. It's Anne Boyle's address. "Eight ninety-five Swidler. 9A. Got it?"

"That's what my screen says."

"Four-oh-five Harris? 11A."

"Exactly."

"Eight-eleven Bryce. 3E."

"You mean D, right?" Hazel says hopefully.

"Not E, like Emily?" The nausea coming in a giant wave now.

"D like Dog. Dentist. Donkey. Delilah."

Hanging up, Voort tells Mickie, "I went to the wrong apartment." He can barely breathe. "I found the mistake."

Long pause. Excruciating pause. Then Mickie says, "Just because you made a mistake doesn't mean it's related. And D sounds like E on the radio. Anyone could miss it." But they both know cops are supposed to double-check addresses on false calls. You never leave a doubtful call without checking to avoid just this kind of stupid mistake. And Voort is running for the building now, as if speed can reverse history, punching in a different buzzer this time and thinking, *It wasn't a phony phone call at all but maybe it won't relate.*

Nobody is home at 3D, so he goes back to the old lady, buzzes, buzzes, and when they get upstairs she's in the hallway. Time speeding up and slowing at the same instant. Everything Voort does going faster. Everything necessary from anyone else moving at a crawl.

"What's wrong?" asks Estelle Moore.

Voort calming enough to ask the name of her neighbor, the absent occupant of 3D.

"Achmed Giza's lived here about four years. He's a very nice young Moroccan. A carpenter. He brings me Thai food sometimes."

"And before him? Who lived next door six years ago?"

"Why, that poor man did," she says, shaking her head at a painful recollection. "I felt so bad for him." Her frown deepening. Her memories disturbing her.

"His name?"

"Oh, the things that happened to poor, poor Wendall Nye."

EIGHT

Wendall Nye, who will one day enthrall and terrify the city, buy semiautomatics at out-of-state gun shows, study poisons, read up on explosives, memorize road maps for escape purposes, waits for silence to encompass the room where he faces thirty-two sullen faces. The blinds are drawn. At times like this, he likes things dark.

"Who am I?" he says.

A groan goes up from the first row, as on goes the tape recorder, on clicks the slide projector. Wan light illuminates the enlarged photo he took of a muddy, rain-soaked field. Just puddles. Ruts. A bit of melted snow.

"They warned me that I will die here in terrible pain."

The word "die," of course, gets his tenth-graders interested. The quiet deepens, as the more intelligent ones cannot resist the process of trying to figure out another of Mr. Nye's dumb mysteries.

A shot of the ocean now. Green. Turgid. White-capped.

"I escaped the mud but now I may drown."

"Are you a sailor?" asks a girl in the first row.

"Dummy," says the boy beside her. "Why show a field if he's a sailor?"

"Because he's goofy," cracks a tall boy in back, where the wiseasses sit, and the class breaks up. Laughter erupts in waves, tsunamis of mockery. Wendall just smiles.

Perfect, the future murderer thinks. Per-fect.

Stars glitter in the sky now on-screen, white and brilliant, achingly far away.

"I'm afraid I may be upside down," the tape-recorded voice says.

Dorky Nye. Silly Nye. Civics and history teacher Wendall Nye who can't present *normal* lessons like other teachers, no, *he* has to barrage his classes with stories and mysteries he creates at home, poring over scripts at midnight after driving the five boroughs in his broken-down Honda, snapping photos at weird angles so his students are never sure what they're looking at in the frame.

The real Nye, not the tape, challenges the kids. "Is this really an advanced class? Or did you wander in by accident?"

The tape gives the next clue, high and wavery, as if coming all the way from Mars or Venus. He taunts his kids with partial truths, oblique references. "If I don't die and succeed in my mission, millions will adore me."

Click.

A small fishing boat below. A shot of icicles.

"Cold. I'm so tired, but I mustn't sleep or I'll die!"

The kids, despite themselves, are rapt now. It happens every time.

"Are you a man or a woman?" a girl asks.

"How can not sleeping kill you?" taunts a boy.

"Wait! I know! You're Charles Lindbergh, the first man to fly across the Atlantic!"

The Eiffel tower fills the screen. Wendall's never been to France, but he borrowed this shot from one of his research books.

"Yes!"

He has taught them this way, about Revolutionary war hero Ethan Allen and about President Woodrow Wilson, has produced tapes late at night as the voices of journalist Jacob Riis, Mother Teresa of India, Pope John Paul when he was in jail in Russia. Nelson Mandela. Simon Bolívar. The kids laugh every time the lights go off, but each spring his classes score higher in state tests, win more merit scholarships, get accepted by better colleges. Later they keep in touch by letters and e-mail.

"You were a real friend, Mr. Nye," they write. "I didn't realize it at the time."

"Why do you care so much?" other teachers ask him in the faculty room.

"What's the point of being a teacher otherwise?" Wendall replies. It's what Dad used to tell him.

"Who cares about this good citizen shit?" Gus Minetta, the English teacher, had grumbled just this morning, but Wendall had felt sorry for the man, beaten down by bureaucracy, salary, cranky parents, disinterested students. Minetta had drawled, "Wendall, you're like some throwback to the nineteen-fifties. Some Norman Rockwell character. A fucking innocent in a madhouse filled with gangs."

"I love the kids."

It is six years before the death of Gabrielle Viera, the last Thursday class of the day for Wendall Nye. Wendall thrilled as always when the students figure out a mystery—but excited too because he sees from one or two irritated faces that they're about to graduate to what he thinks of as each year's second phase.

The last normal afternoon of Wendall's life, and he's hoping, *I need one of them to get mad at me.* Only eight minutes of class time remaining as he gushes on and on about the great hero Charles Lindbergh, how he popularized aviation, how millions adored him, like the guy was some kind of rock star. *Come on . . . get mad . . .* smearing on the praise about how *terrific* Lindbergh was, how *meaningful* even in this corner of Brooklyn . . . Wendall leaning back against his desk, in his work uniform: brown cloth jacket, khakis, Weejuns, crisp white shirt and striped, out-of-style tie.

And *bingo,* he thinks, spotting a hand shoot up on the left side of the room—where the troublesome kids sit.

"Who cares about some fucking dead pilot? What does he have to do with *us?*" a boy in row five demands to know.

Laughter. The kids are waiting for the wiseass to get in trouble, and Wendall—a good actor—pauses, stares, lets them think he's losing his temper and watches the blood lust come into their eyes. Thirty-one kids staring like gawkers at an accident at the thirty-second, waiting for punishment to be dished out.

"Excellent question," Wendall says.

"It is?"

"A thinking man's question."

The boy, thrown off by praise, recovers cockily. "That's why I asked it."

"We study the past to understand the present. Of *course* you're more interested in our current world, Mister Huff. *You* tell me what you'd rather study? *You* pick the next assignment."

"You mean, anything I want?"

"It has to do with social studies."

"Girls!" a boy calls out. "That's social!"

"The beach!" a girl suggests. "Let's take a field trip!" *Hahahahaha.*

But the boy in row five takes the challenge seriously. He's not used to being consulted about things. "Well, it has to mean something to *us*, Mister Nye! Now!"

"You sound just like a voter. Remember how we discussed how few Americans vote? How they feel ignored? Good! So tell us what's important to you."

Not mocking the kid. Being respectful. Fingering the Bics he keeps snugly in his shirt pocket nerd pack. A habit when he's concentrating.

Nye urges, "Tell us something that bothers you, that you'd like to change."

The boy blurts out, "The cafeteria food stinks."

Huge laughter. Other kids shout, "Yeah!" "It smells like shit!" Kids who were watching the clock minutes ago are now listening. There's nothing like complaint to focus attention, Wendall knows.

The boy smiles, bolder now, performing for his classmates. "Today they didn't even *name* lunch right," he says. "The sign said, 'Roast Loin of Dork!' And it tasted that way!"

Wendall nods, looks amused, draws the others into it. "Anything *else* about the school you'd change? Adults don't take your opinions seriously sometimes, but the way I figure it, you spend seven hours a day here, so conditions are important to you."

Lots of things bug us, they say. The hallways need painting. The window bars make us feel like prisoners. The metal detectors slow us down in the morning.

The Huff kid says, "If that wobbly third-floor railing breaks, someone could get hurt! They oughtta fix it."

"Good. What you're really asking," Wendall says, loving the fire in their eyes now, "is how *government* works, how taxes get spent, not just your parents' taxes but *yours*, because every time *you* buy a candy bar or a dress or even those ridiculous puffy jackets that are so popular, *you* actually help pay my salary."

"Then you're fired," shouts a kid in back. Wendall joins in the laughter this time, but also comes up with an idea he's never tried before. A new assignment. A fun mystery. One big reason he lets the kids pick assignments each year is, it keeps him on his toes. Keeps him learning things too instead of just teaching.

"You know what might be interesting?" he asks the class. "What might be fun?"

Reaching for his camera, he's thinking happily, dooming himself, *I better hurry if I'm going to make a new tape this week.*

Voort parks the Caprice outside Nathan Hale High School in Park Slope—only eight blocks from Estelle Moore's apartment—and hurries down busy commercial Seventh Avenue toward the entrance.

"If Wendall *is* our guy, I can't believe he'd just go back to work here," says Mickie. "So if he's here he's probably not our guy."

"Then let's hope he's here. Or taught class today."

There's no excuse. Simply no excuse, Voort thinks, mortified, after calling Santini to admit his mistake of six years ago. Voort burning with shame as he remembers Santini's silence at the news, the cool condemnation, never mind how supportive the detective's words had been after that.

"Thanks for telling me promptly. I'll put the computer girls on it." Meaning that even as Voort heads up the steps now they're checking Wendall's old address to access bills, records, his social security number, and once they find that all kinds of other useful information will swim up on the little green screens. Auto records. Lawsuits he's entangled himself in. A new job.

Santini had said, "Get over to that high school in case he's still employed there. If we get an address for him I'll let you know. The old lady told you he had an accident six years ago?"

"Maybe six. She wasn't sure. She said he was hit by a sanitation truck. Accident or hospital records ought to pinpoint a date or hospital where he was sent."

"But what would a truck accident have to do with someone screaming in his apartment? A truck didn't drive into his living room and run over him there."

Pushing away the humiliation, Voort had tried to figure the thing out, turned the crazy, disconnected bits around in his head. "He's had surgery. He's in pain. A neighbor hears him screaming, but by the time we get there he's passed out. Because believe me, even though we went to a different door, if anyone had been screaming we would have heard it in the hall. The walls in that place were like paper."

Santini had said, "Uh huh," meaning maybe yes, maybe no. "Anything else I can help you with, Voort?"

"A longer list of Phillip Hull's clients. I was thinking that firms sometimes bill for jobs after they're finished, not while they're doing them. Who'd Hull work for *five* years back?"

"I'll see what I can get for you." Santini had signed off then, promised to call right away if the records girls came up with something, gone off to inform Chief Ramirez of Voort's blunder. Odds are the press will be broadcasting the news within the hour.

My job now is to find Wendall Nye, not worry about myself.

A single New York City high school can serve more students than a small liberal arts college. Nathan Hale High, judging from the architecture, has been here over fifty years, like the other Park Slope High, John Jay. The building fills a whole block, looms above the nearby restaurants and shops in three stories of sooty granite, doorways arched like a French cathedral's, city, state, and United States flags dangling limp in the late afternoon. Two-story-high windows, gridded with wire, bring to mind Sing Sing prison. Gothic towers top cornices, as saw-toothed as castle ramparts.

Brooklyn meets Notre Dame.

The Blue Guy guard at the entrance eyes their shields and directs them toward the first-floor principal's office, his casual wave telling Voort that detective visits are no big deal here.

"What do you want the teacher for, molestation or drugs?" the Blue Guy asks.

The building feels empty, especially with after-school programs slashed because of budget cuts, making the likelihood of finding anyone here after five even worse. The place strikes Voort as gloomily institutional, not a setting for inspiring teens. The hallways lack the light airy feel of wealthier public or private schools. Voort sees scuffed floors. Double locks on classrooms. Scrubbed vestiges of graffiti still visible on the glazed cinderblock. He makes out a couple of Brooklyn gang logos. SPACE-BOYZ. FOXYG'S.

5:43.

Normally once I've identified a suspect I have days to work on it, not seven hours.

At least—nice surprise for a change—the principal turns out to be here this late, alone, doing paperwork in his office. A small, balding man in a tweed jacket looks startled when Voort and Mickie walk in, but recovers quickly when he sees their badges. His tortoiseshell reading glasses come off, and Dr. Birnbaum—as his nameplate says—closes a manila folder. The glasses hang around his neck on a string.

Voort says, "We're interested in talking to a teacher who may work here. Wendall Nye?"

"Oh God! Is he in trouble?" There's no mistaking the concern that instantly replaces the stern look on the principal's face.

"Then he still works here?"

"No. He quit years ago, but he was popular with everyone. I hope nothing happened to him. Wait a minute! I recognize you. You're the detective who was on television. My God!" says Dr. Birnbaum. "This is about that grudge killer! What does that have to do with Wendall? My wife just called me about that. It was on the news."

Voort slows things down, keeping his disappointment from showing, explains that Nye is sought for questioning.

"He may have useful information but not even know it," Mickie adds. "He may be able to help us stop this before the next killing occurs."

Birnbaum seems eager to help and leads them

from his office into the larger secretarial area, where he fumbles for a key to open a steel file cabinet. "My secretary leaves at five, but we occasionally keep a forwarding address or new job in here. Nye. Nye. Ah! Nye!"

I wonder if Santini has found a home address by now.

"I'm so relieved nothing's happened to him," Birnbaum says, rummaging through an inch-thick file of papers. "He was the most dedicated teacher. I can't tell you how many parents called when he left—and when parents phone it's usually to complain. Not in Wendall's case."

"He loved kids," Voort says.

"They loved him back."

Dr. Birnbaum looks up from over the top of his reading glasses. "I was shocked when he phoned and quit on me. He hardly missed a day before that. The other teachers used to tease him. They nicknamed him The Postman, from that old saying: 'Neither rain nor sleet nor flu will keep me from my appointed rounds.' That was Wendall."

"Dedicated," Voort says.

"Fantastic."

"But then he just quits. Was that after his accident?" Voort says.

"God, that truck," the principal nods, back at the file. "He said he would need months to recuperate. I told him I'd keep his job waiting, but he said—and this is the kind of man he is—it wouldn't be fair for the *kids*. The *kids* needed someone permanent, not a sub. Always worried about the kids. That's why they responded to him. Sorry. We have no forwarding address or new school."

"Did you visit him after the accident?"

Dr. Birnbaum colors. "He said he didn't want to see anyone. He was pretty banged up."

"Maybe another teacher kept in contact?"

"I can ask tomorrow when they come in. But that could be too late, couldn't it? The radio said you're afraid there might be more killings today."

Voort suggests calmly, not feeling calm at all, "I can call teachers at home if you give me their numbers."

But the principal frowns, as if this is harder than it sounds. "Problem is, the Board of Ed gave us a seminar last week on legal issues. There was a suit involving giving out home numbers without permission. But I suppose I could call the teachers myself and hand you the phone if they're there."

"Thanks," Voort says. "By the way, is the date Nye quit in your file?"

The cellphone is ringing. Caller ID indicates it's Santini.

"What a coincidence! That accident must have happened during this exact week six years ago," Dr. Birnbaum says.

And six years ago, Wendall Nye climbs from the outbound number 3 train at the Brooklyn Borough Hall subway station, clutching a small leather travel bag containing his camera and tape recorder. When he reaches the street, he finds at four-thirty that the daylight is still strong, the afternoon warm enough to make him sweat lightly as he hurries down Joralemon Street. He's trying to think of an opening line for his next "who am I?" tape.

Brooklyn was once a separate city, with its own mayor, council, judicial system. It is so big it comprises an entire county, and its municipal buildings—borough president's office, state supreme court building, sanitation workers building—cluster impressively in a downtown satellite area inside the larger city, near Borough Hall. The neighborhood houses a mix of city services and unions. Reaching Livingston Street, Wendall turns left, passes some parked TV vans, and pulls the Nikon out, then pauses atop the gray granite steps to number 110.

He aims the lens artfully up the tall, sheer side of the building, and as he clicks off shots for his next slide show, the first line he's been seeking finally comes to him.

I am a king and my palace is this building.

Wendall pushes through the revolving door and starts snapping shots in the crowded marble lobby. Cops manning a security checkpoint. Visitors opening attaché cases and showing IDs. From *inside* the door, looking out, he shoots the TV news vans with their mobile antennas telescoped high.

Journalists watch me every day, hoping I make a mistake.

At the security checkpoint the guard opens the back of Wendall's tape recorder, removes the two double-A batteries and holds them up as if weight will prove them real.

"Another reporter, huh?"

"I'm a teacher," Wendall says proudly, showing ID.

The cop becomes friendlier. "We got the *New York Times* up there, and about a hundred lawyers. Union reps. Trump's people. But you're the first teacher I've seen."

"Then the hearing is still going on?"

The cop rolls his eyes. "If they haven't killed each other. Last night the shouting went on 'til after six."

Wendall plans to tell his class, *When I give a command, over one million subjects obey.*

On the tenth floor, the elevator spills Wendall out with the packed car of riders. The hallway is crowded with people trying to push through double doors ahead, into a hearing room. People strain to hear a man's voice coming out, magnified by electronic speakers. People jotting notes, cupping their ears.

Over one hundred thousand people work for me.

The voice saying, "We're dispensing more money here than the annual budget of some African countries . . ."

Wendall pushes into the hearing room, which he is surprised to see looks rather plain—like some VFW hall or paneled basement—considering the vast sums being discussed. Rows of folding chairs are packed. There's standing room only. The audience is focused on a dozen men and women seated in front at a long dais.

It's funny, Wendall thinks. *I've worked all my pro-fessional life for the Board of Education, but I've never actually been this close to them before.*

The speaker—the dark-suited chancellor—announces with an air of authority, "Due to cost overruns we face a shortfall. Instead of the three bil-lion we expected to be allocating from the state bond initiative, we have only one left."

Wendall feels a nudge in his ribs. A reporter on his right—judging from his notepad—has spotted Wendall's camera and assumes Wendall's covering the hearing too.

"That asshole can't talk plain English. They wasted or lost over two billion dollars over the last few years. Now they have to decide which construc-tion and repair jobs to yank from their five-year plan."

"Who *are* all these people?"

"Lawyers—who do you think? For the city. For construction companies. Unions that'll lose work when jobs get canceled. Everyone's fighting to keep their pet projects going." The reporter rubs thumb, index, and middle fingers together, in the universal sign for greed.

Click. Wendall gets a great shot of an angry-look-ing man in a gray suit—a lawyer probably—in the first row.

Click. He snaps the security marshals, the Board of Ed's private bodyguard unit, attentive and off to the side, ready to move fast if the board is threat-ened.

The chancellor assures the crowd, "Every attempt will be made to maximize funds we have left."

"*Stop!*"

The commotion starts behind Wendall, out in the hall, and suddenly the crowd is turning toward the blare of cowbells and bicycle horns. *Click*, goes Wendall's Nikon, as protesting parents surge into the room. In the viewfinder he sees signs waving. SAVE PS 194!

"Crooks!" screams a man. Wendall gets a close-up of the marshals moving to block the tide.

"The roof on one-ninety-four is shot! The classes are crowded!"

Wendall is snapping marshals grabbing signs, taking away cowbells. One mom—clutching her toddler's hand—manages to break through the marshals and get right up to the board.

"*Who took the money?*"

Reporters grinning, writing.

"Sweetheart contracts! Thieves! Liars!"

The chancellor waves the marshals away as they reach the woman. He doesn't want to look insensitive to three million parents who will be watching on TV tonight. He calls for quiet but it isn't working. He bangs a gavel, but the pounding just adds to the noise. He tries to look dignified, but he's more administrator than public speaker, more backroom strategist. He's probably regretting that he ever left his old post in Boston to take this one in New York.

Click. Wendall gets the harried-looking chancellor trying to explain.

"Ma'am, costs go up. The whole country is in a recession. Some of these projects started out as repairs, as you can see in the handout here . . ."

Click. The chancellor waving a report.

" . . . but the repairs turned into major reconstruction jobs when structural problems showed up."

Wendall watching the furious woman enlarged in his viewfinder, shouting, "Who supervises *you* when you cancel a project?"

"As I explained earlier, the law requires oversight when we approve work but not if we eliminate it. The process is complicated . . ."

"*And fucked up,*" someone shouts.

" . . . and to avoid just this sort of accusation we hired outside experts to make recommendations on where to cut jobs . . ."

Wendall snaps the marshals dragging the woman out, but unlike the gleeful reporters he's frowning now himself. His plan had been to show his class, step-by-step, the civic decisions necessary to fix one school's wobbly railing. But now he's thinking, *That railing really could become dangerous. I hope they didn't cut repairs scheduled for the school.*

"Can I see that handout?" he asks the reporter.

Wendall flips pages now as the meeting resumes with a semblance of order. Wendall sees with alarm that repair work on both Park Slope highs, John Jay and Nathan Hale, are listed as "delayed."

The chancellor says, "It is impossible to put off *any* project without angering someone, and we've tried hard to ease the pain and concentrate our dollars where they'll do the most good. Our next witness will explain the process. Believe me, with millions at stake we do not make decisions casually."

"Yeah! You give it to your cousins!"

In the viewfinder, Wendall follows a tall, distinguished looking gray haired man—obviously the "outside expert"—pushing his way to the microphone, carrying a folder. This man helped take my high school out of the running, Wendall thinks.

The chancellor announces, "I'd like to thank Phillip Hull for the special work he's put into our plan."

NINE

TV stations across the metropolitan area are broadcasting the "grudge killer" story nonstop. Channel Two shows an aerial shot of Central Park as an announcer asks, "Will one of New York's finest turn out to be dirty?" Channel Five features Voort's townhouse. "Will two more be murdered tonight?" NBC shows flanking shots of Gabrielle Viera and Phillip Hull.

"Police advise you to stay indoors," the anchorwoman says. "Too bad, because our NBC weather predicts a clear, starry evening."

At Nathan Hale High, Voort's in the hallway outside Arthur Birnbaum's office, returning Paul Santini's call while the principal tries to reach teachers at home, hoping to come up with an address for Wendall Nye.

"Your teacher's looking ve-ry interesting," Santini says, a new note in his voice, belief, telling Voort that the detective's not just doing Eva favors any more. He's excited too.

Santini says, "He was in Maimonides Hospital, all right, like the old lady said. For two weeks. But he never reported any accident. A truck hits him and he never calls the cops? Gimme a break."

"But his injuries were real if he was hospitalized," Voort says, frowning. "What else do you have?"

"No police record. No credit problems. No lawsuits. Just the perfect citizen, who quit his job, divorced his wife, and moved away from his family. But we got a current address from Motor Vehicles. By the way, the doctor who treated him was named Vijay Mathur. He's on duty now, at the hospital. We checked."

"The ex-wife?"

"Trekking in Turkey."

Turns out Nye lives only seven minutes away by speeding squad car, a mile off the southwest corner of the park in a slightly run-down neighborhood populated by Russian immigrants, black families who've escaped slums, newly arrived Tunisians, Mexicans, Pakistanis, and older whites living on pensions, many who've lived here since the Korean War.

The local Western Union office is mobbed by a crowd of people wiring money to the homeland. A private mailbox drop serves those who'd rather have checks sent to a safer place than their homes. Supermarkets have posted sales on ham hocks, chicken legs, black beans. An Afghanistani restaurant advertises LATE DINNERS DURING RAMADAN.

"Even if he *is* our guy, how did he know I went to the wrong apartment?" Voort says as Mickie parks.

"How did he know the name of a cop who never showed up?"

Nye's building is red brick, and as anonymous as a Stalinist housing project, like all others on his block. The only difference is the address over the front door. Nye doesn't answer the bell to 1C—that would be too lucky—but the super calls down when they ring.

"Yeah, yeah, police. Everything's gotta be done in five minutes. The clocks in New York oughtta be set for five minutes. Can't a guy sleep?"

Minutes later a lean, stooped man meanders from the lobby elevator at a pace guaranteed to enrage cops. Suspenders hold his patched wool trousers and swell with his belly and sleeveless undershirt. His large feet snap on backless slippers. His breath, when he opens the foyer door, smells like a Bowery bar.

"You want Nye? For what?"

"Questioning," they say as he leads them back to the elevator. One-C turns out to be in the basement, between the laundry and boiler rooms. The heat is off, but the temperature is scorching anyway. Garbage and recycling bins line the cinderblock hall, which smells of trash, detergent, Lysol, rat poison, and strawberries.

"Wendall!" The super bangs on the door and shrugs. "He's probably at work. He's a laborer."

"Can you open up?"

The super wipes his large nose with his wrist. "I thought you only want to talk," he says shrewdly. "How can you talk if he's not here?"

Voort envisions what he hopes will lie behind the peeling paint—the kind of evidence he's found in other apartments over the years. Clipped articles. Photos of victims. Crumpled-up notes in a wastebasket. DNA on a hair strand that can be matched to a bit of skin.

Mickie repeats, *"Can you open up?"*

"Yeah, if I wanna lose my job. I need a warrant. That's instructions from Ustinov Realty and they own this place. They got sued after a drug bust last year. The cops just wanted to talk then too. Next thing, I'm in court."

The super sets his jaw. "Call Ustinov, not that they'll answer. Leave a message, not that they call back."

"Does Nye have a window?"

"It's in the alley. But he keeps the shades down so perverts can't see in."

Mickie says, "Con Man, call for a warrant. "And *you*," he tells the super, "show me the window."

"Five-minute hours. They oughtta change the watches. Every five minutes, the dials start going around again."

From the laundry room comes the blare of a TV quiz show as Voort reaches Eva, who switches him to Commissioner Aziz's number for a decision. Normally he'd call a judge for a warrant, but today Aziz—Mr. Civil Liberties—wants to clear any sensitive work. Waiting for the commissioner to come on the line he runs his palm over the door, as if information could pass into him through osmosis, as if by touching latex he can absorb knowledge through an inch-thick slab of wood.

"You have something, Voort?" Aziz asks, coming on the line. Voort makes his pitch but in the ensuing silence his excitement starts to sink.

"I need more," Aziz says.

"But he lied about the injury."

"You can't prove that, and even if he did, people don't report accidents for lots of reasons. He was at his girlfriend's; he didn't want his wife to know. He worked a settlement out privately with the trucker. My cousin Lou lies all the time. You have no motivation. No weapon. A lot of interest and no cause. *Get cause or I'm not sending you in.*"

Voort argues. "I'd agree at any other time, but today is different. Give me a warrant on Viera. Don't even mention Hull. If it gets thrown out later and Nye's our guy you can still prosecute on Hull. But we'll stop him!"

"And if he's *not* guilty?" Aziz says as Mickie returns from the alley, shaking his head. "You want me to announce we want Nye for questioning? Fine. You want a warrant? Do your job. If you'd done things right six years ago we might not be looking for Nye today."

Aziz clicks off.

The electronic bracelet gives Voort shocks— annoying jabs when he shakes hands, touches metal, and, as the day grows warmer, passes his wrist close to a doorknob, light switch, even his own gun.

"You know what that thing reminds me of?" Mickie says as they head for the hospital. "One of those magnetic bracelets you buy in health food stores. My neighbor swears it stops his arthritis. Hey, like, healthy vibes."

"Then maybe we can get you one too for *your* birthday."

Voort gets a shock from the elevator panel at Maimonides. He gets one showing his badge to Dr. Vijay Mathur, who they find on the fourth floor leading a half-dozen interns on rounds in the plastic surgery ward, and whose cooperative smile dissolves the second Wendall's name comes up.

"I remember him," the doc says unhappily. He is tan, astute, fortyish, and strikingly handsome in a square-jawed Omar Sharif way. Could be he's gone under the cosmetic knife himself. Voort notes the thick, graying hair as youthful, adding dignity to raw vibrancy. Mathur tells his students, "Perhaps you can wait here? Detectives, perhaps we will walk down the hall?"

Mathur gives orders in the form of questions.

"You are the grudge killer," he says with a slight Indian accent when they are out of the students' earshot.

"I'm trying to catch the killer," Voort corrects.

"Do you think Nye is writing those notes?" From the corner of his eye, Voort sees Mathur's left hand in a fist, fingers digging into his palm. The right hand presses against the thigh of his medical coat. Fingers drumming.

"Why are you scared, doctor?"

The drumming stops. "I am not."

Voort's feet hurt and his neck is throbbing. He tells the doctor, "Some people have poker faces. Some don't. My advice is, don't ever play. You want to tell me what happened now? Or do you want to drag this out?"

Mathur glances at his students as if judging whether they are far enough away. Then he sighs. "I have often wondered about that man. I am not surprised to see police because of him. I did him a favor."

"Favor," Voort repeats.

"Perhaps a cup of coffee?"

"We don't have time for a cup of coffee. If you're following this thing you know that."

Mathur's Adam's apple glides up and down when he swallows, and he swallows more often when Mickie stands close. Voort lies to soothe him. "I'm not interested in what you did. Just him."

"You have to understand. He was in terrible pain."

"His injuries?"

"Ribs cracked. His legs . . . well, I could not believe he made it to the hospital by himself in a taxi. He didn't even arrive in an ambulance. And his face . . ."

"Tell me the part I need to know."

Mathur pulls out a handkerchief and dabs his forehead and cheeks. "He said a truck hit him."

Down the hallway, doctors make rounds. An attendant mops the floor. A nurse hurries into a room with a tray. Dinner service is being rolled on a cart from an elevator.

Mathur says, in a lower voice, "But the injuries in front and back were inconsistent with being knocked to the ground by a vehicle. The facial bones were shattered as if hit from different angles, many times. With a two-by-four, for instance. A rifle butt."

"*Rifle butt?*"

"That is merely a reference. I was a medical officer in Kashmir, years ago, you see, in the Indian army. I examined terrorist suspects. Rules are different there. It was necessary for soldiers to be rough sometimes."

"With rifle butts?" Voort says.

"They were terrorists and you treated them as such."

Voort says, "You saw a similar pattern on Nye?"

"Multiple wounds on the face, chest, legs. A bad mugging could do it. I had a patient once who was a heavy gambler and had not paid his debts. I had a woman who was almost killed by her husband. They were . . . like that."

"Did you ask him about the truck story?"

Mathur looks unhappy. "I am a good doctor and he was in terrible pain. He was crying; he was terrified. He kept insisting, 'Yes, a truck! Stop asking! Help me!'"

"So you just dropped it."

Mathur glances down the hall at his interns, future doctors he undoubtedly advises never to cheat or, Voort realizes, understanding now, to falsify insurance claims.

Mathur tells them, "Of course I did not drop it. But I told him if a truck hit him his HMO would demand a police report before paying his bills. Insurance companies sue the driver in situations like these. Even in a hit-and-run they wait for the driver to be apprehended."

Mathur shakes his head in a way that reminds Voort of the sympathy Nye received from his old neighbor, Estelle Moore, and from the principal at Nathan Hale High. Wendall Nye seems good at eliciting sympathy from people. "He was sobbing. He did not know what to do. He was a bad liar, but I think just an average man. He reminded me of Kashmir, because sometimes when the soldiers beat a man and made a mistake, you know, got the wrong person, they threatened him. They said, 'We'll come back if you tell.' Wendall Nye was terrified of the police. He didn't say it. But I saw it."

We have to get into that apartment.

"You helped him," Voort prompts.

"I suggested," Mathur says, "that his pattern of injuries would be more consistent with, say, a shelf of heavy objects, paint cans for instance, falling on him at home. And he said, 'Write that.' So it is on his medical form."

"Then why did he go back to telling the truck story when he got home?" Mickie asks.

"Perhaps he had no shelf like that and his neighbors knew it. His family certainly knew it. Inexperienced liars change their stories all the time. They are not good at it. I can only guess."

"Shit," says Mickie.

"Look," Mathur says. "You may not believe this, but I don't break rules usually. There was something special about this man. You looked in his eyes and saw more than pain. It was crushing. You wanted to make him feel better. It's not an excuse."

"I'll keep you out of it if I can," Voort says, meaning it.

After all, you didn't make a mistake, I did. You helped him and I drove off. You shouldn't have to pay for that.

"No way Aziz will keep us out of that apartment now," Mickie tells Voort as Mathur trudges back to his students.

But Voort's not so sure. He feels acid eating at his belly. "It's still circumstantial," he says, reaching for the phone, remembering Aziz's words: "If you had done things right six years ago we might not be looking for Nye."

What more could I be doing?

Voort seeing it then, and calling out, "Doctor!" Voort rushing up to the man as twelve fascinated residents stare back at the cop they recognize from TV.

Mathur's frozen in the doorway of a room where Voort glimpses a large black man in bed looking back.

Voort asks, "He needed follow-up care. Right?"

"Of course. Therapy. Surgery. I rebuilt his face."

"So he visited your office, right?"

"Way to go, Con Man," Mickie grins, understanding now.

Voort says, "He filled out one of those patient information forms. Right? Wrote his name? Allergies?"

"What do allergies have to do with it?"

"Call your office. Where can we get a fax at the hospital, immediately?"

Dr. Mathur looks uncomfortable. "Detectives, please. A patient information form is privileged. I cannot do this."

"Oh, we're *following* rules now?"

Dr. Mathur flushes, looks at his students, slumps, accepting finally that things have degenerated beyond his self-interest. "I suppose if I were reading a fax and you happened to be standing over my shoulder, you would see."

Five minutes later the three men are in the hospital administration public relations suite, where a fax machine buzzes and a sheet of paper begins wheezing out.

PATIENT INFORMATION FORM.

It moves fitfully, in starts and stops. Voort grabs it before Mathur can. Screw the read-it-over-my-shoulder game.

WENDALL NYE.

"Look at the Y," Voort tells Mickie, holding the fax side by side against the copy of the note from Central Park.

"Oh God," says Mathur, his eyes wide.

"The two's also the same," Mickie says thoughtfully.

Doctor Mathur tells them, "A street beating is different from professional. Professionals pick exact places and hit those places over and over, you see."

Outside, the sun is going down through the window. Shadows grow. Darkness is coming. Voort feels Wendall out there somewhere, the man who Mathur tried to help, who Arthur Birnbaum recalled as gentle, who Estelle Moore felt sorry for.

"Con Man," Mickie says, "watch yourself. Put a coupla cousins on your block, just in case."

Voort phones Aziz for the warrant.

It's 6:50.

"It's funny what you think of at the oddest times," Wendall tells his tape recorder as he strolls up Second Avenue near Fifty-fifth toward the office of Aiden Pryce. "You try to keep your mind on things, but the weirdest thoughts come out of the blue."

Wendall the priest. Wendall the cleric enjoying the fine warm evening. Father Douglas Daly, from Tampa, as he signed the register at the Nordic Hotel, limps from an old "injury" during the tail end of rush hour—through the east side of midtown, anonymous on the packed sidewalks in a tan raincoat open to show his priest's collar. Longish sideburns. Brown contacts. Phony goatee. Wig styled five years behind New York length, perfect for the South.

Another attaché case, this one in battered purple, holds the articles he needs to dispatch Mr. Aiden Pryce.

"I was afraid last night that fear would be the problem, but it's memories that seem to be distracting me. Sometimes they are so strong I have to almost physically push them away. Here's the murderer the whole city is looking for and am I worried about *that*? Concerned about messing up? Going over how I'm going to get out of a thirty-eighth-floor office after killing the boss?"

He pauses at a newsstand, looks down at the *Post*'s special edition front-page headline: WHO'S NEXT? but suddenly, in his mind, he's hearing a man's voice booming, "Wen-dall?"

"Dad . . ."

Seeing Scott Nye in a grimy jacket, shit-eater boots and filthy jeans, smelling of diesel fuel like he did every morning, tromping into the kitchen of their Bay Ridge apartment.

"You look tired, Daddy."

"Good tired. I worked hard."

Scott kissing Mom and falling into the chair at the eat-in table. Scott putting down the Transport Workers Union duffel bag stuffed with his hard hat and orange work vest.

What tunnel did you work in last night, Daddy?

"Where's that report card, Bud?"

Scott the soft-spoken. Scott of the fearsome muscles and mashed-in face, sculpted by amateur heavyweights during half a dozen Golden Gloves fights, the peak of *that* never-to-happen career. Brown cowlick still oddly boyish above a visual history of punishment. A contented man home from the subterranean city he maintains while millions sleep: washing graffiti off walkway tunnels, dropping poison for rats along the Flushing line, hosing dirt off platforms made filthy by the day's passage of four million shoes at Times Square, Grand Central, 125th Street.

"A in math. A in English, Wendall!"

"I studied hard like you said, Daddy."

"Teachers knock themselves out for you. They're heroes to me. And I'm proud of you!"

Wendall spoons cornflakes while Scott reads the *Times* and Mary cooks buttermilk pancakes, extra crispy bacon, and cinnamon-flavored oatmeal. Wendall downing a big glass of U-Bet with two hands while Scott pokes his index finger at the paper, following the news religiously, word by word.

"A good citizen reads the paper every day."

Pointing out every article about municipal workers. Bus drivers. Fire marshals. Getting a kick out of the brotherhood running the city behind the scenes.

"Daddy, on TV a man called city workers lazy."

"Then he never cleaned a tunnel at two A.M."

Cut.

Wendall's at Brooklyn College now, in the timeline, and it's time to pick a major. Kids going for MBA degrees, dreaming of BMWs and beach houses in the Hamptons. Kids picking theater as a major, seeing themselves winning an Oscar, or at least a Tony. Journalism for the resentful. Liberal arts for the confused. Wendall thinking, I want the Peace Corps, except Peace Corps means two years overseas, and Wendall's fallen in love with the girl in Sociology 101. She's the one who suggests, in his room one night, "What about teaching, Dell? You like kids."

Jump.

Six years ago now and Dr. Phillip Hull addresses the rowdy Board of Ed meeting while Wendall snaps photos of the enraged audience. Hull testifying, "Projected population will rise on the east side of Manhattan so we advise continuing that construction program. Attendance will stay steady in Brooklyn. That seems a place for trimming work."

The chancellor adds with unassailable confidence, "These self-evident numbers are a basis of our decisions."

Nye thinking, "That's no way to figure out which projects to cut. What about the quality of the building? The light? The kids who need relief now?"

"Phillip Hull will take a few questions," the chancellor says coldly. To Wendall, Hull seems friendlier, open, possibly reasonable. Or so he thinks.

Surprising himself, he gets in line to ask a question, formulating his remarks as the man four spots ahead demands that boiler repairs to John Jay High in Brooklyn be put back on the list.

Hull looks sympathetic. "I don't make the final decision. I just advise."

Hull tells the woman two spaces ahead, "With this terrible recession, Wall Street profits drying up, tax money drying up, everyone has to make sacrifices."

"Mister Hull has time for only one more question," the chancellor says.

Tough luck, Nye.

Minutes later the great El Numero is hurrying from the room, on his way to dispense more statistics at other meetings, while Wendall trails ten feet back, trying to lodge his protest as the reporters close in.

He fights to get through, but the reporters are better at it. Pushed to the side, he maneuvers toward Hull, but the man steps into the elevator and Wendall gives up. *What's the point anyway? He's never going to listen to me. Even if he did, what good would it do?*

"But it bothers me," he tells Marcia that night at dinner. "I should have at least tried. I always tell the kids, try. It sounds hokey, but we spend months studying people who didn't give up."

"You did try. Besides, the board looks at the big picture. Not one railing."

"I still feel like a hypocrite."

Twelve years of marriage has gone well for both of them. The apartment is modest; one bedroom for Wendall and Marcia, one for thirteen-year-old Ben, currently watching *Star Trek* reruns in the living room with his best friend, Jack Fine. The family could afford better, but extra money gets deposited into Ben's college fund so he can go to a good school later if he wants, and if he qualifies.

The furniture is Ikea assemble-it-at-home. The art is glassed prints from the New York Transit Museum, the Smithsonian in Washington, the Museum of the American Indian. Wendall the history buff.

The TV, recliner, and nine-year-old Honda outside were inherited when Marcia's mom died. The curtains are end-of-the-year clearance. The pile was 80 percent off at ABC Carpet, not the main store but the warehouse.

"You know why I love you, Wendall? You're the same now as you were in college. You believe in things nobody else does. Politicians are honest. Corporations do the right thing."

Marcia spoons out leftover meatloaf, steamed stringbeans, mashed potatoes, and pours glasses of dark, sweet apple juice—Wendall's favorite—on sale this week at Associated stores.

Marcia says, "All the bad stuff in the newspapers just washes over you."

"It's a question of how you see things. Even during Lindbergh's day there were crooks, Marcia. This country works, for the most part. I believe that."

"Well, no teacher is going to convince the Board of Ed of anything with two billion dollars gone."

"I convinced you to marry me, didn't I? I must have excellent powers of persuasion."

The sweethearts hold hands while Ben and Jack cheer on Captain Picard on TV. Aliens are attacking the spaceship *Enterprise*. But diligence repels the attack.

"Boy Scout," she says, and kisses Wendall's cheek.

Marcia goes on about how tomorrow she'll play mom-escort for Ben and twenty-nine other eighth-graders, climb onto a tour bus for a trip to D.C., baby-sitting the gum-chewing horde while they visit the Lincoln Memorial, White House, Senate building, maybe watch the elephants and donkeys fight it out. Is Wendall sure he doesn't mind spending a couple of days by himself?

I'll try to talk to Phillip Hull while she's away.

The worst mistakes lurk inside mundane choices. Lives hinge on whether you hail a first or second taxi in line.

Next day, school out, he climbs out of the subway at Columbus Circle and walks toward Phillip Hull's office address, which he found on the Internet.

He seemed to have influence on the board's decisions, and he seemed reasonable.

So that the day's not a total loss he's brought the camera to take shots of Hull, if Hull allows it. But when he reaches Forty West Fifty-seventh, Hull passes him on the way out, rushing off just like yesterday. The guy's a human whirlwind, a Johnny Appleseed of statistics, dispensing them through the land.

I'll stick with him, just for a block or two. I'm not really following him. Maybe I'll get a chance to talk.

Wendall hoping that Hull's merely heading to a newsstand or lunch counter, somewhere he can sidle up, pretend it's coincidence, say, "Aren't you Phillip Hull? You're not going to believe this. I was at the meeting yesterday too!"

New York City is one of the easiest places on Earth to follow someone. No one pays attention to people behind them, and a million pedestrians would block the view if they tried.

He sure is in a rush, and he looks nervous. Not like yesterday.

Hull moves north, which tells Wendall he's not heading for the shops along Fifty-seventh Street. He's on foot, so he's not going far, otherwise he'd hail a taxi. He seems distracted enough so, waiting for a light to change, he doesn't move when it does. He just stands there.

He's heading for the park! Great! I can "run into him."

Phillip Hull, shoulders bent, moves briskly past the Wollman ice-skating rink, closed in May. The trees are budding. The popcorn men are out.

He stops abruptly, as if someone had just called to him. Wendall, a hundred yards back, sees another man come out of the merry-go-round and walk up to Phillip Hull.

Beautiful day. The sound of organ music fills the air. Moms and nannies wheel preschoolers toward the ride, or buy them ice creams at the refreshment stand, or stroll past Wendall, who has his camera up, adjusting his two-hundred-millimeter lens for a better view.

I recognize that other man! He was one of the lawyers at the meeting yesterday!

Hull and a man in a gray suit seem to be having an argument. Hull shakes his head vigorously. The lawyer seems to be trying to calm him down. Hull turns away, but the lawyer must have said something else, because Hull wheels back and the argument starts again.

Finally, the man in the suit walks off while Hull just stands looking defeated, and his immobility is, for Wendall, opportunity. Gathering resolve, he heads for Hull.

Hull walks a few steps and plunks down on a bench.

"Aren't you Phillip Hull?"

Whatever Nye expected to see in the man's face, it is not terror, and yet the confident speaker from yesterday practically jumps at Wendall's words. Wendall tries to calm him, says he was at the meeting too. "Taking pictures."

"Pictures?"

Hull seems to notice the camera for the first time, and his eyes grow larger. Horrified, he whispers, "Pictures."

"For my class."

Staring at the camera, Hull laughs wildly.

Clearly the mention of photos has made things worse. Hull squints up at Wendall, who realizes he's in the light. Cooperatively, he moves to the side. He starts off again, calmly. "There's this railing at our school . . ."

"Railing?"

"I know this probably sounds unimportant to you, but if it isn't fixed . . ."

"*Who are you?*" Hull demands, at which point Wendall understands that the meeting he's just witnessed was no accident, was supposed to be private. Relieved that he can explain things better, he says, "Oh, I didn't take any pictures just *now*."

"Now? What did you see?"

"I mean . . ." But of course this approach isn't

good either because *telling* Hull that he saw the man in the suit doesn't seem like the best idea at the moment.

"I'm sorry. I'm a teacher."

"How do I know?"

Which seems like the oddest question, considering the intensity with which it is delivered, but identity is easy enough to prove. Wendall shows his faculty ID, which provides his name and the school where he works and his social security number. It's like saying, See? Nothing to worry about.

Hull sits staring at it, finally handing it back. But Hull does not want to talk about a railing.

"I have a meeting," he says, standing, having regained a slight bit of dignity.

So Wendall never gets to tell him about the railing.

Never even has a real conversation with him.

Never sees him, the instant he's back in his office, sweating, trembling, pulling his cellphone from his pocket.

Never hears him tell the man he telephones a name, Wendall's, and the name of Wendall's school.

TEN

A True Temper sledgehammer weighs only eleven pounds, but wielded by an NYPD tech services sergeant, it strikes doors with enormous force. Wood shatters. Paint bits fly. Detectives and Blue Guys shield their eyes against splinters.

"How'd I know Nye'd changed his locks?" whines the super of Wendall's building, standing directly behind Voort.

"Keep him out of the apartment," Voort orders the Blue Guy team. His new Sig Sauer nine-millimeter pistol is in his hand.

Reaching through the shattered door, Voort flicks the light switch, and sixty watts of illumination floods the I-shaped former storeroom now serving as Wendall's apartment.

The first part of a search is the most dangerous, Voort knows. Assume the suspect's not hiding in a closet, bathtub, under a bed, and you're the one more likely to leave the premises on a stretcher, not him.

The super adds, "He especially wasn't supposed to put in any dead bolt."

The detectives slip inside, Voort left, Mickie right. A two-man pincer movement with the door open behind them so the support crew can see in.

The window must lie behind the bedsheet curtain at the far end of the apartment. Light glows from freestanding lamps. Kitchen nook to the right, Formica eat-in table to the left. Living area straight ahead, and beyond that, workout bench with weights and a room that must be the bathroom.

Mickie the ex-marine says, "Neat as the barracks."

The living room contains two mismatched sitting chairs facing a rickety pine coffee table. The Queen Anne model's ripped. White stuffing bulges from the seat cushion. The purple velvet recliner has a broken front leg that's been replaced by hardback books.

"Furniture by Sanitation Department," Mickie says. "Big sale at the curb before the trash truck arrived."

Voort motions him toward the bathroom.

The place is cramped, claustrophobic, shiny neat except for the homemade bookshelves—cinderblocks and planks—packed with hundreds of hard- and soft-backed volumes. Books on top of other books from floor to ceiling. Books squeezed together to push the cinderblock bookends halfway over the edge. Books stacked by the bed, where Wendall must read by Tensor light. No photos. No knick-knacks. No baseball souvenirs or high school trophies. No art on the walls. Not even a calendar.

Voort smells Mr. Clean, lubrication oil, and a humid odor of deteriorating paper that reminds him of library stacks and NYPD archives.

All the money here seems to have gone for the top-of-the-line Dell computer on the homemade desk—a door laid atop battered steel file cabinets—and for the barbell set and workout bench which face Wendall's old twenty-inch TV.

"Works as a laborer all day, lifting, then goes home and lifts again," Voort says, feeling the obsession in the shiny weights, and sweat marks on the frayed carpet.

No one under the bed, since it's a mattress on a box spring. Stepping out of the cramped bathroom, Mickie signals, no one in the cell-sized shower.

All clear now, in this combination jail cell and college dorm room.

Anger and intellect here, big time.

Rage and control.

No pets. No luxury foods or clothes or entertainment-type electronics. No weapons so far. No photos connoting any family or social life. Canned food in the pantry cabinet. Big casserole pot in the fridge half-filled with stew Wendall must eat night after night. There's enough here for six.

"Probably ten thousand single guys live like hermits in Brooklyn," Voort says, "whether they're ex–high school teachers or not. But what changed this one?"

From out in the hallway, the super calls to them, "He's usually home by now if he's coming home. He stays away sometimes."

"Where does he go?"

"How do I know?"

Mickie calls back to the Blue Guys, "Shut the door. The apartment's clear."

Voort fights off the urge to go faster as the second part of the search begins—the drawer-opening, trash-collecting part. The get-the-toothbrush-for-DNA part.

"I'll take the computer," he says, meaning, Mickie, take the books. Flicking on the Dell, he hears his partner start sliding volumes out, shaking them, flipping through them.

"Con Man, listen to this title: *The Mind of a Serial Killer.*"

"Great."

"*How the FBI Caught the Route 95 Killer.*"

"A special section, huh?" The heat seems to be rising in here.

"*Secrets of Hollywood's Top Makeup Artists.* 'You too can change your appearance. Even your family will not recognize you.'"

Voort goes through the hard drive. Bills. Internet. LexisNexis, which means Nye's subscribed to a costly magazine-newspaper service and can access any article written on any subject.

But nothing illegal yet.

7:32.

Did you research Phillip Hull and Gabrielle Viera here?

As Voort turns his attention to the file cabinets, Mickie's still on titles. "*Business Tactics in the Twenty-first Century.*"

"*Now* we're getting to law-breaking," Voort says.

He finds a couple of expensive Nikons in the top drawer. Telephoto lenses. Wide-angle lenses. A dozen boxes of undeveloped film. His heart starts beating faster.

In the next drawer he sees lots of small rectangular cardboard boxes, microscope-slide cartons labeled: "Ritchie," "Dougie," "184," "Trailer Tapes." Voort finds a couple of pocket Sony recorders, two boxes of double-A batteries, and a rubber suction-cup attachment for recording phone conversations. He sees what looks like two ballpoint pens on the side of the drawer, but recognizes that they're not really pens. He unscrews the first one. Anyone can buy these little recorders at the Spy Emporium at Twenty-sixth and Third or on the Internet.

"Has our boy been out on his own investigation?"

As for the slide cartons, he's frustrated to find the first two empty, and only one cassette tape in the box marked "Riverdale."

Voort inserts the tape in one of the Sonys.

The sound quality is excellent. He hears the whoosh of traffic, windshield wipers, and the blare of a horn. The street sounds get louder, giving Voort the feeling that someone has just rolled down a car window. He hears the growing snap of footsteps on pavement, and he imagines someone rapidly stepping toward a car.

A man's voice says, in a friendly tone, "You made good time, Ritchie."

A second man's voice, gruff but respectful, replies,

"There's no traffic at two in the morning. Where do you want us to put all this stuff?"

"Follow me up the driveway. We'll need the twenty-footers tomorrow. Nobody saw you take anything, right?"

"You think I want to go to jail?"

Static drowns out the rest. *Twenty-footer what?* Voort thinks, keeping the spool spinning in case the voices come back.

Mickie saying, behind him, "Con Man, you better look at this."

But "Ritchie's" back, saying, "We can bring the rest tomorrow night."

"Con Man!"

Mickie holding something out, a photo album, Voort sees. Mickie jabbing his finger at it. Mickie's face so white that Voort shuts off the tape.

"It's pictures and articles about you."

Voort flips pages slowly, his sense of violation growing with each well-mounted shot. Here's Voort in his garden, at home, cut out from the *House & Garden* piece. Here's the *Post* feature on the cop hero who broke the Szeska case, and the *People* bio after he won a bravery citation for Nora Clay. The *Times* series on the Broken Hearts Club, which includes shots of Voort's office, Voort in the Jaguar with Camilla, Voort at the federal courthouse and at Zepp's Jazz Bar in the Village, his favorite hangout.

"At least he didn't take these himself," Mickie says.

"Always the bright side."

Voort turns the recorder back on. Static. He tries the "Ritchie" tape.

On this one, a different man's voice is talking to "Ritchie."

Ritchie: She's hot to see you again.

Man: If my wife fucked like that I'd never leave Garden City. How much are you guys paying her?

Ritchie: A gentleman never tells! But there is a favor you can do for us.

Static. The damn tapes veer between superb sound and maddeningly obscuring static. Then Voort realizes that the static is the exact same wavery pattern on both tapes.

He asks Mickie, "*Is* this static?"

"No, it's the Cleveland Symphony."

"I'm serious. It's the same pattern. Listen. High. Low. High. Rhythmic."

"You should have eaten something."

Voort shuts it off. "Mickie, did you ever hear a white-noise machine."

"You mean the ones that make sounds like waves? The forest? Rain? You think it's a white-noise machine?"

"I'm just saying that's the same sound over and over and it starts every time we're about to hear something extra good."

"I think you need a nap."

Voort opens the bottom file-cabinet drawer and

sucks in his breath at the sight of manila folders. He flips through the labels.

Ritchie. Dougie. Inwood.

But all of them are empty.

What the . . . ?

Voort tries the file labeled "Riverdale."

"It's photos," Mickie says, frowning. "But of what? A house? Is that a rock wall or the wall of a house. Either Wendall's the worst photographer in history or I'm at the Max Protetch Art Gallery. The avant-garde killer. That's all we need."

Voort tries examining the shots from different angles. But the more they find, the less things make sense. "I'd say the photographer's lying on the ground, shooting up in rain. See? The smudges are rain on the lens. Here's a roof overhang. It's a Tudor house! Here's the wood beam running along the stone."

"Nothing in the 'Brooklyn' file," says Mickie.

Voort opens "Travel" and his heart rises into his throat.

This time he's looking at long-range shots of Gabrielle Viera on Sixth Avenue. Clearly the doomed woman has no idea she's in a viewfinder. He sees Gabrielle disappearing into the building where she was murdered. Gabrielle getting into a cab. Gabrielle walking a miniature white poodle in a park.

"I'll be there in twenty minutes," Eva says when they call. "Good job, Voort."

Two minutes later, with the brass on the way, Voort finds a discarded version of the grudge-killer note crumpled in the wastebasket. A file marked "Hull," also there, includes notations detailing the man's daily lunch visits to Central Park, and a street map of Riverdale, in the Bronx, with several streets highlighted in yellow, but none of the streets connecting.

"We got him," says Mickie.

"Yeah? Do you see him?"

"Give yourself a break, Con Man."

"Where is he?" says Voort.

"When the dead come back, they look the same, but the molecules have been rearranged inside their brains, hearts, bloodstream. Our thoughts are different. Having died once, we don't fear the possibility of it happening again. In a way that makes us free."

At 7:06, Father Douglas Daly, as his Florida license says, is returning to Second Avenue after being told by Aiden Pryce's secretary half an hour ago that Aiden was "delayed. Do you mind waiting? Would it be an imposition if you came back?"

"Of course I minded, but I said I'd just stroll around the neighborhood. There's extra time built into the schedule. If there's one thing the dead excel at, it's knowing how to plan."

Wendall lingers outside the building to complete a last thought.

"That's because when the dead come back, they bring a single-mindedness they never had when they were living. They're not interested in eating, drinking, raising families. Having jettisoned those desires we focus energy on plans. Time is nothing against the power of incompletion, and incompletion is what drives the dead to life."

Father Daly shows his clerical ID to the private security guard in the lobby.

"Can I ask you to open your attaché case again, Father? Sorry."

"No need to apologize. You make me feel safe," smiles the priest, showing his folded *Post* and Bible and vial of "holy water." Security guards in New York buildings, he has noticed, never pat down visitors, so this one will never find the Glock stuck in Wendall's belt—which will go back into the attaché case once he's in the men's room upstairs.

"What happened to your head, Father?"

"I got hit during a robbery with one of our very own silver candlesticks."

"Sheesh. Robbing a priest. That's disgusting."

Waved past the security station, Father Daly rocks on his heels as an arriving elevator disgorges workers.

At this hour he's the only one going up.

"Am I babbling?" he says, alone in the elevator. "Well, I have the conceit of knowing that my every utterance will be analyzed later by armies of psychologists and social scientists and reporters, all trying to understand the single-minded process that reverses death."

Fifteen, says the floor indicator.

Muzak, "Tie a Yellow Ribbon," plays over the hum of winches and cables and the groan of machinery fighting gravity as it lifts Wendall higher into the enclosed sky.

"But in the midst of this single-mindedness, I must admit, what surprised me, future listeners, is that even in a dead man feelings can change. I'm talking about you, rich boy. You see, birthday boy, my hatred of you is different than the others . . ."

Floor thirty-six.

"Because you were supposed to be different from them. More later, folks. I've reached floor thirty-eight."

The outer hallway is empty at this hour, lined with locked offices and open bathrooms. Ringing a buzzer, entering Aiden Pryce's waiting room, Wendall reminds himself, *Look meek.*

As Penguin publishers' *Closing the Deal* advised, "When you arrive at a meeting, you are walking onto a stage. Playing your part means adjusting your posture, speech, and facial expressions to your adopted persona. Are you a respectful supplicant? A confident rival? Benign future partner, perhaps? Make the image fit the role."

This may be the most dangerous role today. So be careful.

Shoulders hunched slightly, Father Daly steps up to the receptionist beneath the Blue Knight Security logo. The London *Times* had described the company last year as "one of New York's top private security firms," Daly'd read on the Internet, along with companies like Kroll and Beau Dietl & Associates.

Considering the star-studded list of clients the

Times mentioned, he'd expected more of a glitzy corporate setting. Instead the place feels more bare bones and functional, as sexy as a motor vehicle bureau.

Rather than high-end modern chrome and leather, or a more leathery Harvard Club decor, he finds a large L-shaped room where the gum-chewing receptionist occupies a small booth overlooking a waiting area featuring two faux leather love seats—thankfully empty of clients—facing each other over a glass-topped coffee table. Beyond that, Father Daly sees white partitions separating cubicles whose owners have hopefully left for the day.

Pretty plain for an outfit that does bodyguard work for the Venezuelan consulate, according to the London *Times.* Morgan Stanley, Citicorp, Ford, and other *Fortune* 500 companies have hired the ex–high-level cops staffing this place to uncover fraud, protect executives, and break up industrial espionage rings.

"I am *so* sorry, but Mister Pryce is still tied up on a call to Washington," the red-haired receptionist says between chews of gum. Father Daly sees a small gold cross between her excellent cleavage, shiny against her white sweater.

"Would you like coffee?"

"No stimulants for me, thanks."

Nearby, the few operatives present—big-bellied guys with striped shirts and gaudy ties, ex-cops or military, are putting on off-the-rack jackets to head for home.

Killing time, Father Daly scans more articles mounted in the waiting area—as if he has not already read them. Aiden Pryce loves publicity. There are pieces from *Rolling Stone*, *Wine Connoisseur*, the *Washington Post*.

"Pryce was a highly decorated NYPD detective lieutenant before going private," *Rolling Stone* says. "He inherited control of the company three years back when the founder died. He's often seen around town in his Hummer or Rolls-Royce, and frequently can be found at the Wine Bar at the swanky new Hotel Geneva, yukking it up with anyone who's anyone, from tennis star Adam Adamski to reputed Russian mob boss Iaunno Vivichek."

"Who is Mr. Pryce talking to in Washington?" Wendall asks the secretary, like a potential client wowed by the man's contacts.

"Senator Ryker's office. About software, Father."

"I'm a dinosaur when it comes to such things."

"Aiden invented training software to help police departments fight drug smugglers, y'know?"

"I hate violence."

She whispers, as if Aiden could possibly hear her, "Senator Ryker's trying to get federal money to pay for the software. Y'know, a grant?"

"Theresa?" shouts a man from the rear of the office—muffled so he must be behind a closed door. *"Did Father Daly show up?"*

She tells Wendall, "The intercom is busted." She shouts back, "Yes, Aiden."

"Give him coffee!"

"I offered it already."

"What do you want, a fuckin' medal?"

She turns red. "He has a filthy mouth, but he's a very nice man," she says.

"That's what the articles say."

"He's very generous." Now she *really* blushes.

"Can I turn on the TV while I wait? Watch the news?"

Wendall sits back on the love seat, flicks on the Zenith, and NY1 swims up with an excited announcer saying something about a break in the "grudge killer" case.

Wendall sits straighter.

"We're expecting an announcement from police at the apartment in Brooklyn," the announcer is saying.

Brooklyn, thinks Wendall?

The announcer saying, "Our mobile unit and police are converging on the scene."

When a huge case breaks—when a suspect is identified—half the brass in the city want to be in on the good news. Wendall's apartment has never been so crowded. Aziz is here, and Eva. Santini is here. So is Deputy Mayor Thomas Lamond Deans.

The forensics team is clipping carpet samples, bagging toothbrushes for DNA, gathering hairs from the wastebasket, checking labels on cameras and on Wendall's laborer wardrobe, hoping to pinpoint where the suspect shops.

Out in the hallway, detectives sort through the building's trash, searching for credit card bills, photographs, or perhaps the tapes missing from the boxes in the cabinets.

"I don't get it," Aziz says. "You have a dozen boxes, but tapes in just two. Play that last part again."

Voort hits the play button.

Man one: How many donuts did you bring?

Ritchie voice: Four donuts.

Man one: Four isn't much. I'm pretty hungry. I was thinking, five's better. Definitely five, with sprinkles."

"Donuts?" says Tommy Deans.

Eva says morosely, "Think stacks of bills."

"Sprinkles?"

"Who knows, but they probably don't mean sprinkles."

Rhythmic static. Then the Ritchie voice says, "Stop worrying, Wendall. The *exposed* wire is *painted* copper so the inspectors'll think the whole thing's that way."

"The super said he's pretty sure the Wendall voice is our Wendall," Voort says. "There's an old construction scam where you're supposed to install copper wire and you put in substandard stuff. Could be that."

"What happened to the other tapes?"

"Maybe there aren't any."

"How do we even know these boxes are labeled properly?"

Aziz frowns. "Who's the guy in Riverdale that they're delivering stuff to in the middle of the night?"

Voort says, "Well, let's add it up. We have some-one talking about substandard wire. We have two guys delivering stolen . . . something. We have a guy getting a gift of a prostitute. Let's not forget the Dunkin' Donuts man."

Outside, Voort knows, the news vans are gather-ing, the crowd is growing, the neighbors are peering from their open windows and checking whatever they are seeing with the pictures being broadcast live on TV.

Tommy Deans suggests moving the conference to a more secure location, so minutes later they're in the laundry room down the hall.

"It's getting bigger. Low-level but rising," Voort says.

Dryers whirl. Clothes go round and round. The TV hung on ceiling brackets shows the building from the street standpoint. At least the sound is off.

"Voort?" says the mayor's buddy, Tommy Lamond Deans.

Here comes the shit, Voort thinks. *They're kicking me off the case because of the address screwup.* "What?"

"I was wrong about you. Maybe you should take off that bracelet. Here."

Deans hands him a key, which is good, like his words. So how come, Voort wonders, Deans looks unhappy?

"I'm not sure how to say this Voort."

"Try directly."

"All right. You're through working at One Police Plaza. You may be through in the force."

"What do you mean, through?" he says. The room turns hotter. He feels as if he's been punched in the stomach.

Deans spreads his hands helplessly. "The more I know you, the sorrier I am about this. But a, there's no statute of limitations on a cop screwup, and b, yours has led to two deaths so far, and a beating, and c, politically, there are times when it's good to have connections in the department, but when you're in trouble's the *worst* time. If we look like we're protecting you, those press vultures will start screaming about special treatment. Your chief and commissioner want you to stay. But the mayor says no and I agree. For the present at least."

Voort feels as if all air has been sucked from the room.

Deans says, "You can appeal if you want. You may even win in arbitration, but we both know that even if you keep a job you'll land up in some backwater office that keeps guys like you away from everyone else. You don't need a pension and you won't need the aggravation. You'll quit."

Deans lets the humiliation hang there. Voort watches paisley underwear churning in a dryer. White socks. Boxer briefs. A pair of jeans, legs flailing. He'd never envisioned his career ending in a basement laundry room.

"There *is* one small chance, though," adds the deputy mayor, the consummate politician, showing the punishment first and then holding out the hope.

"What particular miracle do you need me to perform?"

"Stop him before he finishes. Arrest him *before he kills again*. Do that and maybe we can help you. Either way, you admitted going to a ball game instead of checking out the call. Either way we have no way of knowing if you used to habitually ignore calls."

For an instant Voort feels as if a glass wall has descended between him and the others. Like he's looking at them through the wrong end of a telescope and they've suddenly become part of a different world. He wants to remind Deans of his record, his hero status only a week ago. But he knows it won't make a difference.

Stop him and maybe we can help, Deans had said.

With monumental effort, Voort forces his thoughts back to Wendall. He can't waste more time.

"The thing is," he says, "I screwed up six years ago, but his clippings start *three* years ago. Why wait to get angry? Did it take him three years to identify me?"

"He could have done that by getting hold of the 911 tapes any time," Mickie says. "They're public record."

"Then what set him off? He does nothing for three years and suddenly he's taking pictures and making tapes."

Voort feels an idea coming.

"There's not enough on the tapes to figure it out,"

Aziz says. "Every time something solid's close, the damn static starts . . . or the white-noise machine."

The clothes go round and round, like Voort's stomach. "Which means," Voort says, his idea solidifying, "that it's possible he knew we'd come here. Or planned for it."

"By leaving photos of Gabrielle?" Deans says. "I don't think so."

"By taking everything he needed and leaving what he wanted us to find," Voort says, and raises his hand to stop any protest. "Just consider it. The apartment is spotless. Books organized. Files organized. Even the shoes in the closet organized. He's a planner. Now think about the evidence we've been finding until now. Never prints, DNA, something we can use. Always what he leaves."

"We have prints and DNA now," Aziz says, but he looks receptive. He's worked with Voort before.

"What I'm saying is, just for the hell of it," Voort says, "instead of asking why isn't *more* here, let's ask, why is *this* here? He *leaves* the Viera shot so we know he was involved. He *takes* anything that tells us why."

"You're giving him too much credit," says Aziz.

"I'm speculating," says Voort. "With each note he parcels out information. The first one gave us the idea that today's an anniversary."

"The second gave us the year to concentrate on, and both identified who might find answers. You," Eva says.

"So if, just for a minute, if we look at this apartment as a kind of third planned clue, which is possible since he directed us here, now he's telling us he's investigating something."

"Then why not tell us what?"

"I don't know."

Aziz shakes his head. "And why give himself away before he's finished? Why hand us his name unless he wants us to stop him?"

Voort considers it, stomach burning. "I don't know."

"Now you're making sense," Mickie says.

"He's a teacher," Voort starts off again doggedly, thinking out loud. "A teacher makes a tape. A teacher leaves clues. A dedicated, beloved teacher quits a job, leaves his family, buries himself in a basement and risks his life making tapes of . . . well . . . a lot of people are involved, and it's dangerous. We know that much. Then he starts killing people, so we have to figure, whatever he was recording, he wasn't a happy part of it. He's investigating it. Look at half the books in his shelf. How-to books by private eyes."

"People crack up all the time," says Mickie.

"He has no criminal record. Kids apparently loved the guy. Someone beat the shit out of him six years ago and threatened him if he went to the police. He didn't make his injuries up. And he didn't make these tapes up. And what is it they were threatening him about anyway six years ago?"

Eva looks interested, Aziz unhappy.

"What I'm getting at," Voort says, "and it's just a possibility, is, what if he's *teaching* us?"

Mickie says, "You starting to like the guy? Maybe you and Wendall can patch up your grudge and be pals. You keep your job and he promises not to bludgeon you to death."

It's like an explosion that's been building for over half a decade, Voort thinks, as in the dryers, the clothes go round in a mindless, goofy cadence. Flopping with a rhythm that brings an old nursery rhyme into Voort's head.

School kids singing, *Where it will stop, nobody knows.*

But it is time to stop theorizing now and come up with a strategy. Voort the human sacrifice will stand in the background while Aziz and Eva address the press outside, announce Wendall's name, admit Voort's mistake, make some half-lie appeal to get the man to stop or come in.

Which he won't, Voort thinks. *But we have to try.*

Eva will plead for Wendall to call, will apologize for Voort's lapse and release sketches and get the whole city looking for the ex-teacher.

"Maybe it will scare him off," Deans says, but it's just hope, not belief.

"If you're right about what he's been doing, Voort," says Aziz thoughtfully, "we'll be alerting whomever he's after, whoever worked him over. If the killings are related, they'll be waiting for him now."

Mickie says, "That would save us the job."

"And if it is related," Eva says, "I can see how Gabrielle was involved, being a former prostitute, but what about Hull?"

"He worked for the Board of Education, although I can't imagine how he'd come in contact with a civics teacher," Voort says, wanting to catch the guy, wanting to kill the guy himself, trying not to think what it would mean to be released from the force. "If I were Wendall, I wouldn't trust cops either. Not after what happened to me."

Voort able to think of about two hundred better uses of his time than as a prop for the press.

8:00 now, *and in Manhattan,* Wendall's being told he can go into Aiden Pryce's office.

"Aiden's a big old bear," his cute receptionist says. "I'll be gone by the time you leave."

ELEVEN

Seeing isn't believing. The old saying is a lie.

The city proves it every day. A traffic cop stares, unmoving, as an out-of-control Chevy rushes toward him. A broker watches a jet hit the World Trade Center. Debris crashes down on him as he thinks, the air traffic controllers must have gone on strike. A gunman raises his shotgun at a bank teller, who tells herself, *This is just like a movie.*

The truth is, even when seeing *is* believing, the lag time can kill you. If you want to be fooled badly enough the city will oblige.

And six years ago, Wendall Nye stands in Central Park, stunned, watching Phillip Hull stride away. The first trickle of comprehension is coming that he may have just made a monumental mistake.

I gave him my name.

The carousel music seems to grow louder, the heat to coalesce on top of Wendall's head. Feeling something heavy in his hands, he looks down to see his Nikon, and realizes that he never even snapped a photo of Hull's meeting with the lawyer.

"What did you see?" Hull had demanded.

Wendall answers in his mind: *I'm not really sure.*

In movies, he knows, before bad things happen, saxophone music plays and the camera angle goes close-up on the murderer. It's so obvious that even morons in the audience begin nudging each other and the big mouths whisper, "The shit's about to hit the fan."

In real life, your boring aunt keeps blabbing as the atom bomb lands half a block away.

Wendall thinks, *I saw a terrified man. But why was he afraid?*

He flashes to the urgency in Hull's face as the statistician reached the carousel area, to the lawyer emerging from the shadows and the way the two men had stood so close that their torsos obscured their hands as they talked.

Wendall recalls how, as Hull pulled back, he'd spotted a flash of white between the men for a fraction of a second.

White like a shirt cuff, or vanilla ice cream. But neither man had bought ice cream, and neither had worn white.

White like an envelope?

A loose feeling weakens Wendall's knees and he sits down on Hull's still warm bench.

Do bribes really happen? Of course they do, but people like me never actually see them.

Wendall stares at the spot where the men had

been standing. A German shepherd is there now, on a leash, looking back as it urinates on the path.

Did I even see that flash of white at all?

Instead of an answer comes a recollection of a *New Yorker* article about memory that he'd read recently, about an Ohio bricklayer accused of molesting his daughter. Under police questioning the man had admitted committing all kinds of perversions. But it turned out he'd been so susceptible to suggestion, he'd convinced himself his daughter's fantasy accusations were real.

A psychologist quoted in the piece had said, "The ways you can trick yourself are endless."

Wendall starts to laugh.

He can't stop. It's hilarious. He's aware that the nannies nearby are veering away from him with their strollers, but all he can think is, here's the great picture-taker prowling the city for the perfect image. Finally he gets it in his viewfinder. He never even snaps the crucial shot.

If Hull took a bribe, I ought to tell somebody. But I don't want to get an innocent person in trouble.

His mind shifts to the Board of Ed meeting yesterday.

The reporter whispering, "They lost or wasted two billion dollars."

The protester screaming, "Thieves!"

The F train to Brooklyn turns out to be the wrong place to analyze problems. Rerouting changes have it filled to capacity even at 2 P.M. Staticky announcements blare from the twenty-year-old sound system.

Panhandlers perform an a cappella version of "Up on the Roof." Teenagers shout over the singing, the track noise, and each other. Wendall the straphanger glimpses the front page of today's *Daily News:* big black letters above a woman's lap:

PROTESTERS TO CHANCELLOR! WHERE'D OUR $$$ GO?

Back in Brooklyn, he emerges onto Seventh Avenue near Nathan Hale High, stands staring at the place as if it's metamorphosed from stone into collective consciousness, and waits to see what he will do next. It ratchets up his distress and confusion comes as a barrage of conflicting urges to do something, drop it, explore it, forget it.

Dad in there somewhere, going on about heroic city workers. Hull there too, eyes wide with fright. And Wendall's kids, not as individual faces but a stream of thousands of hands on a wobbly railing.

I wish Marcia were here to talk to about it, but she's in Washington with Ben's class trip.

He reaches his brownstone but turns away, remembering passing a bar around here somewhere.

I don't want to go home yet. And I want a drink.

Even a nondrinker needs a dark place to think sometimes, a soothing brew and strangers to cushion anonymity, whether you talk to them or not.

The Dodger Tavern is perfect, with its long oak bar, its cool glow of neon. Bubbles rise in an old Wurlitzer as Wendall takes a stool beneath old Dodgers pennants and black-and-white photos of Brooklyn's heroes at long-gone Ebbets Field: Jackie Robinson and Duke Snyder swing their bats by a backstop and crouch to field grounders above half a dozen empty booths.

"What's on tap?" he asks the bartender.

"Mister Nye!" the young crew-cut man grins. "It's me, Alan Leuci! Remember me from eight years ago? Civics class?"

"How are you, Alan? And please call me Wendall now."

The bartender beams. "I'm in night school! In engineering. You turned me around, Mister Nye. I used to think your slide shows were stupid, but I never forgot the one about Jacob Riis, the slum photographer. How his photos riled up the whole city, got new laws passed! Try the Black Chocolate Stout."

Wendall downs half the pint, feels the brew cool his belly, spots a folded *Times* Metro section two stools away and a partial headline above the fold, SCHOOL TRIAGE.

"You taught me one person can make a difference," Alan says with conviction as Wendall reaches for the paper. "The tough part's choosing to do something, isn't it?"

The article turns out to be a rehash of what he already knows. The original seven-billion-dollar bond initiative. The list of school construction projects that ballooned in cost. The argument—a permanent fixture of city landscape—between the mayor and the chancellor over which one should ultimately control the daily lives of one million public school students.

Should I go to the police? What would I tell them?

He flips pages. The whole damn paper seems to

relate to the decision he has to make. The *Times* is running a series detailing programs being cut due to the budget crunch. No more subsidized school lunch programs, kids. No more afternoon girls' rugby games. Sorry about those limited hours of operation in junior high libraries.

Go to reporters? They'd laugh or start a witch hunt. Tell the chancellor my suspicions? I can't prove them.

"Are you okay, Mister Nye?"

"Another beer, Alan."

Besides, what if Hull had a personal, embarrassing reason for being in the park? A notion that the *Times*, the city's official recorder of mistakes and humiliations, gives credence in lots of scattered articles today.

Why, here's a piece about a celebrity divorce set in motion by an actor's trysts with his make-up lady.

Maybe Phillip Hull was stepping out on his family.

Here's a two-incher about high-priced attorneys who gouge clients by the hour, charging for work even while they're driving to tennis matches or taking a hot shower.

"If I'm thinking about a case, I'm working on it," insists one Park Avenue lawyer to the *Times*.

Maybe Hull was supposed to be in his office instead of strolling around the park. That's more likely than a bribe.

If liquor reveals the secret person, Wendall's secret self gives strangers the benefit of the doubt. Here's a piece about gay couples trying to get legally married in Alabama, and sure, Hull's not in Alabama, but suppose he's gay, and meets his lover in the park, *and today I showed up with a camera. That would terrify him, all right.*

A woman's voice interrupts his thinking. "I said, 'You seem to be the man I want.'"

He smells perfume before he sees her, looks left, and a gorgeous Latina smiles back. Black eyes, raven hair, drop-dead honey-colored cleavage bulging above the scoop neck of her light-blue merino wool short-sleeve sweater. Of the dozen empty stools in the Dodger Tavern, the sex bomb has sat down and crossed her long legs on the one beside him.

"Me?" says Wendall.

"That's your camera, isn't it?"

And looking down, he sees *two* Nikons, his and hers. Lens facing lens as if the devices comprise a telephoto love couple beside his camera bag on Alan's initial-gouged bar.

"I'm Gabrielle."

"Wendall."

"My sister gave me the camera for my birthday," she says, lifting a Tom Collins as ESPN comes on over the vodka section, broadcasting a show about tonight's scheduled major league games. "Leslie told me it's easy to operate." Her black eyes flash. "Easy? I can't even load the film."

"I'll show you how."

"See? You're my camera angel."

She holds up a sheet of directions in French, German, Spanish. "Everything but easy."

Wendall can load a camera with his eyes closed, as

easily as a blindfolded marine assembling a rifle. The film is snugly installed in seconds. The motor whirrs, advancing things in the Nikon at least into their proper place.

"Bartender, a drink for my camera angel," she calls to Alan in a cute South American accent.

"No need for that," Wendall says, pleased with the praise.

In fact, she's so pleasant that instead of leaving, as he'd intended, he tells himself he can worry about Phillip Hull later. Frankly, he needs a break. He lets her talk him into the drink. Marcia's not home and he's got nothing better to do anyway. He doesn't mind being distracted. There's nothing like a woman's interest to perk a guy up.

"You're a professional photographer, I bet," she says. "That's what you're doing with a camera in the middle of the afternoon, right? What do you shoot? Fashion? Sports?"

"It's just a hobby."

"My sister saw a TV show about a photographer who spends his life taking pictures of popsicle sticks! Can you believe it? What were *you* taking pictures of today? Not sticks, I hope." She laughs.

"I was in Central Park."

"You must have taken a zillion shots. It was such a beautiful day. Do you develop your film yourself? Leslie said I'd get hooked on this stuff and she was right."

"I fixed up a darkroom in my apartment. It's easy to learn to develop film."

"Darkroom. That sounds scary. *Dark*room. That sounds cool."

"It's more like a closet."

She asks if he's developed today's shots yet as Wendall sees that another stout has appeared in front of him, another Tom Collins before Gabrielle. Down the bar, Alan's signaling him, man to man. This round's on me, Mister Nye, you stud. Go for it.

He used to get things wrong in class too, Wendall thinks.

But the truth is, there's nothing more energizing for a man than interest from a gorgeous woman. Strip a guy of job, self-worth, apartment, family, and he'll still believe that Miss Nevada has fallen for him because that's what he's wanted since he was fifteen. Gabrielle's easy to talk to. She's interested in photography. She drinks in Wendall's knowledge-filled answers. How complicated is it to use the chemicals, she wants to know? And, "Do you ever get caught up in your hobby so it gets in the way of social life?"

"My wife understands. Anyway, she's in Washington with my son this weekend," he tells her. "I'll probably develop some old film in the darkroom tonight."

Her eyes brighten. Her fingers toy with her glass. Her long nails—even when they don't make contact—create an itch along the back of his wrist. "Wendall, this is going to sound funny, because I'm not trying to pick you up . . ."

"I know that!"

"But Leslie keeps talking about techniques of development."

"You can be very creative in darkrooms."

She has a great laugh, open and warm. "Well, if you wouldn't mind for a couple of minutes, could you show me where you make the pictures?" Gabrielle blushing. "I understand things better when I see them," she explains.

"You want to come to my apartment?"

"Not if it's a problem, Wendall. Not if you have other things to do."

Wendall standing now, wobbly but thinking clearly. Wendall telling her, gratified, but shaking his head, "When I was seventeen I would have killed for an invitation like that, from a girl as pretty as you."

I love my wife. Sorry.

Gabrielle saying, "Oh, I didn't mean *that*." But of course she did, as her awkwardness makes clear. Suddenly the sex bomb has morphed into an awkward young woman.

"Wendall, I *totally* understand. And thanks for the lesson. You're a good teacher."

Alan looks dumbfounded that Nye is paying his bill, getting up, and leaving the clearly interested beauty queen alone.

Alan waving. "Come any time, Mister Nye!"

"How come the good ones are always taken?" Gabrielle asks Alan when the tavern door closes.

"What am I, invisible?"

But she's off her stool already, on her cellphone, and not too broken up now that Wendall has departed. Gabrielle grabs up her camera roughly, as if she couldn't care less if the dumb thing gets smashed or not.

Alan hears her talking as she strides off toward the doorway, her voice different now, distant, cold, tired.

"He's coming," she tells whomever picked up her call.

Alan thinks he hears her add, "He's alone."

Wendall feels a little better now, even though, reaching home, he sees that the foyer lock is once again broken. The hallway light needs replacing, but he long ago stopped getting mad about it. Living in this building, you learned there's just no point. At his door, fumbling for his key, he hears Mrs. Moore's TV blasting next door. She probably misplaced her head phones again.

"These limited-edition necklaces were crafted by Ukrainian master goldsmiths," cries a shopping channel announcer.

Humming, he lets himself into his apartment, the beer and conversation with Gabrielle having softened his alarm over the meeting he witnessed in Central Park.

I probably imagined the envelope, he thinks, closing the door, shutting himself in.

In the lag time between sensing danger and believing it lies destruction. Wendall frowns, detecting a cinnamon odor which wasn't here this morning, and glancing left through the arched doorway to the kitchen, receives a surprise. One of Marcia's crockery bottles lies on the linoleum floor, its brown granular contents spilling out.

Wendall doesn't grasp it yet. He gets mad at the wrong thought.

If we have rats, if that cheap bastard landlord stopped the exterminator service, I'm calling the health department.

But taking two steps forward, he sees other wreckage. In the half-light seeping through Marcia's chintz curtains he takes in pillows thrown around the living room. Drawers tipped open. Books scattered or half-pulled from shelves.

Get out now.

He's reaching for the knob when two quick blows slam into his kidneys, arch him in agony, and he screams as another pile driver punch drives him sideways into the living room. He hasn't even seen who hit him yet, and the momentum causes him to stumble over a pillow. His falling shoulder smashes into the bookshelves. Toppling, Wendall's trying to turn, flee, cover himself.

The rug comes up at him. The air goes out of him when he hits. From the floor he glimpses a black-gloved fist with a long gold gleam across the knuckles coming toward him for a millisecond. Then it caves in the left part of his jaw.

A high, terrified scream is sounding but is cut off abruptly when the man in the ski mask kicks Wendall in his exposed belly. He has never been hit like this, even as a boy during fights in the school yard.

He hears a sound like snapping wood inside his

chest when the next blow lands. Like ice cracking. Like his skin will collapse in on itself with no bones beneath.

Dad was the fighter. Dad could control pain. Dad knew the footwork, angles, strategy, and never wanted Wendall to learn the nuances, to master more than pedestrian defense. And Wendall's seen fights at school, but they've been loud affairs, all flailing arms and screamed curses. Nothing like the incarnation of fury above him, battering him silently and blowing like a horse.

Then the pummeling stops but the agony seems to radiate along his synapses, travel his ganglia like an overcharged current. From jaw to rib cage to skull to heel, burning its way down his spine.

"All warmed up, Cap?" says the man above. There's no emotion in the words. He doesn't even sound the least bit irritated.

The man asks, reaching out again, "Ready for a bit more?"

Impossible, but he's being *dragged* now over the bunched-up throw rug and wooden plank floor as the man advises, "Spit the teeth out or you'll choke on 'em. You don't want to swallow that stuff. Can you breathe through your nose, Cap? Go ahead. Give it a shot."

He's cuffing me to the steam pipe in my own bedroom.

A wet, warm feeling is in Wendall's crotch now. An ammonia smell rises up from himself.

In the freestanding mirror across the room, he

sees a smashed-up stranger and realizes the man is himself—shirt pushed up over his belly, sleeves bunched where his wrist is being affixed to the feed line of the pipe. One shoe off. One sock dangling. The wrecked face looking back at him isn't the one he had only ten short minutes ago. It's become a raw piece of meat.

Now he can see more than his assailant's mask. The kneeling man beside him wears a blue windbreaker, jeans, tennis shoes.

"I said breathe through the nose, Cap." The man sticks a rag—old socks or underwear—into Wendall's mouth.

God it hurts.

"I know it's uncomfortable so pay attention. I'll take the gag out in a couple minutes, and when I do," the man says, "no noise, right? Nod if you understand."

Nod.

"You know who I am?"

A head shake no.

"That's the first lesson here. The fundamental state of your fucked-up affairs. I know who *you* are. I know where Marcia is. I know the boy's schedule and I've done you a favor, see. I haven't touched them yet."

From the businesslike tone, the man might be a lawyer reporting to the Board of Ed.

"I said *yet*. It's up to you."

Wendall starts to gag, trying to beg the man to leave his family alone.

"One more thing to show you before we talk."

The attacker stands now, and stretches, radiating a kind of coiled athletic power found in small, violent men.

He's picking up Ben's baseball bat. How did that get in here?

"I used to hit lead-off when I was a kid, Cap."

Oh God. Oh no.

"When I take that underwear out you'll talk to me. You'll answer immediately. You'll tell the truth."

Wendall gulps down air finally, but even oxygen touching his throat causes pain now.

"Where's the film, Cap?"

"I didn't take any pictures in the . . ."

The man stuffs the gag back in so fast that Wendall doesn't have time to finish answering. The bat shatters part of his left front leg and his scream seems to go on forever, splintering bone, bursting eardrums, breaking glass, and yet at some level Wendall knows only the two men hear it.

I'm going to die.

"Let's try again, Cap. The film."

"In the camera case."

"Good. *All* the film?"

"Yes."

"Including the shots from yesterday?"

"If you mean from the Board of . . ."

This time the bat comes down on the right leg, below the knee. Nothing in Wendall's life has ever hurt so much.

He's starting to pass out, from pain, from shock.

Then there's some kind of harsh odor in his nostrils and the voice is saying, "Open those baby greens."

Wendall looks up at this crazy Halloween figure in black and blue. He hears sticks rubbing in his chest.

"Where's the rest of the film, Cap?"

Thank God Marcia and Ben are gone, and at least I didn't bring that girl Gabrielle into this.

"In . . . my . . . bag."

The man goes off, gives Wendall a few seconds, comes back holding the opened Nikon and dropping a thin strip of exposed film, which floats like confetti to the floor.

"If you would have just spilled to my friend in the bar—if you would have just bragged to her like any other guy, Wendall—I wouldn't have had to do this. You have only yourself to blame."

Wendall starts to weep.

He hasn't cried like this since his dad died years ago. It's not just pain, but surrender, loss. In the mirror the attacker wipes Wendall's face, but there's no compassion in it. This man understands that collapse signals cooperation, surrender equals trust. Besides, we can't have blood getting in the way of appraising Wendall's expression, can we?

"Here. Drink water, Cap. It'll hurt your lip a little."

It hurts more than a little, and the questions come faster. Why'd he follow Hull? Why'd he attend the Board of Ed meeting? Why'd he bring the camera if he's just a teacher?

Wendall whispering through taste of snot and tissue, "It was a project for my class."

His face broken. His synapses so torn that they've either gone numb or carry a quadruple load of pain. Wendall closing his eyes now, dropping into the hurt as the man walks off but coming back because there's no place inside to escape this. Realizing the man is at the window now, staring down at the street.

"Godamn it," the attacker hisses as if *he's* the one with the problem, as Wendall hears a car door slam outside in the parallel universe where the sun shines and kids play on scooters and men are not cuffed to pipes. The attacker slips back to Wendall, furious. He jams in the saliva-soaked gag.

"Not a goddamn word from you. Not a sound."

He sounds afraid.

Wendall hears running footsteps coming up the stoop outside. Then the footsteps are inside his building.

I don't understand.

But as the footsteps rush up the stairs Wendall's heart rate rises with understanding. A gun with a long skinny barrel, a silencer, has materialized in the masked man's hand.

The man whispers, "Police."

Wendall sends his prayers out, begging any greater force out there—God, men, luck, statistics—anything that might respond favorably. Yes, yes, be the police.

And then he realizes that half-deaf Mrs. Moore

must have heard the racket. This stranger could not possibly have known about the half-drunk Indonesian illegal who "fixed" the pipes on their floor last April, replaced them but never put the wall back entirely between apartments. He'd just plastered over holes inside the wall that had been a flimsy, flat-divider to start with.

Wendall prays as a single repeated word to himself: *policepolicepolicepolice*.

Quiet in the building now, except when he tries to shift his legs, bones are cracking. He imagines cops standing outside the door of his apartment.

No knocking yet. But the intruder is terrified. Mrs. Moore must have heard something—*of course she heard something*—because some nights he and Marcia lie in bed and can even hear their neighbor talking to herself on the other side of the wall, writing recipes in her diary that she recites out loud.

One pinch of nutmeg . . .

Wendall and Marcia so conscious of her presence that, making love, they often suppress cries of pleasure or break out giggling. Marcia insisting that Estelle Moore is sitting riveted on the other side of the wall, only pretending to be hard of hearing, soaking up the sounds of love.

Wendall hears banging in the hall now.

But it isn't on *his* door. It's on Mrs. Moore's door.

Then nothing. Then more nothing.

Then Wendall hears voices from Mrs. Moore's side of the wall.

Mrs. Moore saying, faint but audible, "Of course I

understand that you need to check my apartment, officer."

The damn wall so badly constructed that sometimes at night you can see a sliver of *light* from Mrs. Moore's apartment. The wall so flimsy that she moved the TV so it wouldn't disturb the Nyes when they wanted to sleep.

Another voice, the officer's, now jokes, "We want to make sure a big strong lady like you didn't beat up some poor man in your back room, Mrs. Moore."

Hahahaha! Everyone laughing over there.

It's not her apartment! Look in my apartment!

"I guess I *was* playing the TV loud," Estelle Moore says, and Wendall squeezes his eyes shut, realizing that whoever called the police on this block, it wasn't her. With her damn TV on, she'd never heard a thing.

I'm right here!

The cop saying no problem, and Mrs. Moore insisting that she fetch "you boys some home-baked strudel. I'm sorry you came all the way for nothing, Officer Voort."

Nonononono.

The Voort cop assuring Mrs. Moore, "I'd rather find nothing than something." And an older male voice saying respectfully, "Lady, I'll take nothing every time."

Don't they check addresses before they go in?

But no, they don't, because now the cops start gabbing while they wait for their strudel. Mrs. Moore must have gone to her kitchen.

Wendall feeling the silencer pressed to his forehead as the terrible laughing goes on, on the other side of the wall.

"Heading to Shea with the cousins, Voort?"

"Every year on my birthday."

"You think the Mutts'll trade Aguilar?"

"Manheim can't field. Besides, the first time the crowd boos him, he'll start to sulk. Neither of 'em will do well in the majors."

This can't be happening.

"Two brews . . . two franks with ketchup and pepper."

The stranger relaxing.

The older cop says, "Conrad, maybe we ought to knock on other doors, check other apartments?"

But Voort won't have it. Voort wants to reach his ball game. Voort says, "The calls have been phony for weeks."

And Mrs. Moore is back now, addressing her visitors with that cutesy old lady voice that substitutes for flirting: "One Ziploc for you, and one for *you.* Don't eat it all right away or your stomach will hurt."

After a while there's no sound from the other apartment. The man in the ski mask comes back from the window. His step is lighter. Beneath his mask, Wendall knows, he is smiling.

"If you tell anyone what happened," he says, holding up a photo of Marcia and Ben, putting it into his pocket, "I'll be back. Get yourself to a doctor. You really didn't know anything, you poor miserable slob."

The man goes into the bathroom and comes out a few moments later wearing clean jeans and a yellow windbreaker, carrying a plastic bag probably filled with his soiled clothes. But the photo lingers in Wendall's mind. It seems it was taken a million years ago. It's a beach shot, on Long Island. There's a blanket and a cooler filled with iced tea in it. There's a beach ball and a Frisbee. Marcia's smiling at Ben.

Now the cop is gone, off to his ball game, and with Voort's departure the living Wendall—the part not hurting physically—is dying. The final blow had come from the policeman. That evil existed had always been a given. But until now Wendall had thought other people cared.

I'll have to leave Marcia and Ben. I can't tell them what happened and I can't risk this man thinking I might.

As the stranger takes his cuffs off, Wendall whispers, "I was a teacher."

He's talking to himself though.

From now on, that's how it will be.

TWELVE

"Come in, Cap," says Aiden Pryce, six years later.

The voice is low and gravelly, exactly as Wendall remembers. The face is surprisingly benign despite the thrill of fear that Pryce's closeness brings. Wendall advances toward the well-dressed security man rising from behind a teak desk in the far corner of the office. The smiling face is round and the neat sand-colored beard gives a touch of dignity. The compact body presses against the torso and biceps of the Savile Row double-breasted pinstripe suit. The eyes—the only part Wendall's ever seen in person until now—are the twinkling blue that has haunted his nightmares.

"Fucking senators think they're gods," Pryce says, his handshake firm, warm, and repulsive. "They call and you're supposed to drop everything. Sorry you had to wait."

"It didn't affect my schedule," Father Daly says, accepting a seat across from the desk, trying to ignore his thundering heart. "I'm not needed anywhere for a couple more hours."

Outside the window, from thirty-eight stories up, towers glow across Second Avenue. Wendall glimpses the East River and its commuter ferries, and the lit arc of the Queensboro Bridge to the north. A private helicopter skims past, lower than the window.

"I'll get right to it, Mister Pryce. I have a small parish outside Tampa," he begins, lifting his attaché case onto his knees, feeling the weight of the Glock strapped inside. "One of my congregants owns a successful software company. Actually, he's known throughout Florida, so he prefers to deal with a discreet outside firm. I was coming to New York anyway. He asked me to explore the possibility that you might be able to help him."

"How did he hear of us?" Pryce asks, folding his hands on his desk, smiling.

"One of your corporate clients recommended you."

Wendall feels sweat gathering on his spine.

"My friend—I'll call him Tom for now—has been blessed with a beautiful family, lovely home, and financial success. Some people forget their past when that happens, but Tom's always tried to give back to the community."

"Sounds like a good man," Pryce says.

Wendall thinking, Pryce probably hears this kind of bullshit from thieves, child molesters, and embezzlers a dozen times a year. But they pay him, so who cares?

"If it weren't for Tom, we wouldn't be able to fund

our youth athletic program," Wendall says, unsnapping the right latch on the case.

Originally I'd intended to walk in and start shooting, but the gun bulged beneath my jacket and the articles I read about him changed my mind.

"Your voice sounds familiar," Pryce remarks, leaning forward, pulling his hands back a bit so they're closer to his top drawer.

"Perhaps you've confessed to me some time. I'm in New York occasionally. I conduct mass now and then."

"I'm not Catholic. Besides, discretion, remember?"

"Then perhaps you've heard me on the radio. I'm a guest on *The Celestial Hour* sometimes."

"I'm more the Sinatra hour type," Pryce says in a friendly way. "Go on."

Wendall can smell Paco Rabanne cologne again and see the Adam's apple moving and he remembers how *Wine Connoisseur* had warned of Pryce, "This weapons and martial arts expert looks relaxed but don't be fooled. Three years ago a 'source' in an embezzlement case turned out to be a killer hired to shoot him. Pryce barely escaped a meeting in a park with his life. His amazing reflexes saved him."

Which is why Wendall chose home turf, the office, to relax him.

The article had said, "Since then the accomplished security man has turned into an urban Wyatt Earp. As a matter of policy he keeps his back to the wall in restaurants, and 'when I meet a new person I'm always armed,' says our Cabernet Sauvignon–loving Connoisseur of the Month. 'I NEVER RELAX UNTIL I KNOW WHO'S SITTING TWO FEET AWAY.'"

The cluttered office flaunts the man's connections, achievements, hobbies. The coffee table and wall unit are the same banned teak as the desk. The walls are a hodgepodge of blow-up photos: Pryce on the tennis court with Dick Cheney; at a table at Elaine's; with Elaine, Israeli tennis star Amit Amos, and the current female lead of the Broadway hit *These Fine Promises.* Plaques attest to Pryce's generous support of the September 11th Fund, the National Cancer Institute. A golf cup and Maxflies lie on the plush carpet, and there's a model of Pryce's Piper Comanche on a shelf.

Wendall glances down, and with dismay notices something he missed at first, and that was never mentioned in the articles. Doggie chew toys. A half-demolished rubber bone. A ripped-up tennis ball, still wet. A water dish in a corner below a photo of Pryce with a huge rottweiler.

Where's the dog?

A flat-screened TV, near the photo, is tuned to a Mets game. The sound is off, but the Mets seem to be winning. Their new star, Bernie Vasco, has just slammed a homer. Rounding third, he's waving at the fans.

Is the dog in the outer office? Or behind the desk, on the floor.

"Your friend funds youth sports," Pryce prompts.

And the practiced story comes out. "Tom equipped

the boys' football team. He offered to take the boys to a Buccaneers game. He found when he arrived to pick up the boys that only one fourteen-year-old had shown up.

"What was he supposed to do? Disappoint the kid and take him home?" Wendall says.

"No way." Pryce clearly knows where this is going.

"I see you like dogs," remarks Father Daly.

"Oh, Caesar's not a dog. He used to be a person."

"Where is the big guy?" asks Father Daly lightly.

"Where *did* I hear your voice?" Pryce replies.

Wendall almost loses control then, has to use monumental will to keep himself from lunging at the snaps on the case, going for broke. He starts the story again. Is it possible that only ten minutes have passed since he walked into this minefield?

"Two days later the anonymous letters to Tom started."

"False accusations that he molested the boy."

Get up. Say you have to leave. Shoot him later in the garage where he keeps his car. Or on the street.

He'll see me coming. He'll see through me if I try to go.

"Tom needs help," Wendall says.

"Well, the good news," Pryce says, "is that there's no such thing as an anonymous letter, not when we get through with it. We find 'em every time. And we have a fairly good record of convincing them to, er, back off."

"Tom will be relieved. Also, he understands that fees in New York are higher than in Tampa."

"Do me a favor, will you? Say 'My friend needs help' again. It's your accent ringing my bell."

"My friend needs help."

"Nope."

This isn't like the visits to Phillip Hull or Gabrielle Viera. Pryce is faster and younger and permanently on alert. Wendall drones on, afraid to attack, afraid to leave, reminding himself that when he'd tried to envision potential problems, he'd focused on visual ones, not auditory. He'd feared that despite the surgery and despite two years of steroids and weight lifting and perfecting disguises, Pryce might recall some aspect of his face. *Not my voice. I mean, the guy hit me in the throat, so how could he even recognize my voice from back then?*

He'd even tested his appearance over the last month by "running into" people he knew. His old Honda mechanic hadn't recognized him when he tapped the man on the shoulder in A & P and asked directions to the bread section.

A fellow teacher at Nathan Hale High hadn't even blinked—even though they used to talk every day—when he'd asked if she had change of a dollar at a bus stop.

Wendall says now, "There's a perfectly logical explanation why they got home late from that game. First, the boy asked Tom to buy him Dippin' Dots, frozen ice cream."

Pryce glancing down toward his feet. Is there a rottweiler down there? Or was it an idle shift of the eyes?

Wendall saying, " . . . and later they were on I-275 and the tire blew, so Tom had to change it." He unsnaps the second latch on the attaché case. "Let me show you the note he received," he adds as Pryce's phone begins to ring.

"Hold it," Pryce says, breaking eye contact, frowning down at the number of the incoming call.

And this is it, but as Pryce swivels for the phone and Wendall's hands move, involuntarily his eyes jerk left, drawn to something that's just registered from the TV. To his horror, he sees a crowd outside his apartment house.

The ball game has shifted to a news bulletin.

SUSPECT'S APARTMENT, say words on the screen.

Could that lightweight cop have figured it out so fast?

It paralyzes him at the moment when he would have gotten into the attaché case. And then he realizes that the phone has stopped ringing without Pryce's ever having answered it.

Pryce staring directly into Wendall's eyes now.

"*Now* I remember where I heard your voice," he says.

Voort walks out of Nye's building and into TV floodlights for the third time today, only this time the reporters are quiet, the ultimate sign of respect from this pack. The silence seems directed at Deans, Aziz, and Eva, however. Half of the cameras focus on Voort as if the journalists sense the ax starting to fall.

"We have an announcement," Eva tells the reporters after the introductions. Deans announces "a break in the case," Aziz praises, "the coordinated police effort." Eva looks over the scribbling reporters. She's crisp and positive as if all on stage share credit as part of the same efficient team.

"We have identified a suspect in the killings of Gabrielle Viera and Phillip Hull," she says.

Normally Voort would be experiencing vindication, triumph, the familiar cop satisfaction at identifying the suspect. But all he feels is the dreadful weight of time passing and the rolling consequences of a failure that keep magnifying and getting worse.

"Some day you may decide you'd rather not be a policeman," his father had told him, on his birthday, exactly twenty-six years ago.

"I don't ever want to do anything else, Daddy."

"Your mom and I just want you to know, we're proud of you whatever you do. We'd love you if you ever decided to do something else. Do your best and we'll always respect you."

"Why would anyone not want to be a policeman?" the boy had replied.

None of us ever considered that the decision could be taken out of my hands, Voort thinks now, as Eva's words echo and she frames her joint appeal to the city for cooperation, and to Wendall in the long-odds hope that he will turn himself in.

"We've discovered that six years ago, as a uniformed patrolman, Detective Conrad Voort went to the wrong apartment on an emergency call. He didn't learn about that mistake until today, but as a result a man named Wendall Nye—a former teacher at Nathan Hale High School—failed to receive police assistance while being attacked in his Brooklyn home."

Voort thinking, *The other side only beat you up last time, Wendall. But if they find you first they'll kill you now.*

Eva says, "If you're watching, Wendall Nye, know that Detective Voort will be punished for what he did. But know too that you've been identified as the author of the notes today."

Voort looks into the lights, knowing an old driver's license photo of Wendall is being broadcast into apartments, stores, airports, bars. The building superintendent—turned helpful with the artists—has provided a more recent description that will be a fair rendition as long as Wendall's not disguised.

"We also believe," Eva says, beginning the trickier part of her announcement, "that Nye may have been carrying on his own private investigation of whomever he blames for the attack on him six years ago, and that he may have gathered evidence of a criminal conspiracy connected to the construction industry in New York. We believe it possible that today's killings may relate to that investigation."

Voort can practically feel the ticking of his watch's second hand advancing toward midnight. He hears the buzz of camera lights, the swoosh of traffic. The reporters scribble madly. They're electrified. They're practically having orgasms as the story gets better. Each reporter here will make the front page or have the lead story in tonight's TV news.

"Detective Voort came to us voluntarily and admitted his responsibility for his mistake of six years ago. But the responsibility for the killings today is yours, Wendall. If you are watching this, we know that you have things to tell us. We also have things to tell you."

Yeah, that you're getting the electric chair, Voort thinks.

Eva says, "No matter what you may think, Mister Nye, things are discussable. When it comes to uncovering graft, we're on the same side. Let's join forces and do what has to be done. Stop now. Come in and let's deal with it together."

No way are you going to stop, Voort thinks.

Eva tells the reporters, crowd, city, "If you know Wendall Nye or can help us, call our special number. A tip can save lives. If you have a recent photo, if you even think you can help, don't hesitate. We are literally racing against the clock."

The shouting starts when her words die out.

"Chief Ramirez, what do you mean, *he's* investigating graft? Can you be specific?"

"We found tapes that he recorded but the exact nature of his investigation remains unsubstantiated theory. If it weren't for the time element we wouldn't even release the information at this point. That's why we hope Mr. Nye will share what he's learned with us."

Voort thinks, *We're not sure the tapes are even real.*

Eva says, "No more questions." As if that ever stopped reporters.

"Chief Ramirez! Why hasn't Detective Voort been suspended? You said he'd be disciplined."

"Suspension was considered, but it is only thanks to his work today *and* his prompt admission that we've come this far this fast. Our main concern at the moment is stopping two more murders. Detective Voort remains a valuable part of the investigation but will face disciplinary action at the conclusion of the case. I said, no more questions."

"Chief! If this teacher has a grudge against Voort, maybe he'll stop if you suspend the detective now!"

Eva pauses at the podium. She is expressionless, but Voort can feel her distaste at putting him through this. She tells the press, "Wendall Nye has grudges against a lot of other people too," and leaves the podium as the lights swing to Voort and he files off, ignoring shouted questions.

Everyone is watching this. My family. My friends. Camilla.

Mickie's waiting excitedly as he returns to the lobby, grabs his elbow, pulls him toward the elevator and away from the lights glaring in from outside.

"We have to get to a computer, Voort."

"What happened?"

"We have to put you on e-mail, a chat room actually."

"He e-mailed me?" Voort says, astonished.

"Not him. The ex-wife, remember? Trekking in Turkey? Hazel tracked her down in some monastery in the mountains. No phone, but they have a computer. The trekkers stopped for the night. Santini's on-line with her, but she wants the detective Hazel sent the message for."

Mickie pushes the elevator button, but the elevator is on floor two, taking its time.

"He won't come in, Mick. No way he'll trust us."

"The wife says there's a storm there, and power goes out when there's high wind. Con Man, why do people leave New York anyway? Everything you want is two blocks away here."

"Not what *we* want."

"We'll find him."

Voort shakes his head. "If I were him I'd think the cops could be involved in whatever he's looking at. If he's even looking at anything real, that is."

"Fuck him. We'll get him."

"Someone will."

It's 8:39.

Wendall floats in the outdoor swimming pool at the Green Palm Inn annex in Savannah, lies on a rubber mattress in mid-March beneath clear blue sky, soaking up the hot Georgia sun.

Ahhhhhh.

"Mister Nye?"

He shuts the voice out, smelling coconut butter on his shoulders, feeling a lovely buzz from the afternoon wine, planning his drive with Marcia tomorrow over to Tybee Island to visit the wildlife preserve, see the big beach houses, do the boat tour. He's made reservations at a fine old restaurant this evening. He's arranged for tickets for the Episcopalian Ladies House Tour near the historic riverfront district on Saturday afternoon.

Marcia picked Savannah for their honeymoon and loves the heat, the food, the tours of the old eighteen-hundreds' cemeteries and Regency-style homes.

"Mister Nye!"

The water grows warmer suddenly, and then hot, and boiling pain floods up his legs into his abdomen. The pain grows excruciating, and looking up he sees that the sky has caught fire. Flames melt the clouds. Then someone is poking his shoulder, and Charles, the Inn's owner, is looking down, saying, in a woman's voice, "Wendall!"

How could Charles have a woman's voice?

He opens his eyes and sees a black face above him. The nurse wears white, and her large eyes are blue.

"You were having a dream, Mister Nye. Doctor Mathur will be here at three o'clock. Remember me?"

Wendall at Maimonides Hospital, six years ago, peers up through waves of agony at the young woman.

"Alana?"

"I was in your civics class five years ago. Your chart says you had an accident. I'm sorry, Mr. Nye."

He tries to close his eyes, to get back to the dream.

It hurts.

Alana props up pillows, gives him pills, makes sure

he swallows his orange juice. She's got a soft touch, gentle and skillful, and she talks while ministering to him, telling him *he's* one reason she became a nurse.

"Me?"

"Remember those slides you showed about Clara Barton? How she started the Red Cross? They got me thinking. My neighborhood is filled with kids who get knifed and shot—but there's no Red Cross there. It's why I became a nurse. You used to tell us it's good to be idealistic. We used to laugh at you."

It hurts to talk.

"I better call my wife."

But when he has the phone in hand, and hears the buzzing of her cellphone, he remembers that he can't tell her what happened. He can't even hint about it.

"Who is this?" her voice is saying.

She might get upset and call the police. She'd be so angry she might not see reason in keeping quiet.

"Hello? Is someone there?"

It's hard to think because of the terrible pain. She's probably been trying to reach him since yesterday, leaving calls on the machine at home. Pleading into machinery. Where are you, Wendall?

He has never, in all the years, not spoken to Marcia for a whole day.

Wendall hangs up.

And calls Dr. Birnbaum the day after that.

And Wendall tells the principal, "I quit."

I'm dead now, more useful absent than alive. My classes were lies. My shows were ridiculous. That cop

*just wanted to get to a ball game, a stupid ball game.
And the man who came to my apartment might come
back. If I don't leave Marcia he'll start wondering
what she knows.*

Alana tries to talk him into calling the police, after
Dr. Mathur confides to her that Wendall was beaten
up. You need help, she says. Don't make decisions
while you're depressed. Talk to your family, or the
hospital psychologist, she urges.

What a laugh.

Marcia calls from Washington.

"Doctor Birnbaum phoned! Are you all right?"

"I was hit by a truck."

"You're moving *out?*," she cries, three weeks later,
sobbing hysterically as he hobbles from the closet,
suitcase in hand, as he starts stuffing in shirts, socks,
his plastic razor, his bunched up Hanes briefs.

"I don't want to be married any more. I want to be
free," he says.

*"Tell me what happened! There was blood all over
the floor when I got back from Washington. Why
wouldn't you let me call the police?"*

"I met somebody else . . . a woman. Her husband
beat me up. Okay?"

Each lie drives him further into the graveyard.
The apartment he finds is suitably in a basement,
below the earth, like hell. That he doesn't leave the
city, he realizes later, is because he wants to check on
his family sometimes, when they don't know he's
looking.

Wants to make sure the man left them alone.

Alana tries to call, tries to visit, like she's some Brooklyn version of Clara Barton. The nurse tracks him down during a postop visit to Dr. Mathur's office.

"If you don't want to talk to people, that's your business," she tells him. "If you want to leave your family, who love you, and quit teaching, I hope you'll change your mind. But meantime, you're a mess. You need a job. I can help."

Two months later, using his new cane, he trudges in for his first day of work as a truck driver for the Black War Veterans Committee. He'll be paid in cash by Alana's brother Tony, president and retired sergeant from Fort Bragg.

"Alana said you're fucked up."

The other two crewmembers stare in astonishment at the new driver. One angry-looking man goes up to Tony, raps his knuckles on his forehead as if to ask if he's lost his mind. "Anyone there, sergeant? You hired a *white guy*? Like they don't steal enough of our jobs?"

It's perfect work for a dead man. You don't have to think. You don't have to talk. You steer a van through familiar streets that you've been exploring for years anyway. The BWVC accepts donations of furniture, clothing, appliances, games for redistribution to needy veterans. Give us your old TVs and books and keyboards. Write them off in taxes. Help vets and save with the IRS.

Wendall driving to Hunts Point and Greensboro Avenue and Avenue N and down to the Russian zone in Brighton Beach. Wendall helping Tony lug old couches out of apartments rented by Arabs in Flatbush, a night table donated by Croatians in Astoria, a box of never used, five-year-old Panasonic big screens from W. S. Roth's Discount Electronics. Wendall lugging the stuff back upstairs to the warehouse showroom so veterans can get a cheap start as civilians in New York.

Wendall living on six dollars an hour, cash, in his first foray into the city's underground economy. Getting a five-dollar tip here and there. A six-pack of Coca-Colas. An isometric exercise kit. A busted recliner he can take home himself.

Dead men don't spend much. They don't eat a lot and they don't drink alcohol. They don't buy presents, or sweets, and they don't attend movies. They don't socialize when they're off work. Dead men slip invisibly between jobs and apartments. At night they take long walks alone or sit for hours in front of TVs that they barely see.

He watches Marcia sometimes, from a street corner, from a bus window, or in the park where she sits for hours, crying, but after a few months the crying stops. He notes with gratification when she starts dating again. He approves when she and Ben change their last names back to Marcia's. That will make them harder for the man in the mask to find.

He's filled with pride as Ben gets bigger, enters Nathan Hale himself, and the boy stretches out and tosses baskets on the far side of the school's chainlink fence. Ben seems to be laughing more, although he's been a shy kid since Wendall left.

Safe. So far. *But I can never contact them.*

Every few months it occurs to Wendall that more time has passed. After a while two years are gone.

Tony tells him one day, "You're a good worker, but my sister worries about you."

"We have a pickup in Flushing tomorrow. I know a shortcut," Wendall replies, trying to cut this conversation off before it goes further, and examining the route clipboard.

"Don't you want to make more money? I have connections in the Construction Unions, y'know, vets. Give a guy two hundred, you're in the union. Slip him three more and you pick the site where you want to work, so you're close to home."

"I'm happy here."

"Happy?" says Tony, unscrewing a Tropicana bottle filled with sweet tea, sitting on the van's front bumper with a checkered handkerchief soaking up sweat on his big, bald head. "You're loyal. You're smart. You're a helluva driver. The *last* thing you are is happy, Wendall."

"I'll think about it. Okay?"

"Liar. Drive."

The Black War Veterans Committee is the perfect supplier of needs for a dead man. Clothes? A lawyer relocating from Harlem to Hawaii has donated a sheepskin jacket, two pairs of size-ten sneakers, four medium-sized maroon turtlenecks. So what if they have a few ink stains?

Umbrella? The estate of a dead woman in Bensonhurst donates a huge one with a Walt Disney logo on the top.

Pots? A mat to wipe your dirty shoes on? A plastic shower curtain? Check out the BWVC warehouse on Third Avenue. Wendall finds a see-through curtain with tropical fish on it in a box under a pile of books in back.

The city, Wendall notes, is filled with dead men. Maybe mistakes killed them. Or love or financial disappointments. You can identify them by their dull expressions and the lack of animation in their walk.

"Hey, Wendall? The Knicks donated tickets to the game Tuesday."

"No thanks." He's on a break, idly scanning the day's *Post*, never having broken the old reading habit. He's staring at an article about a policeman named Voort, the richest cop in the city. The *Post* calls the civic-minded hero the inheritor of a three hundred-year family tradition of public service in New York. Voort has things pretty easy.

So that's what the shithead looks like.

The paper going on about how *handsome* the man is, how *smart* and *dedicated*. Who wrote the thing? His lover?

Wendall reads, "After giving a tour of his historic townhouse, the decorated detective sat in his garden sipping laphroaig. 'My father drummed into me, if you don't give a job 100 percent, you shouldn't be in it,' he said."

I'd like to make you suffer too. I'd like for you to see what it's like.

"Hey Wendall, Alana's throwing a party for Grissom on Saturday. He'll be five."

"I'll send a present. I can't come."

But he's not surprised when the doorbell rings that day as he's staring at that Voort article, which he'd ripped out of the paper, and Tony's voice comes over the intercom. Sooner or later he knew Alana would drag him off to some family activity. The only surprise is that Tony's wearing a jacket and tie.

"I found one your size in the warehouse, Wendall. What my sister wants my sister gets. And she wants you at Grissom's party. You can go back to your hole-in-the-wall tomorrow," he adds an hour later, pulling the van up to a neat pillbox home on Astoria Avenue. "But you're going to have fun tonight."

Windows glow with Christmas lights strung in arcs, even in April. Relatives carry wrapped presents up Alana's walk as she waves hello with a cake spatula. She's ridiculously pleased to see them all.

"Uncle Johnny, this is Wendall, my old teacher I told you about. Grissom? This man used to give *me* report cards when I was a girl."

It seems like a thousand years since he's been to a party. He feels as if he is watching the singing and cake-cutting from the other side of a window.

"You play pool, Wendall? We got a little championship match going in the basement." This from Alana's husband.

"How about another piece of birthday cake? Black forest." This from Alana's aunt.

The crowd singing, "Happy birthday to Grissom . . ."

The kid grinning, tearing open presents. The

sweet chocolate seeping into Wendall's taste buds, spreading through his veins and into his heart.

Skiing in Massachusetts with Marcia once, he recalls, he got stuck on the lift and lost feeling in his fingers from the cold. Later he got to the lodge, ripped the gloves off, and held his hands to a fire. As the first twinges of sensation returned, his nerves began throbbing. As full feeling flooded his hands, they started to burn.

Now Wendall sits with the five-year-old boy, plays checkers with him, reads a pop-up book, and some pressure seems to cut off air in his chest. His rib cage presses in on him and constricts the air in his lungs.

"Hey teacher! Help us clean up."

The party's over, the boy's asleep. The adults wipe off the table, wrap up remaining birthday cake, store the boy's new softball mitt and GameBoy in his room during the first few moments of Wendall waking up.

Wendall picks up the day's *News* as he waits for Tony to put on his jacket. Wendall so tired he doesn't realize what he's seeing on page three at first. But then he focuses and his legs go weak. The horrible headline isn't changing into a different headline, isn't going away.

My fault, he screams inside. *Nononoo!*

"Oh, God," says Alana, reading over his shoulder. "I didn't hear about this."

Wendall feeling synapses coming to life, switching on, turning on, overloading ganglia. Wendall breaking out in floods of sweat. Needing to throw up. Like all the little locked doors inside have opened and suddenly he's awash in a river of undiluted rage bursting from wherever he's stored and suppressed it until now.

"Those poor people," Alana says.

"Oh, *man*," Tony says.

Wendall unable to speak. Writhing inside, beginning the delayed metamorphosis. Wendall squeezing his eyes shut as if the man in the mask has returned to his apartment, as if the baseball bat has just landed on his leg again, smashed his shin again, and as if the man is leaning close and telling him to shut up and stay quiet and never tell anyone what happened.

His legs burning with pain. His shins splintering. All of it bursting in on him. *Don't throw up*.

Tony saying we have a 5 A.M. run out to Long Beach—where a going-out-of-business store is donating furniture. We better leave now so we can get up early, but maybe there'll be news on the radio. We can try to listen on the road. Wendall? You okay?

He barely hears. His heartbeat is thundering.

"Wendall?"

He hasn't been okay in years, but the dead man is rising, aware finally. He'll never be okay.

Wendall excuses himself and runs for the bathroom.

The dead man has come back.

THIRTEEN

The Internet is a magnificent invention for assisting liars. A twelve-year-old boy uses it to sell "professional stock tips." A convict goes on-line to offer wooded property in Maine, which *is* wooded, but also worthless swamp. A two-hundred-pound secretary sends doctored photos of herself—acne wiped away, hips trimmed, hairline restored—to woo a lover. A forty-year-old lawyer chats up fifteen-year-old girls and asks them to meet him at a movie.

"Don't tell your mom," he types at 2 A.M. from his study, while his wife sleeps in the next room.

"I want to blow you," the Westchester sex crimes detective planning to arrest the pervert types back.

Now Voort sits down at Wendall Nye's keyboard—there is no time to return to his office—to interview a woman he cannot see or hear and whom he has never met. The ex–Marcia Nye is allegedly waiting to receive his questions in a monastery in Turkey. She could just as easily be hooked into the cybercrime squad's private chat room from a basement in Queens.

He envisions sheer rocky cliffs, a cross topping a stone parapet, a hyena barking as lightning flashes. In his mind the chant of monks mixes with the sound of fingers tapping on a keyboard. The American hiker sits on a three-legged stool like a milkmaid, typing on an NEC Versa 2000C.

"Hello, I am Detective Conrad Voort. Thank you for talking to me."

In person, Voort knows, the opening moments of an interview can provide crucial clues and revelations. Does the source look comfortable? Does he or she come across as a braggart, or as shy? Is there a "tell"—a physical manifestation of stress? Does he pull at an earlobe when he's nervous? Does she play absently with her hair each time she invents a lie?

But with no visible aids here Voort must try to establish rapport while appraising a distraught stranger on the far side of the earth, *and I must not drive her away*.

He types, "I'm sorry you have to learn about what's happened to your ex-husband this way."

Steering clear of using "Wendall" because it will sound flippant if she's a cop hater. Avoiding "Mr. Nye" because if she's protective it will come across as bureaucratic, cold.

The cursor blinks like a heart monitor. The computer functions as silently as a polygraph machine. For all he knows the power's gone down five hundred miles from Ankara, where the Bible meets Microsoft. Jonah meets Bill Gates.

Letter by letter, her reply takes form.

"You've made a mistake."

Careful, Voort tells himself. At the moment Marcia's his best bet for learning what happened six years ago, but without a tone her words could be interpreted as angry, touchy, or simply candid. At least on a phone he could gauge a voice by it's friendliness or pauses, its sarcasm, throat-clearing, sudden inappropriate fit of coughs.

He types, "It must be so frustrating to be so far away. The faster we find your ex-husband the faster we can clear things up. Perhaps this is a misunderstanding, but he may have information that will help us stop two murders."

Santini's said she's been filled in on the basics—minus Voort's mistake—but he goes over the story again to gain her confidence and make her feel like part of what is going on. Two people are dead. Wendall's handwriting seems to match notes admitting the killings and draft notes found in his apartment. Wendall's left evidence indicating he may have been investigating a fraud or theft ring on his own, without having told the police.

"But the evidence is incomplete and Mister Nye has disappeared. The notes threaten two more deaths in the next few hours."

"That's crazy," she types back.

"Have you been in contact with your ex-husband?"

"Wendall would never do those things."

"We need to talk to him, to find out."

"Are you really NYPD?"

Voort sends her his badge number.

"Kim, is this you?"

Deans, standing close, says, "Damn."

"Prove you're NYPD."

Voort sighs. "I know this is a shock. I'm frustrated too. You could break contact and try to reestablish through the NYPD Website, but we might lose power. Time is crucial. Test me."

Don't break off, he begs in his mind.

"How did you find me?" she sends.

"Detectives got your e-mail from your mom in Phoenix, at forty-two McLain Street."

"How did you find my ex-husband's apartment?"

"His social security number." Voort supplies it.

"Is he married again?"

Mickie sighs. Voort types, "He lives alone."

"You're just words on a screen. You could be anybody."

She's going to break it off. He can feel it. Quickly Voort tries, "May I make a suggestion? If I ask a question you don't like, don't answer. If you get suspicious, turn off. But for his sake, hear my questions."

"You're doing fine," says Eva as Mickie massages Voort's shoulders. "Rocks in there, Con Man," Mickie says.

No reply from Marcia.

Then, "All right, but don't hurt Wendall."

Voort is struck again by the support Nye engenders in those who know him, at least the ones who are alive.

He types, "Can you tell me who may have beaten

up Wendall six years ago, before your marriage dissolved?"

"He said a woman's husband did it."

"Do you know the woman's name? Or the husband's?"

"No."

"Do you know who Wendall may have had a grudge against six years ago?"

"He likes everybody."

Mickie grunts. "How many times have we heard that before?"

"Mickie, will you shut up." Voort says.

He types, "Do you have any idea what he might be investigating? We found tapes mentioning 'Ritchie' and 'Dougie.' We can't figure it out."

"They're for his class," she types back. "From before."

"Please explain."

"For teaching." Voort senses relief now on the other end. She types, "He'd give the class fragments and they'd guess the lesson. He taught them about his heroes. Lindbergh. Serpico the cop. Thomas Nast the cartoonist—people who had a big effect. He said lessons were like crossword puzzles and you remembered better if you put them together. He took pictures all over the city. You found his old tapes, that's all, so *there's no crime.*"

Voort considers her words but answers doggedly, "The notes at the killings were addressed to me, not a class."

Long pause. Then, "Why you?"

Voort stares at the screen. The cursor is pulsating over the question mark. Each electronic beat sends a stab of guilt through his chest, and the slow throb of a headache begins deep in his skull.

"I don't know." He moves to the next subject immediately. "Have you ever heard of Gabrielle Viera?"

"No."

"Forgive me for asking, but did your ex-husband ever use prostitutes?"

He holds his breath that she won't get mad, but he had to ask. The only sound in the apartment is the whoosh of traffic outside. The empty file cabinet drawers are open, as if evidence will materialize inside magically if they are exposed to air.

"No prostitutes ever," she replies stiffly.

"Thank you. Did you travel overseas? Use a travel agency?"

"No. Why?"

"What about Phillip Hull? Do you know that name?"

Pause. Then, slower, "Phillip Hull was helping design a Board of Ed construction plan."

"Construction again," breathes Voort, and asks for details. The people at his back bend closer. They have gone quite still.

Long pause.

"Where'd she go" says Eva.

Suddenly there's a rush of letters with no space between. "Ohgodtherailing."

"Railing? Explain."

"BrokeatNathanHale."

Voort asks, "A railing broke? Were people hurt?"
No answer.

Voort repeats, holding his breath, "Who got hurt?"
Nothing.

"Wait a minute. I remember this," Tommy Deans says. "It happened during the last administration. A railing went down at a high school. There was a huge settlement out of court. Three, four kids died."

"Didn't Wendall have a boy who would have been high school age?" breathes Voort. "That's what Estelle Moore said."

"Oh, shit," says Eva. "It was their kid."

Suddenly a stream of words explodes onto the screen.

"Hello, I am Rob Wirth, another trekker. Marcia is crying. We are trying to calm her. Stand by."

Voort sends, "What is she saying? Send her exact words. Type as she talks."

"Ohnoohgodohgodgodgodgod."

All because I didn't go to that apartment.

"MakeitstopwendallpleasenotBenBenBenBen."

Santini says, "The chief and I were in Queens then," as if to explain why they hadn't known instantly about a railing breaking in Brooklyn.

Deans saying, "The press never played it up because there was a nondisclosure agreement. That was Nathan Hale?"

Voort doesn't even remember the incident. Maybe he'd been on vacation. A railing breaking in a school would have made news for a day or two, or later on if litigation started. But there are so many stories in New

York that this one would have died down in a few days, especially if the lawyers were smart and the settlement blocked disclosure.

He types, "Can you get Marcia back to the keyboard?"

"She's hysterical."

"Can you relay questions?"

"The monks are giving her soup."

"Ask if there's a court case about this?"

"At dinner she said something about an out-of-court settlement. To lose a . . ."

TRANSMISSION INTERRUPTED.

Mickie hits the desk. "Damn!"

Pieces falling into place now, and Voort thinking that the construction link and stairway collapse would have become obvious within the next few hours one way or another. But the problem is time.

"Try to get her back," says Eva.

"We need to see all reports on that construction plan," Voort says.

Santini and Deans are already on their cellphones.

"We need Hull's recommendations, and the board's decisions based on them," Voort says.

The public record room of the Manhattan main branch library, on Fifth Avenue, is large and wood-paneled, and rows of shaded green lights illuminate long walnut tables. Researchers pore over federal, state, and city government reports. Recent publications are on paper. Anything more than two years old is viewable on microfiche.

And three years ago Wendall occupies a seat in the center of the room, poring over three fat reports. His heart beats rapidly and his eyes burn from strain after sitting here for seven hours.

It wasn't so hard to figure out where to start looking once I knew what I needed to find.

"Fifteen minutes to closing," calls a voice from the front as lights blink on and off and Wendall cross-references reports, jotting notes in his spiral notebook.

The first report outlines the Board of Ed's original construction/repair plan, completed when the economy was robust.

The second, revised report identifies which projects were proposed for delay or elimination because funds no longer exist to pay for them.

The final report tells Wendall which work survived the cuts, which companies lost out, and more important, which held onto their very profitable jobs after Hull was bribed to change his demographics numbers.

Two billion dollars worth of contracts are shifted around in these reports.

Wendall the savvy citizen now. Wendall who learned the facts of life the hard way, a cynic instead of a dupe. Wendall scanning the bullshit opening statements by the chancellor, beside a photo of his eminence's lying face. There are over 1 million schoolchildren in the city, the chancellor tells Wendall, and over 1,100 schools. There are 75,000 teachers in the city. The annual budget is $9 billion. Transporting kids daily costs taxpayers $22 million annually. Just science lab renovations will run over $31 million.

Which provides all kinds of opportunities for loot-ing, thinks the dead man recalled to life. *A two-bil-lion-dollar shortfall? How many millions of that was outright theft?*

He makes a chart. In the first report, he counts fourteen major constuction companies awarded con-tracts on forty-three jobs planned, including repair work at Nathan Hale.

By the second report, forty-three has been reduced to seventeen, although work at Nathan Hale is still considered important enough to remain scheduled.

The voice from the front calls out, "Five minutes!"

But Wendall is finishing his list of jobs reinstated in the third report and *big surprise! Four contractors kept every one of their jobs as the board eliminated others instead—like Nathan Hale.*

"Closing time!"

Wendall's barely aware of the half-dozen other people in the room getting up, gathering coats, head-ing for the exit. He can't stop envisioning that third-floor landing at recess. The steps clogged with kids. The din of laughter.

Oh Ben. Oh my boy, my boy.

"Sir? You'll have to leave."

Ten minutes later he's sitting on the front steps of the library, between the stone lions, looking out at schoolkids streaming from the closing building, book bags in their arms, then looking at the spiral note-book in which he's written four company names.

A. R. Empco.

P & P Construction.

Victor Dzenky Construction.

Tinker & Waddell.

I scared Hull and then Hull called the lawyer who'd met him by the carousel. Then the lawyer or someone at one of these companies sent the man to my apartment, I bet.

Call the cops?

How high does this go?

Tell the newspapers?

I have no proof.

And anyway, is one company reponsible? Or all four? Wendall thinking now about the big picture after learning from a dozen books about construction fraud. "Bid rigging," he's learned, is when several contractors make a secret agreement to bid high on some jobs, low on others, guaranteeing each other more money for jobs. Featherbedding means hiring workers who are not needed. Add concrete fraud. Drywall fraud. Add bribing people to make sure you keep your place at the public trough.

I'd give a different civics lesson to my class now.

Wendall goes into training, works out obsessively, tries to figure out the next step as he lifts weights, eats steroids, runs miles, takes out books about investigating.

A month into the new regimen, *My Life As a Private Eye* gives him the idea of how to start finding people.

I will figure out this whole system.

I will bring it down.

❖   ❖   ❖

First-time visitors to the *New York Times* come away unimpressed at the great newspaper's headquarters. The facade is sooty, the lobby cramped, and the expressions of staffers pouring in and out are sour, as if they think they deserve better. Or fearful, as if they think a rival may steal their beat.

Wendall waits at the security station in the marble lobby. Space is at a premium. There are no chairs or public phones or even decorations. No glassed-in, hung-up, Pulitzer-winning articles. There's no drinking fountain. No impressive view of presses, which have been moved to New Jersey.

These people look more frustrated than the teachers at Nathan Hale.

"Ms. Garcia will be right down," the guard tells him, hanging up a phone.

Moments later a dark, chubby woman in jeans and a khaki photographer's vest rounds the corner from the elevators and strides on squeaky Reeboks toward Wendall.

"William Winslow?"

"You took photos at the Board of Ed meetings, right?"

"You have an interesting face," she says.

"It was rebuilt after an accident."

"You suing?"

"I'm planning revenge," Wendall says as she signs him into the guest book and they head upstairs.

In the elevator he repeats the story he told her on the telephone. He publishes a small newsletter dealing with educational issues. He's planning a series on budget problems at the Board of Ed. He lacks funds to hire a full-time photographer so he buys occassional shots from professionals. "I can't pay much. My circulation's only four thousand. It's not like I'm the *Times*."

"Here are my shots from that meeting."

Her contact sheets, filed by date, are laid out on the portable light table. Wendall peers at miniature shots with a magnifying glass. Despite his grief and rage, they bring an unexpected nostalgia. He'd forgotten the pleasure he once got doing this in his own darkroom.

But the pleasure dies when he sees the lawyer from the park.

"Can I buy a copy of this one?"

"Why not?"

"Do you write down the names of people in photos?"

"Of course. When we publish photos we always ID the subjects. I keep the names in my computer log."

A few minutes later she announces, "He's a lawyer. His name is Redmon Crichton. He works at Tudor, Tudor & Lux on Park Avenue, or he did three years ago when I took this."

"Do I pay you for the slide? Or the *Times*?"

Ms. Garcia pauses.

"Will you attribute the photo in your newsletter?" If you attribute, pay the paper."

What she wants is fairly clear at the moment, and Wendall pulls out his wallet.

"I won't attribute."

"A hundred and fifty cash, okay?"

*   *   *

The offices of Tudor, Tudor & Lux are designed with a rustic Victorian touch, as if the great Disraeli might stroll from the conference room at any moment, don his hat, and stride toward a horse-and-carraige waiting on the cobblestones, instead of plunging forty-three stories to the ground, which is what would happen if anyone tried to walk directly outside today.

The couches are Empire style, low and plush, and the oak furniture looks as solid as the admiralty. Wall prints show British gentlemen at the opera and at Buckingham Palace, and solicitors at court facing bewigged magistrates as they argue eloquently over affairs of state.

Trudy Osborne, Redmon Crichton's executive secretary, has worked for him for eighteen years and knows his idiosyncrasies, wife, mistress, and the way he likes his initials on his cuff links embossed in mistral script, not Colonna. She's helped him handle the Metropolitan Museum of Art's Temple of Dendur reconstruction, the West Side/Trump air rights contract, and the Nikkai breach-of-contract claim after the Tokyo market plummeted. She's quiet, smart, and tough, and gets a large salary for anticipating his wishes, knowing when to bother him with questions, knowing when to handle problems herself.

At 9 A.M. on the morning after Wendall visits the *Times*, Trudy answers Crichton's phone to hear a man on the other end sounding middle-aged, hesitant, fumbling.

"This is, uh, William Winslow at the, uh, *Post*," the voice says. "We're doing a series on construction lawyers. This *is* Mister Christianson's office, right?"

"Crichton," she corrects sharply, sharing the lawyers' natural antipathy toward the fifth estate.

"Sorry. This handwriting's terrible. I wanted to check. Is Mister, uh, Crichton the lawyer for A. R. Empco?"

"He never represented them," says Trudy, who knows well that inquiries about *real* clients are to be answered, "I'm not allowed to give out names."

"Wait, this is the wrong list," the fumbler says as Trudy rolls her eyes. "I meant Victor Dzenky Construction. He represents them, right? This handwriting's a bitch."

"Dzenky is represented elsewhere," she says, knowing the appropriate firm but sparing them a call from this pest.

"I'll call back," says William Winslow.

Idiot, thinks Trudy, hanging up.

Six hours later she fields a call from a "Jack Feinstein" at P & P Construction, who seems more sure of himself.

"We've been going over your billing records from three years ago. We think there might have been an overcharge," he growls.

"That matter was settled," she tells him. Billing discussions are routine and she recalls a little tiff with P & P some time ago.

"I'll check this," says Jack Feinstein.

He never calls back either.

Rude man, Trudy thinks, dismissing him from her mind.

The Internet, Wendall's books advise, can turn the shy wallflower into a top-notch investigator. Without leaving home, follow people! Learn their credit ratings, driving records, loan applications, mortgage history.

Each night after his two-hour workout, Wendall turns on his Dell, keys into databases, hunts P & P in cyberspace.

Lawsuits? The company has deflected several over the last five years, according to court records. And LexisNexis, the database of newspaper and magazine articles, adds that key witnesses in civil suits have recanted testimony three times in the last two years.

Finances? The senior partner owns a $2.3 million home in Riverdale, a fully paid off Mercedes and a four-wheel-drive Land Rover, an insurance policy valuing personal property inside the house—including jewelry, paintings, and antique furniture—at over another two million.

No outstanding debts. Credit rating tip-top. The *Journal* thinks that P & P wants to get into big development.

Wendall goes back to LexisNexis and at four one morning finds himself cross-referencing P & P with every other company or person linked to them in the news.

The sky outside is lightening when up comes Blue

Knight Security and a piece on its recently appointed president, a former NYPD detective lieutenant and former VP in the firm named Aiden Pryce.

His eyes are burning. The letters are swimming. He's been fueling himself with cups of Folgers for the last few hours, and his head buzzes from caffeine and his intestines hurt from acid. He reads how Pryce accepts all kinds of cases: divorce work, security work, fraud investigations.

I need to sleep.

He reads that Pryce helped P & P Construction "convince labor thugs threatening to shut down a site to back off."

I should lie down. I have to be at work in three hours.

Then he scrolls forward and freezes when he sees Pryce's quote to *Forbes* magazine. Wendall's tirednesss disappears. His adrenaline starts pumping.

I found you, he thinks triumphantly.

"I love my job, Cap," is what Pryce has said.

The Are You Talking to Me bar on Reade Street in Tribeca is surrounded by converted warehouses, pricey restaurants, and lots of new office and residential construction since the World Trade Center attack. The bar is long and dark and its walls are hung with photos of neighborhood film star Robert DeNiro. Four P.M. is the start of its busy hours, the time that construction jobs let out.

"Hey, look who's here! Sargeant Tony!"

Wendall and Tony push through the boisterous

crowd, and it seems to Wendall that his boss knows half the guys here.

"Atten-tion," cries a guy with a Bud in his hand.

The man Tony's brought Wendall to meet, Bobby Moldea, occupies a rear booth by the busy kitchen, and is a dark, muscular Czech in a black T-shirt with a stud in his left ear. He's playing chess with a fat man in a wheelchair whose forearms are tatooed with a bishop and a rook. Moldea noisily sips from a highball glass filled with shaved ice and milk.

"This the guy you called me about, Tony?" he says, when Tony and Wendall sit down. "He looks old to be starting out. Whaddaya, Wendall? Thirty-six?"

Wendall slides bills under the table as Tony says, "If he doesn't work hard, fire him."

"If we did that we'd lose ten percent of our dues payers." Bobby grins, and moves a bishop. "Check, you asshole," he tells the man in the wheelchair.

The fat man moves his castle immediately. "Check yourself, you moron turd pig," he says, grinning.

"You'll be doing shit work, Wendall. End of the day, your muscles'll kill ya. Carrying iron. Hauling garbage. The stuff you'll be doing, usually a kid gets it."

"I'll work hard, Mister Moldea." Wendall nods, studying his new union card made out to Wendall Nast. *How to Track Down Almost Anybody* had taught him how to apply for a false birth certificate and social security card, and to avoid detection as long as he paid his taxes and bills on time.

He's already accumulating identities *in case I need them later.*

"Mister Moldea, I was hoping to work in Manhattan."

"Checkmate, you pathetic crippled fuckhead," Bobby says, taking more cash from Wendall. "No problem."

"I want to work on the high school going up in Washington Heights."

"It could take months to get you in there," Bobby replies.

"Then give his money back," Tony says.

"Hey, it's a recession. Guys stay on the job longer! What do you want, I should kick someone out?"

"Kuwait City," says Tony. "The Humvee breaks. The ragheads are coming." Tony goes whiny. "Tony, Tony, my piece is jammed!"

"I *said* give me time. Meanwhile, I'll put him somewhere else. Okay?"

It takes eight months, but Wendall gets the assignment and arrives for work as a laborer on brand-new David Dinkins High School, which is still in the early stages of construction, thanks to huge and costly delays. Turns out there were defects in the original architect's plans—to the advantage of P & P.

Wendall, paid employee of P & P Construction, gazes around the massive pit. Bulldozers roar. Cement trucks rumble. Riveters wield blowtorches and sparks fly against the sun.

"Hey you! You dead? Get to work," a foreman orders.

I'm here, he's thinking. *But what do I do now?*

FOURTEEN

"I remember where I heard your voice before," Aiden Pryce tells Wendall sixteen months later, in Pryce's office.

So great is Wendall's fear at that moment that his control almost breaks. His sphincter loosens and dribbles out a hot dab of urine. His back is soaked without his being aware that he ever started sweating. His testicles beat against his thighs.

"And where was that?" he manages to ask in a semblance of a normal voice, as some instinct of self-preservation keeps him from rushing for the door or ripping open the attaché case.

I'd never be fast enough against this man.

Pryce pokes the air, seemingly oblivious to the fear he's created. "You gave a eulogy at one of the World Trade Center funerals, right? Was it at Saint Mary's? In Queens?"

"It wasn't Queens."

About to say yes, he'd reminded himself even as his mouth was opening, *Stick to the original story.*

Don't give details he can test. He's been to Queens.

As North Point Press's *Negotiation Strategies* had warned, "Do not allow your opponent to throw you off balance, a tactic older than Sun Tzu's *Art of War.* Expect the odd probe, thrust, lie, revelation. You never know the other man's motives, but know to hold firmly to your path."

Wendall can't keep his voice from going shaky, but he lies with inspiration, knowing that his answer must explain why he sounds upset.

"I gave a eulogy for my sister-in-law, but it was in Tampa. She was visiting a friend at the Trade Center when the first jet hit."

Pryce's smile drops away and he blushes actually, looking embarrassed. He radiates sympathy. "I'm sorry, Father. And I've never been to Tampa."

Dropping the subject of where he's heard Wendall's voice before. Just like that.

Those terrible funerals, Wendall recalls as the meeting resumes, had gone on for months. Each day, churches and synagogues throughout the city had been filled with mourners. The eulogies had been endless, and an even more awful aspect had been the lack of hearses, coffins, corpses. There had been few to bury of the thousands lost.

But now he shakes away memory to see that his lie has provided an unexpected benefit, not only deflecting Pryce's suspicion but changing it to contrition. The security man steps away from his desk, where *Wine Connoisseur* had inferred that he stashes a gun in the top drawer.

"How about a glass of water?" Pryce asks. "You probably haven't even had dinner. I can send out."

Pryce's back is to Wendall as he slides open a panel in the wall unit. Wendall sees the shine of bottles and a flash of a silver ice bucket behind.

"I'd like to kill every one of those hijacker bastards. Were you and your sister-in-law close?"

"Losing someone close is one of the worst things imaginable," Wendall says, seized by a wave of grief.

"I have Stoli or Maker's Mark, if you want."

"Water's fine."

And, *this is my chance,* Wendall sees as Pryce stoops at the minifridge to extract a plastic bottle of Aquafina.

But his grief intrudes. A wave of paralyzing agony comes as he sees Ben on the basketball court the last time he'd spied on the boy. Wendall remembering a tall, lanky, terrible player. A kid who had trouble dribbling and relied on a two-handed set shot. Wendall seeing himself behind the fence, watching Ben miss, then turning away before the disgusted kid could spot him, and glimpsing a stray cat on the sidewalk, fleeing by running under a parked car.

Even animals shunning him back then.

"You okay, Father?"

He downs half the water. Pryce stands so close that Wendall can smell the man's cologne. For an instant his clever answer has saved him. *But the dead can't really come back,* Wendall sees, *except in dreams.*

The security man's inadvertent probing has shown Wendall what lies beyond midnight tonight—

whether he is successful or not—and it is not satisfaction but endless debilitating grief.

"I'm not a turn-the-other-cheek kind of guy," Pryce says as his ringing phone summons him back behind his desk. "Help yourself to more. Hello? I'm in a meeting," Pryce tells the caller. "No, the Mets were on, not the news. Slow down. Tell me what happened."

Mouthing to Wendall, "This will just take a minute," as the panicky buzz from the receiver slowly draws Wendall's attention fully back to the room.

"I said, calm down," Pryce says.

He waves his hand toward the wet bar and pokes his index finger at his mouth as if to say, *Snacks there too*.

Then suddenly he seems surprised. "Conrad who? He said the teacher did *what*? Hold on."

Turning to Wendall, he says, "Would you mind waiting outside a minute. Feel free to use the phones or . . ." and then frowning, reconsidering, and reversing himself. "Ah, stay here. It's no big deal."

He was afraid I'd pick up an extension. There's no one outside to stop me from listening in.

Wendall puts the glass on the desk blotter, strolls to the shelves, and pretends to examine books. As the caller keeps talking he sits down again, opens the attaché case, and reaches to feel the grip of the silenced Glock inside. He unsnaps the flap securing it.

"You're losing me," Pryce says. "*He's* been investigating or the police have? Because *he* couldn't investigate himself out of a toilet stall in Grand Central."

From the responding buzz Wendall can tell the caller isn't convinced, although the permanent cocky expression on the security man's face doesn't change.

Pryce draws in a deep breath. "You want to what?"

There's an oily feel to the Glock, and Wendall smells peanut butter, an odor that's come to him ever since childhood when he starts to get agitated. He even tastes Skippy for an instant. The top of his mouth goes dry.

Pryce shakes his head vigorously. "You were overreacting six years ago and you're overreacting now."

Pryce swivels away so he's facing the window. The back of the chair blocks Wendall's view but not his profile reflected in the window.

Pryce says, hushed but audible, "Tell me I'm not hearing this. You're on the verge of the whole deal working out and you're even thinking of leaving? It's not about what the police *say*, but what they can prove, and if they could prove anything they wouldn't be asking for help."

Wendall leans down, glances under Pryce's desk to assure himself that there's no dog behind it.

"Then put Arlene and the twins on a plane and let *them* go to your ranch," Pryce tells the caller, swiveling to meet Wendall's gaze in the window. Twirling an index finger at his head as if to say, *The jerks I deal with sometimes!*

Pryce adds, "Look, he'd need a damn car bomb to get at you if your guys are there. I'll come later, and I promise you we'll stop," he wraps up, glancing at Wendall, "your, uh, husband."

Hanging up, Pryce says, "That was a client in Scarsdale. The husband's threatened her, and the local cops are accusing her of . . ." and then he stops because his gaze has dropped to the Glock pointed at him over the top of the attaché case.

Pryce emits a genuinely amused chuckle. A slow smile spreads on his face. "A priest."

His confidence on the surface at least remains unbowed.

"You have a sense of humor, Cap. And the surgeon did a helluva job on your face. Night and day."

"I always wondered if it was Crichton who called you six years ago, but he's dead of cancer now."

"Who's Crichton? Telemarketers! Who gives them our numbers? That's what I want to know?"

"How many guards are up in Riverdale, Mr. Pryce?"

Pryce says, "I was thinking I knew your voice, but I only had a couple minutes before to hear it, if you know what I mean."

Rolling back toward his desk, hands floating toward the top as if seeking a surface on which to rest.

"So I was thinking eulogy, churches. I was thinking . . ."

"Stop."

Wendall is calm now, but a residual dot of sweat hovers at the corner of his left eye. Then it flows into his eye. The stinging makes the eye water and he shuts it. He wants to rub it but knows he'd better not.

Pryce's right hand is still closing on the desk, from four or five inches away.

"What big deal is about to work out?" Wendall says.

"You gotta put more force into it, like, *Make my day!*"

The fingertips touch the desk, palm dipping out of view as Pryce says, "Also, you left the safety on, Cap."

Wendall fires over the man's shoulder and hears a quick snapping noise, the bullet traveling through the thick window, webbing it, and Wendall's already aiming at the face again as Pryce uncurls out of his flinch.

Hands up now. The picture of cooperation.

Pryce even rolls back from the desk the tiniest bit as if a few pathetic inches represents triumph for Wendall. Pryce simply not seeing the metamorphosis in the man.

"How'd you find Gabrielle?" he asks, starting up again. "That was one hell of a job, digging *her* up? I should hire guys like you."

"What deal?"

"When my nephew orders me around he says, *Simon says* first. You gotta love 'em. Kids."

"You killed mine."

Which is what gets through finally, Wendall gathers from the flattening of Pryce's eyes.

"The cleaning crew's in the outer office, Cap."

Wendall starts to tighten his finger on the trigger and Pryce says quickly, "What do I get if I tell you? I left *you* alive and you're the one who threatened Hull."

"I never did."

"You didn't?" Pryce frowns. "Then I was misinformed. They told me you knew he was pumping his secretary. You wanted money. You had pictures."

"Nobody told you that."

"You're right. Look." He sighs. He'll talk straight now. "Our friend in Riverdale knows you're coming and what *you* don't know is there's a whole *system* looking for you now. Guys in bars, emergency rooms, parking lot attendants. A *system*, Wendall, and everyone in it—even if they don't know each other— knows if they find *you* they've done a favor for people who will make them happy."

"Thanks for the warning."

"Even if the police get you first, you'll never reach court, and *you*," he says logically, "don't even know what's going on. I'm sorry I hurt you," he says, "but I'm the one who told them you weren't a threat. They wanted me to do worse six years ago."

"Tell me the deal."

Standing, Pryce rolls his chair back with a slight movement of his hip. It further frees the space around his hands. He says with pride, "I never hurt a kid in my life."

"The stairs collapsed at the school."

"Ahhhhh." Pryce takes a second to consider, and seems to reach a decision. He idly scratches his chin as he says, "Look, you need to get out. What do you say to a hundred, no, *two hundred and fifty . . .*"

He moves so fast that Wendall's shot hits air where he'd been standing. The man's dropped behind the desk and Wendall leaps left but he's not trained in this. He's firing and moving but he's an amateur and he's wild. He hears crockery breaking on the bookshelves. There's a *boom* and something smashes into his right hip, driving him back and toppling him as he keeps firing. The pain is ballooning and he sees Pryce's reflection in the window.

Pryce rolling on the carpet and another shot sounding.

Wendall on his knees. Wendall's fingers clicking on an empty gun.

And he knows then that he's failed, sees in that brief instant that he will die here. He's too slow to move. But then he realizes that Pryce isn't firing.

Pryce is lying on the carpet, near the chew toy.

Wendall hears a gurgling sound like water bubbling in a fish tank.

Which is when, from the side of the desk he hears Pryce say in a voice gravelly with pain, "Fucking bounce."

It's hard to move. Wendall pushes himself to his feet. He cries out and his gun falls. *There's blood on the wall.* He fights off dizziness. Warm liquid runs down his legs, beneath his pants.

Pryce squints up from the floor, amid blood-soaked papers.

"Like skimming a rock, asshole. It bounced off the floor. What a laugh."

A great gush of blood bursts from his mouth. Pryce coughs and starts shivering. His whole body is shaking.

Then his whole body relaxes.

Wendall bends beside him, sees that Pryce's chest is not moving.

We have guys in emergency rooms, Pryce had said, not that Wendall intends for either of them to go to a hospital.

He wants to laugh suddenly, remembering a line from Crown Publishers' *Your Big Deal.* It was, "Expect unpleasant surprises."

Well, Wendall thinks, it hurts badly, but I was able to move around last time. There's a lot of blood, but it doesn't mean I've been seriously injured.

I always guessed today would not end well for me.

He's rational, though shaky, and when he looks out no one's in the outer office and he sees no cleaning equipment or purse or jackets—nothing left by people exiting in a rush. Banks of overhead lights cast a white glow on empty cubicles. Still, the cleaning crew will be arriving soon, Wendall knows.

Possibly any minute.

I have to write a new note. If Voort knows who I am I can't leave the original.

I have to think.

There's a sense of things culminating as he locates a clean sheet of Pryce's stationery amid the mess of files and blood on the desk. He uses a felt-tipped pen from Pryce's coffee mug pencil holder.

It makes no difference if he leaves fingerprints now. Or hair, footprints, DNA.

The message he folds into a business-size envelope is the shortest yet. The glue tastes bitter on the flap, as if his taste buds have altered. He writes

VOORT on front. He places the envelope on a cleared area of the desk.

Moving as quickly as the pain allows, he cleans off his hands and face in Pryce's private bathroom. He wraps a towel against his side, using a belt to keep it in place. The pressure hurts but he thinks he's stopped the blood flow.

Besides, I only need to walk three blocks.

He finds a raincoat in the main room, and as Father Daly shuffles from the office he sees the floor's cleanup crew emerging from the elevator. He nods to two men rolling a blue plastic bin filled with mops and brooms down the corridor and listening to a transistor radio broadcasting the Mets game. The taller man says, "Padre." The smaller wipes reddish sauce off his khaki uniform with a paper napkin. Stitching on the pocket says "Juan" in emerald green.

In ten, maybe fifteen minutes, Wendall figures, they'll let themselves into Pryce's office. Unless they're illegals, they'll call 911.

The pain in his side is radiating up and down along his whole body now. With each step a hot pain flashes down his leg.

Father Wendall pushes the "down" button on the elevator, as the transistor radio down the hall informs him that the Mets are up 3–2 in the game.

"Anything can happen," the announcer says.

Wendall thinking, *The whole city is looking for me anyway. Risk is what separates the living from the dead.*

* * *

At 9:51 the first of tonight's plays, concerts, and dance performances is letting out at Lincoln Center. The heat is still rising and crowds of well-dressed arts lovers fan across the plaza from half a dozen entrances to the complex, heading toward Broadway or Columbus Avenue, for restaurants, subways, or parking garages.

It's been a pleasant evening on the town.

Voort and Mickie push past the fountain toward the entrance to the Vivian Beaumont Theater, in the rear of the plaza. Huge posters in the window announce tonight's play, *Michael and Mara*, and show a middle-aged couple wagging fingers at each other as two school-age sons look on.

Reached by pager by no less than the mayor, the chancellor of the public school system is allegedly waiting in the theater manager's office. The mayor had advised Dr. Martin S. Oslo to stay put until the detectives arrived.

"Con Man," Mickie says. "If you're kicked off the job, I go too."

"Tell them that and they'll fire me faster."

"We don't need them. We're rich, man. We'll retire. Or go into business together."

"We are in business together," Voort replies, touched by Mickie's loyalty. "My family business. It's three hundred years old."

The crowd's mood is languid. There's no sense that anything more serious than a traffic jam lies in the future. A few people frown or slow, recognizing

Voort, but no one speaks to them as he and Mickie push into the entrance.

Identifying themselves to a security man, they are ushered immediately down two carpeted flights of stairs to a small office behind the box office cage. The chancellor, recognizable to Voort from TV, rises from behind a desk in a corner. He's a tall man with thick corn-colored hair in a close cut, a plain light brown suit, and tortoiseshell reading glasses that underline his blue eyes and elongate the rectangular face, patricianlike now, but with age it will lengthen like a hound's.

The handshake is dry and vaguely distant. Then again, Voort's presence here means possible scandal for Dr. Oslo.

"I sent my wife home. This is Robyn Townley from our construction office. I sent for her when the mayor called. She's familiar with the details of our capital improvement plans and her recollections may save you time."

The woman, who Voort judges to be in her thirties, has a mussed, fresh, roused-from-sleep quality. Her baggy black pants and matching jacket accentuate a feminine healthiness in cut and color. Voort takes in red bangs. Green eyes. A thin silver necklace. A pleasant talcum smell.

"I brought all three reports with me. We can check details if you need."

The room is small and functional: windowless, with a chipped pine desk, a trio of black file cabinets, a cushioned sitting chair for Robyn, and a mixed smell of burnt coffee, tart furniture polish, and years of cigarettes.

"We planned the largest school-building program in a generation," says Chancellor Oslo, as if size excuses error.

"Let's hope this whole mess has nothing to do with your program," Voort says.

"From your mouth to God's ears," Robyn says.

Voort gets to it, explaining that at the moment, theories about Wendall's motivation center around revisions to the plan and the fact that repair work at Nathan Hale High was delayed because of them.

"While you were on your way here the news broke about his son," Robyn says. "I have a two-year-old. I can't imagine losing a child."

"We want to know which contractors benefited most from the revised plan," Voort explains. "Wendall may blame them for what happened. It doesn't mean they're guilty. It just means he thinks so."

The chancellor adjusts his posture, sits straighter. "Those plans were revised only after input from principals and school boards, and after public hearings," he says. A defensive tinge has already come into his voice.

"I appreciate that, sir, and I'm sure the contractors will turn out to be honest."

Not if Wendall's tapes were real, they won't.

"Robyn?" the chancellor says, meaning, answer the question.

"Well, I'm not sure what you mean by benefit, because no contractor was awarded new work," she says, "but several kept their big jobs. They were fortunate."

"By coincidence," Mickie says.

"Down boy," Robyn says, easier going when challenged than her boss. "Our office of construction *does* supervise work, you know."

"Then why the giant shortfall?"

The chancellor sighs. It's the two thousandth time he's been asked the same question, Voort supposes. "Bigger original costs on contracts than we anticipated, even *after* competitive bidding. Rising labor contract expenses. Delays that ran up to twenty thousand dollars a day. Legal difficulties, and my predecessor never acknowledged these problems. Her people just buried shortfalls into each next year's budget."

"Ignored them, you mean," says Voort.

The chancellor sighs again. "Look, before I cut our building program I eliminated supplies, staff, programs. Prices have risen in all areas of the economy over the last five years. But when it happens in schools, people scream scandal."

"Especially when billions disappear," Mickie says.

The two detectives have agreed that he'll be the irritant tonight, if necessary, and Voort the nice guy.

"How come I'm always the irritant?" Mickie had said.

"Because you're a natural."

"My wife says that."

Now Voort asks courteously, "Have any of your internal audits revealed other discrepancies? Things you may have handled internally but not told the police?"

Robyn shakes her head. "It's a public process all the way through."

"Was the initial shortfall solved by the cuts six years ago, or are you still having problems?"

The chancellor looks unhappy. "The economy is worsening. We continue to need ways to lower costs."

Especially if there's wholesale looting going on.

"Is there any correlation between companies that kept their jobs and jobs which ran up big surprise bills?"

The chancellor and Robyn exchange glances. Robyn answers, "Off the top of my head, yes. But let me explain the safeguards in the process, because our original expectations don't necessarily accurately reflect costs. The board hires architects to come up with plans, and our own engineers to design specs. Then, interested contractors study the specs and submit sealed lump-sum bids. They don't enter the process until after the specs are complete. They can't possibly influence the specs."

"Robyn, thank you for that explanation. Off the top of your head, which major contractors kept most of their big jobs under your revised plan?"

"Victor Dzenky. A & R Empco." She nods, looking up to concentrate, showing the curve of slender neck. "P & P."

"And which of those also worked on projects that came in at far higher cost than anticipated?"

"Dzenky and P & P. But we don't just hand over

money. There's a checks-and-balances system to prevent drainage."

"Worked pretty well," Mickie says, scribbling notes.

"As a matter of curiosity," Voort continues calmly, "of the companies you just mentioned, will any also survive this new upcoming round of cuts?"

"There aren't officially any new cuts yet," Dr. Oslo breaks in. "And I don't see why that's relevant. My impression is you're interested in what happened six years ago."

"We're interested in what's occurred today."

"If I can go off the record . . ."

"We're always discreet."

"The board is in the middle of negotiations now on a rather innovative way of limiting cuts. Early disclosure might cost us tens of millions of dollars."

"Hurt bargaining positions, you mean," says Voort.

"It's just that I fail to see how negotiations that weren't even under consideration six years ago might relate to this former teacher."

"Well, if there's a pattern of fraud we may be able to access it on this end and work back. Let us be the judge."

The chancellor shakes his head unhappily. "I wish I could be that open-ended. I want to help, but I need to keep the children in mind. I don't know how it works in law enforcement, but in education you don't release news prematurely unless you want a fight on your hands."

"Oh, it's the same," Voort agrees. "But we wouldn't release it."

"Leaks always start with trust, unfortunately. To be frank, I've been following this story on the news, and my understanding is that the whole problem arose because of some error on your part, Mister Voort, not a lapse on ours."

"And it looks to me like at least one of the companies Robyn mentioned is one you're negotiating with now. Sir, we've got evidence that somebody is screwing around on your projects, and a logical starting point is people who've made big profits on them. I'm not accusing anyone yet. But do you want to be shielding them?"

Voort's hotline is ringing.

The chancellor looks miserable.

"I need to talk this out with the mayor," he says. "I can have an answer for you within an hour, but I'd rather not discuss it unless you can prove how it relates."

"We can't afford to lose an hour."

"I can."

It's 10:23.

"You look good on TV," Camilla says over the cellphone. "If you get fired you have a future at NBC."

"What did you find out?" he says, appreciating the levity.

"You know, lover, if they screw you over, you *could* always go to the press."

Voort's outside the theater office in the empty lobby. A cleaning crew vacuums the carpet, empties ashtrays. Mickie's still with Dr. Oslo and Robyn, trying to convince them to open up.

"Camilla, just tell me what you found?"

"Your cousins came through at Tudor, Tudor & Lux with the names of clients we didn't know about. The lawyers were cooperative for a change. Then again, the partner who did the work died of cancer a couple years ago. Crichton was his name."

"And the clients?"

"Pelham Shipping. Access Computers. P & P Construction."

"I love you," says Voort, his pulse heating up. *Maybe there's a chance to stop him, to save some people.*

"You better," says Camilla. "But wait. P & P rang a bell because *Target* tried to do a show on construction fraud and federal contracts a few years back. I called my old number two, Susan Mitchel, and I was right. P & P handled some major jobs in the nineties. I cross-referenced Phillip Hull and P & P. Nothing. Gabrielle Viera? Nothing."

"P & P was convicted of fraud?" The ticking feeling moves to his head.

"Allegations only. Bribing inspectors. Contract fixing. Scaring off competition. But no proof."

"Who investigated?"

"Justice. Federal housing. Us. Susan e-mailed me the file. We would have been sued if we'd ever used it, but it's on the screen in front of me right now."

"Any reward you want is yours, my sweet."

"*Anything?*"

"Except asking Julia to leave."

A sigh. "P & P was a father/son business until Robert, Sr., killed himself in ninety-six, in Riverdale. He was sixty-one years old. In good health, apparently. He just turned on his Lexus and listened to Imus on the radio until he drifted off. No note."

"That show could drive anyone to suicide," Voort says, and repeats, "Riverdale," remembering the file by the same name that Wendall had left in his apartment.

"Camilla, who took over the company?"

"Robert, Jr., branched into Manhattan jobs after that, joined exclusive clubs in the city. Made influential friends. Gave to charities and candidates. Within a couple years the company's winning contracts downtown, but just like the Bronx, their projects always develop cost overruns or legal problems, settled by our now deceased lawyer, Crichton. Judges excuse themselves from trials. Competitors stopped bidding against them. One case did go to court and the other side screamed jury payoffs."

"P & P won, I take it," Voort says dryly.

"A few years ago they got into development. Bigger projects. A condo tower in the East Village. Rumors of mob involvement. But no one's ever proven anything. Not the Justice Department. Not the *Times*. You know what they say, Voort. Where there's smoke, you can't see a thing."

"How come people keep awarding them contracts?"

"Last time I checked, rumors aren't grounds for

denial. You want Robert's address in Riverdale? He's on Beauchat Avenue. Eight-eight-eight-four."

"How about a last name?"

"Didn't I tell you? P's for Priest. Robert Priest."

"My other line is ringing. . . . Voort!"

Santini tells him, "We found number three."

Voort squeezes his eyes shut.

"It's Aiden Pryce at Blue Knight Security. The office is all shot up, apparently. I'm on my way there now. A cleaning crew called it in. They think they saw the killer leaving. They said the guy was moving funny, like he was hurt. Detectives from the one-seven are there. Meet me there?"

Do I head for Riverdale and Robert Priest, or the scene? I can't make the wrong choice.

Voort asks, "Did Wendall leave a note again?"

"They're opening it now. I'm on the line with them. I wanna tell you, Voort. I knew Pryce when he was a cop. Everyone always thought he had sticky hands."

"That's not the point."

Voort switches back to Camilla and says, "Can you use those computer skills and contacts of yours and see if you can link P & P with Blue Knight Security and its president, Aiden Pryce?" Voort spells the name.

"I work harder for you than when I had a job."

"But I give better bonuses."

"Hmmmm. Very true."

Something the chancellor said is bothering me, but it's not the part about P & P, so what is it?

But Santini's back, announcing himself with a sigh.

"Looks like you aced your term paper, Voort."

"What does the note say?"

"Well, there's another cassette in there, the Ritchie voice talking to a hooker, telling her to blow a guy and not take money, but the note just says, 'To Voort.' And under that a big A-plus, in black felt tip. That's all."

"Double our guys checking emergency rooms. Fax Wendall's photo and sketch to doctors."

"Me, I always got Cs in school. Looks like you're out of detention. But I don't get it. You identify him and he gives you an A for *that*?"

"It's sick, all right. Unless he wants to get caught."

But inside his frustration Voort also experiences a vague pulse of pride, like he used to get in school when a test came back with a high mark.

This is perverted. Am I trying to please this guy or catch him?

Santini says. "Maybe there will be more on the tape."

"My guess? He's saying we're on the right track. He's been steering us all day and we're doing what he wants, doing well in his eyes."

"In *his* eyes doesn't mean doing well."

With an hour and a half to go, do I meet Santini or head for Riverdale? If it's Riverdale, I've limited myself to one possibility. But at the scene I can dispatch detectives anywhere if I find something new.

Voort pulls Mickie from the meeting, takes along the reports, and fills Santini in as they head for the car. He gives Santini the names of the three construction companies.

He says, "Get people to the homes of the owners of those companies, for protection. But I also want to know if any of them made defensive preparations. Have they left town? Do they have bodyguards? Are they *expecting* him, is what I mean. And have your guys go through Pryce's files, see if he worked for one of those companies."

"You think Hull was bribed?"

"I think a lot more happened."

"Look Voort, what the mayor and Deans is doing to you is shitty."

"We get Wendall first, then worry about the rest."

"Fine, uh, you know the call-in line's been ringing off the hook since Eva went on TV, right?"

"Get the bad news out, Paul. I hear it in your voice."

"Callers are saying, 'He's the greatest teacher I ever had, the nicest guy I ever knew. What are you cops trying to do to him?' I just want you to know, Voort. My cousin owns a private security firm in Atlanta. If I recommend someone, they're on the job."

Voort feels sick. "Thanks."

"And the worst part is, we can't *use* Wendall's tapes even if he came up with something. Aziz says they're inadmissible. Recordings without the knowledge of . . . you know the law. Unless the court okayed a tap, it doesn't make a difference if the guy said he'd shoot the president and then he did. Nye's tapes are useless in court."

How could one mistake do all this?

"See you at Blue Knight." Santini is gone.

Mickie pulls into traffic, shooting south down Broadway, siren blaring. Looking down on the seat, Voort sees the crumpled bag of sandwiches that have been sitting there since noon.

"Riverdale," he murmurs.

"What about it?"

"Wendall left a file that said Riverdale, so does he *want* us to go there or is *he* going there? And if *he's* going there, why's he happy that we found the file? Or is he happy because we got everything wrong, and the note's a trick. I'm not seeing something."

"It's nice to know we've almost got this solved. Look at the bright side. Maybe Wendall's bleeding to death."

"Maybe I interpreted the fucking note wrong. Maybe it has nothing to do with teaching and he's killing random people like you said all along. He's a nut."

"We'll save the last guy, Voort, and figure it out."

"Yeah, save the crook."

Mickie cuts through Central Park, exits at Fifty-ninth, blows through red lights on the way to Fifty-sixth. To the west, it looks like a storm is coming, never mind the earlier weather report.

"Well, we're heading away from Riverdale at about forty miles an hour," says Mickie. "You'll feel better if you eat something. Those sandwiches aren't bad."

"Why do I think we're making a mistake?" says Voort.

FIFTEEN

The temperature tops ninety, smashing records, causing power failures, driving a mammoth heat-lightning storm into the city from across the Hudson. Out on the street again, Wendall sees immense blue-white flashes explode over the towers of midtown. Roiling clouds blacken out stars as they rapidly come on. He smells ozone, exhaust, burnt electricity.

"I don't feel so good."

Nobody pays attention to him shuffling east down Fifty-sixth, off First Avenue. The few pedestrians out are busy gaping at the approaching light show or rushing home to beat the violent storm.

"I'm a little dizzy, but not dripping blood I think. And I never thought I'd say this, Voort, but when I stood over Pryce—when that man was as dead as my son, Ben—my rage against you passed away and I saw that I'd blamed you for things that weren't entirely your fault. I made you a scapegoat. It was easier than doing something, and easier than thinking about my own mistakes."

A squad car glides past, its driver a pale silhouette twenty feet away from the arrest that would make his career. Oblivious to the error he is making, he will tell his wife tonight, "Other cops get all the breaks. Never me."

"The student passes the teacher's expectations," Wendall says into his neck microphone. "But the student's created new problems for me. I'm impressed with you Voort, the way you admitted your mistake. The way you put my clues together. But did you have to be *so* good?"

Blue bolts hiss and seethe in the sky.

"Six years ago you almost killed me by ignoring me, and now you've done the opposite. But the question is, are you playing catch-up? Or do you know where I'm headed?"

He stops and leans briefly against a building, to catch his breath, and then pushes himself off. He passes a closed antique shop, shuttered pizza parlor, lit apartment building. The air is still and hot and electrical explosions make a strobe show in the sky.

The clerical collar is gone, discarded in Pryce's elevator. The attaché case lies in the recessed entrance of a tobacco shop, where he'd needed only seconds to change from priest to artiste, donning stylish black-framed glasses, a faux diamond stud in his left ear, and a soft black beret, the affectation completing the transition from man of abstention to flamboyant figure of excess.

Wendall the painter, actor, filmmaker wheezes

over the pulsing pain, "A few tiny changes vastly alter perception."

He reaches a small open-air parking lot fronted by a razor-wire fence, across the street from the bridge. Cars inside are squeezed bumper to bumper and stacked on hydraulic lifts. OPEN 24 HOURS, says a sign on the attendant's shack. ASK ABOUT OUR SPECIAL PRICE IF YOU PARK BEFORE 5 A.M.

He hands the attendant the stub he'd received yesterday when he'd left his Nova here but kept the separate key accessing the trunk. Inside are files he'd removed from his apartment, one neatly folded transit-cop uniform, one combination hat, rumpled dark suit, hanging sideburns, and a long beard to make him resemble a Hasidic Jew, night-vision binocs, new wallet with false ID, eight thousand dollars in cash, two clips of nine-millimeter bullets, one spare silenced Glock, an old Ronzoni carton filled with months of tape recordings, and eight manila envelopes, sealed, stamped, ready to be express-mailed to the networks and newspapers. They contain the results of his twenty-one-month investigation.

"Are you all right?" the attendant asks.

"I just got out of the hospital."

"Forty-eight bucks, my good friend," the thieving attendant says with an Eastern European accent. "If you leave the car more than twenty-four hours, you pay the bigger rate."

He wipes donut cream from his thick lips and shambles off with Wendall's cash in his pocket instead of putting it in the register. He'd probably rip off the pope, the president, the first arrival from Mars, Wendall thinks, but watches as the man begins shifting cars around to free his rented Nova.

"Are you in Riverdale, Voort? That is what I need to know."

He tips the attendant, checks the trunk, bumps out of the lot, and turns on all-news radio.

He heads north on First and takes Sixty-second to the FDR Drive. Lightning bursts over the East River and towers of Harlem.

Keep the car steady.

But the pain makes him pull over at a rest stop for a minute. He adjusts the compress on his side.

On WCBS he hears, "A fifteen-thousand-dollar reward is being offered by Hull's company for information leading to the arrest and conviction of the killer."

"That's probably less than Hull took as a bribe."

The ABC announcer, trying to sound horrified, comes across as thrilled instead. "ABC has learned that Nye's son was one of three students killed when a railing collapsed at Nathan Hale High three years ago."

"Oh, God. I miss you, Ben. Marcia."

Sitting instead of walking restores some energy, and moving again, he's able to breathe slightly better now, although the pain is not diminishing at all. The Willis Avenue Bridge—one of two spans off the island lacking tollbooths or police—takes him over the East River and spills him north onto I-87 in the Bronx.

Check the rearview mirror for cops.

But the only thing he sees of note there is his new, glinting ear stud.

"All those books by costume designers were good but missed a main point. Disguise is more than physical. It's a melting away of self into nothingness, a surrender of will enabling others to imagine who you are."

Switching channels, he hits a phone-in show.

"I agree with the last caller," an agitated woman is saying. "Wendall Nye was one of *my* teachers too, and it's *terrible* that the police just assume he's guilty. What happened to innocent until proven guilty in this country?"

Wendall takes the Major Deegan Expressway to the Mosholu Parkway exit. He winds onto the Henry Hudson, going south.

"And another thing," the next caller says. "*I'm* a parent now, with a little girl in first grade. They fired her assistant principal and nineteen teachers in our district. All the PTAs in our area have teamed up and called the mayor's office and Senator Rush's office to demand a federal investigation of this whole Board of Education mess."

Wendall feels tears forming at the edges of his eyes.

RIVERDALE, 1 MILE.

Over the last few months he's made sporadic visits to this wealthy neighborhood, scouting the oak-lined streets and carved-up estates, fine homes, private tennis courts, yacht club, and tracks abutting the Hudson.

He's checked which apartment buildings have doormen. Which have roof decks. Which ones provide parking to visitors like him.

On Riverdale Avenue, the four-lane-wide commercial strip, he passes shops and strip malls, behind which loom apartment buildings, and behind those, he knows, are small narrow streets and expensive private homes.

"Let's hear what Joe in Little Neck has to say," the talk show host is saying.

A gruff, older-sounding man comes on. "Nothing excuses murder. We need to enforce laws."

"Amen, Joe."

"Wendall Nye should get the chair if he killed those people. But I'm mad at the police too."

"Why, Joe?"

"Well, the cops announced that Nye's conducted some kind of investigation but won't say what it is except to ask him to share results with *them*. It stinks of a cover-up, if you ask me."

Suddenly Wendall hears a siren and sees the flashing red roof light of a squad car in the rearview mirror. The car rushes past, leaving his heart pounding. As it makes a hard right at the next light the caller says, through worsening static, "I'd also like to know how an amateur managed to uncover some multimillion-dollar scam when our police never found a thing. That also says cover-up, and so does the way the police are keeping that rich detective on the job."

Wendall pulls into an apartment house parking lot

and a space marked "Visitors." The storm has worsened, and massive explosions of thunder reverberate after each flash of light.

He sees no one as he painfully opens the trunk and removes the clothes he needs, then changes slowly in the front seat. He stuffs his hand into his mouth to keep from crying out from the pain.

Minutes later Wendall the Hasidic Jew opens the front door of the high-rise apartment building. He's wearing the rumpled dark suit, scuffed shoes, rough long beard, and long *payos*, or hanging sideburns. Riverdale has one of the largest Orthodox Jewish communities in New York.

The lobby door is locked—as he knew it would be—but Wendall waits until he sees a man outside walking toward the building from the parking lot, carrying a briefcase. Wendall pretends to press a buzzer and talk into the intercom as the man reaches the outer door. He's getting dizzy, though.

"I don't *want* to come up, Gloria," he says as the man enters the foyer. "I'm not feeling well."

Which the man can certainly see is true.

"Okay, I'll come, but just for five minutes," Wendall says, catching the inner foyer door after the man uses his key to go through.

"Have you been following this school construction scandal," Wendall asks the man in the elevator. His curiosity is real.

"Why bother? You can't stop this stuff," the exhausted-looking guy—probably home late from work—replies.

❖ ❖ ❖

In Manhattan the lightning storm grows fiercer, starting to affect power around the city. As Voort and Mickie reach Fifty-eighth and Second they see that streetlights are broken. Street lamps are blinking and sizzling and whole apartment buildings have dimmed down.

"This is weird, Con Man. No rain. Just these explosions. Where's the rain?"

"We're not going to stop him."

"You've saved more lives than any ten cops. Aziz has to keep you on."

The radio emits static and police-band transmissions are getting mixed up. The sky goes green. An enormous shaft of lightning strikes the top of the Queensboro Bridge. "You know, Mick, ten years from now, when I have a kid and he's old enough to understand the portraits in my house, what'll mine show? A cop going to the wrong apartment? Making a mistake?"

Between the static bursts and a stream of police emergency calls—traffic smashups, in the storm— they barely make out that Wendall Nye has been spotted in the East Village.

"Sure he has," Voort sighs. "And in Little Neck. And in Red Hook too, all in the last ten minutes."

A different dispatcher announces brokenly, "Nye was seen driving over the Willis Avenue Bridge, wearing a beret."

As they pull up to Pryce's building, seeing the squad cars and unmarked cars, four beeps sound, signifying that a citywide police emergency broadcast is about to begin. Bending close to hear better, Voort makes out that One Police Plaza is releasing a new description of Wendall, garnered from witnesses at Pryce's building.

"He was dressed like a priest," the dispatcher says.

Mickie's already turning the car. Voort doesn't need to say, "Goddamn it. Priest and Priest. *Riverdale.*" But he does anyway.

On the dashboard clock, 10:45 becomes 10:46.

On the top floor, Wendall takes a stairway to the roof deck, which is empty thanks to the mammoth electrical storm overhead. He's moving very slowly from the pain. He extracts the military quality night-vision binocs from his jacket, and from the northeast corner of the deck has a splendid green-tinted view of a Tudor mansion four blocks away.

He wheezes, "You there yet, Voort? I lost time in the car."

All the lights are on in the mansion and, as Wendall watches, a man with a German shepherd on a leash walks around the house and disappears in back. A well-dressed woman and two small, twin girls hurry out with suitcases, get into a Range Rover in the driveway, and quickly drive off.

"One squad car arriving. Two. Here comes the army."

In an upstairs window he catches sight of a lone white face peering out at the street as the man talks frantically into a cellphone. The face swings up. It seems to be looking directly at Wendall. But that is impossible. Wendall is too far away.

A sudden stitch in his side doubles him with pain, and when he looks again the curtain's back in place.

He's just about to go back to the car when another flash of movement outside Priest's home attracts him.

Through the hurt, Wendall sees two Voorts step out of two black Caprices.

He whispers, grimacing, "Another A, detective. Perhaps I'll manage five by midnight. Not just four."

When the horn rings at quitting time each day, Wendall's arms and shoulders are on fire. His calves and thighs burn. His neck hurts. He's been carrying iron and planking and bricks all day and can count where new muscles are growing by all the places where he hurts.

"Want to make some extra money?" the timekeeper asks.

It's hard to imagine that the huge pit in the earth will one day be a high school, but Wendall's seen blueprints in a visiting architect's hands. The cafeteria will be on the north end, by the rear entrance. The science labs will look out on the basketball court.

"I could use a few bucks," Wendall says. "Why not?"

"Keep it between you and me, okay?"

They're alone in the P & P trailer on the site, and the timekeeper is nineteen-year-old Joey Priest, the owner's nephew and a pal of Ritchie the foreman, Dougie the union steward, and a fat electrician named Al Crane.

His job recording hours that guys work would be easy to automate, but the company wants a human doing it. The job's a perk.

Joey Priest sits with his shit-kickers up on the trailer desk, keeping cool under the roaring air-conditioner as he sucks down a canned iced tea. *His* muscles never hurt. He jabs his Bic at the clipboard where he records hours.

"If you ever want to take a few hours off, I'll put in for your full time, and even overtime, and then you give me twenty percent of the extra, okay?"

Wendall grins. "Monday morning I think I'll sleep late."

"Just remember. Twenty percent."

It's a start, but a long way from a stairway collapsing, so when he gets his next paycheck he heads down to the jewelry stores near Madison Square Garden. He picks out three brand-new Festiva watches. A hundred bucks apiece.

"Joey, do you know anyone who might pay twenty-five a pop for these? They're worth a hundred."

"Are they real?"

"Whaddaya think? I gotta work here too, y'know."

Joey buys one and so does foreman Ritchie Mayhew. Dougie the steward buys one, and a day later Ritchie sidles over when Wendall's loading wheelbarrows. He's a tall, powerful man, a perpetually smiling blond with a long ponytail who wears cutoff T-shirts that show his biceps and has his shoulder tattooed with a picture of a naked brunette in high-heeled shoes. "Can you get anything else?" Ritchie asks.

"Like what?"

"My kid needs a DVD."

So Wendall buys one and brings it in, like he stole it.

"How much?" says Ritchie.

"I didn't pay so why should you? My father used to tell me, better one favor than one hundred bucks."

"One favor," says smiling Ritchie. "Come into the trailer." It's after hours, and the second the door shuts, the broad smile on Ritchie's face flattens a bit.

"Empty your pockets, Wendall. Take off your boots."

The door opens and in walks Dougie and Joey and three-hundred-pound Al Crane. All the other workers went home at four-thirty. The night watchman isn't due until five.

Wendall says, "Hey, what is this? Remind me not to give you guys presents any more."

They pat him down. They check his clothes. They go through the trunk and unscrew the dashboard of his fourth-hand just-purchased Escort.

"You think I'm a *cop*?" Wendall asks, humiliated and terrified.

"Who told you to sell shit on my site?"

Joey and Dougie stand at his back in the trailer, and Ritchie's in front, boot up on the chair.

"Nobody, Ritchie. A guy had them on my block."

"So you decided to set up a shop and attract cops."

"I'll stop."

"What favor do you want?"

"I needed a few bucks. I'm sorry."

And I'll quit this whole stupid thing if I get out.

As Wendall dresses, Ritchie pushes off the chair. His smile seems to shift around so his left lip curls a bit. "What favor?"

Dougie and Joey move closer. Al blocks the door. Wendall figuring his whole genius plan is about to crash and burn from this stupid mistake on the first round. Wendall unable to think of any other answer than the one he planned.

"All I wanted was, I mean, I work hard, but my back hurts from carrying shit all day, y'know? If you had a chance, I thought maybe you could get me something easier to do."

In the pause he feels sweat pouring from his face, despite the air-conditioning. "Forget it, okay?"

But Ritchie breaks out laughing, so the other guys do too.

"You stupid asshole. I'll buy you a beer."

But the test isn't over, he realizes, not from the way they wedge him into the back of Joey's new Cherokee. Wendall between big Al and big Dougie, on the West Side Highway, heading north. It's incredible how far away the other cars seem—how far even the lock on the door seems.

"Where you from?" asks Ritchie over the front seat, like he's making innocent conversation.

"Queens."

"Married?"

"My wife left me," Wendall says. "The bitch."

"You're old to be getting into the union," Ritchie says as they cross into the Bronx.

"Never too late to start."

"Ever done time, Wendall? The Tombs? Attica?"

Ritchie's smile flickers. It has ripples. It reflects light.

"No jail? No record if we checked, *paisan*?"

"Beautiful girls," breathes Joey, pulling into the parking lot of a strip joint. DIAMOND CLUB, says a sign showing a female ankle above a high-heeled shoe. At six the lot is half-filled with cars, the place close to the Sawmill parkway so it draws in commuters heading home to Yonkers, Tarrytown, Katonah.

Watch naked babes dance, guys, then go home and close your eyes when you're in bed and imagine those slender bodies are under you, not your whiny, fat wives.

"Beer's on me," says Ritchie, which strikes the other guys as funny. They always laugh when Ritchie wants.

I never should have started this.

Ritchie orders a pitcher of Bud, and three glasses. Dougie asks for Coca-Cola. "I'm in AA," he says.

"AA. Asinine assholes," Ritchie says to more laughter.

Three girls dance on a runway, grind against poles, run their hands over their bodies, mouth the words of the hit song "Ram Me" as they watch a TV monitor where the video is being shown.

The place smells of beer, perfume, sweat, mold. Wendall's nerves are screaming and he waits for something terrible to happen. But Ritchie just talks about the Jets' chance of reaching the Super Bowl. Dougie tells about two sisters he's screwing. The younger one is prettier, but the older has a corkscrew motion which is out of this world.

Why did they bring me here?

Three new dancers take over.

It's getting dark outside.

After a while Ritchie stands, makes no move to pull out cash and says, "Dougie and I have a drive to take. Wendall, is that a wallet in your hand? Put it away."

"Aren't we paying?"

"Not here. We drink free."

When they get outside, it's dark, and the streetlights are broken. Ritchie seems edgy, distracted. "We'll drop you home," he says, guiding Wendall into the back of the Cherokee again. "And pick you up in the morning, get you back to the site, *paisan.* You won't need to go get your little car."

They're going to pull over. They know I'm phony.

The radio blasting and nobody talking as they head across the urban wreckage of the Bronx and over the Throgs Neck Bridge into Queens, where thank God he had the foresight to rent a room under his union name, just a cubicle in a private home with a bathroom down the hall, two hundred dollars a month. No lease for Wendall Nast.

Wendall out of his league here. Wendall knowing

only one thing, and it is: *They're going to kill me.*

"Be outside at seven tomorrow," Dougie says as they drop him off. "I'll pick you up. Get some sleep."

Within a month he's going out with the guys regularly, to the freebie strip bar, a moussaka place in Astoria, a sports bar in Riverdale.

"How come we never pay?" he asks Ritchie.

"Why, you *want* to pay?" Ritchie grins back.

He goes to Dougie's house in Flushing, meets the wife, eats ravioli, and watches the Yanks. He fishes for blues in Montauk with Ritchie and Al. When the charter boat captain tries to overcharge them, Ritchie goes ballistic. Very bad temper, Wendall thinks, never able to relax.

My investigation is going nowhere.

Four nights a week he sleeps in Flushing. Others he hits the Internet at home and stays up until dawn cross-referencing P & P Construction, Aiden Pryce, Phillip Hull, and every member of the Board of Education. He checks credit ratings, mortgage information, lawsuits, cars owned, and minutes of board meetings he finds on-line or buys from the records section on Livingston Street.

He learns nothing, and he's four months into his investigation.

I'm a failure at this too, he thinks, always on guard, always watching what he's saying, having trouble sleeping.

Then he gets a break.

*　　*　　*

"Want to take a drive, Wendall?"

They're in the strip joint and it's Friday and the drink tonight is margaritas. Joey's home with his wife, who's two months pregnant. Al's in Miami. Dougie sits disconsolately in the third seat, grimacing each time he turns to watch the dancers. He's in pain.

"I'm mowing the lawn and I turn sideways. Next thing I know I need a fucking plastic disc in my fucking back."

"Dougie, we'll drop you off. Wendall, you and me'll take the drive tonight."

Ritchie, Wendall knows by now, likes company, likes to be boss, and show off, and hates to use his own, new BMW on certain errands. An hour later they're barreling along the Grand Central Parkway in Wendall's Escort, toward the Southern State Parkway and Long Island.

"Get off at Rockville Center and turn left on Tesser Place. Park in front of number three-three-three-two. Stay in the car."

Ritchie rings the bell of a nice-looking colonial, where shrubs border the mowed lawn. Tulips grow under the bay windows. Ritchie talks earnestly with a nervous-looking man who answers the door, nods often, and peers at the Escort as if memorizing the damn car.

Afterward, Ritchie stuffs a hundred in Wendall's pocket. And that night on the Internet, Wendall finds that the house belongs to the principal of a Queens junior high school. His credit rating is terrible.

He owes thousands to stores, banks, the IRS.

Well, it's a start, puzzled Wendall thinks.

Not much has changed two months later except Wendall's *more* on edge. The guys go drinking and play poker, and every week or so Wendall drives Ritchie somewhere: a judge's house in Bay Ridge; a union vice president's house in New Rochelle; a Riverdale Tudor mansion belonging to the owner of P & P, who he also sees at the construction site and strip bar from time to time.

"He owns the place," Ritchie says.

Each time a fragment of theory falls into place Wendall experiences a surge of optimism but realizes he *still* has no evidence on P & P. Not a thing.

The foundation is up on the school now. The walls are up for the principal's office. But Wendall's obsessing about the trailer. Often he sees strangers going in and out of that construction trailer—or he sees people whose homes he's driven Ritchie to. Ritchie in there sometimes, and lots of times men in sharply cut, expensive suits, except they aren't architects because they don't carry blueprints, and they aren't lawyers because lawyers like to put on hard hats and walk the site to examine whatever work—costly delays usually—they're fighting over in court.

What the hell do they talk about in there?

So Wendall goes back on the Internet, types up "equipment" and "surveillance," and what do you know, the "Spy Guy" and "Espioshop" pop up.

"We sell the top covert wireless video and audio

surveillance systems, like law enforcement professionals use. WARNING. Using these devices may be unlawful in your state or country. It is the buyer's responsibility to use the equipment in a lawful way."

Yeah, right.

Wendall is astounded to learn what he can buy. There's the wireless clock-radio camera, hidden TV camera, briefcase camera, video-pager camera, and cameras in Walkmen, smoke detectors, wall clocks, lamps.

"Allow seven to ten days for delivery."

Or, he sees, deciding audio is more desirable, for between three hundred and eight hundred dollars there's the micropen recorder, phone recorder, button mike, air purifier mike, wall-outlet mike, sunglasses mike, and parabolic long-distance mike, like Fox uses at football games.

"WARNING: These devices are not intended for use in surreptitious audio interception."

But how do I get one of these things in the trailer?

A month goes by, and then one night he finds himself playing poker at Ritchie's nineteen-hundred-square-foot Tribeca condo loft with Tony, Al, and two "advisers" for Blue Knight Security. Dougie's in the hospital, scheduled for surgery again.

"Wendall, you want to take over the timekeeper job when Joey's on vacation? You asked for a favor when I met you." Ritchie grins and taps his forehead. "I never forget."

And two weeks later, Wendall finds himself on a

stepladder in the trailer, switching smoke alarms so the new voice-activated transmitter will broadcast to a receiver he's hidden inside the door panel of his Escort. The new alarm looks normal enough. Like the old one, it has a red light that blinks on top to let you know the battery works.

Ritchie walks in and stops, eyeing Wendall frozen on the ladder. Ritchie's gaze moves from the alarm in Wendall's hand to the one on the ceiling.

"Worried about fire, *paisan*?"

"The old one was busted, Ritchie."

"Was it now? Busted?" Ritchie looks thoughtful.

It's got to be the thousandth lie Wendall's told, the thousandth time he's sure they've caught him. Every minute is a lie in the way he walks, works, even in what brand of beer he drinks. Some days, like now, the strain of telling a specific lie makes him want to scream, or quit. But even during quiet times the weight of nonstop deception exhausts and depresses him.

Once or twice at home he's broken out laughing, realizing, *These guys are my only friends.*

"You got gas?" Ritchie asks now in a hard voice.

This time they head south into Brooklyn and across the Verrazano Bridge to Staten Island, where they've never gone before. Ritchie has him buy two plastic jerry cans at a Pep Boys. Ritchie waits while Wendall fills the cans with gasoline at a BP, his heart starting to thump faster with apprehension. Ritchie directs Wendall to a ranch-style home—just a frame—going up in a new subdivision.

"Spread the fuel. Light the match. Drive away like shit."

"No." Wendall thinking, horrified, *I have limits*.

"It's just wood, *paisan*. Nobody lives here."

"It's arson."

Ritchie smiles when other guys would look angry. He smiles when other guys would look worried. He has as many smile variations as Eskimos have words for snow, and his grin now is broad, friendly, showing very white teeth. "That place is insured up the wazoo. Do you think any of the other things we've been doing for months is legal? I vouched for you."

"I didn't ask you to."

"Yes you did, in every way except saying it. Burn the fucking house."

Ritchie's smile slides around and lifts the left edge of his mouth and softens the blue in his eyes. He shrugs.

"Or don't burn it and we turn around and go home. Nothing will happen to you. I promise."

After Wendall starts the fire, Ritchie has him park a few blocks away until the glow of flames tinges the sky and they hear fire engines. Wendall feels like throwing up.

"Ever burn a log in a fireplace, Wendall? It's the same."

Later, on the Internet, Wendall finds that the site belongs to someone named Bernice Cavanaugh. And Joey mentions that his uncle bragged about Cavanaugh Contractors withdrawing bids on two Board of Ed jobs.

I still can't prove a link. Or find Gabrielle.

In his dream that night Nathan Hale is on fire but Wendall's unable to evacuate his students. He's tied to a chair while his panicked class can't get out. The room gets hot. Flames lick the windows. The kids are screaming about a stairway collapsing, and Ben's in the class, and instead of the fire-drill bell he hears Voort over the intercom, saying, "Manheim for Aguilar" over and over again. Wendall wakes screaming, drenched with sweat.

Next day, he converts half his savings to a money order and mails it anonymously to Bernice Cavanaugh. He needs the other half for weapons, ID, contingencies.

But at least on the site, the recorder in the smoke alarm is working.

Wendall starts wearing a wire when he and Ritchie take their drives after that. He figures they probably won't frisk him again. After all, they're friends.

SIXTEEN

Robert Priest's Riverdale mansion turns out to be a three-story Tudor with a pitched slate roof, granite walls, and embedded beams running diagonally down the front. The center hall blazes with light behind two-story-high windows. Ivy covers flanking wings. Balconies overlook a carriage house and a trio of parked antique collectible cars: a crimson '58 Mercedes, a cobalt '60 T-Bird, a cream-colored '60 Seville, its huge fins like rocket stabilizers gleaming in the light storm.

The whole neighborhood seems to seethe and sizzle like an electric mosquito killer on a summer night. Oaks predate Lincoln. Homes cost two-million-plus. Extensive properties—carved-up former estates—line a maze of quaint, narrow lanes smelling of flowers: It's not exactly the rest of the world's vision of the Bronx.

10:51.

Mickie halts the Caprice before a patrol car blocking Priest's gravel driveway. Another blue-and-white and an empty, unmarked LTD sit empty behind that.

"No ambulances. No tape. He's alive," Voort says.

"This could be the house in Wendall's photos," Mickie says. "But so could a thousand others, I guess."

"Couldn't he just take normal pictures like everyone else?"

"We beat Nye here, Voort. We'll stop him."

Before they reach the front door they're intercepted by a uniformed lieutenant who introduces himself as Antoine Sullivan, and is a lithe, powerful-looking man with fine Somali features. Sullivan says he's been instructed to hand control of the scene to Voort when he arrives.

"I got two of your cousins in my precinct. My captain's your cousin Dieter. My sergeant's your cousin Brett. Captain Voort passed along a message."

"Happy birthday?"

"Word for word, it's: 'Fuck Deans and fuck the mayor. You'll be a cop when they're gone.'"

"Delusion is the family bond," Voort replies.

Sullivan gives a rundown on defensive preparations. The lieutenant and another uniformed officer man the first squad car—serving as guardhouse. Blue Guys from the second car are in the backyard, a heavily wooded area bordering three other properties but at least offering a ten-foot-wide strip of mowed lawn between Priest's private forest and a deck offering access through a sliding glass kitchen door.

"All doors are locked," Sullivan says.

A plainclothes team, also on foot, is making circles through neighbors' yards and across streets, hoping to intersect Wendall if he approaches. All three teams are in contact over secure field radios.

"Priest's wife and twin daughters left just before we got here," Sullivan says. "For the airport."

"Did he mention how long the trip's been planned?" Voort asks with great interest.

"Well, his wife called him while I was with him, asking him to make sure the kids' teachers know they're traveling. I'm guessing the trip came up fast," Sullivan says.

"So you're saying Priest sent them away *before* you told him he might be in danger," Voort asks, impressed with the lieutenant's perceptiveness and knowing that if Cousin Dieter sent him, he's good.

"I had the impression he knew Wendall might be coming before we got here. He's in the house now, upstairs. I've got a man with him, but figured I'd concentrate the rest out here."

Voort smells rain now, and the combustible combination of electricity and humidity. But rain isn't falling yet, and he pivots to survey the area, trying to remember the FBI's tips on securing defensive perimeters that he heard at One Police Plaza a year ago, when the department had feared a car bomb attack during the Szeska case.

He points out a dark line of apartment buildings five blocks away, rectangular hulks looming in lightning flashes.

"Anyone check those roofs?"

"I told you. I kept my guys here."

"Order a search. If they find anyone—even a

woman, fireman, old man in a wheelchair—two IDs. No exceptions. Wendall's been switching appearances all day."

"I'll call the precinct. We're shorthanded here."

"No one enters the house unless you recognize them or they show two IDs. Even brass."

"You think he's dressed like a cop?"

"It's possible. Also, could you move the first squad car? See where the side street hits the property at the T? It's a straight run to the front door from there. Block that direction so he can't build up speed."

Sullivan sucks in his breath. "A car bomb?"

"There's no reason to think he'll come that way. I'm just being safe."

Sullivan rubs his cheek worriedly, looking younger than he had a moment ago. He hands portable radios to Mickie and Voort, then starts to turn away, but Voort calls him back. "I'd appreciate your other impressions of Priest."

Sullivan nods as if he's been thinking about it. "It's funny. He had two guys with him when we got here, guests, he said, but they were edgy and more like . . . from the way they deferred to him my guess would be employees. Heavy guys. Armed maybe. He got rid of them."

"License numbers?"

"There was no reason to get them."

"Names?"

"Joey Priest and Dougie . . . Lopes, I think."

Joey and Dougie were names on Wendall's tapes.

Sullivan frowns, reluctant to continue.

"Go ahead," Voort prompts, sensing more and trusting the man.

"Well, it's just a feeling, but Priest seemed frightened of *us*. He relaxed when I said we were here for his protection. I wondered why he'd thought we'd come at all."

"Three police cars pulling up to anyone's house would rattle most people, don't you think?"

"This was different. People see cops, they get scared it's going to be bad news. He seemed more afraid for himself. He was sweating like a pig even though the AC's on in there at subarctic level."

"One last question. Would you say his reaction was consistent with being unsure if you'd come to protect or arrest him?"

Sullivan grins. "I understand Nye's been making tapes of payoffs in the construction industry. At least that's what I heard."

Voort thanks Sullivan, who turns away to revise his preparations.

Voort thinking, *How will Wendall hit this place?* And also, *What am I still missing?*

"Let's meet Priest," he tells Mickie. "I always wanted to protect a scumbag who looted two billion from the city. It's been my life's ambition."

"What about guilty until proven innocent," Mickie says, wagging a finger. "And his share might only be only a few million. Besides, if we save his ass they won't fire you."

Voort says, "Sweating like a pig, huh? Do pigs really sweat?"

* * *

From Voort's years on the force he knows that evil—when it comes—can appear in mundane shapes and sizes: a nine-year-old school girl; a cripple in a wheelchair; a miniature collie wagging its tail in the instant before its mood turns bad.

But the man unwinding from the leather chair as Voort and Mickie enter his study is still a surprise in his blandness, considering Camilla's description.

The body is tubby, the face forgettable, the hair thickly combed back with gel, the eyes two black raisins set in dough. Priest's the fat kid from fifth grade who grew up and made money and stayed the fat kid. No wonder he needs the AC so high. The fleshy neck sprouts from the sweat-moist collar. The white button-down, open-collared dress shirt is Barneys. The slacks are Yves St. Laurent, as are the black suspenders. The watch is a Rolex. The whole package is prosperous and out-of-shape and Voort sees a mass of half-rolled, weighted-down blueprints on the big desk in front of drawn curtains. The man's been working, or trying to, holed up in his study/bunker while cop guards circle outside.

Voort spots a small table to the side with a white cardboard model development displayed on top.

"Tell me you got him," the builder starts off in a low, hard growl that instantly makes the fat-boy impression vanish. "Tell me my taxes went for something better than paying police to goof off while a psycho runs loose?"

The anger doesn't bother Voort. Angry people

make mistakes, and anyway, men handle fear in different ways. Some go quiet. Some make jokes. Anger is as good a response as anything else.

"I understand your frustration," he says.

"I bet you do." The builder's tone tells Voort that Priest's been following Voort's problems on the news.

The room is big, and like many people who occupy Tudors, Priest's gone Olde English in decorating the place. There is a suit of armor on the stairway and foxhunt scenes in the hall. The desk is thick oak with fat legs. A DeCourt wall tapestry shows a medieval battle. Priest can plot real-estate strategies while Saxons hack at Normans overhead.

"Sir, we're doing everything we can to arrest this man," Voort tells the developer. "In fact, there's a good possibility that he has no plan to come here at all."

"You don't seem to have eliminated *any* possibility. You don't seem to know much."

"Yes sir, we've had less than a day to put this together, but my chief told me to answer any questions," Voort says agreeably, knowing that a frightened man's queries often reveal more than his answers.

His eyes flicker again to the table model vision of Priest's contribution to urban progress. Plastic trees bloom atop the cardboard tower. Plastic runners circle a track on an extension deck nearer the street. Plastic cabs line up as plastic doormen smile at plastic residents. Folks who live in cardboard towers are rich enough to avoid taking subways home.

"Questions?" Priest says. "With forty thousand cops on duty how come William Nye runs around all day free?"

"His name is Wendall."

"William. Wendall. Whatever."

Voort now notices the crystal tumbler filled with ice and amber-colored liquor beside the blueprints. *I bet you can tell me things about Wendall that I don't have a clue about. How can I use the booze to get you to do that?*

He remains polite. "Nye's been planning this day for a while, Mister Priest, and probably staying out of sight between attacks."

"Well, I don't understand how you even decided I'm a target. Aiden Pryce? That just came over the news. It's tragic. Awful. He worked for me."

Not that you seem curious about what happened.

Priest takes a drink. "But the travel agent? The statistician? What links me with *them*? I never met them. I don't even *make* my travel arrangements. My secretary does that."

Voort feels as if he's tuned into the longest running song in the city's crime history. Cops call it "Never." When he was a child, his uncles used to make up words to "Never" using old Broadway tunes, and get the whole family howling.

> *Never robbed that bar.*
> *Never saw that knife.*
> *Never stole Joe's car.*
> *Never hit my wife . . .*

Priest says, "Explain how you decided this teacher has a grudge against me."

11:21, and the stake-out radio crackles to life.

"I got a white Nova on Beauchat."

All three men in the room pause.

"False alarm. He's turning," the radio says.

Priest shakily finishes his drink as Voort sees that the ice cubes haven't melted. The man's drinking fast. *Does he always do that?*

Priest growls, "I never worked on any Brooklyn school. If a railing collapsed, what do I have to do with it? And what's this crap about an investigation *he* made?"

"Actually, we exaggerated," Voort lies. "That announcement was for Nye's benefit. We stretched the truth to get him to come in."

Priest, who was rising with the empty glass, probably for a refill, stops.

Voort nods. "We never found anything solid. He left tapes, but they're just him accusing people. You. Other contractors. Hell, the president even. We've got guards on at least ten other people, not just you. Nye read the Board of Ed plan and just picked out names and accuses everybody."

Mickie adds, "He *says* his tapes are evidence, but they're not. It's like talking a nut off a roof. You say anything to move him back from the edge."

"Guards on ten other people?" Priest says hopefully.

"There's no proof. No links."

And actually, come to think of it, I've heard noth-

ing solid against Priest on those tapes, Voort realizes. *It's part of what's bothering me.*

Sullivan's voice on the radio says, "I got a yellow cab on Beauchat Avenue, slowing . . ."

They all pause again.

"It's speeding away."

Priest says, shakily, but friendlier, "You guys want a drink?"

"Yeah, but I'd be fired," Mickie says.

Voort holds a hand up to refuse. "Maybe after. Sir, what we've reconstructed is, someone beat up Nye six years ago and possibly caused brain damage."

"Those x-rays were bad," Mickie says, shaking his head.

"I don't know if we'll ever find out who did it," Voort says. "For all we know, maybe it *did* have something to do with schools, but his tapes are pathetic."

Priest pours himself more Johnny Walker at a side bar. "Hmmm. I almost feel sorry for him."

"Well, I don't," Voort snaps. "He's killed three people. I promise you, he shows up here and he's dead."

"Thank you, detectives. I shouldn't have barked at you before."

Voort waves it away.

"Hey, if I were you I'd be pissed off too," Mickie says somberly. "We're here for you."

And now it's time to go for it, Voort thinks as Priest slurps down another two fingers worth of Johnny Walker Black.

"Doctor Oslo asked us to assure you, sir, that nothing that has happened will affect your deal. He said to tell you, nothing's going to change."

Priest lowers the glass slowly.

Voort says, "Doctor Oslo said he's not going to let some nut wreck . . . his exact words were, 'a win-win situation.'"

"He said that?" Priest says. His eyes are quite focused now.

"Millions of dollars saved. Jobs saved," Mickie says, repeating words they'd heard from the chancellor. Voort hoping, maybe Priest is drunk or scared enough for this to work. And if it *does* work, that it will be relevant.

11:29.

Voort says, "I don't think Doctor Oslo would have told us normally, but . . ."

Mickie picks it up. "We were looking over reports and we saw part of the new stuff."

Voort says, "So Doctor Oslo explained the rest, but made it clear how much this means to the city. We didn't tell that reporter from Fox TV a thing when he asked."

Which is a mistake, apparently.

Because Priest starts to laugh.

"Which one of you is Billy Crystal?" he says. "Which one's that Jim Carey guy?"

"Excuse me?"

Priest is grinning, though. "What do you think? I have two drinks and fall for bullshit?"

"It never hurts to try," Voort says, controlling his disappointment and smiling back. At least Priest isn't angry, so Voort rolls with the mood.

"*You guys are checking me out?*" Priest says, shaking his head. "It's hilarious. I'm the one he's after and you check *me* out!" But he seems strong now, and the mix of confidence and fear before is puzzling, unless he's got a mood-swing problem.

Or is he confident as long as he's not in physical danger? He started calming down when I told him we were guarding ten other people too, that we weren't sure he's a target.

"Look," Priest explains, "I've built things for the defense department, Lockheed, the housing department. But on a day-to-day basis, for sheer paranoia, nobody beats a school board. Joe Blow gets on a school board and he turns into Machiavelli. You know who Machiavelli was?"

"Third baseman for the Cubs?" Mickie says.

"*Hahahaha!* Look, I have no problem talking about the deal. The chancellor's the paranoid one, not me. It's just a question of how to announce it. He's always afraid publicity will screw things up. I say, let it out."

"It's that model, isn't it?" Voort says, following Priest's glance and suddenly recognizing other structures on the board. He'd missed them before because the big tower had distracted him. But he knows the block. He sees the old Jefferson Market library and the stores lining Sixth Avenue. Balducci's market. The new Tower Records. It's his own neighborhood.

"It'll revolutionize education," Priest says proudly, following Voort's glance.

"What is it?" Mickie says.

And Voort, going to the model, awed by what he is seeing, resting his hand on top of the tower, says, "It's a school."

"Wh—aaaaat? Thirty stories high?"

From the radio comes a crackling noise, and Sullivan's voice, "The yellow cab is back."

Priest freezes. The transformation is stunning.

Sullivan says, "It's slowing. It's going past. Hell, the driver's in a turban. He's Indian. He's gone."

Another piece falls into place for Voort.

Priest isn't scared of being arrested. He's scared of pain. He's a physical coward.

Priest lets out his breath, regains composure, and turns his attention back to the model. "Imagine walking around the city. What do you see? Highrises. Offices. *Space* is gold in Manhattan. Space! In Los Angeles it's water. In the Big Apple, space. Now imagine turning a corner and you see a school, and how many stories is *that* usually?"

"Two," Voort says, seeing the brilliance of the scheme. "Three tops. You negotiated air rights with the Board of Ed. That's it, isn't it, sir? You bought the right to build on *top* of schools."

"Bought it? We *gave* away work on the low floors as long as we get everything on top. It won't cost the board anything, hardly. It'll free up money for all sorts of things."

"How many schools are you doing this with?" Mickie asks.

"Two to start. If it works, there's like three hundred schools in the city, plenty of them sitting on prime real estate. Using wasted space, gentlemen, is the solution to solving this terrible budget crunch."

"You'll make millions," Voort says, as the lights dim and the air-conditioning falters, but starts up again.

Voort hears the patter of rain hitting the roof. The storm's finally broken.

Hell, maybe we did scare Wendall off.

But he doesn't really believe that will turn out to be the case.

"The board'll *save* millions," Priest says. "So why shouldn't I make money too? I get zoning. I get tax breaks. They get a new building. For years the board was wary of private involvement. Now they're going broke. They need help, big time. Well, there's a hundred kinds of private assistance out there. Win-win all around."

First you rob them blind and then you get control of the wreckage. Is this what sent Wendall over the edge?

Then the radio pulls his attention from the model as Sullivan's voice cries, *"It's the cab again. This is it! This is it!"*

"He was waiting for the rain," Mickie says.

"Stay here," Voort orders Priest, which is unnecessary as he's not the type to run toward danger.

Priest looks around wildly.

Voort and Mickie rush for the door.

What's the old line? When the world ends, it won't happen with a bang but a whimper? When the big ending comes, it will be the smallest, softest sigh. A slow last breath. A bit of vapor dissipating into air.

Sullivan's got the driver on the ground face down when the detectives reach the front lawn. The rain is a torrent. Voort can barely see fifteen feet ahead. The thunder is earsplitting and the cab's a yellow blur, its door open, its bumpers hemmed in between a squad car and the Caprice. Two more Blue Guys bend over the figure on the ground, holding him steady while their boss snaps on cuffs.

Closing on the "Indian" driver with the turban, Voort sees a paper bag on the lawn beside him that wasn't there before. There's clearly something in it, and Voort is thinking, *What's in that bag?*

Then Sullivan turns the man over and Voort thinks, *This is all wrong* before he even sees the face, before the head swings around and he sees terrified eyes and dark skin and long flowing hair, the beard going mushy from rain as the turban slides off.

"It's not Wendall."

Sullivan saying, "Huh?" and the driver saying, "Please, sirs. He said to deliver the bag."

"Who?" demands Sullivan as if they don't know.

"The Jewish man."

"Where was he?"

"On Riverdale Avenue. I was at the 7-Eleven," the man babbles, shaking with terror and staring at the armed Blue Guys who seem almost as frightened as he.

Voort orders them, "Put those guns away."

Some awareness in him building now . . . growing.

The driver shivers as rain presses his silk shirt to his body and blasts the trees and the earth seems to reverberate.

"The Jewish man said there was a study meeting. He said to bring this food at eleven-forty exactly. He said there would be another big tip. Twenty dollars."

"Food?" says Mickie, looking down as if becoming aware of the bag for the first time.

Sullivan's eyes widen. "Move back! Everybody! Fast!"

And things are speeding up, the cops are retreating and Voort doesn't move, he just stares at the bag and he knows Sullivan's warning is wrong because *Wendall would have known if cops were here the package would never reach Priest inside the house.*

Mickie asks as he reaches for the bag, "If we're all on the front lawn who's guarding the back?"

Someone yells, "The back!" as Sullivan runs for it, shouting, 'One of you get inside!'" The great defensive perimeter has shattered in a second. Cops head in all directions. Mickie runs into the street—the unguarded route—to see if anyone is coming. The Indian guy is crying for help. "These handcuffs hurt me, sir!"

And Voort upends the bag—still trying to figure this out—and of course only sandwiches fall out. Warm sandwiches wrapped in cellophane, and Cokes and napkins and then something smaller too.

Something two inches long lies on the grass. Something plastic, rectangular.

Another tape?

But why send a tape, unless . . .

Voort sees the answer then, finally, shoving the tape in his pocket.

He's not in back either.

Mickie's in the street and Sullivan is gone and the cops have disappeared. Voort is alone with the driver who keeps saying, "These handcuffs hurt very much, sir. Very, very much."

Normally, revelation is one of the best moments of an investigation. All threads link together. Things that made no sense an hour ago line up to form trains of logic and become so clear that you wonder why you never saw them before.

With each tape you told us more, Wendall. And you want us to listen to this one now, don't you, because if we do we waste the last minutes while you finish up.

Voort runs for Mickie, who's looking wildly up and down the street in case the attack comes from either direction. He's brave to stand in plain sight but, Voort is suddenly certain, utterly useless at stopping what is about to occur.

"The keys," Voort gasps. "The car keys."

"You're *leaving?*"

"He's not coming."

"Are you out of your mind?"

"He was *never* coming here," Voort shouts over the rain.

"What are you talking about? The cabbie spoke to him. He could be in the damn house already."

Voort grabs his partner, reaches for Mickie's

pocket as Mickie says, "Okay, okay," and hands over the keys.

Voort runs for the Caprice, except the cab and a squad car have wedged it in. A whole damn street to park on and the cars sit bumper to bumper because their drivers are conditioned—New York style—to distrust easy places to park. There's not even enough room to build up speed and push the taxi or squad car out of the way.

The radio at Voort's belt squawks out Sullivan's voice. "Back doors locked!"

"You leave here and you're through," Mickie says, behind him. "You heard what Sullivan said. Even Priest knows he's coming."

The taxi key is not in the ignition. The squad car key is certainly not there so Voort has to go back to the taxi driver, has to try to calm the soaked, panicked man—telling him someone will *get* the cuffs off eventually—so the driver lets Voort pat down his pockets for his keys.

"They are not in my pocket? They must have fallen on the grass when that man knocked me down."

The Blue Guy in the house reports over the radio, "I'm with Priest. He's fine."

Voort drops to his knees on the lawn.

He tries to explain to Mickie as he crawls in the mud, frantically looking for keys, "He's quiet. Dedicated. Students loved him. He's Jimmy Stewart in *It's a Wonderful Life*."

"Don't do this, Con Man."

"A hero worshiper. He wants to do right," Voort says sifting through grass. "Those biographies on his shelves. *He still reads them.* Serpico went to the *Times* and got the Knapp Commission established . . ."

The driver, understanding the urgency if not the situation, is scanning the ground too.

Voort says, "Thomas Nast's cartoons raised a stink and helped bring Tammany Hall down. Wendall's heroes roused public opinion."

"By killing people?" But at least Mickie's starting to look.

"Come with me, Mick. I need help. Wendall left the last note after he knew we'd found the Riverdale file. You know why he was glad we found it? *He wanted us here because he had no intention of coming. He has a different job in mind for us.*"

"You figured him out in ten hours, huh? I'm not going with you because you're wrong. I'd do anything for you, Voort, but you're just not right this time."

"There! Keys! Oh, it's aluminum foil," says the cabbie.

"Camilla said it," Voort insists. "*No one gets proof against Priest.* We *assumed* Nye had proof, but we never heard it. Those tapes are low-level. A hundred bucks. A bribe."

"Voort, who cares if he got proof or not?"

"He does. That's the point. *He does.*"

Voort gropes in a puddle. "If he had real proof, all he had to do was go to the papers, but he never got it. He needs help to finish what he started. The tapes, the murders, it's all to blow the thing open. In the end he needs the rest of the city to drag the whole mess down."

"There! Keys!" the driver says triumphantly.

Voort reaches for them. "Don't you see? No matter how much he hates Priest, how much he *thinks* the guy's guilty, he won't actually hurt someone unless he has proof."

"You don't know that."

Voort stands as Mickie blocks him, pleads with him. "You're throwing it away, Con Man. Even Aziz and Eva will back off. You'll never get your job back. Stay here. Protect Priest. You'll have a chance."

Voort shoves the keys into Mickie's cold hands. "It's my call and my risk so just move the fucking taxi. And it's not me he's after. He knows I made a mistake."

"Who is it then, genius?"

Voort's soaked and cold and there's no more time to argue. There may not be time anyway, he thinks, grabbing for the keys back, but then Mickie says, "All right, goddamnit. I'll move it."

"Thank you."

In the Caprice, the dashboard clock reads 11:46. Voort hits the accelerator and drives off alone.

SEVENTEEN

Lots of people are frightened tonight.

Dr. Arthur Birnbaum, for instance, principal of Nathan Hale High, is too scared to leave his apartment.

This has been the worst day of my life, he's thinking. Worse than when the stairs collapsed. Worse than when I had to speak at the funeral. And it started when those detectives showed up at the school.

Eleven-forty-five now, and Fox TV's following the Wendall Nye countdown at his back as Birnbaum stares down sixteen stories from his living room to rain-washed Riverside Drive. He's praying to the god of self-preservation—the god who watches over fools like him—to save his marriage, job, life.

Birnbaum sends his terrified will out like a mantra. *Don't be after me. Be after someone else.*

From a back bedroom of his six-room apartment, his wife's voice calls to him, "Artie, are you going to walk Doodles or not?"

In response, Birnbaum hears a soft whimpering from the floor and glances down to see his ten-year-old bulldog staring up at him, head cocked. Doodles always goes out at eleven. Doodles has been going out at eleven for a decade, which makes the dog's nightly habit, in canine years, the equivalent of seventy years old. Doddering but well-trained, Doodles is clearly in bodily torment, shivering and shaking and not understanding why his master isn't grabbing the Extendo-Leash and a plastic bag and crying jauntily, "Okay, sports fans," the signal that another bladder-emptying, bowel-clearing jaunt in Riverside Park is about to begin.

"Honey?" Amy warns. "He'll go on the rug!"

In the kitchen, the phone starts to ring, jerking Birnbaum's head in that direction.

Be a wrong number. Be a solicitation. Don't be who I think you are, he prays.

The ringing stops.

And from the TV, Fox News's hot young announcer, Lou Mostazzio, says with his customary thousand-watt smile, "The big question is—who is number four, and will the police stop this crazed teacher before he kills again?"

Coanchor Sheila Chang nods with practiced worry. "Our Fox team will stay on this story until it wraps up."

I didn't know what I was getting into, Arthur Birnbaum thinks, as if that excuses anything he's done, which he knows it does not.

"Honey, if you don't take him, I will," says Amy

Birnbaum, padding barefoot into the room in her nightgown and purple robe. "What's the matter with you? You look sick."

"I think it was the tuna casserole."

"Poor thing! I'll take Doodles."

"No!" He'd never forgive himself if Wendall showed up and harmed his beloved Amy. That would compound his mistakes beyond redemption, Birnbaum miserably knows.

Woof!

All his demons seem to be gathering tonight, as if they've been waiting while he's accumulated debts and tipped a balance, and now they will roar howling out of the storm outside or even from the again-ringing phone.

"It's a call for you," says Amy, from the kitchen. "Some man."

"Hello?" But Birnbaum knows damn well who it is. At least Amy's wandered out of earshot to the window, to watch the lightning and rain.

He winces as a familiar voice demands, *"Paisan,* are you going to walk that fucking dog or not?"

"I thought I'd wait until after the news."

"You mean you'd hide and hope he shows up somewhere else. You want me to talk to Amy?"

"No! We went through that."

"Then amigo, get your ass *aqui* now!"

"I'll be right down," Birnbaum whispers, his compliance soothing the cursed voice enough to soften it. First you use the stick on Arthur Birnbaum. Then you offer sweets.

"Arthur, I told you. We're here. We're watching. If he comes, you're protected. Believe me, this isn't the only place he might show up. Odds are you'll walk the dog. Nothing'll happen. You'll go to sleep."

"I don't see you down there."

The voice sounds amused. "What do you want, I should stand in the middle of Riverside Drive with a sign saying 'Here I am, Wendall'?"

Click.

Birnbaum feels the blood flow out of his knees, vaporize through his pores, evacuate human muscles, and leave them as flimsy as glass, to shatter if he moves.

As he sets the phone into its cradle Amy comes up behind him. She hugs him. She's so close he can smell her Aphrodesia, still enticing to him after seventeen years.

"Who was that, at this hour?"

"That new math teacher," Birnbaum lies.

The AC is on and the lights have faded to a brownout yellow, and in the urban glow outside rain falls straight and hard and air currents rattle Birnbaum's windows.

Birnbaum looks down at the little dog, who is in agony.

He hears himself say, "Okay, sports fans." The tail stump jerks and Doodles's right ear, the one that still moves, lifts a half inch.

Birnbaum praying to God as he forces himself to put on his summer-weight rain slicker, *Please help me. If you do, I promise to really stop this time.*

Woof!

Birnbaum takes the umbrella from the foyer closet, scarcely believing that he's actually going outside. But man and dog waddle into the hallway and watch the arcing elevator needle rise toward 16, the floor on which Birnbaum's lived off and on since he was a boy. He inherited the place from his dad. He's walked dogs in Riverside Park during the crime years and the safe years. There was Nutsie the Labrador. Corkie the Jack Russell.

"Don't rush him, honey. Let him finish," Amy calls from down the hall, as the elevator arrives.

Amy—despite the fear he feels—even now looks good to him, still sexy at forty-three, so much that guys still watch her when she shops at Fairway, guys even try to pick her up when she goes with her friends to Mozart at Lincoln Center. But Amy is loyal and loving and a good mom to their son, who's off at Choate.

Still, nobody is perfect, even Amy. And Amy's most glaring imperfection where Birnbaum is concerned is her hatred of sex.

Which is what got me into trouble, he thinks as the elevator doors open like some gateway to hell, which come to think of it is the direction in which the claustrophobic box is taking him. Doodles whimpers like a sinner facing judgment. That sinner is me, Birnbaum thinks.

Sex. Amy *used* to like it, *love* it even. Tiny little Amy, when they first dated, had seemed joyously insatiable to Arthur. Let's do it in the park, she'd say.

Let's do it with the curtains open. Let's do it in the backseat of the rental car. Arthur, are you actually going to sleep? It's only 2 A.M. Wake up!

Amy had seemed to exist as a pure manifestation of passion. Amy had been the embodiment of every sexy magazine picture, movie actress . . . hell, even naked mannequins in the East Village Pleasure Shoppe windows.

Ah. the wonder years!

But then, after twenty-four electrifying months of marriage, after Griffin was born, the eagerness had started to dissipate. Nightly sex had shrunk to four times a week, which was still great, actually, and then three, which he knew because he counted, and anyway, three was still pretty good. Even two was adequate.

One was subadequate, but bearable.

And now they were down to once every . . . when *was* the last time she'd wanted to have sex anyway?

Christ, it was three months ago!

"This happens to every couple," she'd said when he complained about it. "Every couple slows down. It becomes like a routine. It gets as interesting as Velveeta. By the way, are you going bald on top?"

Now the elevator door opens and Doodles strains to pull Birnbaum outside. He can hear the rain echoing in the marble lobby.

Woof!

Noel the doorman peeks his head into the lobby from the front foyer. "I wondered where you and Mister Doodles were."

Where was I? Hiding upstairs and following every second of TV coverage. Praying that this awful day would play itself out while I escaped and the cops never figured out the mistake I made when I talked to them before.

Noel says, "Whooeeeee, Doctor Birnbaum! It's raining like back in the Dominican Republic!"

As he steps outside, an odd memory comes to him. When he'd been an English teacher, before becoming an administrator, he'd used to teach film to advanced placement classes, and one of his favorite classics had been the old comedy *Pat and Mike*. Pat had been a woman tennis player, talented and confident, but whenever her boyfriend had shown up at a match, her composure had gone to pieces. The camera had reflected this by making tennis balls look enormous, the net seem miles away, the racquet to become itty-bitty, even the people in the stands seem as if they were laughing at her.

Just the way, as Birnbaum passes out of the safety of the building, Noel the doorman seems to shrink behind him into a speck on the rainy horizon.

Woof!

Doodles strains to get across the street to the park periphery, but Birnbaum thinks, I have my limits. I'll stay on this side, near buildings. I don't see any "protectors" out here.

Sex.

He's remembering how sex or the lack of it had gotten him in trouble. One night, after work in Brooklyn, after a long day when his ignored dick had grown hard any time a cafeteria attendant or semiattractive teacher had gone by, Arthur had driven to the Rookie Lounge under the Prospect Expressway, ordered a nine-dollar Budweiser, and gaped with pulse-quickening excitement at the strippers gyrating a few feet away.

Harmless entertainment. A way to relieve pressure. A week later, he'd come back.

"We're *not* going to the park, Doodles. Do it here, okay? One time you don't have to go to the park."

11:52.

Cut to six years ago and *principal* Arthur Birnbaum—the respected educator, revered administrator, canny budgeter of resources and adviser to the Board of Ed, not to mention a regular wise-old-Moses when it comes to resolving faculty disputes—*that* Arthur Birnbaum has turned into the slinking Mr. Hyde strip-bar addict when night falls.

Which is how he meets Ritchie, who knows of better clubs, especially one up in the Bronx.

Woof!

And Ritchie tells him, "Why look when you can touch?"

"I'm married."

"Changing subjects?"

"I would never cheat on my wife."

"Cheating? Why is it cheating if the wife won't do it? Why are *you* cheating if she screws like a rabbit *before* you slide on the ring and stops after that? I hear this all the time. I'll tell ya' who's cheating. She is."

"You are handsome. You are strong. I can't get

enough of you," says the woman Ritchie introduces him to, who has an apartment two blocks from the Diamond Club.

"Actually, there's a favor you can do for me too," Ritchie tells him a couple of guilt-ridden but gloriously illicit weeks after that.

"What do you need, cash?"

"More like a professional favor."

"Let me guess. You have a relative in my school, and the kid's having grade trouble."

The two of them in the Diamond Club and a very nice little black girl on Arthur's lap, doing things to him with her butt that make him feel seventeen years old again.

"Well Artie, it's a small thing, actually. In fact it isn't you should *do* something, but that you shouldn't."

Arthur still paying only half attention as the ax slowly begins to fall.

Ritchie saying, "You know that report you told me about? The construction thing?"

"I didn't tell you about a report."

"You mentioned it," Ritchie nods with certainty. "Y'know, the report about whether they're going to delay work on your school or not."

Birnbaum, no idiot in nonsexual matters, starts to feel uncomfortable. His dick's shrinking to soft proportions and sweat trickles down the lower part of his spine.

Ritchie says, "You know the part where you're supposed to let them know if you have problems with the recommendations? Protest if the school *desperately* needs the work they're rescheduling, which we both know it doesn't?"

"But it does."

"Since when are you an expert, Artie? Go along with what you read in the report. Don't protest. Send it back. The work's all done. Don't make waves."

Arthur, stunned, feels his head reeling.

"I won't do it," says Arthur, pushing the black girl off his lap.

Which is when Ritchie pulls out pictures, *pictures*, for God's sake, out of some sordid grade C movie.

Birnbaum feeling like throwing up. "Tell Amy. I don't care."

"Hey, if you don't mind, I don't."

But Birnbaum does mind, of course, and not just because of Amy, but because it would turn him into the laughingstock that he secretly knows he is.

"Why me?" he asks in surrender.

"We checked out eight or nine principals, actually, at different schools where work'll stop. You're the pervert, *paisan*."

"Why those schools?"

"I just do what people tell me."

But Birnbaum figures out the answer later. It doesn't take a genius to do this kind of math.

Delaying work on Nathan Hale frees ten million minimum to go somewhere else.

And now it is 11:52 and the steaming rain is falling, and as any resident of Manhattan will tell you, weather is more severe on the island's western or landfall side. Birnbaum lets Doodles drift away from the doorway, toward the corner. It's the only way to get the dog to relieve himself.

He also recalls painfully the mistake he made this afternoon with Voort.

I never even mentioned the stairway collapsing. I went on and on about Wendall, how I worried about him, yet I stayed away from the stairway. I was too nervous to talk about it, afraid I'd look as guilty as I feel.

Doodles finally doing the long awaited deed.

"Rrrrrrrr."

Doodles stares into the rain and Birnbaum sees someone hobbling toward him up the dark, quiet next block. In his reverie he's let the dog inch him to the corner. No other people are out here other than the approaching figure.

Unable to move, locked in place, Birnbaum stares as the apparition of pain shuffles toward him, dragging a foot. The man—it's too bulky to be a woman—seems to be in agony. He clutches his side. He leans against a pole.

It's just some old Hasid. Lots of them live on the Upper West Side. Except why doesn't he have an umbrella?

Then Birnbaum catches sight of two other figures—men also—quickly crossing the street from the park side, approaching the Hasid, stopping him, gripping his arms as they talk to him in low tones. Neither of the men carry umbrellas either.

Then the two men from the park seem to push

and drag the hurt Hasid back across the street. The injured man seems to be resisting.

I don't want to know what's happening. I don't want to watch.

"Move it, sports fans," he tells Doodles, turning toward home, feeling his heart pounding, yanking the leash. When he gets back inside he never looks back. He walks Doodles to the elevator. He feels steaming rain falling off his slicker onto the marble floor.

It wasn't him. Those men probably know each other, he tells himself, wiping Doodles off once they're upstairs in his front hall. But his breath has caught in his throat.

The TV is off now in his apartment. Amy's in their bedroom, thumbing through this week's *New York* magazine, and its lead article: "Cheap Eats for the Recession."

"Where's that cute little tushie of yours?" Birnbaum says, sliding under the covers and needing sex badly, or at least physical contact. "I want your cute little tushie."

"I have my period," Amy says. "Read a book."

At seventy miles an hour, a Chevy Caprice with police lights flashing can make the run to Seventy-ninth Street from Riverdale in less than eight minutes. Slowed by floods in the left lane below 157th Street, Voort reaches the exit at 11:56.

He's finally got Santini on the cellphone, as he steers with his free hand.

Voort saying, "Birnbaum never even *mentioned* the stairway collapse, and Oslo said that jobs weren't eliminated without three-way okays."

"Are you telling me," Santini says angrily, "that you're *not* at Priest's house?"

"Birnbaum goes on and on about how much sympathy he has for Wendall. The stairway killed that kid and he doesn't even mention it? That principal signed off on the work."

"You left your post because of that?"

"All of it! The tapes. The clues. Principals were *on* those tapes and Nye's killings directly relate to the stairway. Even if I'm wrong, someone should be there!"

"I gotta go. We think they spotted Wendall near Dzenky's house in Queens!"

Click.

You're finished on the job, Santini's tone had said. *You left your post. Nobody will help you now.*

Voort skids around the rain-slick exit and splashes onto Riverside Drive, past fancy prewar apartment buildings on the right side and the park on the left. It's in bloom, its forest of oaks and elms blocking any view of the river even without the cyclone-force rainstorm. There's a stone-wall boundary running along Riverside, from where winding paths meander down steps from entrances spaced every block or two. Voort's strolled the park scores of times when he dated girls in this neighborhood. He held their hands and walked past playgrounds, basketball courts, dog runs, benches.

His siren is screaming now.

If you're here, Wendall, give up and run.

The rain is Jurassic. The Caprice sends up spray as it barrels beneath a blinking light and halts in front of a purple awning reading 112 RIVERSIDE. The entrance is on Eighty-third actually, but a Riverside Drive address is more prestigious. A small, black doorman in a summer-weight uniform watches from under the awning as a sopping Conrad Voort gets out.

"Arthur Birnbaum! What apartment?"

"He is in 16C, sir."

Voort holds the badge. "Don't call him."

"He just went up with the dog."

Voort halts, realizing this means the principal is safe at the moment. Jerking his hand at the storm, he says, "You mean he was out there a minute ago?"

Voort thinking, Riverside Drive is the perfect spot for an ambush, so if it didn't happen there maybe Mickie was right. Maybe I've come to the wrong place.

"Rain or snow, Mister Doodles goes out for his walk."

"Mister who? Oh, the dog. Birnbaum went up alone?"

"Except for the pup."

"Is there another way up to his apartment besides the elevator?"

The doorman seems puzzled at the question, but answers anyway, unflinchingly polite. "The basement is locked and you couldn't get upstairs from there anyway without a key to the service elevator. If I don't see you, you don't get up."

Voort feels throbbing pain coming into his head now, and he sees that he is ending this day the way he started it, by the learning of a massive miscalculation.

I came here because I panicked. I was wrong.

Oh, he'll go up and question Birnbaum. There's nothing else to do. But as he starts past the doorman another thought comes to him and he asks, "Did Doctor Birnbaum take Doodles into the park tonight?"

"Usually he does, but tonight he stayed by the corner. This rain! Only those crazy men went to the park."

"Crazy men?"

"The Jewish gentleman and the other two. I watched because I thought it was Mister Levy, from 8F, at first. He's Orthodox and he comes home late and I thought he was coming up to Doctor Birnbaum. But then he fell and his friends picked him up, and they all walked off."

The doorman shakes his head. "No umbrellas. No raincoats. Going through that entrance over there, down into the park. Why would anyone do that in this storm?"

Voort yells thank you over his shoulder.

Voort runs for the park.

EIGHTEEN

Midnight.

Voort's birthday is over.

In Central Park, the Delacorte clock chimes as its rotating statues, Alice-in-Wonderland and the Mad Hatter, glide forward in their endless circle. At Times Square, the subway platforms are half-filled with party-goers and workaholic commuters going home. SoHo bars are full. Kennedy Airport's runways are lined with jets awaiting takeoff for overnight flights to Europe. The Mets game is delayed in its tied eighteenth inning, and the DiamondVision screen in center field broadcasts local news to riveted viewers. The city awaits news of Wendall.

Who is, at the moment, barely alive.

Pain brings him back to consciousness, makes him wish for a return to darkness and peace. His nerve endings are on fire. His spine is a solid mass of agony. Alternating waves of heat and cold have his leg spasming. Something hard and cold presses against his cheek.

I'm in a public bathroom, on the floor.

The conversation above him seems close, then far away. He gathers that the men there have been ordered to abduct him if possible, kill him if not. They'd sat outside Birnbaum's apartment so long that police patrols had noticed their car, so they'd parked it four blocks away and returned on foot in the rain.

"I hate parking on the Upper West Side," one voice says.

"Like we're gonna drag him around the neighborhood so everyone can watch," says voice number two.

It's Ritchie, Wendall thinks through the pain.

"He's awake."

Razor-bright light drives into his eyes off the shiny urinals and sink. *The bullet must have shifted when I hit that pothole.* All he knows is, he never thought he could experience pain worse than six years ago, but the meter is blowing off the charts now.

Two sets of shoes move close to his face.

Ritchie tells him, kneeling down. "We figured you were SSI when we found the smoke alarm. Then we figured cops. We never figured it was just you. A teacher."

Two faces up there, expanding and contracting. Ritchie's partner is a man Wendall's seen over the months, going in or out of different construction trailers on different sites. He works for Blue Knight, according to the tapes. He's a bland-looking man with a round face and a soft body, and through the pain Wendall recalls that he's the one who first mentioned Dr. Birnbaum by name on the tapes, while running down a small list of principals and Board of Ed staff they'd bribed, blackmailed, or threatened.

"I remember when you installed that fucking alarm," Ritchie says in a voice so soft that, considering his rage, it can only come from supreme self-control. As if a possible answer exists that might save everyone in this room from the storm Wendall has unleashed.

Ritchie whispers, "Months of tapes. Where are the tapes, Wendall?"

"Newspapers," Wendall gasps, the air like razors against his trachea. There's no point in lying. He feels as if there is a hole in his side and oxygen flows right out. "And . . . TV."

"But you made copies, right?" Ritchie's voice is part rage, part hope, part prayer. Copies could help a defense lawyer, or cause appropriate people to disappear before the police come for them.

But the police have the other copies now, and anyway, no sound comes out of Wendall. Smiling Ritchie isn't smiling anymore. His handsome features have compressed and shrunk so his eyes seem closer and his mouth is a ball, a ballistic little "O" the diameter of a bullet. The black in his pupils seems to have spilled into the irises. His whole body seems poised to explode. The slightest increase in decibel level, hint of a false answer, or simple relaxation of restraint will release his attack.

"Where else, Wendall? Where else did you put mikes?"

"My car."

Ritchie can't help it. He hits Wendall in the face so hard that his neck snaps back, and the pain drives down into his spine and up from the wound at the same time. His synapses can't handle it. The agony is so extreme that he imagines it can disintegrate mortar and brick and explode lightbulbs and lift the roof.

"I'm taking a piss," the bland guy tells Ritchie.

Ritchie is almost crying with rage. He knows he's not supposed to hurt Wendall yet, but he can't help it. "I brought you *in*," he cries. "I was your friend. They're blaming me. Me!"

"Kill me," Wendall says.

"Yeah."

"Now," Wendall begs.

"After you answer, you piece of shit."

It's just like six years ago, like no time at all ever passed between beatings. Ritchie's next blow lands in his abdomen, near the wound. His scream echoes off the bathroom fixtures and walls. Sound becomes liquid and flows and sprays like disassembled molecules to wash on the floor.

"What do you have on Robert Priest?"

"Nothing."

"Don't lie, Wendall." Ritchie's face seems broken up now, a jumbled mosaic of pieces like a Cubist painting.

"I tried but . . . never . . . got it."

"How did you find the woman? Gabrielle Viera? Nobody mentioned *her* in the trailer. Nobody even knew her name."

The hole in Wendall's lungs must be getting bigger because no matter how deeply he draws in air, it doesn't seem to be reaching the rest of his body. The lightness starts inside the top of his head and seeps downward. The tips of his fingers feel numb, and the floor is going from cool to cold.

His answer is so low and whispery that Ritchie has to lean close. "Mug . . . shots."

He flashes back for a fraction of a second. It's not a conscious effort. It's almost hallucination. Finding her had been the hardest part. But the *Wine Connoisseur* article on Pryce had provided the answer—when he bragged about his contacts in the city, about how he hired prostitutes and petty thieves in investigations sometimes.

Wendall flashes to Brooklyn's Seventy-eighth Precinct, sees himself lying to detectives there and telling them he'd been pickpocketed by a bar girl.

"Can I look at mug shots?" he'd asked the detectives.

"Why not? There's only about fifty thousand of them," a bored, skeptical detective had replied.

But diligence had triumphed, just as it had for Lindbergh, Serpico, Nast. He'd found her two weeks later in a computer file, when, scrolling through pictures, he'd reached the letter "V."

He'd lied to the detective. "It's no use."

"Stay away from hookers," the detective had advised.

Now pain brings Wendall back and he sees that the future is not so different for him and Ritchie.

Ritchie's voice will be all over the radio by tonight, if it isn't already. Nothing Ritchie can do here will change his fate. Even through his diminishing capacity for thought, Wendall is surprised that Ritchie has even stayed in the city. Or has the choice been taken from him? Is the bland-looking man here to help look for Wendall, and to keep an eye on doomed Ritchie too?

Either way, the pale man has gone into a stall and stands with his back to Wendall, waiting to urinate.

"Godamn prostate," he says over his shoulder. "Can't piss. Can't fuck. Can't bend over any more."

"Wendall?"

"Wha . . ."

The pain seems to change light and make it dim, and Wendall squints because he sees more people in the room now, but he can't make out faces. Schoolkids stand behind Ritchie in the corner. Hanging back and looking like silhouettes behind a gauzy curtain, or is anyone there at all?

"What are you staring at?" Ritchie says, turning.

"You don't see them?"

"No more shit, *paisan.*"

Ritchie's hands reach and claw at him and the pain rises up and Wendall hears screaming. Someone is begging Ritchie to take his hands off, to stop.

Then another voice is shouting too, and it's a voice familiar to Wendall. Is it from the tapes? Is it from the trailer?

"Freeze!" The voice is saying. "Police!"

❄   ❄   ❄

It's six minutes earlier—at 11:57—when Voort enters the park at Eighty-third Street, charges through the gap between stone walls that the doorman had pointed out. There's no one in sight, and at least half a dozen possible directions in which three men could have disappeared.

His Sig Sauer is out. His shoes flap on the pavement. The city has vanished and hard rain falls like he's in Indonesia, not New York. Like it's Zaire or the Amazon. The hot, steady downpour is so thick that it seems to replace oxygen. Land becomes ocean. Water pounds elms and pours off leaves and gushes down the hillside to squish into his shoes and spray off his eyelids. It makes the ground suck at him when he leaves the path and pushes into the woody part of the park.

He has failed again. He'd almost caught up.

I couldn't even convince Mickie to come with me.

Perhaps if there were *no* rain he might hear footsteps or shouting or spot figures ahead or glimpse foliage bouncing where they'd passed.

Instead, like the last man on a planet, he steps onto the path again, lets his running feet choose a direction and take him past the empty basketball courts and the empty dog run and past a locked, bolted playground. . . .

Voort halts, breathing heavily.

Turning back, obeying the little voice in his head, he thinks, almost unconsciously, *Did I see a light?*

There it is.

It's coming from behind the spiked gate, from a

small building in the playground—a public bathroom probably. Someone probably left a light burning earlier, like half the city's residents do every night. But he steps to the entrance, which is barred, of course, by a padlock and chain. Looking through iron bars, Voort's eyes sweep the playground. He sees empty swings and monkey bars. There's a new sandbox and new seesaws. The whole kiddie park was remodeled before the city's budget surplus evaporated. There's at least a quarter million dollars of equipment in there.

The lock on the gate turns out to be a thirty-dollar Ironguard. Typical.

He's turning away when a scream erupts from behind the closed window of the public bathroom.

Fumbling with the padlock, Voort sees with rising excitement that it's broken. The chain is simply wrapped around bars to make it appear that the playground is sealed.

The gate slides open noiselessly. The bathroom is eight feet away on his left. A shadow moves in the window as he glides forward, presses against the outer wall, inches to the corner, spins to catch by surprise any guard who might be there.

There's no guard.

Voort hears a man talking inside the bathroom but he can't make out words through the door.

Hasn't Wendall endured enough?

He hits the door with his shoulder. He goes in fast. He shouts "Freeze! Get against the wall!" The Sig Sauer is up, gripped in both hands for better aim, better control.

It's *exactly* the way he's been trained to assault a room, with one key difference. In training sessions at the department's mock town in Staten Island, two police officers always make the assault.

Two. Not one.

First officer covers the middle of the room. Second takes the corners, instructors always say. *Remember. Never less than teams of two.*

Excellent advice, actually.

Especially in this instance.

Because Voort realizes in even the first millisecond that he's in *major* difficulty here, because maybe *three* men came in here, but all he sees are two.

One man, who must be Wendall, is on the floor in a heap, a hat on the floor beside him, and a wig.

A young, tough-looking man with a ponytail is standing up, his hands raised above his head without Voort even ordering it.

Convict.

Less than a half second has passed, and *where's the third guy? He's got to be behind me, in a stall.*

Excellent deduction, Holmes.

Clearly, the architect who designed kiddie playgrounds around here never took one-man police assaults into mind. He put the toilet stalls to the *left*. He put the sinks, urinals, and towel dispensers to the *right*.

And now, in the next millisecond, Voort hears over his own voice the splash of urine in a toilet bowl.

Too late.

Voort's gun is swinging as someone rams into him from behind, the force driving him toward the ponytailed man, whose arms are coming down and who looks so terrified that if he's going to fight instead of giving up, he must be desperate.

Instinct against numbers, and now even *Wendall is moving* on the floor, and for Voort it's down to reflexes, down to those Saturday afternoons he used to spend in the gym basement with Dad and his uncles, playing defense games, three against one, the relatives training him long before he ever even *saw* the police academy. Infuriating him by leaping out of closets, surprising him from behind, making him cry with rage

And now, pushed toward the man with the ponytail, he uses the momentum to add to his force. He lets it make him stronger. He lets it increase his power as he drives the Sig Sauer into the exposed spot on the man's chest. There's a grunt and a hard, dry, cracking sound like pinewood snapping in a fireplace, and the man's eyes widen. He clutches his chest. Whatever damage Voort has done has reduced him from brawler to patient.

Which is fortunate, because less than two seconds have elapsed and there's still the man behind Voort. *Wendall is crawling toward the door,* but there's no time to do anything about that because stall-man is unbending from a crouch. He'd reached for an ankle holster. His gun is coming up and his dick is hanging from his open zipper and Voort, bringing up the nine-millimeter, sees that *he had to get me off-balance while he went for the gun.*

The two shots go off simultaneously, exploding

and echoing and Voort feels something hot sizzle past his ear.

The man in the stall stops moving. His gun clatters to the tile. He frowns as if he just remembered an errand he forgot to run. Considering the fact that he's sinking to the floor, the expression is all wrong and almost comical. His elbow comes to rest atop the toilet seat.

Voort sees the web of red soaking into the man's rain-soaked shirt. He slides the gun away with his shoe.

Three men down. Voort standing.

The room smells of shit, powder, rain, wet clothing.

Wendall's sitting up in the doorway, framed with each lightning burst. His left leg is out and his right won't stop spasming, scraping a black leather shoe against tile. Some escape tropism is at work, trying to get him outside.

He's like a half-crushed bug with its legs still twitching.

I did it. I stopped him. I got the other guys too.

A selfish thought, but it occurs to Voort that it is just possible that he's saved his career.

At that moment, all the lights go out. Power's finally completely failed.

"Voort . . ."

The croak comes from the figure in the doorway. In a lightning flash Voort realizes that Wendall's marshaled enough strength to actually start to rise. It seems impossible. It seems superhuman. The dead seem to be coming to life again, at least for a few moments more.

Wendall says, "You . . . came . . . this . . . time. . . ."

"Yeah."

Lightning creates a strobe effect, turns the dead man in the stall into a mannequin.

Señor ponytail sits ass on the floor, back against the wall, breathing jerkily like a bass out of water. Voort figures he's broken ribs in there. Either that or the tough-looking guy has no capacity for pain, unlike Wendall, who's still moving at the door. Voort moves back a step to give himself a view of Wendall and Ponytail at the same time.

The teacher, meanwhile, has managed to push himself to his feet. He needs to use the door frame for support. Pain has robbed his voice of intonation, transformed it into a series of flat exhalations, air and information driven out by a sucking sound like a pump moving up and down.

"I was hard . . . on . . . you . . . Voort."

"I better get you to a hospital."

Wendall groans and grips the doorjamb and sinks to his knees. But he straightens again.

"And . . . prison."

Well, yes, but Voort had been reluctant to dwell on that.

Voort says, "Mister Nye. I can't just let you go."

"I . . . know."

"A jury might find you innocent." Voort finds himself hoping for it.

"Yes . . . they . . . might . . ."

He cuffs the man with the ponytail. He won't need to do it to Wendall. He tells the teacher as he hears the snap and click of the lock, "You could have come to us. You could have brought the tapes. Those people deserved jail, not killing."

"You're a . . . good policeman."

Voort sees in the next flash of lightning that the pools of rainwater at Wendall's feet have turned pink.

"Thank you, Mister Nye. That means something to me."

What am I saying?

Voort says, "You can't just be a vigilante. Do you know what the city would be like if people did that?"

The man nods, half standing against the doorway. "I'm finished now . . . Voort."

"I know good lawyers."

"I'll . . . need . . . one. . . ." Wendall shakes all over. Voort realizes that the man is actually laughing.

Voort's whole body is burning. His mouth is parched and he feels the nausea that came the last time he shot a person. He lets himself be sick. He turns away to do it. He almost wills it to happen. The ponytailed man gets to witness Voort's professional suicide here.

Wendall's gone, of course, when Voort looks back at the doorway.

Anything less would have surprised me.

Rain beats down harder.

It seems like it will never stop.

NINETEEN

"He got away, Con Man?"

Twenty minutes later Mickie Connor's on the phone in Robert Priest's study in Riverdale, where Mickie and Priest have been locked in since Voort drove off. Electrical power's gone out all over the metropolitan area. Candles flicker on the desk and computer. Ebenezer Scrooge, meet Steve Jobs. Priest's behind the desk, sipping from a tumbler half-filled with Johnny Walker. Although tipsy, he's still following every word that Mickie says on the cellular phone.

"It doesn't sound like he'll get too far, Con Man. And you brought down two of them. You did a helluva job."

Outside, cops patrol the property with flashlights. The beams don't penetrate far in the rain.

Mickie says, "It sounds like he was about ready to collapse. Hell, find him and I bet things still work out for you. Nobody else even thought to go down there. Only you."

There had been a time when a man like Robert Priest would have owned a generator to provide electricity in the event of a blackout. But it's been so long since there's *been* a blackout that people stopped buying generators years ago.

"Con Man, good luck."

Mickie hangs up. He tells Priest, "Looks like you were never the fourth victim. He was pissed off at his old principal at Nathan Hale. But Voort stopped the guy."

"Thank God," says Priest.

"It also looks like Aiden Pryce shot him up badly."

"I'll feel better when they get him," Priest says.

"Me too. What a day."

Truth is, for the last twenty minutes Mickie's been holding his temper while Priest distracts himself by going on and on about the benefits of corporate/school partnerships. Downing drink after drink while seeming only mildly intoxicated, except for his nonstop monologue about saving troubled schools, donating scoreboards and gym facilities, and some "very wealthy individuals I know" who have a great interest in philanthropy.

"All they ask is a tiny plaque with their name on it. And maybe, as long as the kids have to buy lunch anyway, would it be such a gigantic problem if they supplied the food?"

"They sound like great guys," Mickie had said.

"Let's face it," Priest had said, as rain pounded the

house. "The government? Who relies on the government? The government wastes money right and left. The government couldn't run a candy store."

"When you're right, sir, you're right."

A couple more scotches and Priest had admitted that he even has a couple of ideas for changes in curriculum. Little things that he'd like to talk to the chancellor about. Tiny slants in ways to teach history and art.

"I mean, if you're funding something, you ought to at least be able to get your opinion heard, Mickie. Can I call you Mickie? I'm not talking about control, Mickie. Just input. A lot of these teachers, well, let's face it. If you can do things you *do* them. If you can't *do* anything you teach."

"Everyone should have input," Mickie had said, worrying about Voort.

Which is when Santini had called, and then Voort, filling him in on what had just happened in Riverside Park and passing along new instructions to pull protection off Priest. Cops are needed all over the city to handle blackout problems. Traffic lights are out of commission. Accidents are blocking roads. Callers are alerting 911 dispatchers about minor looting in the South Bronx.

"You mean you're leaving?" Priest asks.

The change in him is startling. The lectury confidence has disappeared, and he seems so vulnerable that Mickie actually finds himself through his disgust feeling a little sorry for the man.

But he alerts Sullivan on the radio to wrap it up

here, send the uniformed people back to the precinct house for reassignment and the plainclothes people to Riverside Park, so they can help in a grid search for Wendall Nye.

"But how do you know he's in the park?" Priest insists when Mickie clicks off.

"Either way, you're cool, Mister Priest. He wasn't after you. He certainly won't be going after anybody now. He's hurt. He's probably down. We're on all the bridges watching for him, and traffic's screwed up anyway."

"I'd feel more comfortable if you stuck around while I call some friends over," Priest says. At least the phones still work.

Mickie nods. "Good idea to call friends if that will make you feel better. But we gotta go."

Even in candlelight, the sheen on Priest's white forehead is unmistakable.

"Good luck on the new school, sir, and just make sure the doors stay locked." Then Mickie walks out of the room and house, and from the second-floor window Priest watches all the cops drive away.

That detective is probably right. There is absolutely no reason for me to be scared.

Robert Priest, master developer, master planner, mobbed-up murderer of his own father, stands in his huge foyer hallway surrounded by tapestries and oriental carpets, and with all his reach and wealth he can't even turn on fucking electricity to switch on his home alarm. It's like year thirteen hundred, not two thousand. Thank God for the phones. Reaching his nephew Joey, he orders the kid over here right away, along with a couple of friends.

I'd call Aiden, but that isn't possible anymore.

Make sure the doors are locked, the detective had said. Well, what the hell is *that* supposed to mean? Priest thinks suddenly. Weren't the doors locked all along?

So he starts going around the house, his scotch in one hand, a flashlight in the other. He feels like a burglar in his own home.

Front door locked. Good.

Living room windows locked.

Dining room fine, and downstairs bathroom also.

Den okay. Guest bedroom sealed. *I'm going to call the police and complain about those officers leaving early,* he thinks, growing slightly more confident and much more indignant as he approaches the last room that provides direct access from outside.

Priest totters into his huge eat-in, skylighted, stainless-steel kitchen, antsy as a five-year-old hearing thumping noises outside a window at 3 A.M.

He's known for years that he is a physical coward, has been aware of it since age five, when he wet his pants in terror when another boy in the playground ordered him to hand over his plastic shovel. In school he'd avoided contact sports. In college he'd never, like the other kids, ventured into rougher, exotic parts of the city. As a man he'd gotten rich and hired protection, and it was *them,* through Pryce, who'd murdered his father and scared off his competitors, and they are the ones who have been out looking for Wendall Nye.

But until tonight he hasn't had to directly face his secret flaw in years. In fact, he'd convinced himself that it wasn't there anymore. After all, he's ordered men killed. He's risked arrest and imprisonment in business. He's matched some of the most ruthless men in the city, word for word, when they talked about "stuffing" the opposition, "silencing" critics, "beating down" anyone blocking their objectives and plans.

Those detectives saw who I am. I know it.

It makes him angry at Voort and Mickie, and distracts him as he walks into the kitchen.

Which means that it takes a fraction of a second longer than it would otherwise to realize that a man is slumped at the table, four feet from the open glass door.

Priest freezes, his eyes fastening upon the gun that lays an inch from the man's hand on the table, by the sugar bowl. The room lights up with each lightning flash.

He can't move, can't turn. His legs feel weak. Neither man speaks and Priest doesn't move for a couple of seconds. The terror, alcohol, and diminished response capacity are mixed up. The earth seems to have disgorged this man, and the half-dead voice emanating from the figure makes Priest's already shaky legs like rubber.

" . . . sittttt . . ."

It is not a human voice. It lacks intonation. It's a

voice that comes with the smell of rain and wet earth, so detached from life that it might have come from an alien manipulating a human's vocal cords.

Priest forces himself forward, still holding the flashlight, never taking his eyes off the wet gun. The chair scrapes like fingernails on a blackboard. He smells shit and something fouler, dirtier, torn from inside the man. He forces his eyes from the gun and up the slumped, shadowy body to the long "beard" and wide-brimmed hat, and he breathes in a urine odor now along with a sweet, thick aroma like he smelled once at an auto accident, where he was too frightened to help pull bloody victims from the car.

Wendall slides down an inch. His breathing comes in insufficient gasps. He is clearly in agony, and Priest recalls Mickie saying the man was "all shot up."

I'll just sit here. I'll do what he says. Maybe he'll pass out.

" . . . Robertttt . . . Priest . . ."

The gun's not exactly in his *hand,* but pretty close to it, much nearer to Wendall than to Priest.

" . . . you killed . . . my sonnn . . ."

"I didn't."

Priest's not sure where it comes from, his ability to speak. It's the equivalent of a braver man's charging toward firing guns across a battlefield. His only thought is to delay Nye until he collapses, or until Joey arrives with help.

"Wendall? That's your name, right? I don't know who told you things. I don't know what you think I did, but you're wrong. I promise you."

The man slides down another inch. The breathing is barely audible.

"The police said you think I was involved. But I never worked on that school, never even visited that school. I can't imagine why anyone linked me to what happened. . . ."

Wendall groans and presses his free hand to the lower left side of his abdomen. Priest sees that the clothing is stained darker on that side.

"Would you like a glass of water?"

Wendall shakes his head no. He doesn't waste speech. He doesn't want water.

The free hand comes up and for a terrifying instant Priest is sure he is going to be shot. But Wendall just gropes in an inner pocket. He extracts something small and silvery, which he pushes across the table. In a flash of lightning Priest sees the metallic glow of a tape recorder.

"Playyyy . . . the . . . tape."

This cannot be good. This is actually terrible. There is no way anything of benefit to Priest could possibly be recorded on the cassette in there. But Wendall's free hand, *covered with blood,* touches the gun now, so Priest picks up the tape recorder and hits the button marked "play."

He hears a faint whirring.

He almost faints himself because he recognizes the voice on the tape. It's Aiden Pryce.

Pryce says, "You were overreacting six years ago and you're overreacting now."

My God, he was in the room with him.

Pryce says, "Put Arlene and the twins on a plane."

Priest begins to cry.

He's four again, a baby. Tears roll down his cheeks and fall on his collar. His whole body is shaking. His collapse is complete. There is nothing he can think of to counter what he is hearing. His mind has stopped working.

All that comes out is a whimper. "Please don't hurt me."

The man across from him is motionless.

Priest sobs, "I'm sorry. Sorry. Sorry."

Wendall slides down a little more and his head loses any remaining animation. His chin dips. There is the sudden tart stench of fresh urine in the room.

"I told Pryce not to hurt you. I just wanted information. *He* decided to beat you up."

Wendall issues a noise from deep inside his body. It is not communication. It is an emanation. It sounds like *ssssssstt*.

"We thought you knew more about the arrangement with Hull. We never thought kids would get hurt. It was only a short delay. A few months."

On tape, Pryce is saying, "Nobody ever linked you . . ."

Wendall's hand drops off the table. The curled fingers hang an inch from the floor.

"Mister Nye?"

Priest makes himself stand up. Wendall doesn't move.

Priest inches forward. He touches the gun and slides it toward him, away from Wendall. The man, incredibly, is still breathing, processing oxygen, but with each breath the chest shudders like a lawn-mower running out of gas.

"You don't look good, asshole."

Priest getting angry now, because after all, he has the gun. And there is no anger greater than a coward's when he feels safe enough to release it. No rage greater than a man who knows, in his heart, that he is afraid.

He broke in. He's wanted by the police. I got the gun away from him.

"You nothing. You . . . *teacher.*"

Priest's never really pulled a trigger, but it comes easy, just like flicking a fuse switch. But there's no explosion. Just a hollow click of metal hitting metal.

Priest starts laughing. There weren't even bullets in the thing.

Hell, hit him with it.

Then Priest backs a step because the wounded man is stirring. It's impossible, but the man seems to be gathering himself. He's pushing his chair back. He's *standing.* It cannot be happening. Priest wants to scream.

"Trick or treat," says the man in another voice, the detective's voice, Conrad Voort's voice.

The other one, Connor, steps in from the patio.

To Voort, Connor says, "Happy birthday."

To Priest, he says, "Nye died in Riverside Park. Put your hands behind your back."

TWENTY

Room 104 at One Police Plaza is where detectives get rewarded if they become heroes.

Room 1209 is where screwups get fired.

One-o-four is a midsized auditorium with a raised stage facing rows of spring-action chairs cushioned in dark blue velvet. When young detectives dream of glory, the dreams usually end in room 104, before reporters, brass, and proud or grieving families.

Twelve-oh-nine is bare and small with a no-frills table in front. There's no police flag, city flag, or U.S. flag. A trio of comfortable chairs serve whichever officials have unpleasant duties that day, and disgraced detectives stand while handing in their gun, badge, and whatever final paperwork is deemed appropriate to accompany their professional demise.

Detectives lauded in room 104 usually sit while their superiors stand up and give speeches.

Detectives humiliated in room 1209 stand up while their bosses sit down and give speeches.

One morning a week after Robert Priest's arrest, Commissioner Aziz sits beside Voort on the podium in room 104, along with Chief of Detectives Eva Ramirez and Deputy Mayor Thomas Lamond Deans. The mayor is at the podium, addressing reporters; Voort family members, and Camilla and Julia, side-by-side, occupy the first row.

The mayor's never met either woman, but he's thinking while he speaks, *Gorgeous*.

"For conspicuous bravery," he is saying, "for unflinching police work in the face of criticism and great odds . . ."

Mickie, in the third row, gives Voort a grin and thumbs-up. The reporters who were ready to crucify him a week ago gaze up at Voort as if he's won the Nobel Prize.

"For his honesty in admitting his lapse . . ."

The award won't be a promotion, Deans had told Voort, because technically you can't promote a man under investigation. "But it won't be demotion either. You're in exactly the same position as you were when Gabrielle Viera died. Considering the shit you were in, that's quite a feat."

The mayor says, "We all make mistakes, and the better of us learn from them. We all also occasionally disobey orders, and when we're lucky or smart we turn out to be right. Eh, Detective Voort?"

The reporters laugh.

Julia waves proudly from the first row, stunning in an emerald silk dress suit that shows off her petite, lithe body. Even her smallest wrist actions impart a blatant femininity, a chemical invitation wafting across twenty feet.

Camilla's in a cream-colored jacket and skirt, her long hair down, her long legs crossed, her long fingers tapping on her little pocketbook, the deep blue of her eyes visible even from the stage. To Voort, there's something luscious in her posture, the arch of slender back, the curve of tanned neck and the long fingernails. He imagines he can smell her perfume even at this distance. It's impossible, but they say smell is the most powerful sense.

After all, I fooled Priest by actually putting on Wendall's shit-stained clothes. Once Priest smelled that, it never occurred to him that I might not be Wendall.

This room, for him, has marked so many of life's passages. His grandfather's retirement happened here, and his father's promotions. His awards after the Nora Clay and John Szeska cases were given here, and so were the terrible nonstop press conferences after the Trade Center went down and he spent days with Mickie sifting in the wreckage and manning the DNA section at the arsenal, using computers to help match up mailed-in toothbrushes and combs and underwear with body parts that workers had pulled from the pit.

This is not a room where detectives actually accomplish things. But it is the room where the department publicizes or explains them, the room where the Blue world officially reveals or conceals.

"Thank you, Detective Voort."

Applause erupts. The pin on his chest has no

weight to it, but when he moves back to his chair it provokes the slightest rubbing sensation against nerve endings beneath his shirt.

Afterward he stands in the hallway and answers reporters' questions. The journalists seem to have completely forgotten their antagonism toward him two weeks ago. Suddenly they've decided that he represents the best of the department, not the worst. Priest's arrest has begun eclipsing news of the police graft scandal, and seems to be turning the public image of the cops around.

"How did you *feel* when you found Wendall Nye lying in the park, Detective?"

"How do you *feel* about Robert Priest being out on bail? And Voort, Voort, how many times did he pull the trigger when he aimed that gun at you?"

"No comment on a pending case." Now that press cooperation is not needed to catch Wendall, Aziz has ordered a return to traditional PR policy.

It's noon when they finish, and he's glad, because one perk detectives get after award ceremonies is a few hours off. He's got the rest of the day to relax. Outside, the sun is hot, the sky blue, and Julia and Camilla wait—not exactly together any more—in the bright plaza outside the building.

Julia smiling.

Voort smiling.

Camilla smiling.

What could go wrong since everybody's smiling?

He takes their arms, Julia's pliant, Camilla's soft, and he walks the women toward the arch of the municipal building that will spill them onto Tribeca's main east-west artery, Chambers Street.

"Julia, thanks for coming. It meant a lot to me. And I want you and Donnie, Jr., at the house until you find an apartment close enough so he can keep attending the same school."

"That means so much."

"But," he says, turning to Camilla, "Camilla and I haven't had a lot of time together lately. A guy needs time alone with his one true love."

Julia stiffens a little. The arm slowly withdraws.

She says, "I thought we could all go somewhere, have a picnic."

He strokes her cheek with his forefinger, but in a brotherly gesture.

"Another time."

You let futures pass by with a word or a gesture. You block off opportunity with the softest brush of a fingernail against a fragrant cheek. Julia stands there a moment, absorbing changed possibility. But she's still bright and smiling when she says, "I'll leave you two alone."

Slipping his arm around Camilla's waist, Voort feels her whole body relax.

Julia says, "See you later, Conrad, Camilla."

High heels can make a woman look sexy or unsure, depending on why she's walking away from you. Julia has suddenly lost some allure to Voort. But as she moves off he notices men on the street watching her, and he feels a pang of closure, no question. And of male regret.

Then he gently swings Camilla around and they walk toward the Hudson.

"That was a bit rough on her," she says.

"Would anything less have made you happy?"

"No," she says.

"Why do I have a feeling that you've got a specific destination in mind?"

"A belated birthday surprise. We never got a chance to celebrate before."

They stroll through a neighborhood rebuilding itself. Big trucks move in a stream south, carrying steel and concrete toward the old World Trade Center site. The clang of construction is a welcome sound, a triumph of creation over destruction, of industry over decay. Chambers Street is clogged with Tribeca Film Festival attendees: movie makers, film reporters, actors in town for film premieres. The festival will be launched tonight on the steps of city hall, with the showing of the Chinese hit comedy *The Plum Bun*. Manhattan Community College students flow in and out of the campus west of Greenwich Street, and Voort and Camilla stroll past P.S. 234, the two-story elementary school that serves public school students from Battery Park City.

COP BREAKS BIGGEST SCANDAL IN CITY'S HISTORY reads the banner headline on today's *Post*, stacked at a newsstand.

CROOKS TO DA: LET'S MAKE A DEAL reads the headline on the *News*.

The article will detail what Voort already knows. Ritchie Zahn, Wendall's old foreman, has already agreed to turn state's evidence, as have two of Pryce's investigators. Lawyers for other construction companies want to work out deals. The ex-president of the Hod Carriers Union, also on the tapes, is negotiating immunity.

Fact is, whether Wendall's tapes constitute admissible evidence or not, twenty million people are reading the unedited transcript sections every day—in New York, in the state capitol, and in Washington, too, thanks to the *Washington Post*.

CONTRACTS TO BE INVESTIGATED reads the top-left headline in today's *Times*. COURT VOIDS DEALS.

At the Hudson River they turn north, Voort knowing now where she is taking him. He feels as if he has not enjoyed an idle stroll in months.

"I could have stopped him from leaving that building, you know," he tells her. "I could have held him there until an ambulance came."

"Should you have?"

Voort can't answer. He doesn't know.

The bike path is sunny and warm and they pass Stuyvesant High School, which under the canceled plan was to serve as the base for a thirty-story condo tower built by Robert Priest. They pass the miniature golf course and jazz pier and halt at a locked chain-link fence around Pier Twenty-six's boathouse.

Camilla uses her key on the padlock. She locks the gate behind her when they go in. They're both members.

Inside kayaks are stacked in booths and the place smells of wood and resin and salt and river. The breeze is out of the Atlantic, so it smells the way it might have three hundred years ago, when Voort's cabin-boy ancestor first arrived in the New World, sailing into this harbor in Henry Hudson's *Golden Hind.*

They change into bathing suits that they keep stored in the newly installed locker section.

The day is warm enough so they don't need wind-breakers. Summer prematurely arrived with the lightning storm two weeks ago.

But as Voort heads for his Perception seventeen-footer, Camilla says "Wait," and he sees her unlock the storage area, where, inside a fenced-in room, are stored members' paddles, vests, spray skirts, and wet suits. The neoprene suits are for winter use.

"Happy birthday, Voort."

"A knapsack?"

"Open it outside," she says, lugging the heavy red bag through the double doors to the pier.

"It's a folding kayak!"

"I got one for each of us. I figured, if we go some-where wild, like, say, Alaska, we can take the Feathercrafts on the plane, load 'em on a pickup, drive where we want, and paddle our hearts out. That is, if you can ever get away. Me? I'm unem-ployed."

"I've never been to Alaska," Voort says.

From inside her knapsack, she pulls out an enve-lope.

"Who put *this* here? It looks like airplane tickets."

The Feathercraft K-1s take a half-hour to assemble, and he finds the work pleasantly distracting. She's practiced already. She shows him how to insert the shock-corded tubes into each other, fit on the plastic cross ribs, and make skeleton sections over which they slip the urethane skin. When they're finished, the K-1s are seventeen feet long, sturdy, and easy to slip into the water. They paddle out toward the Statue of Liberty.

The tide is out. The river is calm. In the harbor, ferries chug back and forth from Staten Island. Square-prowed tugs push barges. A big car carrier steams in from under the Verrazano Bridge. Voort's muscles feel good as he paddles, and the sun is hot and soothing on his shoulders. Camilla, the kayaking champion, races ahead, her blonde hair flashing as her paddle sprays diamond bits of light. She is an animal on water. She is the top half of a beast. Looking at her he is reminded of the Aztecs and the way, seeing Spanish conquistadors arrive in Mexico on horseback, they had believed themselves to be observing single creatures composed of man and horse.

I'm sorry, Wendall.

Voort turns the Feathercraft around. Bobbing, he has a view of southern Manhattan. He sees the new American Express building and the joggers on the bike path. He sees the low purplish haze of dust and car exhaust that has replaced the forest his ancestors saw when they arrived at the harbor.

He will never look at the sky over this part of the city without experiencing a pang of grief for his cousins and the others who died in the World Trade Center. He feels as if he is looking at a hole in the sky where mountains used to be.

Then Voort turns back, and Camilla is already a low, red speck on the calm water, diminishing as she closes on the Statue of Liberty.

Thank you, God, for what I have. Thank you for protecting the people close to me. Make me better. Help me not screw up again. Help me be the person you and I both want me to be. Help me be a hundred percent for Camilla from now on.

Her voice comes to him from over the water. Bright. Happy. Musical.

"You coming, lazy?"

"I'll beat you there!"

Voort puts his muscles into it.

On the water, from this angle, the city seems gone.

SIMON & SCHUSTER
PROUDLY PRESENTS

AT HELL'S GATE

Ethan Black

Available in hardcover August 2004
from Simon & Schuster

Turn the page for a preview of
At Hell's Gate. . . .

"What's the thing you must never do, but you can't resist doing?" asks the street preacher on the loading dock. "The extra step that you can't stop from taking? The excess that brings you to Hell's Gate?"

It's what I did tonight, thinks the man in the front row, sinking down, trying to hide, knowing he's chosen the wrong place.

It's too light in here. Too big and empty. The men chasing me must be right outside.

The street preacher wears coveralls. The eleven p.m. sermon takes place on a hot September night. The once-a-week "church" is an abandoned warehouse garage in the South Bronx. Bare bulbs illuminate folding chairs that hold a smattering of half-sprawled, half-asleep prostitutes, homeless men, and even one long-haul trucker who knows he shouldn't be here but couldn't resist looking for a certain redheaded hooker. She'll infect him with AIDS forty minutes from now.

I should have just gone to work tonight. I should have driven the taxi. I should never have come to Hunts Point. Save me, anyone, prays the fugitive in the front row.

"For each person the temptation is different. But the result is the same."

The man in the front row pulls down his Mets cap

and turns to squint toward the smashed-in garage door. Three silhouettes—large men, from the shapes—have just materialized in the shadows back there. Their heads move side to side as they scan the audience. Their features are invisible, but the fugitive feels as if their scrutiny carries weight, and darkness, coalesced into human form, needs a few more seconds to gather power, to attack.

"Hell's Gate," warns the bald, bearded preacher in a soft voice, "is as small as the last digit of a phone number you know you shouldn't be dialing, as delicious as one too many sips of scotch before you drive off on an icy night. It's as logical as an urge to please someone you love: a parent, a boss, a child."

The shadow men glide forward.

"You men! We have extra seats in the front if you'd care to sit."

The attention freezes them, but they resume moving when the preacher's attention shifts to the trucker and the hooker, who are whispering together in the third row.

Only a few years ago here—before fire closed the place—big eighteen-wheelers would back up to this dock in the Hunts Point warehouse district each night to unload fat prosciutto hams from Parma, sweet Vidalia onions from Georgia, bananas from Honduras, crates of baby peas, yellow squash, corn, black beans. Food biblical in its proportions, to feed New York. Bounty grown, manufactured, or genetically engineered from all corners of the earth.

"If you are here, friends, you have known temptation."

Homeless men eye folding tables laden with freebie Tropicana orange juice, freebie Dunkin' Donuts.

"You never dreamed you'd live in a wasteland like this."

The shadow men halt in the dark areas flanking the front row; two on one side, one—the biggest—on the other.

I never should have followed them into that bar, the man in the middle of the first row thinks. Or asked them that last question.

He looks pathetic, more boy, less man. His khaki shorts are as grimy as his black Keds high-tops. His sweat-stained T-shirt swells with a pear-shaped body that's been out of shape for years. His Mets cap is pulled low over black-framed glasses. Only his biceps show muscles, as if they're the only part of him that gets exercise.

He might win an arm wrestling contest. He'll never win a race.

I shouldn't have asked them about their job.

"Hell's Gate is the name we New Yorkers call the body of water only half a mile from here," the preacher announces to the blast of a tug horn, a requiem floating over his congregation in a low F flat. "It's a ship grave-yard, right in our city. Down there lies the broken sloop *Irene* and the schooner *Diadem*. The tug *Vixen* and the brig *Guisborough*. The wrecks of the *Flagg*, the *Planter*, the fine old *Hannah Ann*."

I'm too scared to stand.

"Imagine those struggling sailors as the water closed over them. But my friends, they'd reached Hell's Gate long before their ships."

The man in the front row bolts.

He runs up onto the loading dock, toward the star-tled preacher but away from the men. Charging past the preacher, he glimpses wide bottle-green eyes and white palms coming up, as if to ward off an attack.

The man plunges through a half-sealed doorway into the abandoned main warehouse. The dark assumes geometry. Blocky forms of burned-out machinery rise up in opaque light seeping through mesh windows, or flooding through holes smashed in sooty glass. The runner weaves past stripped-down conveyor belts, rusted blackened crane hoists, stilled winches, pushcarts robbed of wheels.

Dim, through the wreckage, he makes out an exit door at the far end of the big room.

He bangs his shin but keeps from crying out, more from vocal-cord paralysis than self-control.

Someone call the police. He sends his will out as a prayer.

The only answer is the sound of footsteps behind.

A flashlight beam swings in the dark.

What is about to happen will never make the newspapers. The homeless people of Hunts Point don't talk to police. The trucker's not about to admit he left a $110,000 rig parked alone. The preacher will make no inquiries because in this neighborhood that would violate an unspoken bargain.

Which is mind your own business, preacher, and pimps and pushers won't bother you.

Maybe the agreement will bring me to Hell's Gate one day, the preacher sometimes thinks.

"I won't tell," the man in the Mets cap yells as he batters his way through the two-by-fours half-nailed across the exit. Doubled with exertion, he pants back onto the street.

I won't tell.

Outside, Hunts Point presents itself as deserted block after block of warehouses, razor-wire fences, and bars in which the liquor served is more of a side business. The rare private home is squeezed between tire shops. Squad cars—when they come—seem more lost than appropriate in a place where most vehicles lack even parts to be stripped. Street names—like Tiffany and Casanova—suggest that geography itself would rather be somewhere else.

In the distance, through gaps between warehouses, the running man sees the lights of Manhattan, beyond the East River shoreline oil terminals.

"Get away from meeeee!"

His sneakers slap against glass and roadway. He realizes that he's run the wrong way. He crashes into a chain-link fence topped by concertina wire. Moonlight illuminates a municipal sign beside a long hole cut in the fence.

Tiffany Street Pier. Keep Out at Night.

Beyond that the dark river churns toward the roughest part of the harbor. The late summer air seems as thick as water down there.

I can't swim. The man pounds down the pier.

And of course here they come, as silent and purposeful as African wild dogs he once saw on TV in a *National Geographic* special. He'd told himself not to talk to these guys, but had been unable to resist asking one five-second question, the one that had made their eyes turn hard.

"Please don't hurt me."

Sinking down on his knees, he feels the moist scrape of wood and smells the tarry odor of resin. He's afraid to make eye contact as the men reach him. When a hand appears at face level, he sees the tiny tattoo below the knuckle of the index finger. He'd noticed it in the bar, a picture of an old-style cutlass side by side with a barracuda. At the time the image had made him think of pirates.

Henry Morgan. Blackbeard. Calico Jack. Captain Greaves.

When the finger crooks now, the barracuda's mouth seems to open.

"I don't know what you're doing. I don't care what you're doing. I'll go away and never come back," the man in the baseball cap whimpers.

The Mets cap falls into the water.

The hands, when they touch him, are gentle.

He hears a siren in the distance.

It's much too far away.

"So this is Hell's Gate," Camilla says.

Voort opens his eyes and shields them against noon sun that is as warm as a first rush of anesthesia. The gorgeous blonde on the beach towel to his right wears a black string bikini right out of a teenage boy's dream.

Voort loves her long hair. Her trim, tight athlete's body. Her tanned, smooth skin that highlights her fierce Irish blue eyes.

The green birches and oaks behind the strip of beach are filled with migrating tanagers. Two foldable kayaks, yellow for Voort, red for Camilla, lie pulled up where they'd left them two hours ago.

"I can't believe we're in the middle of New York," she says.

"Ready to head back through the Gate?"

"Falling asleep during an argument doesn't win it."

"I fell asleep because I was tired."

"You're tired because you've been carrying the load for Mickie for weeks. You're working without a functioning partner. If you get in trouble, who's going to save your nicely muscled ass, Voort?"

A good day, despite the edge to the banter. A relaxing day. His first day off in two weeks.

"Whatever's wrong, Mickie will work it out," he says, knowing that in all likelihood he's just lied.

Brushing her hair, she leans close. Even when she's irritated her lips fascinate him. "That's interesting because you don't even know what it is," she says. "You say, 'Hey, Mickie.' He says, 'I know.' End of conversation. What is it with guys?"

"They give all their attention to their gorgeous fiancées," says Voort, who knows Mickie's problem well enough and has been jeopardizing his job by protecting his best friend.

"That's the most pathetic, condescending and bald-faced attempt at dropping a subject I ever heard," Camilla says, grinning.

"Yeah, but you liked it," Voort says, smiling back.

There's something about a woman when you finally decide on her, Voort thinks. It's a solid feeling that makes all the old questions disappear. You sleep more deeply. You're filled with a kind of certainty you'd never known existed before. You understand things you've been missing.

"At least talk to Mickie," she says.

"You know what they say about Irish women?" Voort stands and starts gathering up the remains of lunch. "They never die. They just get smaller and smaller from wind erosion. After a while nothing remains but a complaining voice by the fireplace."

"You know what they say about Dutch men?" she counters. "They never die because they were never alive in the first place."

"Okay, I'll really talk to him this time."

Her kiss still gives him a jolt. Any disagreements between them these days are nothing compared to the obstacles they've overcome. He flashes back to some of their history. There was the initial three-month period when the richest cop in New York had started dating the tough, beautiful TV producer. It had been the most sexually thrilling time of Voort's life, and her day-to-day temperament—the rhythms of her quiet times—had matched his own. But there had also been some extra quality that defied definition. Some primal connection that had driven him wild.

He'd been so infatuated he'd found himself praying for her in church each day, including her in the supplications he sent out for the family.

God, he'd say, help me make her as happy as she makes me.

Now as they store the remnants of lunch in the kayaks he remembers the second phase, when she'd started disappearing evenings, seeing a shrink, as he later found out. He'd learned of a betrayal so bad it seemed impossible he could ever forgive her.

She wanted to come back but I said no.

Which is why he'd been amazed to find himself ringing her bell one day after the Szeska case had concluded. They'd become friends again, and then lovers, and now—four years after they met—what exists between them lacks the spicy danger of the early days, but it's a mix of trust, respect, and chemistry, with just enough unpredictability thrown in to make him anticipate happy surprises in the upcoming years.

"Last one through the Gate has to limit the wedding list to two hundred," he says.

"Then it better be you, because that's how many Voorts we have at the house every night."

In the foldable Feathercrafts they push into the swift water toward Hell's Gate. At this hour flood tide is flowing in from Long Island Sound, heading south toward the East River, which is churning north. The collision zone is the S-shaped curve ahead.

Beyond that Voort sees the towers of Manhattan.

"Yippee!" Spray flying, Camilla drives her foldable out of a bubbling whirlpool and up a four-foot wave. She's a former college kayak champ, a TV news producer laid off by NBC. She spends hours each day at the Hudson River boathouse, building custom models for private clients, having made the transition from professional woman to unemployed athlete without a hitch.

Voort keeps pace easily, a lean man, with good shoulders, bronzed by the sun and powdered by beach salt. He's the guy who women notice in offices, churches, supermarkets, jazz clubs.

Overhead is the railroad bridge linking Queens with the soccer fields of Randall's Island. At Voort's back is Brother Minor, the island where he and Camilla had eaten their picnic of warm French bread, smoked Gouda, pink strips of prosciutto, and ice-cold Evian water. No people live on Minor. Its ruins and woods are filled with migrating birds. Even farther astern, from the prison windows at Rikers, inmates jeer at anyone on the water who's having fun.

"Watch out, Camilla!"

A big square-prow tug chugs toward them, twin engines roaring, diesels set at full thrust to push through Hell's Gate. The captain blows his horn at the kayakers—to him, Voort guesses, irritating specks on the waterway. Pleasure seekers who have no place clogging up a business highway, a commercial thoroughfare for real river men, not a playground for yuppies and their two-thousand-dollar toys.

"Fuck you too," Camilla shouts, getting out of the way easily. She's dainty as a schoolgirl one moment, tough as an eighteen-wheeler driver the next.

The tug sends up a wake that hits a wave that churns into a whirlpool. Seventy feet below, from a mountain of rock, tons of water bubbles up toward the sand barge towed by the tug's thick ropes.

"He's trying to slow me down, Voort."

"That, Camilla, is impossible."

Ahead, something white and big spins in a whirlpool. I hope that isn't what I think it is, Voort thinks.

Is that an arm?

The day so far has been a journey—as any metropolitan trip is for Voort—through three centuries of family history. It had started at eight this morning when they'd carried the foldable Feathercrafts in their knapsacks from his house on Thirteenth Street, a property Voorts have occupied since the end of the American Revolution, when the Continental Congress gave the family the land and any structure built on it in perpetuity, tax-free.

"It was a reward for keeping the British from landing in New Jersey," he'd told Camilla on their first date.

They'd walked under the FDR Drive to the Twentieth Street "beach," a strip of sand, rock, and washed-up pilings jutting twenty feet into the East River. They'd assembled the shock-cord frames and rolled on the Duratek skins of the foldables as fascinated onlookers, chess-playing oldsters, looked on.

"The British chained American POWs together in prison ships, off this point," Voort had told her.

The ninety-minute journey upriver had taken them through a panorama reminding him of family tales. Here was Roosevelt Island, to which Voort cops had ferried the city's orphans at the turn-of-the-previous-century. Here was the UN, where Voorts had held back protesters hundreds of times since the building opened its doors. Here was North Brother Island, to which Voort had rowed the waitress Mary Mallon—"Typhoid Mary"—to live out her days in isolation.

"She sang all the way out," Voort had told Camilla.

Fact is, Voorts have protected the city since the Dutch first settled it. They patrolled the mud streets on foot in New Amsterdam. They drive electrically rechargeable Hondas in Central Park today.

"What's that in the water, Voort?" Camilla says now. "My God!"

"He moved! I think he's alive!"

Voort paddles hard to give the man something to grab, but a whirlpool sucks away the body.

I'm caught too.

It's impossible to keep the kayak stable and reach out at the same time to grab a black-Ked-clad foot. Then the foot is gone but fists are spinning above the surface, as if the man twirls underwater like a Rollerblader enthralled by music on headphones, like skaters in Central Park.

The maelstrom pushes the forehead to the surface.

I was wrong. He's been cut up by propeller, or ship. No way is that guy alive.

On land, meanwhile, in Astoria Park, people are starting to realize something dangerous is happening twenty feet from the shore rocks.

Voort tips left, rolling dangerously. He's going to get dumped. He thrusts the flat of his paddle into the current and uses its counterforce to right himself. Camilla has driven her Feathercraft into the floater to try to push the body to shore.

"Together!" she shouts. TV producers have a need to produce.

They inch the corpse toward the softball field in Astoria Park.

The game has halted. Players in red or blue uniforms line the rocks, spread out to help if the kayakers can get close enough. Men extend bats, which are much too short to reach.

"Grab it!"

Someone screams, "Watch out!" and Voort spins the kayak left to avoid a heavy timber shooting past.

Camilla hits the riptide suddenly and her kayak gets caught between currents. She spins. She flips. She's upside down. Voort's heart goes to his mouth, but in that fraction of a second she surfaces again, cursing, long hair flying, muscles straining as she drives the prow into the body with renewed force, gaining another two feet.

"Camilla, get to shore and call 911."

A fisherman has removed the hook from his line and replaced it with bobbers and weights, to cast it farther as a makeshift lifeline. Falling toward Voort, the red and white plastic bobbers resemble Christmas tree decorations dropping from the sky.

"Camilla, go ashore! I'll follow the guy!"

But the current gives them a break, spurts them toward shore so the ballplayers haul up the body and kneel and grab the kayaks. Hands reach, grip wrists, pull hard until Voort and Camilla half crawl, half scramble onto land, blowing hard, out of breath.

The last thing Voort needs is some two-hundred-pound ballplayer shouting in his face, but the guy is doing it anyway.

"I'm a cop," he yells as Voort notices the team name—Thespians—on the man's blue shirt. "Are you crazy to go out there? You goddamn people! Crazy nuts! Your buddy's dead! Are you out of your mind?"

"The current's not even a class two," retorts Camilla, puffing up to them, coming to Voort's defense. She's right, Voort knows. Without the body to handle, passage would have been simple. They plan to honeymoon on more difficult stretches of water in Andalusia four months from now.

"Camilla, you hurt?"

But she looks fine and says, "Your cell phone's in my front compartment." Meaning, to call 911.

Camilla adds, "Excuse me, honey."

She leans over and throws up.

Voort introduces himself to the cop and takes over. He orders the off-duty Blue Guy, "Keep everyone away." He adds, recognizing shock in the man, "You did a great job. Tell your pals thanks."

After calling 911 he phones his partner, Mickie, on Long Island, at his waterfront mansion.

No one answers there. Nor does he get a response on Mickie's cellular phone.

Which has been the way things have been going even

when they're on duty lately. Mickie's just not there.

Hell's Gate churns behind him as Voort bends and examines the body, the gashes, feels for breaks, studies the face. It's cut up but not puffy, so the death occurred last night or today, Voort guesses, maybe as recently as the last few hours, although his experience with floaters is limited, so he could be wrong.

The arms took a beating. The right hip seems caved in. The skull has suffered one hell of an impact, probably from boat, rock, timber, whatever shredded the T-shirt down the man's back. Blunt objects in the river flow down every few moments, coming at targets in multiple choice.

"Who is he?" Camilla asks, beside Voort again, staring down in horror, and yet he hears in her voice the TV producer's ability to dehumanize a situation, the instinct—whether she's working or not—that never goes away.

Voort orders her away from the body.

"I found him, buster."

A quick look from Voort and she's backing away.

"Do you think," she asks, "he jumped or fell?"

Voort kneels again, frowning. "Look how his pockets are all turned inside out. The current didn't do that. People did."